THE ALUSIAN'S
QUEST

LAUREN STINTON

THE HOUSE OF ELAH
Book 2

For Hannah, in honor of her wedding.
Every Hannah should get
the man of her dreams.

acknowledgments

As always, I want to thank my "crew": Brooke Ewers, Cherish Brunner, and Ashley Van Winkle. Thanks for all the encouragement and for meeting my deep, fiery need to read my books aloud and/or talk about the drama happening in my characters' lives.

Thanks also to Susan Stinton (hi, Mom), Jane Lambert, Blair Reynolds, and Ben Moulton, who read the manuscript and gave me incredible-though-sometimes-violent-and-bloody feedback. You guys have made this a better book.

Trace, you have magic. I'm pretty sure that in certain lighting, I would be able to see sparks flying off your fingertips. Thank you for designing my book. You've done a great job.

Finally, I also wish to acknowledge Delanie Specht— you'll always be a pirate in my book. (Ahem.) Start on page 371, my dear.

part one

God of the Sun

$\mathcal{F}$inlan did not understand why he would ride through the gate of Ausham and start to smell the sea.

The salt in the air was as strong as if he stood on the shore, facing waves that lapped at the toes of his boots, the fresh wind flowing across his face. Ausham was surrounded by four days of thick forest. Finlan had not been able to smell the sea on the outer side of the wall, a mere twenty feet behind him. He had not even been able to smell the sea five days ago on the banks of the Redaman River, and it was much closer to the coast than this place.

How was it that Abalel's city seemed so familiar to him? The smell instantly wrapped his old, wrinkled heart in peace. He felt like he had stepped into his grandfather's house on the rocks beside the sea. This felt like home to him, just because of the smell.

Issen-El, he thought in surprise, *how is it that you are here? This is the home of the god of the sun, not the god of the sea.* But Issen-El did whatever he wanted. Propriety had never been one of his concerns.

Entan Gallowar, the blue-eyed Alusian, turned and gave Finlan a warm smile. "Welcome to Ausham, Finlan. It is a good day to be here, for today, many things change." Entan urged his horse forward.

Finlan liked the boy well enough, but he did not always understand Entan's sporadic desire to create trouble with his words. *Today, many things change.* What did that mean? Was it truly necessary to say? Finlan doubted it. He rubbed the top of his old wrinkled head and looked around.

The place was filled with trees. He saw pines and thagbrush, purple oaks and miresen-well, and a host of other green-leafed entities. Ausham was a seat of power in this country. The king came here and consulted with Abalel's prophets. But what Finlan saw now suggested that Ausham was not more than a village in the woods—a place for loggers or hunters. Other than the guards standing watch at the gate, he did not see any people.

They rode for half an hour. Then the trees parted, and they came upon a deep clearing. A large stone building rose up at the distant end of the green. It was full of windows and lined with engraved steps, marble pillars, and guards at attention. The architecture was magnificent. *Now this is what I expected,* Finlan thought. This was no village in the woods—this was something of weight in the world, a place capable of influencing kings and governments.

At the base of the steps, Entan dismounted without a word. Finally, after five days of travel, it would seem they had reached their destination.

"What is this building?" Finlan asked as servants appeared from some secret, hidden region and claimed their horses. He rubbed his lower back with both hands. So many days in a saddle had not been a blessing for his old bones.

Entan stepped close to him and asked intently, "Do you know what a skroel is?"

Finlan pulled back at the boy's sudden severity. "A what?"

"A creature that is half man and half reptile. They often appear as snakes."

Why would Finlan ever need to know about that? It sounded terrible.

Entan nodded toward the steps and began to walk toward them. Finlan hurried to keep up.

"They can alter their forms," Entan continued. "They can appear as a snake, or they can appear as a man. They are similar to lycanthrope, except these beasts have scales and not wolves' fur. The blood is dangerous, and they use it as poison on their weapons. They prefer a crossbow. If the bolt itself does not kill, the blood will in a short period of time."

Finlan still didn't understand his need to know these things until they reached the top of the steps, where the boy paused. He turned his head and looked down at Finlan. Entan was tall. Much taller than an old man from the coast, the stock of fishermen. Finlan smiled to himself. Somehow, he had become rather fond of this white-skinned creature standing before him. This Alusian was nothing like the last one Finlan had experienced. Thoughts of the female still made him shudder on the inside of his bones.

"Finlan," Entan said, "a skroel tried to kill Myles

Hileshand not an hour ago. The creature is dead now, for he made the attempt in Ausham, surrounded by Abalel's prophets." Entan rolled his eyes once and scoffed in the back of his throat. "A fool's errand indeed, but the enemy deemed it worthy. Myles Hileshand is the key of prophecy."

Finlan knew all about Myles' prophecy. Entan had told him. They had discussed it at length. All in all, the old prophecy was rather short. The more popular lines spoke of a man who would hold the Ruthanian throne in his hand, but according to Entan, that part of the prophecy was not the most important. It was a side note. A fact that almost did not matter. The most important part, Entan said, was that the man who held the Ruthanian throne would speak Abalel's name in Ruthane and remind the people what they had lost.

Finlan's heart pounded. "Is Myles all right?"

Entan laughed again, and this time, he appeared to mean it. He seemed genuinely amused. "Of course he is. What else would you expect him to be, Finlan? The skroel are difficult to apprehend when they are unexpected. What man, on his own, can escape an unseen death? Yes, Myles is fine."

Those who hear Abalel's voice live in this city, Finlan thought. How could Abalel's prophets have allowed that vile creature to enter? There was a hole somewhere in their defenses. Had they not been paying attention?

Then Entan the Alusian said something that made no sense whatsoever. "The skroel was killed quickly, before he could draw his weapon, but there is hope he will be successful yet."

Finlan looked at him sharply. "What?"

As if they spoke of fishing or horses or any other *tame*

topic, Entan turned and smiled at him.

Entan Gallowar was friendly. Finlan knew this. They had talked and shared one another's company. On their journey through the woods, they had spent many hours speaking of Issen-El and all Finlan had learned of him during a long and faithful lifetime. Surprisingly, the Alusian had shown true interest and listened intently to Finlan's information regarding the god of the sea. Their conversations had been entertaining; Finlan had actually enjoyed them. *Carrying on with an Alusian. Imagine!*

But Finlan had never seen this expression on the boy's face before. The look was unnatural. This was not a friendly look. There was something wild about it, something that did not appear quite sane.

"Entan?" Finlan asked. "Are you all right?"

The creature suddenly groaned. "Oh, this I despise." He blew out his breath and, for a moment, seemed very disturbed. He lowered his voice and said, "Wait, Finlan. You will see. It is very important that you see it, that they all see it. A high price for anyone to pay, but it will be worth it in the end."

"What do you mean, Entan?" Finlan asked.

But this time, the Alusian did not explain himself.

The guards knew Entan Gallowar and pushed open the main doors for him. The boy had told Finlan that he was the abbot's nephew. Apparently, he was on the grounds fairly regularly, for no one asked him his business or tried to stop him.

"What do you mean?" Finlan repeated as they entered the atrium. "What do you mean—you despise this? What is worth it in the end?

Entan took hold of Finlan's arm with a strong grip.

"Abalel's council hesitates, when it is not the time for hesitation. It is the time for understanding. The prophecy is true. It is here. It is time; they cannot hesitate. They need to see that what they have believed for so long remains good. What they believe is steady and firm. It will not betray them. They need to see this, but they lack the courage."

Another set of guards waited at the end of the atrium. Finlan watched the guards' faces. Clearly, they did not hear Entan's words; they didn't respond with concern. Again the doors were opened for them. The Alusian pulled Finlan through the opening into the large room on the other side.

It was like stepping into a market in the middle of a sprawling city. The ceiling was suddenly several feet higher, and it was made of clear glass, so the sky could be seen. Huge lamps hung from golden brackets along the upper walls, making even the thought of shadow impossible. The lower walls were bare except for windows larger than Finlan was. The curtains were tied back, the glass panels pushed open, letting in the light and the afternoon air. Oddly, Finlan could smell the sea even more strongly in this room and wrinkled his forehead, looking around. Why would he smell the sea inside a building?

A raised dais sat on the far side of the room. Before it stretched row upon row of wooden chairs, but none of them was filled. Men stood talking in groups. Finlan estimated he saw about four hundred people. Several of them wore white or purple robes. *Priests,* he thought. There were children present as well; Finlan saw a few boys as young as six or seven years of age.

His iron grip wrapped around Finlan's arm, Entan took them left, toward the western corner of the room. They stopped to wait for a child who darted around their legs.

The little boy looked up at the last possible moment, realized he was knocking into an Alusian, and nearly tripped over his feet as he threw himself in a different direction. His approach had been that of an excited child—his exit was terrified.

Entan, what are you doing?

The men they approached were examining a crossbow.

Finlan's heart tightened when he saw it. *The skroel's crossbow.* He had never seen anything like it. It was as black as pitch, with symbols drawn across the wood with some sort of white ink.

These men also recognized Entan Gallowar. A few of them immediately looked somewhat nervous, but most did not. Specifically, the man holding the crossbow responded in a positive manner.

"Entan," he greeted. "You've returned." The man was tall and broad, as if he had been lifting heavy objects since boyhood. There was a faint touch of gray near his temples and a thin white scar across his forehead.

"Hello, Garran," Entan said and let go of Finlan's arm. "What do you have there?"

Finlan knew it was a ruse. Entan didn't need to ask the question. He knew exactly what the man was holding.

Finlan groaned deep in his chest. Dread built within him. "What are you doing?" he whispered to the boy.

Hearing those words, Garran glanced down at him. His brows came together, a faint flicker of concern passing through the dark eyes. "And who is this?"

"This is Finlan," Entan said.

To Finlan's surprise, recognition leapt through Garren's expression. "Finlan," the man repeated. "Now, *Finlan* is a name I have heard many times in the last several days. 'Tis a pleasure, sir. Amilia and Myles speak well of you. They were pleased to hear you would be joining us. Myles is here. Somewhere."

Finlan scanned the crowd but did not recognize any of the faces in this room. He had been hoping to see Myles right away—or the sister who was not his sister. *But perhaps it is for the best,* he thought, bringing his gaze back to Entan. Something was not right here.

"Finlan has come to speak with my uncle about the sea." Entan nodded toward the weapon. "May I see that?"

"Of course." Garran did not hesitate. He did not question the boy's motives. He didn't seem to see what Finlan saw. He passed Entan the weapon. "Look at the etchings there. Have you ever seen anything like this? A dark but beautiful weapon. I knew the skroel had magic, but I did not know they had anything like this."

"Where are the bolts?" Entan asked.

Finlan reached out and took hold of the boy's arm. "Entan," he cautioned.

Entan looked at him. Finlan had never seen a look like this before. It drove spikes of cold through his stomach, and without meaning to, he released him and took a step back.

One of the men held up a leather satchel, also black. The same strange white symbols covered the strap. Without a word, Entan carefully reached into the bag and brought two of the black bolts out into the light. Entan had been right, Finlan saw—the ends of each bolt were smeared crimson. The blood glistened. It had not dried.

Finlan shuddered, his apprehension growing. *This is not right. Not right at all.*

"Careful there, lad," Garran said with an easy smile. He was unconcerned.

Entan did not have a smile anymore. "Oh," he said quietly, "I will be very careful."

"Finlan!" a familiar voice exclaimed.

Finlan had to remind himself to keep breathing when he saw Myles approaching. The young man smiled at him. He appeared well, despite whatever misadventure he had faced this morning. He was all right. He was fine.

Slowly, Finlan's strange fear began to ebb. He *knew* he did not need to be afraid of Entan. He knew that. The Alusian blood was thin in this boy; there was no reason for Finlan to be wary of his actions. Entan had proven that day after day, bringing him here and looking after him. Entan was Alusian, yes; but he was a good boy.

Finlan heard the skroel's bolt click into position. Entan had loaded the weapon.

The sound had the same effect as a scream. Conversations throughout the room cut off. Four hundred men fell silent in a moment, their attention captured by that single metallic click. Finlan could suddenly hear the sound of his own breath.

Myles took two more steps, and Entan leveled the crossbow at his chest. The welcoming light melted from Myles' eyes. His steps slowed. He cocked his head, as if he didn't fully believe what his eyes were telling him.

There is hope the skroel will be successful yet.

Surely not, Finlan thought, shaking his head. *Surely the Alusian does not mean to complete what the skroel failed to do.*

But he did.

In front of the entire room, the creature released the first bolt. At this close range, it was impossible for him to miss. The blow staggered Myles' steps, drew him around. It wasn't pain that filled his features; it was surprise. He stared at Entan, shoulders bowed, his body half turned away from him. Finlan saw blood appear along the back of his tunic. The bolt had cut clean through his chest, penetrating the skin on the other side.

Before the shock could be overcome and his actions realized by the rest of the room, Entan fit the second bolt in place.

Garran reached for him as Entan lifted the crossbow, but Entan was Alusian, and he was quick. Sliding away, he shot Myles again, this time in the back. Finlan grimaced as he registered the sound of metal breaking bone. The bolt lodged firmly between Myles' shoulders.

The man collapsed to the ground.

The room came alive.

Finlan stood there in horror as Entan was tackled to the floor. The black crossbow skidded across the marble.

chapter **2**

When Entan Gallowar saw his uncle's face, he started crying. Tears wet the floor beneath him. The boy's hands had been bound behind his back, and large men held him to the ground. It could not be a comfortable position. Standing by himself, Finlan stared at the boy and could not fathom why he had done this. Myles had survived all manner of things, only to be shot down now, by an Alusian's hand.

Jonathan Manda, Entan's uncle, was as old as Finlan. A long white beard hung down to the middle of his chest. His face was weathered and dark, as if he had spent so much time in the sun that it had marked him permanently. He had a face like that of a ship's captain.

Jonathan did what Finlan had been doing: He stared at the boy on the ground. One of his hands came up and found his chest. He seemed to think that if he pressed hard, he could slow his heart. Finlan felt the man's sorrow and recognized the disbelief burning through the other's expression. Finlan had liked Entan, too. Now he simply did not understand.

Men knelt around Myles. The young man had not died yet. The rough sounds of his gasps could be heard through the room, and Finlan wanted to cover his ears.

One of the men kneeling beside Myles had Myles' face. *This must be Marcus,* Finlan thought. This had to be the brother. Which one was the father, the one called Hileshand? He glanced through the other faces and could not tell. None of them had that particular look of anguish a father would have in this situation.

Why? Why did you do this, Entan? Entan was very fond of his uncle Jonathan. Finlan had heard some lovely and rather exciting stories about the abbot of Ausham, who could hear Abalel's voice clearly. Finlan had been looking forward to meeting him. Not once had he imagined circumstances such as these.

"What have you done?" Jonathan asked his nephew.

The pitch of his voice was much higher than Finlan had been expecting; it was like the squeak of an animal. Did he always sound like this? It was a unique voice for an abbot of Abalel's school, which was a position of prominence.

The boy wept. "Pairs."

"What?" the uncle whispered.

"Pairs. They always come in pairs. The skroel do not fight alone. One…" Entan stifled a sob. "One goes to the intended victim. The other goes to someone that man cares for. If the first is unsuccessful, the second kills the loved one. You know this!"

One of the men dressed in a white robe lifted his arms and said, "Yes. We know the skroel work in pairs—we are not children." The man was completely bald. His head gleamed as if he had rubbed it down and polished it. His voice was everything the abbot's was not. It was clear and deep, a broad voice, and Finlan supposed he had spent much time speaking to crowds. The man stared down at Entan and treated the Alusian like a foolish youth, a reprimanded schoolboy. "The woman is protected. Her father is with her even now."

So that was why Finlan couldn't pick Hileshand from the crowd; he was with Amilia, keeping her safe. *Good,* Finlan thought. That made sense. Finally, something made sense.

Leaning back, the bald man projected his voice, saying to the entire group, "Amilia is safe. This time, the heathen gods of death sent only *one* creature. They could not send the completed pair—this is Ausham. We would have known if there were a second anywhere within the gates."

Finlan saw a handful of nods. Most of the men agreed with him.

On the floor, Entan laughed bitterly through his tears. "They never send only one. You should listen to Abalel more and yourself less. You have lost your wisdom, counselor."

"*Eurackain!* You will be silent in the presence of Abalel!"

Unwanted, he called him—it was the same Paxan word used for weeds that grew in a cultivated area, where they were not supposed to grow. Finlan blinked several times and pressed his hands together, feeling pain in his heart. The bald counselor used this word to describe the abbot's nephew, and he used it in front of the abbot.

But who would be able to say anything about it? Entan had just killed a man, in front of them all. The man dying on the floor was a dear man. One who had just been re-turned to his father.

Poor Myles. And poor Amilia. Finlan would weep for her as soon as he was alone.

Marcus rose to his feet. His resemblance to Myles was uncanny. Finlan had seen this hard look before.

Marcus glared at the counselor. "Abalel *more,*" he repeated tightly. "Yourself *less.*"

The counselor sneered at him. "You would defend this Alusian even as your brother bleeds out on the floor? It would seem the female chose her companion wisely."

The room dropped into silence. Everyone stared at Marcus.

Marcus held the counselor's gaze. Entan could not tell what he was thinking, except that they were harsh thoughts.

"You teach that when Abalel says something will happen, it will happen," Marcus answered. "You teach that he does not speak half-truths, nor does he forget his words or change his mind, as a man would do." Marcus pointed at his brother, and that was when Finlan saw the depth and nature of Marcus' emotions—Marcus did not grieve. He was angry. "Either we trust Abalel or we don't. Either he is true, or he isn't. Which is it? Abalel has given my brother a prophecy, and he does not go back on his word. Now is not the time to hesitate, Orrien. You hesitate—when you should be moving forward."

A shiver wrenched its way up Finlan's spine. *How...?* Marcus spoke the same words Entan had spoken in the atrium. *Abalel's council hesitates.* How did Marcus come to think like an Alusian?

Marcus shifted his weight and slammed his booted toe against the bottom of his brother's foot. It was a firm strike. Myles groaned. Every man present sucked in his breath, startled.

Finlan stared with wide eyes. Myles had taken a bolt through the chest and another through the spine. The brother had gone mad.

"On your feet, Myles," Marcus ordered gruffly.

When his order was not obeyed immediately, Marcus frowned. "Myles!"

He made as if to kick him again, but his brother hissed, "Don't touch me."

The air ground out of his lungs as Myles pushed himself into a sitting position. Blood drenched the front of his tunic. Scarlet had pooled on the floor. He trembled once and then calmed, drawing deep breaths. Finlan could hear every inhalation.

The temperature in the room lowered. The smell of the sea grew strong again. *What is this?* It was beginning to scare him now. He had never experienced this before—the strong smell of his beloved sea, with no reason for its presence. In his cave on the mountain, there had been a reason: the trapdoor set in stone. But what was this? *Issen-El, what do you do here in this strange place? With strange men?*

Myles sat there with one hand bracing himself on the floor, the other covering his face, his head lowered. A bolt protruded from his back. The bolt in his chest was buried deep and could not be seen.

No one moved.

The counselor had fallen silent. None of those in robes made a sound. When Myles had been on the floor, they had whispered to one another in alarm, all of them, but now the room was quiet.

"Let him speak," Myles rasped.

The men holding Entan relaxed the force of their grips but did not let him up.

"The bolts are dipped in the blood of the partner," Entan replied. "Each skroel carries the blood of the other. If I had not injured you in this way, with both bolts, the second skroel would have attacked the woman. But now he will not, because he feels your blood. He will report to his masters that you are dead, and the woman's life will be spared." He swallowed. His face was wet, but the tears had stopped.

"Which woman?" Myles asked softly.

"Hana Rosure." The Alusian paused and amended, "Hana Gaela."

Not Amilia. The arrogant counselor in white, the one who treated Entan as if he were a child—he had the wrong woman. He had been mistaken in his assumptions.

"Who is Hana Rosure?" one of the others asked in a quiet voice. He was standing near the counselor and was dressed in purple. Finlan thought that perhaps the man was a student here.

The question was asked of the abbot, but Myles was the one who answered.

"My mother." Myles pulled his hand away from his face. His eyes were red. Blood covered his lips. He leaned over and spat on the floor, ran the back of his hand across his mouth.

Marcus donned leather gloves and offered his brother a hand, palm up, which Myles accepted. Once on his feet, the man staggered for balance, and Marcus grabbed his arm. He held on to him.

"Good?" Marcus asked.

Myles stood there. He did not quickly move again. He

drew in a deep, full-lunged breath, like an Alusian. He released it, repeated the process. Deep breaths.

Every man in the room gaped at him.

Turning his head, Myles looked through the crowd and found the face he wanted. He pointed toward the man gripping the skroel's satchel. "Bring that to me."

The black satchel was placed in Myles' hand. He flipped it open and withdrew one of the bolts. He was not careful with how he touched it. The skroel's blood mixed with his own. "Get him up," he grunted and examined the bolt in his hand.

The Alusian was dragged to his feet. Entan sniffed loudly, like a little boy. His face was wet and blotchy, the blue eyes bright from his tears. They seemed to gleam.

Myles handed the skroel's satchel to his brother but kept the bolt he had removed from it. On his own, he walked slowly to the Alusian, each step a little firmer than the last. He recovered. The blood he had lost weighed down his tunic, made it thick and heavy. He fiddled with the bolt in his hand, getting the skroel's blood all over his fingers.

The blood is very dangerous. Finlan doubted it was meant to be touched like this.

The room waited to see what Myles was going to do with that bolt. Finlan wagered that in this moment, Myles could do anything he desired, and no one would stop him. The thought would not even enter their heads—for Myles should be dead. He had been shot in the chest, near the heart, and also shot in the spine; Finlan had heard the bones break. Myles should be dead.

Myles lifted the bolt. "What would happen if I touched you with this?" He brought the skroel's blood near the

Alusian's cheek. The bolt had a sharp point. It would not be difficult to push it through skin.

Entan did not move. He did not react in any way, but Finlan heard the uncle take a quick breath, alarm in the sound. Jonathan's wrinkled hands rose, fingers spread in caution, yet he didn't say a word. There was nothing that could be said.

In his typical calm fashion, Entan answered, "If you broke my skin with that, I would die in a short time. In a matter of hours. The skroel's blood is highly poisonous for everything but a skroel. Forgive me for doing what needed to be done." He paused. The intensity returned to his blue eyes, and he stated, "Next time…just take the hit. Let him attack you."

Next time? Whispers stirred the crowd.

Myles' grip tightened on the bolt. "And here I thought you weren't going to tell me my fortune."

The sarcasm seemed to fall flat. Entan nodded as if he didn't hear it. "The skroel will attack you again. There are some who recognize the skroel's attack as it occurs and choose not to resist it, offering themselves as a sacrifice to save the ones they love. The skroel are cruel, the children of Viceese—a bitter god of death and pain. The next time you are attacked by a skroel, accept the blade. It will be easier. For me."

Myles pushed his thumb against the bolt's bloody point, cutting his skin. With a slight frown, he pulled his thumb up to his lips and sucked the blood away, his blood and the skroel's blood both together. "Is my mother involved both times?"

"No. The next time, the skroel is paired with your father."

Finlan had heard many things about Hileshand, Myles' father.

Something dropped to the floor behind Myles' boots. Several men gasped. Audible disbelief swept that side of the room, through the men who had a clear view of his feet.

Myles turned to see what had happened, and Finlan saw what the others had seen. He added his own sounds of amazement. It was the end of the bolt, the visible piece that had been protruding from Myles' back. The bolt had broken, or melted. A twisted piece about two inches long lay on the ground.

What is this? Finlan did not know if this cold emotion thrilling through him now was fear or something much better than fear. *What is this?*

Myles reached up and rubbed the hole in his chest. Loosening the ties of his tunic, he pulled the fabric down and examined the wound. The bleeding had stopped. He pressed his fingers against the opening, but it was as if it ignored him; the bleeding did not restart. Next he reached behind him and felt for the hole in his back. He bent and twisted, tried to find it and appeared to be having trouble. Nothing restricted his movement.

Straightening, he grunted deep in his throat and shook his head once, his look becoming fierce, yet it was not anger. Finlan saw the bolt tremble in Myles' hand, and as the man drew breath, Finlan heard the unsteadiness of it. This was not anger; it was concern. Perhaps even fear. This was a reaction Finlan could understand. He did not know what he had seen here today—but he knew it was glorious, something no one had seen before. The words Marcus had spoken roared through Finlan's head: *When*

Abalel says something will happen, it will happen. He does not speak half-truths. Abalel was very powerful, to save a man's life in this manner.

Myles glanced at the guards holding Entan. "Let him go."

They obeyed instantly and released the Alusian. As Marcus pulled a knife from his belt and cut the creature's bonds, Myles dropped the bolt he had taken from the skroel's satchel. It hit the floor and rolled toward Garran's feet. The man sprang away.

Swiftly, Myles turned and headed for the door, his steps broad and purposeful. Blood covered the back of his tunic. Finlan stared at him. They all stared at him.

Marcus watched him go, an amused, knowing smile on his lips.

Myles did not make it seven steps before the room erupted with a chorus of exclamations, and dozens of men surrounded him, blocking his exit.

chapter 3

Half a mile away in one of Ausham's guest-houses, Hileshand and his daughter, Amilia, waited in the sitting room. It was the only room in the house that had fewer than three windows. Ausham was devoted to the god of the sun, and subsequently, there were many windows, letting in as much light as possible. The skroel could use a window as easily as they used doors. A few years ago, Hileshand had heard a story of how the skroel had killed a target who had been living by himself in a secure room. Every door had been guarded, every opening sealed along the ground. The only unguarded point was a small locked window set high in the wall. It was closed before the death and hanging open afterward. The fewer the windows, the safer the room.

Amilia sat on the couch, her lower lip protruding, her arms folded in disgust. She had not responded well to the morning's threat. Hileshand had seen no tears from her, but she pouted like a child. She loved his son, and she did not appreciate the forced distance, especially when there appeared to be no reason for it. According to Orrien, the very bald, very *vocal* student counselor, only one skroel had entered Ausham.

The men at the gate were seers. They could look at a man and know his intentions as easily as a farmer could look at storm clouds and know that rain approached. They were very skilled at sensing danger. They had known about the skroel before the attack but were yet uncertain about his point of entry. He had not come through the gate, nor had he touched the wall. They had seen only one of the creatures. Orrien was right—only one. But Hileshand was cautious, and pouting had no effect on his willpower. Twenty men surrounded the house. Captain Isule stood guard on the front porch, watching the sitting room's windows from the outside, while Hileshand kept watch inside the house.

Isule met his gaze through the pane.

Hileshand saw a line appear between the sea captain's brows. Isule turned and looked behind him. A moment later, a soldier came through the trees, jogging toward the house up the path.

After two hours of silence, Abalel's council had finally sent word.

Isule received the man first and after a brief conversation, motioned for Hileshand to join them.

"Wait here," Hileshand told Amilia.

Her blue gaze snapped to his. "What? Why?" She was five months pregnant. She had been able to hide it for a time, wearing clothes that fit her comfortably, but not well; she was rapidly losing that ability now. Rising up off the couch, she gripped a square pillow in one hand and lifted it slightly, as if it were a weapon. "Why?" She stood on her tiptoes and peered around his shoulder to see Isule with the messenger. "Why can't I come, too?"

He would have smiled at her consternation, had she not appeared so serious. "Wait just for a moment. I'm going to see what he says first."

The pillow rose a little more. "Hileshand—"

He stepped into the kitchen and took the door that led onto the porch, closing it securely behind him. Hileshand had seen this soldier before. He recognized the peculiar jut of the man's cheekbones but couldn't remember his name. It began with a *C*, and it was an odd name, something foreign—a name as odd as the man's face.

"Your daughter is safe," the soldier said. "As Orrien stated, the second skroel is not in Ausham."

"There is always a second," Isule murmured.

Hileshand glanced at him. "Do they know where the second is?" he asked the soldier.

The man nodded. "Hana Rosure."

Hileshand stared at him. His heart stumbled. "What?"

The soldier waved his hand in a dismissive gesture. "There is no cause for concern. It has been taken care of, but there is a story to it, and I should not be the one to tell you. Come quickly, sir. They wait for you."

Hileshand returned to the sitting room, where his daughter glared at him.

"Well?" she demanded.

"Yes, we can go now." He motioned for her to come to him. The second skroel had been sent to Hana? He could not think of that. He couldn't consider it. "Hurry."

The scene that awaited them in the Council Chamber was not the scene Hileshand expected.

Myles and Marcus were sitting on the dais—Marcus in a chair on the right, Myles in a chair on the left, with Jonathan Manda standing between them, his hands clasped in front of him. Marcus looked relaxed. He was sort of sprawled in the chair, his elbow hooked around the chair's arm, his legs stretched out in front of him. Myles, however, had been stripped to the waist after a severe injury. Blood covered his chin and jaw, smeared across his forehead, on his hands, all over his chest. Amilia gave a strangled cry when she saw him. Her fingers dug into Hileshand's arm. What had happened?

Jonathan Manda called to Hileshand from the dais. "Come up here."

Hileshand left his daughter with Captain Isule in the front row and slowly took the dais steps to stand at Jonathan's side. He stared at Myles and the blood that coated him. There was much blood. He had tried to wipe it from his lips and had succeeded only in smearing it.

"Are you all right?" Hileshand asked quietly, when he could form sounds again.

Myles nodded. "Yes."

"You are certain?"

A slight smile this time. "Yes."

Hileshand had left his sons in peace. The guards had killed the skroel out on the green—Myles hadn't even seen the skroel. A slew of expletives swamped Hileshand's head. "What happened?"

Myles shrugged, both hands lifted.

Jonathan related what had happened. His nephew, Entan Gallowar, had shot Myles twice. Once in the chest and once in the back. "There is always a second," Jonathan said. His voice echoed through the Chamber.

Every time he spoke, he reminded Hileshand of a

child who had not matured beyond five or six. He did not have the voice of a spokesman; he didn't sound like a man who directed the throne of Paxa in worship, but that didn't matter. He had a significant gift to hear Abalel's voice. The entire nation respected him, much more than they had respected Constance Perebole, his predecessor.

"The second," Jonathan said, "was sent to Hana Rosure, and Entan saved her life."

Myles and Hana. Hileshand reached up and ran his hand over the lower half of his face. *Hana.* He and every other man here had instantly assumed the skroel would seek out Amilia, whom Myles intended to marry at the end of the week. Genuine in his Furmorean view of the world, he refused to travel with her again until she was his wife. He wished to give her the opposite of what she had known and treat her with the highest level of integrity possible.

Myles had been shot twice. With poison-tipped bolts.

Jonathan put his hand on Hileshand's shoulder. A touch meant to calm him and redirect his attention. Hileshand recognized the look Jonathan gave him now. The abbot had heard Abalel's voice, and he was about to speak in response to Abalel's words.

Jonathan motioned to the twins. "Tell me about your sons, Hileshand."

Hileshand drew a breath and replied, "Apparently, I can't turn my back on them for a moment."

He received two identical grins in reply, and the tension began to ease in his chest. His concern grew quiet, turned over, and became something entirely different. "These are my boys. They are mine." Pride swelled in his heart.

"And are they called by your name?" Jonathan asked.

One of them was. Marcus was. And in truth, it did not matter to Hileshand what Myles called himself. Nothing would be able to shake the foundation that Myles had laid in Hileshand's heart. Myles was his son, through and through, and he would remain his son; it had nothing to do with his name.

But Myles smiled, appearing completely at ease. He nodded once. *Yes.*

"Yes," Hileshand whispered. The word tripped at the back of his tongue, and he cleared his throat. "Yes, they are. Both of them."

"You are familiar with Myles' prophecy," Jonathan said soberly. "He will have power over the Ruthanian throne and be able to direct its course."

Hileshand smiled, the pride rising through him again. "I believe the exact words were that he would hold the throne in his hand."

Marcus started laughing. He tossed a wide smile toward his brother.

Jonathan nodded. "True."

For a moment, the Chamber was still. The crowd sat in silence.

"Hileshand," Jonathan said slowly, "as you know, our council here in Ausham watches the activities of governments. Abalel shows us what occurs in Ruthane, Galatia, and other nations before the word of man reaches our gates. By the time the actual news does reach us, it is our history, for we already know it."

"Yes," Hileshand said.

"Abalel speaks to his prophets. Before any action of political import is taken, he reveals that action to us. Only rarely does Abalel keep his secrets." Jonathan started frowning. "This morning, we received news that was unexpected, something we had not heard before. A courier brought it to us. General Link Claninger of Ruthane has assassinated his king. Habeine is dead, his government overthrown. A new king has been instated in his place." Jonathan studied Hileshand beneath a wrinkled brow. "The new king of Ruthane is Korstain Elah."

Marcus came out of his seat and then, realizing he had moved, sat back down, shock etched through his features. He looked at Myles, but his brother appeared rather bored.

Myles had never met his blood father. This news did not seem to interest him. If anything, he seemed faintly belligerent toward the prospect. A mild scowl formed a series of lines between his brows.

Hileshand made certain he had heard correctly. "Korstain Elah has gone and made himself the king of Ruthane?"

Jonathan nodded stiffly. "Yes."

Hileshand remembered the man unfortunately well. Korstain Elah was intelligent, capable, and thoroughly ambitious. If there was something he desired, he committed himself to the task and would not cease until victory was his. *The throne of Ruthane.* His ambition had taken him to the height of any man's achievement, but at what cost? Hileshand looked at Myles. He looked at Marcus. Both of these men had been stepping stones for their sire. He had traded away their lives without hesitation.

Hileshand had been on duty the night the twins were born. The moment Korstain's wife had gone into labor, Korstain had set about drinking himself into a mumbling stupor. It was as if he had known what was coming—that he was going to lose her. He disappeared with a bottle in each hand, and the servants had rushed around in a panic, trying to find him before his wife died.

Korstain Elah, king of Ruthane. Myles was Korstain's firstborn, but his position as heir had lasted for all of five minutes. Then the priest had carved the half-moon into his chest and sent him with Hana Rosure to the temple, in accordance with Temple Law. The position of heir had then transferred to Marcus. If he had been allowed to keep it, Marcus would be the succeeding prince of Ruthane. That was an odd thought.

Korstain had remarried when Marcus was four years old, and there were other sons now—two that Hileshand knew of. They had been seven and five the last time Hileshand had seen them.

"Korstain has already proven that he has no intentions of following in Habeine's footsteps," Jonathan continued. "He executed the priests of Oelemah and Etnyse, who were Habeine's counselors. The temple has called for his death but does not have the power to bring it about through force, for the military supports him."

Jonathan rubbed his hands together and looked at Hileshand steadily. "Hileshand, it is time to consider Myles' prophecy again. A man—named Hileshand—will hold the Ruthanian throne in his hand. In light of these new facts presented to you today, what do you believe this prophecy means?"

Myles did not care about a single thing related to Korstain Elah. Why would he? The man had proven himself worthless. Not only had Korstain shown his true character to Myles, but he had also gone to greater measures and revealed it to Marcus, who had loved him as a father. It was a grievous matter to get rid of a child at birth, but it seemed much more grievous to get rid of a child who was *known*, who had been raised and cherished in the household. The ugliest highwayman from the poorest city had more value in Myles' eyes than Korstain Elah.

But as he watched Hileshand's reaction to Jonathan's question, Myles found himself growing curious. Hileshand stopped moving. His face paled, and the muscles contracted in his jaw. Myles had never seen this sudden look of rage before, and he felt the seriousness of the situation with greater clarity.

Hileshand looked at Marcus. His gaze shifted to Myles.

Myles frowned at him, asking the question without words. Hileshand clearly perceived the question but looked away from him, unwilling to answer.

"Would you like to discuss this in private?" Jonathan asked quietly.

"There is nothing to discuss." Hileshand did not match Jonathan's tone. He was not quiet.

"You have not heard the full prophecy in years. On the contrary, there is a great deal to discuss."

Hileshand leveled a glare at Jonathan, his old friend. "I say there isn't."

Myles heard nervous, quiet comments ricochet through the room. He saw frowns appear in the crowd sitting before the dais—scowls directed at Hileshand's back—and he still did not understand why the man was angry.

Jonathan nodded. "Then we will speak at a later time."

Before Hileshand could argue, Jonathan motioned to the counselor, and the room was dismissed.

Myles held up his hands and twisted away as Amilia approached him. "Wait," he said. "Don't touch me. Don't, Amilia."

They had taken his tunic and burned it, but that did very little to relieve his problem. Myles needed to be picked up and tossed into a lake. Repeatedly. He was right to be concerned. Most of the blood on his body was his own, but not all of it.

Standing on the dais steps, Marcus watched as his brother retreated, trying to keep the girl who loved him at a distance. Amilia appeared at a point near tears. She followed Myles, speaking words Marcus couldn't hear, and Myles backed away from her. The men parted and gave them room. It would have been amusing, had it not been Amilia, if it hadn't been Myles. Amilia was beautiful, even when her brow was furrowed with anxiety and worry.

Marcus looked away. He needed to get beyond this, whatever this was, as soon as he could. She was going to be his brother's wife. He did not begrudge either of them for that; he was happy for them.

He sighed. *So very happy.*

The abbot came down the steps behind Marcus, stopping to watch Myles and Amilia as well.

"Will it always be like this?" Marcus asked.

Jonathan's brows came together. He did not seem to understand the question.

Marcus clarified. "The skroel. The *atham-laine.* Things trying to kill him and failing."

"I don't believe so," Jonathan answered. He pulled his hand down his beard and repeated, "No. I don't believe so."

The room was slowly emptying. Several steps behind Jonathan, Hileshand stood by himself on the dais, his arms folded, his brow lowered.

Nodding toward his father, Marcus asked quietly, "Do you know what he knows?"

Hileshand responded now in a way that jolted Marcus

with its familiarity. He had seen this look before. One night during Marcus' thirteenth year, thieves had attacked their camp. Hileshand had fought like a madman and thoroughly destroyed those who had been intent on bringing them harm. Whenever Marcus considered his decision to refer to Hileshand as his father, it was this expression he saw in his mind. It was a look of strength, severity that promised protection, no matter the cost. In Marcus' mind, it was the look of a true father.

Jonathan looked at Marcus with something that resembled pity. "I don't think he *knows* anything. I think he simply suspects what Korstain Elah is about to do, now that he has obtained the Ruthanian throne, the prize he wanted."

"I don't understand you," Marcus said.

The pity in Jonathan's eyes became more pronounced. He fidgeted with the end of his beard and sighed. "You don't see it, do you? But no, I suppose you wouldn't. You are familiar only with Korstain's betrayal. That would not be an easy weight to carry, and I'm sorry that it is yours." Jonathan shook his head. "Consider the facts. How does Korstain think? What is the driving force of his thoughts? It is his ambition. He has what he desires now—he has the throne, and he has taken measures to preserve that throne. He is thinking ahead."

Marcus began to suspect what Jonathan was about to say. The possibility turned his stomach.

"As king, he cannot have an estranged son roaming about the country. It could lead to upheaval, even war. His enemies could seek you out and attempt to use you for their own purposes." Jonathan glanced back at Hileshand, and his voice filled with the notes of sympathy. "Hileshand is afraid he is going to lose his sons."

chapter 4

Bryce Gallowar, Entan's father, had lived in Ausham for sixteen years. Gallowar was a carpenter by trade and one of the few men within the city gates who had never attended Ausham's School of the Prophets. He had, in fact, not even stepped foot into the Council Chamber, not a single time, and he held this as a matter of pride. A man of great talent, Gallowar could make anything with his hands. This remained true despite a logging accident five years ago that often kept him in a chair. On a good day, Gallowar could stand for thirty minutes at a time, sometimes a little longer. During the winter months, that number dropped considerably.

This morning, Bryce Gallowar sat near the front windows of his main room, his legs covered with a red blanket. He was Hileshand's age, perhaps a little older. Entan had his smile, Marcus realized.

"Father," Entan said, and for a moment, he sounded like a normal man, with no Alusian blood. "This is Marcus Hileshand."

"The Alusian's companion," Gallowar said, nodding. He said it simply, as if he understood it and nothing about it compelled him to shake in terror. It was a very different response than that of most men in this city. Gallowar shrugged and offered lightly, "I have heard much about you, Marcus. Some of it was good." His eyes filled with humor.

Bryce Gallowar had been married to an Alusian whose father was a full-blood. The Gallowar bloodline was the only mixed-Alusian line Marcus had ever heard of. Entan had told him that no others survived.

Gallowar appraised Marcus in silence for a moment and then nodded to the chair opposite him. "Sit with me. Entan, pull the other chair out of the study."

As his Alusian son stepped from the room, Gallowar said, "I suppose I know why you have come to see me."

Marcus sat down. "Your son says you are very wise and that your opinion of the Alusian is based in truth, not in fear."

Those were Entan's exact words. He had also said, *If you yet require courage for the task set before you, my father can help you. He knows the Alusian better than any man alive.*

The brows rose, and Gallowar wryly replied, "My son tried to kill your brother."

Marcus smiled faintly. That was true. "Entan seemed to know what he was doing."

The humor trickled through Gallowar's eyes again, and he glanced at a small portrait sitting on the mantel. The woman in the picture was lovely, and the artist had painted her as white as a winter field; Marcus assumed the woman was Gallowar's wife, Selia, who had died when Entan was a small boy.

Thinking of Gallowar's wife brought Marcus around to the wedding he had observed this morning. *Myles and Amilia.* Following Furmorean tradition, the ceremony had taken place at dawn, with the abbot overseeing the vows. No one had minded the hour; nearly the entire city had come to attend the wedding of the man who did not die.

Marcus was grateful it was over. Now, perhaps, he could move forward and put aside this ache in his chest.

Entan returned with the chair and sat down. "Father," he said, "Marcus would like to hear about my mother. Would you tell him the story you told me?"

Bryce Gallowar referred to his wife as "my Selia." He did not call her by her name alone; consistently, there was a "my" in front of it. She remained the light of his heart, even years after her death.

Marcus thought of Bithania and wondered how any man could fall in love with an Alusian. According to Entan, Alusian females did not differ from one another in temperament. They were all much the same. Stubborn. Elitist. Difficult to touch. Meddlesome.

Except Bithania. Bithania is different. All the others are matchsticks, while she is the fire itself. She will say harsh things to you, Marcus, and I apologize for her in advance. The image she gives of the Alusian is not the image we wish to present of ourselves.

Entan insisted there was warmth in the female soul, but Marcus had never seen it in Bithania, and to be honest, he could not even imagine it with her. He had spoken with her at length, and there had been no warmth.

But here Gallowar was, attesting to the contrary. He had loved an Alusian female—*a matchstick,* as Entan had put it. A fire ready to start.

"Her family lived outside my town," Gallowar said. "No one ever saw the father. He was a full-blood, and he did not follow any suggestion of Paxan culture. His wife, a Paxan woman, would come into town for supplies, and she often brought my Selia with her. The first time I saw her, I was six years old, and she was four, and I remember the sight. I thought she was beautiful, even then."

Gallowar smiled. In this moment, he did not seem sad at her loss. "I saw her every few months for five years. One day, I found a piece of quartz in the river. I thought it was beautiful, and it reminded me of her. It glistened and glowed pink in the sunlight, and I knew she would think it was interesting, because I thought it was interesting. Perhaps it would give me a chance to talk with her. So I carried the stone in my pocket for three weeks, and finally, her mother came to town again and left my Selia in the wagon. I stood by the wheel and smiled up at her, and she just stared at me."

Gallowar laughed quietly. "She wouldn't talk to me, so I just left the piece of quartz on the wagon seat. I told her it was a gift."

"Gifts are important," Entan said suddenly.

Marcus looked over at him. The Alusian sat there, arms folded, watching Marcus intently, as if there was something he wished him to understand.

"Gifts are important," Entan repeated. "If you give me a gift, I know why. If it is a bribe, I know it. If it is out of fear, I know it. But if you give me a gift from a genuine heart, it will mean more to me, as an Alusian, than it would mean for a man without the blood, because I know why you gave it. Remember that."

Marcus nodded, feeling a bit like a child at school.

"Two nights later, Selia's father came to my father's door." Gallowar snickered. This story seemed to give him a tangible level of amusement. "Scared the wits out of my family—me as well. I had never seen the father, but I immediately knew it was him because my Selia looked like him. He asked my father if he could speak with me privately and promised he would not hurt me, or anyone in my family. My father, with strong trepidation, gave him permission, and the Alusian took me out behind the barn. He had the piece of quartz, the one I had given my Selia, and he put it back in my hand."

Gallowar's eyes gleamed. "He told me, 'You cannot give this to her yet. It is not time. Wait ten years and then come back.' And that was what I did. My Selia was the prettiest girl I had ever seen. I didn't care what the others said about the Alusian. I didn't care about any of that. I thought she was perfect. So when I was twenty-one years old, I went to her door, stone in hand. I knocked and her father opened the house to me. 'I have a gift,' I told him, 'for your daughter.' My Selia was standing behind him. She smiled at me, and I was..." Gallowar paused, seeking the right words. "There are few things that have come close to making me feel what I felt that day."

"Had you spoken with her at all?" Marcus asked.

Gallowar chuckled. "Very little. Just when her mother brought her to town. But that didn't matter. I knew. I knew she was for me, that she was mine."

Entan spoke up again. "It can be like that."

"What can?" Marcus said.

"Boerak-El has no boundaries and does not follow traditions of man. My father was directed by him and responded to his direction. He loved my mother without details, without actually knowing her, yet when it was time for him to know the details, they were given to him. It can be like that. With Boerak-El, the story can happen without a man's full understanding. It is because Boerak-El knows the details and has been directing the man accordingly for years. If that does not make sense to you now, it will make sense to you eventually." Entan shrugged. "Boerak-El does whatever he wishes to do."

Even bend the laws of life and nature. Marcus nodded slowly, a familiar question rising up within him. He had been wondering about something. "How do the Alusian age? It is different than we do, isn't it?"

Entan studied him with what appeared to be surprise.

Gallowar looked back and forth between them.

"Aye," Entan finally replied. "We mature as men do until our twentieth year. After that, we age according to purpose, not according to year. Some live for centuries and some die as children, but neither of those timeframes is considered fair or unfair, because always the purpose is known. It would not be wise to live beyond your purpose."

"True," Marcus agreed. "How old is your grandfather?"

Entan scowled at him. "Marcus, you think you know something, and I do not know what it is."

Marcus laughed at him, truly entertained. "I *think* I know something? Thank you for that. Your confidence in me is overwhelming."

Bryce Gallowar laughed. "The grandfather is old. Very old. He has a purpose that has not been completed, and he was born a long time ago. I have spoken with him four times in my life, and each time was a…unique moment."

He abruptly changed the subject. "Tell me about your quest with Bithania."

No one had asked Marcus this question. His father, the abbot, Abalel's council members—they avoided this topic with care. No one wished to address it. Marcus knew the answer to Gallowar's request, at least in part, but he wasn't certain how to express it in an understandable way. Boerak-El was not considered an enemy within Ausham's gates, but neither was he considered a friend.

"The quest," Marcus said at last, "is not harmful. I think it will even do me good in the end, for I trust Abalel more than I have ever trusted him in my life, and it is *because* of Boerak-El."

"Have you said any of this to the abbot?" Gallowar asked.

Marcus had *tried* to say these things to the abbot. "A little," he answered and glanced out the window. Gallowar's house did not face the street. It was set back in the shadows of an old oak grove, and the view out the window revealed very little but trees. Anyone crossing from the street to the house would not be seen from this room.

Gallowar followed his look. "Are you expecting someone?"

"Yes. The abbot."

Gallowar's head tilted with interest. "Jonathan has a class that starts in less than an hour. He's been teaching the same class, at the same time, for twenty years."

"He's making an exception today."

Entan smiled, seeming pleased. "Boerak-El speaks to Marcus, Father. He tells him interesting things."

Gallowar stared at his son, and then he stared at Marcus. After a moment, a smile cautiously spread across the older man's mouth. Marcus saw strains of uncertainty in his look, but they did not appear to be fear, as it would have been with any other man.

"What else do you know about Bithania's quest?" Gallowar asked.

"I don't know much about it, actually. I do know that every Alusian quest is different, and this quest is, perhaps, more unusual than some. Simply because it hasn't been done before." Marcus hesitated. This would be the first time he spoke these words aloud, the first time he voiced something that had been told him in private. "Boerak-El wishes to remind his people of something they have forgotten. I will remind them." He shrugged. "That is all I know."

Gallowar frowned. "What could the Alusian forget?" He looked at his son. "Is it possible for an Alusian to forget something?"

Entan answered without pause. "Yes. Yes, it is very possible for an Alusian to forget something—and to forget it so thoroughly that we begin to resemble men."

Heavy insult indeed, Marcus thought wryly.

"Of what are you going to remind them?" Gallowar asked.

Marcus shook his head. "I don't know." The words he was about to say would be curious words to speak in any part of the country, but here in Ausham, they seemed especially peculiar. "Boerak-El will tell me on the way."

chapter 5

Jonathan Manda enjoyed Finlan immensely. The old fisherman from the high country bore a simple wisdom that was gentle and friendly, and he had been faithful to Issen-El all his life.

Abalel was the Ruthanian name of the Creator, the god who brought life to the world. Most called him *the god of the sun* because it was an accurate symbol of his nature: He was the one who caused all things to grow. But for a simple fisherman who had grown up on the shores of the Paxan Sea, the bringer of life would be what was before him: the sea, his livelihood. The sea was also an accurate symbol of Abalel. The god was the same; only the name was different. Jonathan had lived in Paxa his entire life, and he had never come across any inconsistencies between Issen-El and Abalel. Abalel never contradicted himself; he was, however, very fond of presenting himself in such ways that men could search him out and find him. For Finlan, Abalel used the sea.

On the day of Myles and Amilia's wedding, over the noon meal, Finlan suddenly put down his cup and exclaimed, "Jonathan! Did Myles tell you we have gifts for you?"

Jonathan cocked his head. "Gifts, Finlan? No, he did not say anything about gifts."

Finlan nodded, as if he could understand how this information had slipped Myles' mind. "Well, they do not bear your name. Perhaps he did not consider this, but I think this is how it should be done. You are the abbot now—you should have the old abbot's gifts."

Jonathan looked across the table at Hileshand and Antonie Brunner, the redheaded scribe out of Tarek. Both men shrugged at the same time. They did not know about this either.

"The old abbot, Finlan?" Jonathan asked. "What do you mean?"

"Aye. Constance Perebole. We came to Ausham to bring gifts to Constance Perebole. That's why we're here."

Jonathan stared at him. It felt like his heart squeezed into stillness, then violently jolted back to life. *No, this cannot be right.* Only one of Hileshand's sons had a prophecy. The other son did not. *Not Marcus.*

But then the familiar words snapped into place in Jonathan's head, and he realized he and his council unexpectedly possessed a significant problem.

Many prophecies were delivered in riddle, rhyme, or some form of prose, but this one had come to Ausham's council in pieces, like a child's game that had to be put together in order to be seen for what it was: a prophecy about a first counselor. A man who would be the liaison between Ausham and the Paxan government. It was a fairly prominent position, and it was never bestowed carelessly, for the first counselor represented the School of the Prophets and therefore Abalel himself.

"Myles…?" Jonathan began. He had to clear his throat and try again. "Myles has a gift for Constance Perebole?"

"Not *a* gift, Jonathan," Finlan proudly corrected. "*Many* gifts. Entan said the man has been dead for twenty years, so I think you should have them instead."

Jonathan gripped the edges of the table. "Myles has gifts for Constance Perebole?" He noticed Hileshand's frowning study and ignored it.

"Gifts for you," Finlan repeated.

"But *Myles* is the one who brought these gifts?" *Abalel, what are you doing?* The prophecy could not be for Marcus, the Alusian's companion. None of the council would accept him willingly. Marcus was the Alusian's choice for companion *and* Abalel's choice for first counselor? This had never been done before.

"We both brought these gifts—you'll see. I will go get them." Finlan went into the other room and returned with his bag. Untying the straps, he took hold of the bottom of the bag and turned the entire thing upside down.

Little pieces of wood clattered across the table and rolled. Hileshand captured three of them as they attempted an exit near him. Jonathan caught one. He held it up and examined it. It did sincerely appear as nothing more than a piece of wood.

"Gifts from Issen-El," Finlan declared. "He has been giving me these little pieces of ash wood for years. Some of them are very old indeed. I had no idea what they actually were until Myles—"

A sword materialized in Hileshand's hand.

Finlan pointed at him with joy. "Yes! You know how they work. Myles had to show me." He gestured to the pile of sticks on the table. "Weapons, all of them. Gifts from Issen-El. All of them bear the same name: Constance Perebole. I knew we needed to bring them to him. This is why I left the mountains—to bring Perebole his gifts, but then Entan told me he was dead, so I assume Issen-El means them as gifts for you, Jonathan. Why give a gift to a dead man? No, the man must be *alive* to receive a gift. Otherwise, it is not a gift."

Jonathan did not move.

"Something amiss?" Hileshand asked, tossing the sword from one hand to the other and putting his free hand to the abbot's shoulder.

"Finlan," Jonathan said, urgent, "why do you say these are from Myles, if you are the one who brought them?"

Finlan picked up one of the sticks and made stabbing motions in the air as he answered Jonathan's question. "He knew what they were. I never would have known if he hadn't shown me, so they are very much gifts from him as well."

Abalel, this cannot be right, Jonathan thought.

Immediately, as if in answer, the words of Bithania Elemara Amary came thundering back to him, hitting him like a frigid wave of the sea. Just before she had touched Marcus with Boerak-El's power, she had belligerently told Hileshand, *Your son has a greater part in Ausham than you know.* She had seen the future and spoken prophecy.

Entan. That boy. What did he know that he had not told? He did this at times—he knew what Abalel was about to do, yet he did not offer his wisdom to others.

Jonathan turned his gaze to Hileshand. "Where is Marcus?"

Suspicion began to pool in Hileshand's eyes. His tone took on a faint but distinct edge. "I believe he is with your nephew. Why?"

What could Jonathan say? What could he tell his friend Hileshand? Nothing came to mind except that Bithania had been accurate. *The female was right.* Marcus Hileshand *did* have a greater role in Ausham than any of them had realized.

A single knock on the door, and it opened before Bryce Gallowar could reply. The hinges squealed.

"Entan? Bryce?" Jonathan called.

Gallowar looked at Marcus. "So he misses his class after all. You were right. When possible, a man should be accurate with his fortune-casting, especially you." His eyes twinkled. He lifted his voice and replied, "In here."

Jonathan stepped into the sitting room. The abbot seemed agitated, flustered. He wrung his hands.

Hileshand was with him. He gave Marcus a brief smile and lifted both hands in a shrug behind the abbot's back. He did not know what transpired here.

"Marcus, Entan..." Jonathan took a deep breath and squeezed his hands together until the knuckles whitened. "I have questions for you both."

Entan stood from his chair. He did not seem concerned or perplexed at the suddenness of his uncle's appearing; it was a rare day indeed when something surprised him, and whenever he did appear surprised, Marcus felt an intense level of satisfaction.

"Uncle, Marcus has already heard his fortune. He knows the questions you are about to ask."

Marcus did not know the *exact* questions Jonathan wanted to ask, but he did know the topic, and yes, he had heard his fortune. The glimpse of the future that no Alusian wanted to give—*that* was the fortune Marcus had heard.

The abbot made a noise of disbelief in the back of his throat. His gaze flicked to Marcus. "You know about the position of first counselor?" he demanded.

Marcus regretted the surprise that washed through his father's expression at those words. He wished he had told Hileshand everything he knew, in private—but what would he have said? All things pertaining to Boerak-El were like an entirely different language. Hileshand feared for him, and Marcus didn't know how to relieve the pressure.

"Yes," Marcus answered.

Jonathan shook his head and stared at him. "How long have you known—did Bithania tell you?"

"Yes."

Hileshand began to frown, and Marcus sighed. *I know. But what could I have said?*

Hileshand despised Bithania. Before hundreds of witnesses, he had vowed to kill her if she injured his son, and Hileshand did not make such statements lightly. He didn't understand that Bithania *hadn't* hurt Marcus—her touch had not been one that brought sorrow. Instead, it had cleared Marcus' vision and gifted him with the room to breathe. It was not sorrow that Boerak-El had instilled within Marcus, through Bithania's hand.

For a brief time, the abbot considered Marcus in silence. Then the old eyes narrowed. "When will you return from your quest?" He did not say that last word gently. *Quest* came out of his mouth like a curse.

This was not going to be an easy road.

chapter 6

Jonathan waited two days.

Then, in the evening, he pulled out one of his table chairs and arranged it on his short front stoop, settling down with a pillow at his back and a book in his hand. But the book he quickly found to be uninteresting, and no matter how he arranged the pillow, his back complained against it.

The evening was remarkably warm for this late in the year. Abalel had told Jonathan about the warmth and how young couples liked to walk together at sunset.

Sure enough, after an hour, he saw them. They came up the road leisurely, his hand around hers. The two of them were alone—Jonathan had not seen anyone else come this way in several minutes—and they were talking. *Planning the future, no doubt,* he thought and sighed. The situation would be sad if he weren't so intrigued.

"Myles," he called.

Myles and Amilia came up to the stoop.

Amilia smiled warmly, and her husband said, "Evening, Jonathan."

Again, Jonathan released a sigh. This time, perhaps, there was a bit of sadness in it after all. The girl was so happy, and Jonathan knew enough of her past to understand that this happiness was new for her.

Just for a season, he reminded himself. *Remember—it will be just for a season. She will survive it and be stronger for doing so.*

Jonathan pulled himself out of the chair. He was highly distracted now, and the book toppled off his lap. Myles bent to retrieve it for him.

"Boy," Jonathan said.

Myles was not a boy, but sometimes, it was necessary to remind men that certain things, certain truths, remained inside them, no matter how old they became.

Myles looked at him, waiting, book in hand.

"I want you to do something for me," Jonathan said.

There was a slight hesitation. A moment when nothing responded. Then Myles answered, "What is your request?"

Jonathan smiled at his reservation and his willingness both at once. The abbot glanced at Amilia, a step behind Myles, the glow unmistakable on her face. He was about to give this young couple more questions than answers. He did not like this sort of work and avoided it when he could.

This was not one of those times.

"Just stand there," Jonathan said and set his hand on Myles' chest.

The images rose up before Jonathan like moving pictures on a canvas. The colors were bright and steady, depicting scene after scene of Myles' future. This was often how Abalel spoke to Jonathan; he gave him pictures. Jonathan knew how many children Myles would have. He saw their faces and knew their aspirations. He saw Myles sitting at a long polished table with a man Jonathan immediately knew was Korstain Elah. It was surprising how much Myles and Marcus looked like their blood father. The same nose. The same eyes, especially in Myles' case. Jonathan recognized Korstain's scowl, and all at once, he knew the source of several of Myles' expressions. Marcus had a different temperament, but Myles—

Jonathan stiffened as the realization gripped him. Myles was like his blood father. He was *like* him. Jonathan could see the similarities clearly. Could Hileshand see them, too? Was that partly why he had responded so strongly in the Council Chamber, when they had spoken of Korstain Elah and Myles' prophecy? Hileshand could see that the two men were similar, and when two men are similar, they are better able to understand one another.

Everything Abalel showed Jonathan of Myles' future took place in Ruthane. He saw nothing of Furmorea. Nothing of Paxa or any other nation.

And then Jonathan saw something else.

He paused in his thoughts, in his breathing. He looked at Myles closely. "Really?" he said. His intrigue blossomed into delight. Hileshand had never hinted at this; he had said nothing about it. Was it possible Hileshand didn't know? Getting words out of Myles was like getting oil from a rock. Maybe Myles hadn't told anyone.

Jonathan pulled his hand back from Myles' chest and just looked at him. "You have a gift," he said.

Myles grimaced.

"Why didn't you tell me? I could have helped you. Boy, that's what we do at this school—we teach people how to hear Abalel's voice." Myles needed to understand what Abalel had given him, so Jonathan pressed, "There are different levels of gifting, Myles. You can hear his voice as clearly as anyone in the school, and you have had no training whatsoever."

Amilia took her husband's hand. Jonathan observed this simple action and realized that perhaps Myles had kept his gifting hidden from Hileshand, but he had not kept it hidden from his wife. Amilia knew what others did not. Why go to the trouble of hiding it? This was a good thing to have, a *good* gift.

Myles' grimace grew more severe. "I didn't know what it was," he said.

"Well, that can happen at times. There is no shame in that. Many of our students come to us because they want to understand what is happening to them, not because their understanding is already complete."

"No," Myles said. "No, I mean…the gate. Something happens when you come here. Something happens at the gate of Ausham. I thought his voice could be heard by everyone in Ausham. It is his school, where his prophets live. I didn't realize that…wasn't the case." He shifted awkwardly.

"You never heard him speak before you entered Ausham?"

"No, I didn't."

It was no small matter to hear Abalel's voice. Neither was it a small matter for the man who heard it to be on his own, in a country that did not honor Abalel as God. Ruthane had once been an Abaleine nation, a country that followed Abalel's ways, but they had traded Abalel for Oelemah and Etnyse, gods of death that offered favors to men who sacrificed to them. The greater the sacrifice, the greater the favor, which was why Ruthane had adopted heathen practices like killing the chosen twin. Habeine, Korstain's predecessor, had promoted Temple Law to an unprecedented level, and his people had suffered under his fanatical rule.

Myles' prophecy suddenly connected with Jonathan's thoughts in a new way. He saw it in a greater light than he had before. The prophecy declared that Abalel's name would once again be spoken in Ruthane, and that the people would remember what they had forsaken.

And Myles could hear Abalel's voice.

"What has Abalel told you?" Jonathan asked slowly.

Myles sighed and looked at Amilia, who offered him an encouraging smile.

"I need to go to Ruthane because it will be good for Ruthane," Myles mumbled.

"That is true," Jonathan agreed. "He wants to take back what once belonged to him, and he will use you to do it. It is a significant prophecy. Something of great worth."

Myles scowled. It was Korstain's scowl—the exact image Jonathan had seen a moment before. He marveled at how much Myles resembled his blood father. Hileshand had never mentioned this—but he wouldn't, would he? He wouldn't want to see the similarities.

"He also said it would be good for Korstain," Myles said next.

Jonathan could imagine that being true as well. One could not bring light to a nation without also bringing light to its king.

"Is that all?" Jonathan asked. "Is that all Abalel has said to you?"

A moment passed before Myles answered, "Abalel also said that this would be good for Hileshand."

"Hileshand," Jonathan repeated in surprise. How would this be good for Hileshand? Hileshand despised Korstain Elah. He thought Korstain was going to take his son from him. The entirety of Myles' future lay in the nation that had once tried to kill him.

The look in Myles' eyes grew hard. "I don't care about Ruthane. I don't care about her king." Then his voice lowered, and the tone softened. "But I do care about Hileshand. He is a good reason—will always be a good reason—to make a sacrifice."

Myles loved Hileshand, his namesake. Jonathan had seen this again and again. Myles respected him completely. He would do anything Hileshand asked of him, and he would do it with pride, the sort of pride a son has for his father, when he has seen the father's worth and known the father's heart. Hileshand had done well with Myles.

Amilia wet her lips and asked quietly, "When will we go to Ruthane, Myles?"

Jonathan knew the reason for Myles' sudden wince.

Amilia would not be going with him.

part two

Hana

chapter

 All at once, it was over.

The trees stopped at the base of a charcoal cliff—an unforgiving fence she could not climb or cross. The wall of stone tilted backward on itself, giving the appearance of an old man bulging in the middle, and she could not see the top.

They had come so far, and suddenly, they could go no farther. The forest was thick and dark in this area of northern Paxa; the branches had hidden the cliff from view until this moment, allowing just enough room for Hana Gaela and the one remaining nurse, Mimi, to think they had chosen a good route of escape. Instead, they had lost all their options.

The wind picked up. The branches danced, and Hana imagined she heard a dark sort of laughter.

No, she thought. She said it aloud: "No, you will not win." Her voice wheezed out of her. She was gasping.

"Hana," Mimi sobbed. "What are we to do now? The way is blocked—what do we do?"

Each of them carried a child on her back. Little Ramia gripped Mimi's neck with both arms, her dark eyes wide and full of something that was not fear. The emotion wasn't anything safe to name, and Hana would not try. Ramia was three years old, old enough to understand, at some level, what she had just seen. The guards had been killed right in front of her. Her favorite nurse, whom she called *Nana*, had fallen from the coach, and their attackers hadn't seen a reason to spare an old woman. Since that moment, Ramia hadn't made a sound. Hana was alarmed by the look in the child's eyes. She wished it were fear; fear would be easier to mend.

Hana carried Stephan, Ramia's older brother. He was seven and much heavier than his little sister. The sweat rolled off Hana's body, draining from everywhere—her brow, her arms, her chest, her back. She was tired, so very tired. Stephan's weight seemed to have tripled over the last mile.

They had run from the road into a ravine that had no exit. At least one soldier followed them—he was behind them, somewhere down the hill. His name was Fostaine. Until this day, Hana had rather liked him. Jovial and friendly, he had always been pleasant toward her, but his good will had been false. There had been a plan in his heart, the entire time.

Hana swung Stephan off her back and gently set him near the stone wall, leaning him against it. He looked up at her with pain-clouded eyes. She had felt the pattern of his breathing change, and she knew this look he gave her. He was due another dose of his medicine, but there was no possibility of that. In all the commotion, his medicine bag had been left back on the road.

"Are you all right?" he asked her quietly.

He asked her this. Precious Stephan. The disease in his spine had aged him far beyond his childhood years. He spoke and interacted with others like a young man, someone near the end of his schooling. It was when he showed childlike interest that Hana looked at him twice, having forgotten his actual age.

She smiled at him tenderly. She would give her soul for these children. "Yes. May I have your sword?"

With a cautious frown, he passed her the wooden blade—a gift from his father. Stephan carried it everywhere. It was always somewhere within his reach. He was unable to be the warrior he wished. He could not hold a real sword, walk more than a few steps on his own, or draw a breath without pain, but this little wooden sword had become his symbol of hope. He was a fighter in his mind—a boy much braver than many of the men Hana knew.

"Hana," Mimi whispered again, wiping clinging strands of hair from her forehead. "We cannot stop in these woods. The miron will find us. We have to keep going."

Hana turned blazing eyes upon her. "And where would you have us go? Would you wish to go *back*?"

Mimi dragged in air. Her body sagged beneath Ramia's weight, and she adjusted her footing. Sarcastic now, she spat, "You have a different plan?"

"Yes." As calmly as she could, Hana replied, "I'm going to kill Fostaine. Stay here."

"With a wooden sword? Hana—" Mimi shook her head so quickly that it seemed her brain shuddered. "This is our end. We have to go back."

Hana glared at her.

Mimi glared in return. "At least we would live! The children, too. It's a ransom they're after, not our necks. You heard Fostaine!"

Hana could not believe the woman's stupidity. She had seen the simplicity of this mind before, but she could not stomach how it presented itself now. "They killed the other guards!" she shouted, the anger dissolving her weariness. "Men who were their friends! What do you think they would do to *us*, Mimi? They are not interested in our welfare. We don't know what they would do to the children. They are *lying* to us. Why can't you understand that?"

Mimi's face darkened. "You are a child's nurse, and a woman, and you have only a wooden sword. What can you possibly hope to do?"

"Kill him," Hana answered. She looked down at Stephan. "Thank you for the use of your weapon, my lord. I will return it."

Mimi tried one more time. "Hana…"

"Wait here," Hana snapped.

She ran back the way they had come.

chapter 8

Hana found Fostaine at the bottom of the hill. She felt a brief rush of satisfaction when she saw that he was just as winded as she.

Fostaine stopped as she came into his line of sight. "Hana," he said, putting his hands to his knees and heaving in several deep breaths. "Stop. Stop running. Why are you running?"

Her anger returned in a wild burst. "You dare ask me that? Lawvek has been nothing but kind to you. How could you do this to him? How could you even think of doing this?"

He straightened slowly, still trying to catch his breath. "You don't need to argue with me. You don't need to try and change my mind. Obviously, what is done is done. There is no turning back now."

His face was scarlet, and he wiped sweat from his brow with his leather-wrapped arm. He was wearing full armor, the uniform of his station as a guardian of his master's house. He had held a trusted position for multiple years, and the thought of his betrayal was like needles pushing through Hana's chest. Just the sight of his face was repulsive to her. If he threatened Lord or Lady Lawvek, that would be a different matter. Instead, he threatened children. Small children, one of whom could not even stand on his own.

She gripped the wooden sword. "You are not taking the master's children."

He sneered at her. "You're a nurse. And you've naught but a wooden sword. What could you possibly hope to do?" He tapped his metal-clad chest. "Armor, my love. Stephan's little sword will break upon it."

He sounded like Mimi. She glared at him. "I am going to kill you." She was certain of that now. This man was going to die. She would find a way, and she would kill him.

Fostaine laughed, mocking her. "No...no, I don't think so." His tone of voice changed. It raised bumps along the back of her neck. "You have been promised to me. My employer asked what I wanted in exchange for Lawvek's children."

She shivered at the look in his eyes.

"And I knew what I would ask for. He will not have you. It will be only me." He nodded up the hill. "Give me Lawvek's children. Make this simple for us both. I know where they are—they will not be difficult for me to find, whether you assist me or not." A dark sort of smile slid across his mouth, and he said, "There's no need for you to be jealous, you know. I don't want Mimi. I am going to sell her to the miron. She is stupid and dowdy, and from the first day I saw you, you've been the only woman I wanted."

Hana held the hilt of Stephan's sword in her right

hand and gripped the blade with her left. *A wooden sword.* For an instant as she considered the situation soberly, her anger hesitated. *What do you hope to do with a wooden sword?*

Stop it, she commanded. She did not have the option to fear.

She thought of little Stephan, leaning against the rock, his small face twisted with pain. She thought of Ramia, who had seen her beloved nurse die right in front of her and now did not respond when Hana spoke to her. The anger returned in full force. She could feel it in her veins. She lifted her wooden sword. "You are not going to touch me."

"I am going to do much more than touch you," he replied and started toward her.

Hana staggered backward and squeezed the blade into her palm until her hand hurt. "Abalel," she whispered, desperate.

The wooden sword trembled in her hands. She was so surprised that she nearly dropped it. Fostaine misunderstood her response and took it for a different sort of fear. He laughed.

"Give me the sword, my love," he said.

The hilt shifted in her grip. She jerked her hand off the blade as the wood grew cold and damp against her skin. Stephan's play sword began to lengthen, and as she watched, it transformed into a real blade. It was lightweight and balanced in her hand. The blade glinted in the shadowed light that trickled in through the tree branches.

Fostaine stopped. He stared at the blade. Then he lifted his gaze and stared at her. "You're a witch. Well, now, that explains it. This is a spell. I have not been able to think of anything but you. I haven't been able to sleep…" He lifted his hands as if to plead with her. "Don't you see what I've done for you? All of this is for you! I have given you your freedom! I will take care of you, Hana. You will be safe with me."

She wanted to yell at him. What had destroyed his mind? How would she be *safe* with him? Twelve soldiers had left the Lawvek estate five days ago, and seven of them were dead now, killed by Fostaine and the men who had joined with him. She gripped the sword's hilt. "Turn around. Go back. I will not kill you if you go back."

A scream tore through the quiet of the woods. The harsh, braying cry jerked a thick line of shivers up Hana's spine. She looked around quickly. *Miron!*

Fostaine leered at her. "Too late," he said. "Your choice has been made for you. They will take Mimi, of course— no great loss there—but they will also take Ramia. Her death would be a tragedy, would it not? Do you truly wish to be responsible for the death of one so young? We will let her live, Hana. We just need to get to her before the miron do. Put the sword down."

She maintained her grip, keeping the sword level. "Those children are in my protection, and I will never give them to you."

She held a real sword—proof enough that Abalel did not intend her to fail.

Thunder rolled overhead, and the clouds began to drop rain. The leaves trembled as water struck them and bent down to release their weight to the forest floor. Red splattered across Fostaine's face and armor, running down his form in crimson trails. After a quick scowl toward the sky, he glared at her again, wiping his face with both hands.

"What are you doing now?" He sounded annoyed, not alarmed.

But Hana was terrified. *What is this?* As the rain increased, red filled her vision, and she hurriedly ran the back of her arm across her eyes, trying to see. The sky appeared to be bleeding.

Fostaine pulled his sword and approached her. "Witch," he hissed.

His attack was determined and strong but far from deadly. He did not want to injure her; he meant to unarm her. She blocked three of his blows before the hilt ripped from her hand. Stephan's sword spun through the air and buried itself point first in the soil beneath a leaning thagbrush tree.

Fostaine grinned. His look churned her stomach. She could see in his eyes what he intended.

"Now then," he said quietly, "let's review your situation again."

He never touched her. The leaning thagbrush shook violently, and a large black form swung out of the branches and dropped down behind Fostaine, dragging him to the earth. Hana staggered back as the two bodies wrestled on the forest floor. She remembered Stephan's sword and ran for it. As her hand closed around the hilt, she heard the snapping of bones and a single, choked cry.

Trembling, she whirled around.

Fostaine did not get up. The miron did. She held the sword out as it scrambled toward her on its feet and several of its hands.

"Stay!" she shouted, not knowing what else to do.

It stopped and cowered. Multiple sets of hairy arms

extended from the long torso. She couldn't tell how many there were. She had never seen anything like this. The face was *almost* like a man's. The skull was covered with black hair from the top of the head to the jawline; there was no white in the eyes. Several of the creature's hands lifted in an imploring gesture, palms uncovered.

"Make it stop," it whined. The voice hissed like steam through a kettle. "Make it stop!"

She stood there immobile. Make what stop?

Thunder roared across the land. The miron jerked toward the earth, pairs of hands pressed against the sides of its head. Hana had not seen any ears, but it appeared now to cover them.

"He is angry! Make it stop. Make it stop!"

Suddenly, she understood. The realization seized her heart. *Abalel.*

Drawing a breath, Hana pointed at Fostaine's body. "How many more?" she asked, trying to sound stern. It did not work and she tried again, yelling, "How many more? How many like this one follow us?"

The creature was shaking. The blood of the sky ran across its form, matting its hair. "Four more," he cried. "Four."

"Keep them away from us! You will not touch us. You will not come near me or those in my party."

"Yes, yes—kind sir. You are a kind sir. The rain will stop, yes? He will not be angry?"

Sir? These multi-armed creatures attacked and killed women—why did it call her *sir*? She nodded. "Yes. Stop those men, and he will not be angry." She hoped it was within her power to make that promise. She hoped she was right, so this creature would obey her.

The miron bolted back into the tree, swinging up by its hands and gripping the bark with its feet. Despite its size, it disappeared into the branches. She couldn't see it anymore. A tree on the *other* side of Hana started shaking as well, and she lurched backward, jerking the sword up. How many miron were there?

The movement in the trees on both sides of her flowed quickly away, back toward the road. Screams resounded through the woods—those were the miron. They did not sound human. Then other screams joined the first, and these sounded like the cries of men. They were not far from where she stood—Fostaine's men had been close behind.

Hana stood there until the trees stopped shaking and the cries grew quiet. The thunder faded, but the rain continued, the water droplets slowly growing pink, then transparent, then clear. The rain was merely rain now. The blood-like liquid washed away.

Her heart throbbed. She turned and jogged up the hill. By the time she reached the stone wall at the end of the ravine, she was thoroughly drenched.

Mimi was gasping for breath as if she were about to die, little Ramia clutched in her arms. When the nurse saw Hana, she started to weep.

"It's all right," Hana told them. "They've gone. We're safe now."

"The sky," Mimi wailed. "Did you see the sky?"

By Abalel himself, Hana thought in frustration. *That* was what scared Mimi the most? "I most certainly did. Look, Stephan—look."

Hana held up his sword. The blade began to retreat in size. She felt the hilt moving all on its own. The sword grew dull again, transforming back into the toy given him by his father—a simple wooden blade and nothing more.

"Did you see that?" Hana exclaimed and grinned at him. She blinked water from her eyes.

The boy stared at her. "Abalel listens to you," he whispered. "You told me this, but until now, I did not believe you."

Hana plopped down beside him on the ground and leaned close to kiss his forehead. "Yes, little one. Yes, he does listen, and now we are going to find a way to get you home again."

chapter 9

ive hours later, Hana left Mimi with the children in the woods and crept out into the cold silver moonlight spilling across the shoulders of the Yomal Road.

They were five days out of the city of Red Sands. Though not the shortest route, Yomal Road provided the smoothest journey for little Stephan as they made their way to the estate of the children's grandfather. Three times Hana had been a part of this journey. The children saw their grandfather often. He doted on them, particularly Stephan. Lord Keresgrove would read to him for hours at a time and take him by carriage up into the hills to look at the views around the estate. He loved his grandson, and the boy's illness did not dampen his enjoyment of him. If anything, the boy's frailty seemed to make Lord Keresgrove a much more tender man.

This stretch of road between Red Sands and the small city of Yomal was often quiet. One could go for a full day without seeing any other travelers. Hana hoped that had been the case today, and the scene of this afternoon's attack had been left undisturbed. Stephan needed his medicine. He never cried, but Hana could always tell when he was in pain. Tonight, in the darkness of the trees, she had felt the tears on his cheeks and discovered how much he suffered in silence. This was the first time he had gone this long without relief.

She had to get that bag.

The night bore the bitter tones of winter. *First the bag, and then a fire.* She tried to pretend that she felt warmth instead of cold, tried to ignore the way her hands were shaking.

When she found the first body, she squeezed her hands into fists and tried to keep her breathing steady and calm. In the moonlight, she could not tell the man's identity, but it didn't matter; she had known all of the guards. All of the dead. Any still, lifeless form she found on the road tonight was likely to be one of those who had been betrayed, as she had been betrayed. Killed by his friends. Her heart twisted. Her hands shook for reasons other than the cold. How she despised this.

When the killing had started today, the coach had lurched forward and raced for about a mile before their pursuers had managed to stop it. In the ensuing fight between those who killed and those who protected, Hana and Mimi had grabbed the children and run. Stephan's bag had dropped off Hana's shoulder before they had reached the woods. There had not been time to go back for it, but she thought she could remember where she had lost it.

Cautiously, she walked alongside the road. When the overhanging trees did not block the moonlight, she cast a black shadow that slid silently in front of her and a little to the right, leaning into the grass. She found a second body.

The man's head lay at an odd angle, his face twisted away from his chest. Fostaine and his men had not killed him from a distance, with a sword or an arrow; they had put hands to him and broken his neck—a man who once had been their friend. Heat rushed through her, followed by wave after wave of nausea.

She had lost the bag right after they had run from the coach. When she had jumped out the door with Stephan, she had knocked free a small insulated chest that had been sitting on the floor. It had tipped out the coach door and landed in the road. Stephan's bag would be somewhere near it.

It took her fifteen minutes to find the chest. A half-mile from where she started searching, it was lying face down on the edge of the road. Going to her hands and knees, she felt around in the grass she could barely see, sheltered by the shadows of the trees. She found many things that were not Stephan's bag. Her hands came up covered in something sticky. She knew it was blood, and her stomach started a second rebellion. A dead guard lay several feet away from her. This one had some sort of weapon sticking out the front of his armor. It appeared to be an ax.

I need that bag. I have to have that bag.

She heard movement that was not her own and looked up quickly.

The road behind her was empty.

Miron, she thought instantly, but the night remained quiet. There was no animalistic screaming, no shaking in the trees. There had been no sign of the miron since this afternoon, when they had retreated in haste.

As she crouched in the grass and watched the road, a

cloud began to blow across the moon. *No, no,* she thought and watched as the road darkened, the shadows lengthening and growing stronger. She widened her eyes, trying to see.

The noise came again. Footfalls to the side of her, beneath the tree branches. The animal was in the grass, the same as she.

Something growled.

Not miron. It was definitely not miron. The sound was broader, deeper, as if it came from a much larger beast.

Hana stayed where she was, still as a stone. The footfalls slowly approached her, the growling becoming more insistent.

Abalel, she thought and began to retreat, one small movement at a time, back toward the dead guard. *Abalel, again...I need you.*

Her heart felt like it was going to burst behind her ribs. The fear she had felt this afternoon with Fostaine was nothing compared to the fear she felt now. At least this afternoon, she had been able to see her attacker.

She backed into the dead guard, her leg bumping against the cold metal covering his shoulder. Holding her breath, she leaned backward in the darkness and felt around for the ax. Part of the head was buried through the breastplate. She worked it carefully, rocking it back and forth, her eyes on the blackness before her. The weapon loosened its grip in the man's chest, and she grimaced, trying not to think about what she was doing. *I'm sorry, my friend.*

The growl became a snarl. Taking hold of the handle, she ripped the ax free and jumped to her feet. A hard, hot, hair-covered mass slammed into her and sent her toppling onto the road. Her shoulders met the ground with force, the animal's weight bearing her down.

Snapping and snarling near her face. Ax in hand, she shoved the creature away from her. She felt fur on her fingers, skin spread thinly across a rib cage. The animal, whatever it was, was not as large as she had expected, but it was determined. Something sharp slid across her left arm.

She scrambled away and came to her feet. Growls erupted through the concealing darkness, and she swung the ax, aiming for the source of the sound. The blade connected with something that squealed in reply. The ax jerked in her hands. Freeing it with a sharp twist, she took a step forward and slammed the ax straight down, toward the road. The first downward slash hit nothing but stone. The second time, the ax caught something and pulled. She tightened her grip. The creature hissed at her. The handle ripped out of her hands.

Sounds of movement. Metallic clicks on the road as the animal retreated. Crashing brush on the other side. A significant amount of brush. *What was that?* The animal had felt small beneath her hands, like a dog, but when it entered the woods, it made a noticeable amount of noise.

Hana stood there, ax gripped tightly, and waited for the next move, the next snarl out of the trees. She had no weapon. Distantly, she wondered if she had splinters in her palms and fingers from the wooden ax handle sliding hot and quick across her skin. Her arm throbbed. Other than that, nothing hurt.

Nothing attacked her.

She forced herself to breathe deep, calming breaths. Listened to the shadows.

The cloud that had made all of this difficult began to ease away from the moon, and as the light spread across the road again, Hana looked and saw nothing. The creature had retreated completely. Her arm was bleeding. Glistening darkness trickled down her skin and off her fingertips.

Was that it? Was it over?

She heard steps on the road behind her. She spun around.

A man jogged toward her. "Are you all right?" he called.

He was not a soldier. In the moonlight, she saw no armor, but he did carry a sword and it was out of its scabbard.

Run, she thought, but her boots didn't move from the ground.

"Miss?" he said in Paxan, slowing to a stop. His gaze seemed to focus on the blood on her arm. "I heard a commotion. Are you all right?"

"Who are you?" she demanded. Without thinking, she spoke in Ruthanian, her native tongue. She didn't recognize this man. He was not one of Lawvek's personal guards, but that didn't necessarily mean he wasn't involved. Fostaine had spoken of an employer. Perhaps this was he or one of his men, come to collect.

The man put his hand on his chest and spoke in the same tongue back to her, his words succinct and purposefully calm. "My name is Lehman Isule. Are you alone? You should not be alone, miss. There are miron in the woods and, as you have apparently seen, other things as well. May I bring you to our fire? We'll bandage your arm, get you cleaned up." He studied her. "I want to help you."

"What are you doing here? In the dark?"

He put his sword away and lifted his hands. He meant to calm her. Pronouncing his words with care, he said, "There is a hunting cabin just up the road. About a quarter

THE ALUSIAN'S QUEST

mile from here. There are six of us, and we have another
woman with us. Come back with me, and we'll see to your
arm. Your arm needs attention."

Suddenly, Hana realized she was shaking. Her arm
hurt. Her heart tripped all over itself. She wanted to curl
up on the ground and cover her head. Drawing her hands
to her chest, she whispered, "Do you have a lantern? I need
a lantern. I've lost something, something I need to find."

For a moment, the road was quiet.

"Yes," he answered. "We have a lantern."

Isule carried Stephan against his chest. He was gentle
with the boy, and it made Hana think that he had carried
hurting children before. It was impossible to tell in the
moonlight, but he did not seem like an old man, nor did
he seem young. Forty-five, perhaps. He had a short, dark
beard and all of his hair.

Hana held Ramia close, running her hand down the
child's small back as they walked up the road. Ramia did
not tremble against her. She did not make a sound. She
was as stiff as a wooden post.

"It's all right, little one," Hana kept saying. "You can
sleep on me. Close your eyes. You are safe now. Nothing
will hurt you now."

The girl held very still, but Hana knew she wasn't
asleep. This was fear. Trauma. It was not rest. She ached
for her. No child should have to see what Ramia had seen.

"It's all right, Ramia. It's all right now." The words had
no effect.

Mimi cried the entire quarter mile. She could not and
would not stop. They came to a slight trail, nothing larger
than an opening in the trees, and Isule led them forward,

into the woods. Hana had passed this trail about an hour ago but hadn't seen it.

It was difficult to see in the shadows. Gradually, square panels of light appeared in the darkness—the windows of a cabin, just as Isule had said.

Mimi was too distraught to open the door. She tried several times and couldn't, and Hana, rolling her eyes, shifted Ramia in her arms, took the handle in her bloody hand, and shoved the panel back with more force than necessary. Lamplight washed across the front stoop.

Isule entered first, ducking to avoid hitting his head on the doorframe. "We have guests," he announced. "I found people."

"You *found* people?" a man inside repeated. He did not sound alarmed at the prospect of sudden company; instead, it seemed that Isule's words amused him.

For a moment, Hana's tired mind told her she knew that voice, the one she had just heard, but she dismissed the thought. She was exhausted. It was not possible that she knew anyone here.

Mimi stumbled over the threshold and almost tripped headlong into some man's lap. Hana stepped through the doorway after her into a room that was fairly large. Beds lined the walls. A warm fire blazed in the hearth. There were many lamps. People sat around the table.

She heard a garbled exclamation. A chair toppled onto the floor. And then there was someone standing before her.

She looked up into the face of her son.

Someone took Ramia from her. Hana didn't remember when or how; she eventually realized she was holding Myles instead and the little girl was gone. Hana did not cry. She was too stunned to make a sound. He held on to her tightly.

"I am glad," he whispered into her ear. "So glad." Those were the only words he said, and he repeated them several times.

When he released her, she looked up at him. He smiled. She saw the new scars and ran her fingers over them—the jagged lines on his forehead and along his jaw. His smile widened. She knew this look. Something delighted him.

"What happened to your face?" she asked, still in shock. It was a question without any sort of worth, for he could chop off his nose and still be handsome, but she wanted to hear his voice.

He shrugged one shoulder and gestured toward his jaw. His eyes twinkled like sunlight on water. "I actually did this on purpose—so you could tell us apart."

She smiled because he smiled. "What?"

He nodded toward the man who now held Ramia in his arms. The little girl was sleeping at last, her head on the man's shoulder. She drooled on his tunic as he sat with her at the table.

Myles said, "You remember Marcus, don't you?"

Hana's hand went over her mouth. Marcus smiled at her. It was the same smile. The same eyes. The same facial structure. She knew this face. She had loved one just like it for years, and because of that, she immediately loved this one, too. The contract was signed with the first sight of his smile—but she did not know if it should be. What was Korstain Elah's son doing here?

"Myles," she said. "I don't understand. How is he with you?"

"It's a story." Myles shrugged again, as if it were nothing, but again, she knew his look; he teased her. Something amused him. He added, "His father brought him."

His father brought him. He spoke the words lightly, without understanding. His father brought him? "Myles…" she said. He couldn't mean it. Korstain Elah would try to kill him. With Myles' words, old fears came back to life inside her. Old hauntings and whispers of death.

Her son looked toward the other side of the room. Full of dread, she followed his gaze.

She was met with another familiar smile. "Hello, Hana."

The voice she had recognized at the door, the one she hadn't heard in years. *Hileshand.* He seemed easy and relaxed. He was leaning up against the distant wall, his arms folded, his smile steady and warm.

A hundred different memories poured into her head, where they churned like boiling water. Heat burned the backs of her eyes, and the image of him standing there blurred.

chapter **10**

$\mathcal{T}$he hunting cabin was clearly meant to house an entire hunting party and resembled more of a lodge than Isule's description of "cabin."

Stephan lay on his back in one of the beds along the eastern wall, the blankets pulled close to his chin. Captain Isule and redheaded Antonie had gone back out to the road and retrieved Stephan's bag. Hana mixed the boy's medication from instructions she had long ago memorized and spooned the grisly brown liquid into his mouth. The child needed a bath. Grime clung to his skin and made clumps in his hair, but she would see to that later, after his medication had come to life in his bones and eased his pain.

"That man is your son?" Stephan asked her. He asked the question quietly, but no one else was speaking, so his voice carried through the room.

She dabbed the excess from his lips. "Aye," she answered with a smile.

Her married son. Myles had a wife. Hana had known

that one day, it would happen, but he had never shown interest in any of the girls he had known in Nan. Their community had not been large, and every unmarried woman it possessed had shown a clear interest in Myles. Occasionally some bold female would act on that interest, and Myles' response was always amusing. Hana smiled as she remembered the way he would scowl, muttering all the reasons he didn't return the woman's sentiment. There were always reasons.

One time, her husband, Rand, had demanded to know what the problem was, and after Myles had begrudgingly told him, Rand replied, *Mark my words, boy. Women are all the same.*

For Rand, that was likely true. Hana had pretended she hadn't heard the remark.

Amilia was beautiful, with pale skin, hair as white as sand, and striking blue eyes. She sat close to Myles on the bench, her side to his side, his arm around her, his hand on her opposite shoulder. A simple yet demonstrative touch. Hana wondered where her son had learned to do that. She knew he had not seen anything like this in the home of her husband. Rand Gaela had not been an affectionate man. Yet Myles made the action appear easy and simple, as if he were long familiar with it.

Myles was married. The idea felt foreign to her. Hana had last seen him on a slaver's block in Tarek, and now here he was with his arm around a girl.

Stephan's head was propped up on a pillow. His eyes narrowed as he studied Myles sitting at the table. "How did he get his scars?" The interest gleamed in his voice like firelight on a sword blade.

Hana heard Hileshand's rumbling chuckle. He was sitting at the table across from Myles, and he snickered as if the boy spoke in jest. "Stephan," he said, "I could tell you amazing stories of how Myles received his scars."

"I like stories," the boy answered.

"How is your stomach? Are you hungry?" Hana put a hand to Stephan's forehead and felt the dampness of his skin. When the pain was bad, he did not like to eat; she would have to bribe him to do so. The medication required several minutes before it began to work.

"I am fine," the boy said. "I'm not hungry."

"Then sleep, Stephan. You should sleep."

He looked at her from under her palm. "It will be some time before I am able to sleep, Hana." His brows moved in a frown beneath her hand. Quietly, he said, "I…I hurt severely. I would like a story."

His sister had been placed in the next bed. She slept, her thumb in her mouth. Mimi snored loudly in a bed on the other side of the room. She had collapsed on top of the blankets, unmindful of the dirt and blood on her body. She had barely said more than a handful of words to anyone.

"All right," Hana said, "but perhaps you should ask *Myles* how he received his scars."

Marcus snorted his laughter. He was kneeling in front of the hearth and making supper for the second time that night. No one in Hana's party had eaten since that morning. "Myles is not good at telling stories."

The teasing familiarity in his voice caught Hana by surprise.

Myles scowled. "I can tell stories."

"You should tell him about the dragon, Myles," Hileshand instructed, the smile lines deep around his eyes. He attempted, somewhat in vain, to keep his mouth still.

Stephan's eyes widened. "A dragon? I like dragons."

Myles leaned back on the bench. He cleared his throat, held his arms out to either side of him, and began with elegance, "There was a dragon." He ended just as elegantly: "I killed him."

The men laughed at him, and he said, "That's what happened!"

Marcus rose before the fire and wiped his hands on the thighs of his trousers. Directing his gaze toward Stephan, he said, "See? Don't ask Myles."

There was but one story Hana wanted to hear just now. She looked again at Amilia. Myles had been forced out of Furmorea, and yet he had still found a Furmorean wife. The northern territories produced skin like this, white like fresh wood, and pale hair. *This* was the story Hana wanted to hear, but she would oblige young Stephan, at least for the moment.

"Well, then, what happened with the…dragon?" she asked Hileshand. That final word was unexpectedly difficult to say. *My son fought a dragon?* She was tired. She overreacted. She nearly dropped Stephan's medication on the floor.

Hileshand watched her. "Perhaps we should begin with a different story, one that provides a foundation for all the others." And so, instead, he told the story of how Marcus had come to be in his keeping.

Without effort, he did what he had always done and removed Hana's tension. He put her at ease. She had forgotten what it felt like to be in Hileshand's company. She had missed this. She had missed his stories—the sound of his laugh, the way he showed others value. Her husband, Rand, had been good in a different sort of way. He had possessed other strengths, and she had learned to feel affection for him and what made him strong. She had respected who he was.

But Hileshand was different. He had always been different than other men. He had not changed. Being in his presence now felt the same as it had twenty years ago. She found herself wondering what he thought of her. The last time she had seen this face, his eyes had been full of anguish. She had said horrific things to him. She had injured him on purpose, with intent, and that was how she had left him—alone and bleeding.

"I want to hear about the dragon now," Stephan said.

It was Marcus, not Hileshand, who told about the dragon, and the story immediately began to sound familiar. Hana listened with suspicion, and when Marcus began to describe the fighter ripping his helmet in two, she came to her feet.

"That was *you*?" she yelled at Myles. She hadn't meant to be loud, but it was as if her voice suddenly developed a mind of its own.

Myles pulled back slightly. "Why are you shouting, Mama?"

"Everyone in Paxa knows that story. I cannot tell you the number of times I have heard it. Merchants carried it up from Edimane, and now men talk of it the way they talk about the weather." She thrust a finger in Stephan's direction. "He wants to hear it every night! The man who killed a dragon with naught more than his helmet—that was you?"

A smile on his lips, Hileshand shook his head and gave the context for the story. "Marcus and I were passing through Blue Mountain in Edimane on business. We were there for one night only. Immediately after arriving in town, Marcus hears that some of the local *talent* has captured a dragon."

"Talent?" Stephan asked, not understanding.

"He's being rude," Marcus replied with pleasure. He explained to Stephen, "The man was a gamer. He sent slaves to their deaths against wild animals. People would buy tickets and watch as men were ripped apart. It wasn't very nice of this man. He was not someone you would want to invite to your house."

"No, you wouldn't," Stephan agreed.

Hileshand continued, "Well, Marcus wants to see the dragon. He promises that we can leave immediately afterward—he just wants a *glimpse* of the dragon, and that is all."

But clearly, based on his tone, a *glimpse* was not what happened.

Hana sat on the edge of Stephan's bed and watched Hileshand interact with Marcus, Korstain's son. *But not Korstain's son.* She saw the glow in Hileshand's eyes and heard the warmth in his voice and wondered, *What is this? Hileshand has become a father.*

Marcus scoffed. "You wanted to see the dragon as much as I did."

Hileshand grinned and did not deny it. He went on with the story, and Hana gradually began to suspect that he left out certain details. Instead of blood and mayhem, he described the arena built into the mountainside. He remembered the smells, the way the men shouted and screamed around them. Hana felt like she was there, and she tried not to respond to the anxiety that swamped her stomach. Her son had fallen in the arena, and Hileshand had wanted to buy the body.

The body.

She was tired. Why did she react this way? It was all right—Myles had lived.

"Did you hear about the *atham-laine* in Tarek?" Marcus asked Stephan. "The head as big as you are? No one had ever seen the creature before. It was a perfect mystery."

The boy nodded. Hana heard him hold his breath in sudden excitement.

Marcus pointed at his brother. "Myles is a great warrior. He killed the *atham-laine*, just as he killed the dragon. He chopped its head off with an ax—right after he fought a meusone, which also died."

"I didn't kill it," Myles mumbled.

Hana heard all she could. She glared at Hileshand. "What have you been doing with my son?" She tried to say it in jest and failed. Her voice was scratchy.

Hileshand shifted uncomfortably in his chair and frowned at Marcus, who smiled with noticeable satisfaction, unrepentant.

"Trying to keep him alive mostly," Hileshand grumbled.

"Did you hear about the niessith that washed up on the coast?" Marcus asked Stephan next.

No, Hana thought. *Not that, too.*

"I *saw* it!" the boy exclaimed. "My father took me to see it. Did Myles kill it, too?"

Marcus dropped his hands onto Hileshand's shoulders. Both hands, both shoulders. Hileshand stilled beneath his touch.

"No, not Myles," Marcus answered, affection in his voice. "My father killed it."

My father, he said. He stated it as fact, as if he had never had any other father.

"Isule, the man who carried you here from the road—he was the captain of that ship. He stays with my father because he sees what sort of man he is. The best of men." Marcus pulled his hands away and walked toward the fire. He called over his shoulder, "Stephan, are you hungry?"

Hileshand reached up and rubbed his shoulder, the left one, where Marcus had touched it.

Instantly, Stephan replied, "Yes. I am hungry."

Hana looked at him, surprised by the change of mind. He couldn't be feeling better already.

"Good. I was hoping you would say that. I made the entire pot."

Marcus took the boy food himself. He spoke with Stephan quietly, made him laugh, arranged the pillows around him with one hand, was gentle with him. Hana could not have cared for him better herself. This was Korstain's son, who was nothing like Korstain.

Marcus dropped a hand on the child's back as he helped situate him on the bed.

Stephan sucked his breath in. His eyes widened.

Marcus pulled his hand away and put a pillow on the boy's lap, setting the bowl upon it. "Careful," he said, making certain the contents did not upset themselves. "It's hot."

Stephan stared at Marcus, and Hana heard the child whisper, "Are you a wizard?"

She laughed quietly. *A wizard.* Stephen always asked the most peculiar questions.

Marcus winked at him. "No," he said. "I am not a wizard. Eat your meal, Stephan. You'll feel better in the morning."

chapter 11

Hana slept beside Mimi, falling unconscious to the sound of the woman's snores almost the moment her body touched the blankets. Snoring had never bothered her; even as a child, Hana had slept like a member of the dead.

The room was gray-blue with early morning light when she awoke to the prods of a small hand on her face.

"Hana," a tiny voice said. A light slap on the cheek accompanied every call of her name. "Hana. Hana. Hana."

Hana captured the hand and pulled the little body up off the floor, and a flurry of giggles ensued. Mimi grumbled in her sleep as the bed shook. Hana pulled Ramia close and tried to quiet her. She didn't want to awaken Mimi, who never greeted the morning with joy.

"Ramia," Hana whispered. "How do you feel this morning, *goshane*?" She was relieved to hear the girl's voice. The horror had drained out of the bright eyes. Ramia smiled.

"B'eakfast," Ramia said and pushed her hands against her belly.

Supper had been made for her last night, but Hana had been unable to wake her enough to eat more than a few spoonfuls. Remembering the sight of Ramia drooling on Marcus' tunic, Hana smiled to herself. Marcus was good with children.

She glanced over at Stephan's bed.

It was empty.

"That was no dog," Marcus said.

He was crouched on the side of the road, examining tracks in the grassy shoulder. Hileshand stood near him, close enough to see the pleasure on his son's face. There was a smile on his mouth and a glint in his eye, neither of which had anything to do with the tracks he was studying.

Even from a distance, Hileshand could hear Stephan's laughter. The boy had wanted to come up the road with them, but this scene was not appropriate for any child's eyes. They had found five bodies so far, all of them broken. Something had come during the night and broken them further. Isule, Antonie, and Myles had stood watch at various times last night, and each of them had reported growls in the dark and the crashing of brush. No child should see the remains that lay scattered along the road. Hileshand and the others were going to gather the pieces and bury them.

He realized Marcus was looking up at him. "What?"

"Hana said she was attacked by a dog. She felt fur and a ribcage." Marcus pointed at the indentations in the soil. "This is not a dog. It has large claws." He laughed once. "Myles' mother beat away in the dark something much larger than a dog."

Hileshand felt intensely distracted. "Marcus…" He did not know how to put words to this distraction.

A quarter mile behind him, Stephan was playing with Myles near the lodge's short drive. Marcus had recovered a little wooden sword that belonged to the boy, and unexpectedly, the sword could do tricks. It repeatedly transformed itself in the little boy's hand, as if it could not determine which form was the better form in the moment. In Marcus' or Myles' hand, it was only a wooden sword, but in the boy's hand, it seemed to be made of magic.

Hana did this, Stephan had proudly informed them. *Because Abalel listens to her.*

Yes. Abalel did listen to Hana Rosure. Hileshand remembered this well.

Marcus was still looking at him. He stood up slowly, his hands loose at his sides, and waited for Hileshand to speak. He had to be aware of Hileshand's thoughts right now, yet his was not a defensive posture. He simply waited.

Hileshand didn't know what was happening, and he wasn't certain he wished to ask the question.

Are you a wizard? Stephan had asked Marcus last night. The little boy had been wide-eyed and serious, and Marcus had laughed.

No, I am not a wizard. You'll feel better in the morning.

Marcus had been correct—Stephan did feel better in the morning. He played with Myles almost violently, like a small wild beast that didn't know how to be quiet and still. Just after first light, he had slipped out of the house while the rest of them slept and had gone out to find Myles, still on watch. Stephan laughed hysterically every time Myles spoke to him.

Hana will be pleased, Stephan had told Hileshand a few minutes ago. He did not seem surprised at the sudden change in his circumstances. It somehow seemed to make sense to him. Standing straight for the first time in his life, magic sword gripped tightly, all he said was, *Hana will be pleased.*

"How did you heal that boy?" Hileshand asked at last. He would start with a simple question.

Marcus chuckled. "I have no idea. I just..." He shrugged. His voice quieted. "I knew I should touch him, so I did."

When Marcus said nothing else, Hileshand asked, "That is all?"

Marcus nodded. "Yes. Father, I meant what I told Jonathan and the rest of the council. I fully believe what you have taught me about Abalel. I could not change my mind or be persuaded to a different path. This quest of Bithania's—"

He said her name as if she were a woman, something with human blood.

"—it doesn't matter. It will not negatively affect what is real and true."

Hileshand had heard all of this before. He and Marcus had already discussed these things. Marcus was not a father—he was incapable of understanding the iron spike Bithania had driven into Hileshand's heart. Hileshand wanted to take hold of Marcus, shove him into a dark room below ground, and lock the trap door over the top of him, ignoring all threats of violence. He wanted to keep him safe. Hileshand could not predict this quest with the Alusian. He did not know what to expect here. It was not in his hands—and that was difficult for him.

He was unfamiliar with the sense of inadequacy he felt so strongly. Abalel did something here that thrust Marcus out of Hileshand's protection. He could not go where his son was being taken.

Hoarding his last pieces of confidence, Hileshand smiled briefly and said, "I am trying to understand."

His son nodded. "I know." He shrugged again. The motion was smaller this time. "Me, too."

"But I will believe what you tell me, even if I do not understand it." Hileshand meant this. Every word. He made a private vow: *If you fall, I will fall with you. If this deceives you, I will be deceived.* He took a deep breath. He felt like the inside of his body trembled. "I will believe what you say."

Marcus glanced away for a moment, down the road toward his brother. Stephan laughed loudly, and Hileshand followed Marcus' look to see that Hana and Ramia had joined Myles and Stephan on the road. Ramia wiggled to be released from Hana's arms, and the moment her small shoes touched the ground, she took off after her brother.

Marcus looked back to Hileshand. "Thank you," he said.

For a moment, the road was quiet, save for Stephan's delighted cries.

Marcus pointed at the tracks beside the road. "This was a wood dragon," he said.

Wood dragons, despite the name, were not actually dragons. They did not breathe fire and didn't fly, but they could grow quite large and were covered with both scales and fur. They breathed through gill-like contraptions as wide as ribs on both sides of the jaw. The hide was thick and sturdy, like that of the goe'lah. In most cases, they weren't all that dangerous; unless they were startled or otherwise upset, they were just chicken killers the size of horses.

Hana had stepped into the lodge last night with her arm cut open. A four-inch gash. *A dog,* she'd said. She probably had grabbed the head and felt the hair-covered gills in the dark.

A dog.

She was remarkable.

Marcus was staring into the woods. Hileshand turned his head and scanned the woods himself. There was a faint breeze this morning and the sound of Stephan's laughter. Except for the cries of birds, the forest seemed quiet. For the most part, wood dragons didn't scavenge during the day. They had ripped the bodies apart last night, in the dark, and they would be asleep now.

But then Marcus said, "It's close by."

"How do you know that?"

Marcus looked at Hileshand slowly, and after a few awkward moments had passed, he said, "Someone told me, Father. That is how I know."

He did not need to explain whom he meant. No matter what Marcus said, no matter the assurances he gave, something had changed for him. Something was different now. *Someone told me.* Alarm washed through Hileshand's stomach. Boerak-El had not left his son alone. The god had spoken to him in Ausham, and he continued to speak to him now.

Hileshand worked to keep his voice calm. "Boerak-El told you there was a wood dragon?" He had a difficult time pulling that image together in his head. The Alusian god who did not speak to men—speaking to a man about a wood dragon. Why would the god of sorrow be interested in doing such a thing?

Marcus frowned. Briefly, he seemed somewhat alarmed that Hileshand had asked.

Boerak-El speaks to my son. Hileshand felt his features pull in a grimace as he recalled the young man's words from just a few minutes before: *I fully believe what you have taught me about Abalel. I could not change my mind or be persuaded to a different path.* Yet Marcus heard Boerak-El's voice. What did that mean for his future? How would this quest affect Marcus? Hileshand would not be able to bear the loss of either of his sons.

chapter **12**

.

Myles' head came up, and he looked toward the woods.

Hana noticed the sudden tension in Myles' expression, but she had difficulty acknowledging it. She watched Stephan chase his sister. The little boy ran as if he had been running all his life. Hana blinked, rubbed her eyes, looked again. It was real, this scene before her. The laughter was real. The delight. Yet her mind was slow to accept the change.

When the children ducked into the woods, Myles called, "Stephan! Ramia! Come back to the road."

Ramia reappeared first, her hands full of yellow ferns. Stephan ran out behind her. He tripped on an exposed root and fell flat, meeting the grassy earth hard. Hana froze, alarmed, but the boy snickered and pushed up onto his hands and knees, spit dirt out of his mouth, and went back to chasing his sister.

Myles slid his arm around Hana's shoulders. She

looked up into his face. A topic. Any topic—if he spoke to her, perhaps her mind would stop hurting from trying to understand what had happened with Stephan.

Are you a wizard? the child had asked Marcus late last evening.

No, I am not a wizard.

But clearly, Marcus was something. He could call it whatever he liked—a wizard, a healer. In Furmorea, men who could heal with magic were often called *sortens,* a simple word meaning "hands," because they touched those who came to see them.

"Tell me of Amilia," Hana requested and saw the light appear in his eyes.

A smirk filled his expression, and Myles replied, "She is pregnant."

"Myles, that is wonderful."

The smile widened. "I know."

"When did you marry her?"

"Three weeks ago," he answered, watched her reaction closely, and seemed quite pleased with himself when, apparently, her face reflected her surprise.

Eventually, he began to tell her a few of the details— by far, not as many details as Hana wanted. Amilia had lost her father when she was twelve, and she had been sold in Tarek to a man named Olah. When Hileshand learned that she might know who had purchased Hana, he had searched her out and bought her from her master. The child she carried was not Myles' child. And yet it was Myles' child.

Hana studied her son for a long time. How was it that Myles had made these choices? She knew he was an excellent man, without a shadow of being anything less. Nothing was amiss in his character or integrity. But Hana found herself repeatedly surprised by him. How was it that he so easily did what her husband had not done for him? Rand Gaela had bruised her heart with his treatment of her son, who was the child of another man. Rand had never been able to accept him and had continuously pushed the boy away, declaring, *I'm not his father. He needs to honor his bloodline. I can't take another's place.*

Who, then, had taught Myles to do the opposite? *My son,* he called Amilia's child, and he did this without effort or hesitation. *My wife,* he called Amilia, clear and strong pride in all his words concerning her. Prostitution was considered a vile practice in Furmorea, but Myles had released the restrictions his country had instilled within him. He spoke of his wife as if she had grown up in a king's palace. It was sweet and tender, and Hana could only stare at him and wonder what had promoted this sense of easy acceptance.

Myles took a step away from her and lifted both hands to the sides of his mouth. "Hileshand!" he called down the road.

The man broke away from Marcus and began to walk toward them.

"Careful, Mama," Myles said suddenly.

She looked up. *Careful?* "In what way?"

"I am giving you fair warning that I am about to have an opinion." Myles nodded toward Hileshand. "He has a way of changing what you think cannot be changed and showing you how it could be better. Hileshand would never let go of anyone he cared for—there would be a severe battle to keep her." Myles met Hana's gaze. "You, perhaps, most of all. What happened with the two of you? Was there someone else?"

When she understood what he was saying, surprise

LAUREN STINTON

rolled through Hana's system. Her stomach dropped. "Myles." She needed to shove that look off his face before Hileshand reached them and heard any of this. "You are being highly inappropriate."

Myles was unconcerned with propriety. "I think that if, at any point, you were ever in love with him, you should consider being so again. That is my opinion. It is my permission, too, if you need it."

"Myles!" she hissed.

He grinned. "What? I gave you fair warning."

Hileshand joined them. "Good morning," he told Hana with an unencumbered smile. He and the boys had been awake for a while; he glanced at Myles but did not greet him.

She felt like the bones of her soul had been turned upside down. Myles had startled her. Where had his information come from? What had *Hileshand* said to suggest there was a story here? He must have told Myles something, hinted at it, and that alarmed her, because the only story Hileshand had did not end well for him. It was a horrific story, when told from his perspective—and from her perspective, because of the guilt.

But Hileshand smiled at her as if she had never hurt him. It was as if he had no memory at all of what she had done. How had he been able to recover so completely? And what did his apparent recovery mean? She saw him, and she remembered everything. The good and the painful. He should not smile like this.

After the slightest of hesitations, he asked, "How are you?"

No words came to her mind. She couldn't say a thing.

His attempt at conversation dropped into an uncomfortable hole of silence.

Then Stephan shouted behind her, and Hana latched onto that sound as a safety net.

"Surprised," she said.

Hileshand laughed. "Yes."

Myles gestured toward the children. "Mama," he said.

Oh, how she had missed hearing that word. She had thought she would never hear it again.

"Would you take Ramia and Stephan back to the house?" Myles waved his hand toward the trees on the right-hand side of the road. "There are wood dragons nearby. They're scavengers—they'll want the bodies."

Hileshand folded his arms and leveled a heavy stare at Myles. "How do *you* know there is a wood dragon?" He placed his emphasis with care.

Myles hesitated, just for a moment, and then pointed at the tracks in the grass. "Wood *dragons*," he said. "More than one. Probably three."

Stephan was not pleased. He pointed his sword at the lodge's door and declared, "I want to fight dragons, too! They're not even *real* dragons. They're like…like ponies with large tails. I could get them with my sword! And Marcus and Myles would be there, so it would be safe. Please, Hana! This is the best day of my life!"

All of her strength was required not to laugh at him. "No, Stephan. No dragons," she said as calmly as she could.

"But, Hana—I could be useful!"

She found it necessary to rewrite her strategy. "Well, Myles wants you to stay inside. You heard him say so."

His expression darkened. He considered this and finally replied, "Fine. But if they kill the dragons, I want to see one."

"If they kill the dragons…then perhaps."

Ramia watched her brother with wide eyes. Hana did not think the little girl knew what a dragon was, but apparently, she found her brother's responses exciting.

Mimi kept staring at Stephan as if he were a ghost, which did not please him either. Eventually, the sword swung around, and he shouted, "I will fight you with my sword, evil washer woman!"

"Stephan," Hana chided.

He ran into Hana's arms, held her fiercely, then cried out at his sister and chased Ramia around the room. From where had all this energy appeared? It was as if he had been storing it up with care for seven years and now, all at once, released it with gusto. Gone was the severe, studious child who acted like a man. Stephan now showed his age—and every age he had ever been. He shrieked and stormed about and called himself a pirate. His sister squealed in delight and darted under a bed as he chased her.

It was Amilia's bed. The girl was still asleep. How could she keep her eyes closed in the midst of all this pirating? Hana shushed the children and dragged them out from under the bed by their ankles.

"But, *Hana*—" Stephan began.

"A different bed," she said. "Go ahead and be a pirate— just use a different bed as your vessel for merciless pillaging, all right?"

Two long hours later, they heard footsteps outside the front door.

Stephan leapt off the bed he had commandeered as his headquarters and rushed for the door. "Marcus! Myles!" he shouted, hope in his voice.

It was Myles.

He stepped away from the door and left it hanging open. Hana saw the scowl on his face and the way the tension rode his shoulders. The easy peace he had displayed on the road had vanished.

Amilia had been awake for about an hour now. She stood up off the bed, and without a word, Myles put his arms around her and pulled her against him, dropping a kiss on the top of her head. There was something fierce in the way he touched her. Alarm rolled through Hana's stomach. *Myles? What is it?*

Myles held Amilia for a moment in silence. "Bithania is here," he said quietly.

Amilia reached up and put her fingers on his jawline. "Are you all right?" she whispered in Furmorean.

Myles hesitated. Hana saw pain flicker through his expression.

"There has been a change of plans," he said.

chapter **13**

Captain Lehman Isule had been there the day Boerak-El had publicly claimed Marcus. He had observed the young man's response to Bithania Elemara Amary, the Alusian female, when she had put her white hand to him. He had dropped to the ground, his body shuddering as if he had taken poison. Something had happened that day to Marcus Hileshand. The voice of a foreign god had changed him. It had put a spell on him and filled his body with fire.

Boerak-El was the god of sorrow and death. What could be worse than having a son claimed by such a god?

Silently, Isule groaned. *It could be worse.* A man could lose *both* of his sons to Boerak-El. Boerak-El could strip that man of his family and take both sons, instead of only the one.

Hileshand had not yet recovered from Bithania's announcement, or perhaps it was Myles' *response* to that announcement that surprised him more. Bithania had told Myles that he was to accompany them, and in very uncharacteristic fashion, Myles had allowed her to direct his steps. He had not questioned her. He had not argued. He had simply mumbled something about gathering his things and walked away, not meeting Hileshand's gaze.

Hileshand's hand was wrapped, white-knuckled, around the hilt of his sword. For the moment, the blade remained in the scabbard, but Isule suspected it would not stay in place for long.

Hileshand did not look at Bithania. The force of his glare was reserved for the Alusian male who had accompanied her here. The full-blood.

His name was Ethan Strelleck, and Isule knew he had played a vital role in the lives of Hileshand's sons. That famous night in Tarek, when Hileshand had defeated an Ethollian sorcerer and Myles had cut off the *atham-laine*'s head—Ethan Strelleck had been with them. He had given Myles the weapon he needed to kill the *atham-laine*, and then Strelleck had gone and saved Marcus' life as well. Isule had heard many things about Ethan Strelleck.

Hileshand stared at the Alusian with a look that resembled hatred. "I once thanked you for saving my sons." These were Hileshand's first words since Myles had walked away, and they were spoken through a clenched jaw. "I trust I did not speak out of turn."

Strelleck looked at Hileshand as if the man had surprised him. A moment passed before he answered, "I was very clear when I told you about your sons. I told you they had been claimed by another. Both of them. So why are you surprised with Bithania's words today? You should not be surprised by them. They are true words."

"Claimed by Boerak-El?! You were not clear in your meaning—or your intent."

"My meaning should have been apparent to you," Strelleck said. "I would not speak for another. If I speak at all, it is because Boerak-El has spoken. If I act at all, it is at his request. I do not interfere in the affairs of men. I listen to his voice."

Hileshand turned to Marcus, who anticipated the question and answered, "I did not know about this. I did not know what she intended. I…" The words faded.

Marcus scowled at Bithania, and she lifted her chin in an unrepentant manner. Isule almost laughed at the disdain that poured from her form. This female would be at home among palaces and kings—she was arrogant enough to have birthed the entire Terikbah royal line by herself. It was cold and remarkable, this attitude within her now.

"You should have said something to me," Marcus told her.

"Why?" With visible contempt, she said, "Why would I have told you? Why would *you* need to know?"

Hileshand almost drew his sword in that moment. Isule saw the muscles contract through his shoulders. This female had taken Hileshand's son—she had ruined Marcus' future and filled him with a bitter magic—and then she treated Marcus like less than a servant. Isule was not a father, but he felt he could understand the emotions involved in this situation. He knew Hileshand loved his sons.

Isule held his breath as Marcus stepped forward. The man took hold of Bithania's forearm, and the creature whirled toward him as if he had slapped her, eyes wide.

"Careful," Marcus said to her face, pulling her close. She staggered to keep her footing. "This is not the image you wish to present."

He released her with force and walked away as Myles had done, back toward the hunting lodge. The female drew her arm close to her chest and watched him go. Marcus had left a handprint on her white skin. Strelleck took an immediate, rather peculiar interest in it, which Bithania did not appreciate. She glared at him, and he ignored her, leaning close and peering at her arm.

Hana approached Hileshand and the others with slow steps, a heavy frown on her face, distrust in her eyes. Hileshand felt responsible. Less than a day she had been with them—a matter of *hours*. What sort of reintroduction was this? This was not what he had imagined with her. He should have told her about Bithania immediately, should have given her some sort of warning. But he hadn't known. He hadn't known the creature intended to take both men, including Myles. Hileshand was grateful for his anger. Without its heated strength in his body, the despair surely would have crushed him. *Why Myles, too?*

Strelleck lifted his head when he saw Hana. "Hello," he said right away and straightened from his inspection of Bithania's arm. He fixed his dark, piercing gaze on Hana's face; the tension visibly eased from his features, and he smiled at her.

He *smiled* at her. It was not a large smile, but it was, by far, the greatest display of positive emotion Hileshand had ever seen from a full-blooded Alusian. Strelleck resembled Entan Gallowar in this moment, who smiled as often as a normal man. Hileshand stared at him in shock. Then he turned and stared at Hana.

Hana attempted a smile. "Hello, Strelleck."

Hileshand nearly lost his balance. He tried to keep his

voice calm. "You *know* him?"

Amusement went through Hana's expression. Gently, she said, "Close your mouth, Hileshand. You'll live."

Hana Rosure knew Ethan Strelleck? *How? When did she meet him?* Hileshand knew he was staring at her yet couldn't move his gaze. The possibilities ran like wild horses through his head, raising a cloud of dust that obscured every other thought. If Hana Rosure knew Ethan Strelleck—

The facts readjusted themselves. Heat seeped through Hileshand's stomach. If Strelleck knew Hana Rosure, was it possible he had also known *Myles* the moment he had seen him on the porch of the King's Southern Inn in Tarek? The innkeeper's wife had told Hileshand—multiple times—how interested Strelleck had been in Myles.

The Alusian could see the future. They walked in prophecy. What if Strelleck had been at the inn that night on purpose? What if he had always known what his god intended with Hileshand's sons, and so he had been there to protect them, if protection became necessary?

Your sons bear the same mark, inscribed by the same god. One of them bears it on his heart; the other bears it in his flesh. But it is the same mark, and the same god desires them to live. So they will live, because he desires it.

It was difficult to forget words that had been uttered by an Alusian.

This was out of Hileshand's control. All of it. He could not predict this. He could not stop the moving pieces.

Strelleck pulled in a deep Alusian breath. He did it again and said to Hana, "You remember my words to you." Had a man made the statement, it would have been a question.

She nodded.

"You do not remember them as well as you should." He motioned up the road. "Walk with me, Hana."

Hileshand watched them walk off together, Hana and Strelleck, and his anger betrayed him. He felt his strength leaving, confusion rushing in to take its place. *Ethan Strelleck and Hana?* Why did the Alusian smile like that? A different sort of heat began to swarm beneath Hileshand's ribs. It wasn't right, this uncommon, un-Alusian friendliness toward Myles' mother.

He registered the sound of hoof beats behind him, coming up the road. When Hileshand recognized the rider, he groaned.

Entan Gallowar swung out of the saddle.

"Hello, Hileshand," he greeted warmly.

"You're late," Bithania complained.

Entan looked at her with mirth, as if her anger had no bearing on his reality. It was an uncommon expression to give her, and Hileshand inwardly braced himself for Bithania's fiery response.

There wasn't one.

"You're still here," Entan told her simply, and after those three brief words, he acted as if he no longer saw her. He looked at Hileshand. "She gave him a gift."

"A...what?"

Entan repeated, "Hana gave Strelleck a gift. Gifts are very important. When you give me a gift, I know why you have given it. We respond very well to gifts, provided they are not given with the intent to manipulate."

Bithania muttered something in Galatian, which was a difficult tongue; Hileshand could stumble his way through a conversation if given enough time, but he was not proficient in the language.

Entan smiled. "Keep your peace, Bithania. I speak true words."

Entan was a brave man.

Bithania blew her breath out in a huff and stalked away toward the lodge. Hileshand, Entan, and Captain Isule watched her go.

"She needs a gift," Entan told Hileshand, glancing at him.

"Oh, I will give her a gift," Hileshand promised, his tone dark.

Entan studied him curiously. "Abalel is known for his mercy, is he not?"

"You speak, yet you say nothing."

"You do not understand the risk Bithania takes with your son, Hileshand. If you understood the circumstances, you might have compassion for her, instead of anger."

Hileshand could not imagine a scenario in which that would be correct. He almost laughed. "I doubt that."

"You know I walk in two realms," Entan said, nodding. "One is of man and one is Alusian. The Alusian value my words, for they realize I understand Abalel in ways they do not. For the same reason, you should also value my words."

Oh, the arrogance of youth. Hileshand recognized it, for he once had employed it himself.

The moment the thought ran through Hileshand's mind, Entan grinned. "Arrogant? I am not arrogant. I am wise." His brows rose. "This is what you need to understand. Marcus is the Alusian companion. It is prophecy. That is what he is, but Bithania was not the one purposed to find him. It is a serious matter when an Alusian breaks trust with another. It is a matter more serious than you can understand. When she returns to the Alusian council, it will not be as one who has done well. You know what it is like to stand before your judges and sense their displeasure toward you. Does this not give you compassion for her? She is experiencing what you have experienced."

The words didn't make sense, and Hileshand scowled. After everything Marcus had endured at Bithania's hand— it wasn't supposed to happen? It was a wrong on her part? "Why did she do it?"

Entan folded his hands in front of him and rolled a shoulder in a shrug, as if the matter was settled in his mind, and so it should be in Hileshand's. "She claims to have heard Boerak-El's voice and responded to his guidance."

"She *claims* this? It is possible she did not?"

"Boerak-El speaks to many of us. Much of the time, that is how he speaks. If he is going to speak, he will speak loudly, so many can hear. Bithania heard something no one else heard. Boerak-El will use your son Marcus either to support her in her actions, because Boerak-El did speak to her, or to tear her down, because she acted on her own."

"Wouldn't an Alusian know when Boerak-El was speaking and when he wasn't?"

Entan's chin rose slightly as he looked at Hileshand, and Hileshand began to feel that he had spoken without understanding. What had he missed?

"Boerak-El speaks as Abalel speaks, Hileshand. Do you consistently understand what Abalel says to you? Is not his voice clear at times, and at other times, it is unclear? It is a serious matter when an Alusian makes an assumption and is wrong in that assumption, for an Alusian hears his voice with much more skill than a man."

Hileshand had never heard of an Alusian prophecy proving false. He didn't know a single story in which their words failed to come to pass. How could an Alusian be mistaken?

For a moment, the road was quiet. The breeze moved through the tree branches, stirring the shadows lying below them in the grass.

Entan inhaled, filling his lungs, and when he spoke, he once again proved that the Alusian missed very little that happened around them, even in the privacy of a man's thoughts. "Myles is much like you, Hileshand. When Abalel speaks to him, he eventually comes to agree with his words. You are correct in your assumptions concerning him and his prophecy—no one will *compel* Myles to do anything. Yet he will enter Ruthane of his own free will. He will embrace his prophecy because you have taught him to heed Abalel's voice."

Hileshand had spoken his thoughts concerning Myles' prophecy only to Jonathan Manda. They had been alone at the time. *I despise the Alusian,* Hileshand thought now, meaning the words in multiple ways, but Entan's ability to hear the thoughts of others apparently wasn't constant, for this time, the creature didn't respond to the insult.

Entan nodded and said, "You have adequately prepared Myles for his future. His prophecy will come to pass only because he has known you, and you cared for him."

Cared, Entan said, speaking of the past. The words contained no hope. In a single moment's time, Hileshand felt himself reduced to nothing more than a teacher, a mentor who could be put aside, now that he had been useful. *No,* he thought. *I know I am more to Myles than that. He is more than that to me. He is my son.* Entan's words cut him deeply. Aware of the tremble within him, he glared at the Alusian. "So much for not speaking Myles' fortune. Why do the Alusian insist they will not speak the future and then they always do?"

In reply, Entan looked up the road to where Hana stood with Strelleck. She was speaking with him, gesturing with her hands. Hileshand could not hear the sound of her voice from this distance. Strelleck had escorted her a good ways away, and there was an opposing wind that carried their conversation into the trees. When the Alusian answered her, he nodded and made hand gestures of his own. His were not as vehement.

Part of Hileshand could not believe he was seeing her again. He and his sons had been anticipating this moment for months, yet with it had come unexpected confusion. How was it that she knew Ethan Strelleck? Hileshand ran his hand over his face and tried to think clearly around all the questions. *A bloody road indeed. What is to come of this?* He felt small and despised the feeling.

Entan smirked at him. "Perhaps I will speak the fortune of your son," he said, "but I will not speak yours."

$\mathcal{M}$yles pulled Amilia into the stable behind the hunting lodge, where the trees were thick and the shadows thicker still. She trembled and glanced at the dark branches latched together just beyond the stable window, but he did not allow her to give her fears much mind. He took hold of her chin and drew her face toward him, kissing her with warmth and passion. He dropped a hand to her stomach, and the kiss intensified until she started crying.

"Don't leave me," she whispered.

He looked down at her, sorrow in his eyes. "We knew about this," he said after a time. His tone was calm, but the words left him slowly. "You and I. We knew it was coming."

Yes, they had known it was coming.

When will we go to Ruthane? she had asked that night in Ausham, after Jonathan had put his hand to Myles and looked through his future. Neither man had been able to tell her when, but both men had been able to tell her that she would not be traveling with him.

Jonathan knew this because Abalel had told him. Myles knew this because there was no way he would thrust her into a situation he could not predict. He was returning to a nation that had once tried to kill him. He did not know what was going to happen, and he would not endanger her in any way. She had cried. He had refused to change his mind.

Now he stood before her and wiped her tears away with his thumb.

She spoke unevenly. "I didn't know it would be so soon. I thought it would be…would be months yet. *Months*." *After the baby.*

His fingers shifted position on her stomach. She realized with his touch that he was telling the baby goodbye, and she started crying again. "What will I do without you?"

"The same things you did before."

She chose to smile then. She chose humor, and the pain in her heart paused long enough for her to flirt with him and say, "*Everything* I did before?"

He scowled at her. "That is not amusing."

She thought it was.

Three weeks. The whole of their marriage had been three weeks. *Do what you did before.* They'd had so little time together, and yet it had been time enough to change her. What sort of person had she been before she had met Myles? What had she thought about? What had she done? The past had been wiped away.

"I cannot do what I did before," she said. "I can't remember what I did before. I don't remember what my days were like without you."

He held her close, her forehead on his chin. He exhaled, and she felt the air move down the side of her face.

"Neither can I," he answered finally.

How were they supposed to do this? How would she be able to live with the distance?

Myles bent down and kissed her again. His hand moved up the back of her neck and began to ease the pins from her hair. He issued an invitation. One last time. She smiled, her vision blurring. At times, her husband had an interesting, entertaining tendency to forget what some would term *decency*. It truly seemed to be forgetfulness. She knew when a man did something "accidentally on purpose," and Myles was not like that. He would see no reason to be. He had almost brought them trouble a few times in Ausham. Almost. But then, she had almost brought them trouble, too. Myles had no shame. He did not even understand the concept.

Her hesitation now had nothing to do with decency; she had no foundation for decency. She looked at the tree branches through the stable window. She would never be able to enter the woods without thinking of the miron. She would never be able to forget the way they had touched her stomach in the dark. She shuddered without meaning to. The window had no pane. The door had no lock. "Myles, are you certain?"

"They will not come near you again," he said and kissed her forehead, her cheek, her nose. "Remember what I said."

"You are *certain*?" she whispered.

He pulled back enough to look into her eyes. He wove his fingers into her hair as he answered, "Yes. Abalel told me. The miron are smart—they remember their fears very well. Nothing is here, *aufane,* my love. Nothing is coming for you. You will never need to be afraid of the miron again."

Abalel had told him these things.

Do I trust this voice you hear? Making the decision did not require much time. She put her arms around his neck and kissed her husband the way he sought to be kissed. He moaned when she responded to his passion in kind.

In this moment—yes. Yes, she would trust. Myles was worth it.

Once again, Bithania took Antonie, too.

At her brisk command, Antonie paled beneath his freckles and then retreated to the stable for his horse. Isule went with him.

Hileshand stood near Hana and quietly explained what no one had thought to mention last night. The Alusian quest. Boerak-El. Marcus. And then he half-heartedly attempted to tell her about Myles and the prophecy that hounded the young man's steps.

At the name *Korstain Elah,* her spine stiffened, and she stared at him.

It isn't right, he agreed with her silently, his gaze mixed with hers. *I know.* But he would not say that out loud, not when she needed peace. So instead, he took hold of the calm Entan had displayed a short time before, and he smiled and said, "It will be all right."

She did not ask questions. He could see the tension in her body. He could hear the unevenness in her breathing. But she didn't say a word, and he wondered at her silence. Why didn't she argue? Why didn't she fight this?

Hana kissed Myles goodbye. He looked at her for a long time without any words. Then he smiled faintly and leaned forward to kiss her forehead.

"I trust you'll remember everything I've told you," he said. Humor filled his gaze. "All of it. I want you to be safe."

Hileshand saw Hana's hands tighten on the shoulders of Myles' tunic. "I remember," she whispered.

Myles lifted his head and looked at Hileshand, the little smile still in place. "Keep her safe." A simple charge. "Both of them." His wife and his mother.

Hileshand was not concerned for either woman; he was concerned for his son. He wanted to save him from this. He wanted to protect him, yet all he could do was nod. "I will."

They left. Three men, two Alusian, and a half-blood.

They returned to the lodge, where Amilia curled up on Hileshand's lap like a child, her arms around his neck. He soothed her tears as best he could, and eventually, she quieted, holding on to him.

She was becoming more and more comfortable with him. She had relaxed with Marcus first, and gradually, her sense of peace had extended to Myles; but it was not until after the miron that she had begun to treat Hileshand as honestly as she treated his sons. He didn't understand how a daughter could possess so much power over a father's happiness. Her pleasure gave him joy; her tears threw him into intense anguish. A daughter was a magician who cast a spell over her father's heart.

The lodge had warmed with the late morning sun. Hileshand considered opening a window but then dismissed the idea. He ran his hand down Amilia's back and didn't wish to give her another opportunity for alarm. She needed comfort, not fear, even if what she feared would never happen. They hadn't seen the miron a single time since that night near the river, when Entan had led Hileshand and Isule to the miron's camp. In that encounter, Hileshand had won his daughter from the enemy. He hadn't merely saved her—he had won the opportunity for moments like these, when she made him feel like a father in ways Marcus and Myles did not.

Stephan and Ramia whispered to one another beneath Mimi's bed. Their nurse, Mimi, seemed a peculiar sort of person. Hileshand wasn't certain how he should classify her. She sat now in a stiff position on top of the bed, her arms wrapped around her drawn-up legs, her back to the wall. She wouldn't meet Hileshand's gaze, wouldn't speak to him. He couldn't tell if she feared him or if she was somehow in denial of his presence.

Hana did not fear the way other women feared. Unmindful of the threat of miron, she had disappeared into the stable about an hour ago. Hileshand had directed Isule to follow her, to watch over her from a distance, and the man remained outside when Hana chose to return.

Hana appeared calm now, her eyes brilliant green from tears she had shed in private. She stopped on the other side of the table and looked at him as he sat there, his little girl in his arms. It was possible Amilia had fallen asleep. She had not moved in several minutes. Hana watched him for a long time, and slowly, Hileshand found himself thinking again what he had thought last night—that the years had left her untouched. She had been sixteen the last time he had seen her. Clearly, she no longer appeared that age, yet maturity had sculpted her well. She was far more attractive now than she had been at sixteen. He hadn't been expecting that, and then he wondered why he hadn't. She was remarkable in every way; of course she would be remarkable in this way as well.

A familiar twinge of sadness moved through his chest. If Hileshand had seemed old to Hana at thirty, he would certainly seem old to her now at fifty. These thoughts he entertained did him very little good.

A slow smile moved across Hana's lips, and the look in her eyes warmed. He could not bring himself to break her stare, even as a distant warning pealed somewhere in the back of his mind. *You give yourself away. She will know your thoughts.*

"Mimi and I need to take the children to their grandfather," she said quietly. "His estate lies beyond Yomal, about eight hours from here. He expects us. I...I don't want him to worry more than he already will."

"We will take the children to their grandfather," Hileshand replied.

But that was all the grandfather was getting. Hileshand would not allow him to keep Hana Rosure.

chapter 15

Late that night, Lord Minton Keresgrove held his granddaughter in his lap and watched Stephan run around the sitting room. Stephan had slept for a few hours on the way here, his head tipped back against Hileshand's chest, his mouth gaping open, and during his brief rest, he had recovered all of his previous energy. His antics were quite wild, with the lateness of the hour and the fact that he had never before done what he did now. In a way, this terrain was completely new to him. He could walk it himself. He could run paths he had only observed. Mimi followed him around, attempting to divert his sword hand away from the furniture.

With his gaze fixed on his grandson, Lord Keresgrove did not appear to be listening to Hana's story, but he was. Every time she paused for more than a breath, his attention snapped back to her.

"Yes?" he said. "And then what happened?"

When she had finished, Keresgrove sat there in silence

for a long moment, his hands on his granddaughter's small arms. Hileshand watched him and wondered at the older man's thoughts.

Ramia was tired. She yawned, releasing her breath from a wide, stretched mouth as she settled down against her grandfather.

"Hileshand," the man said at last. He pulled his gaze from Stephan and looked at Hileshand on the couch. "I have heard of you."

Hileshand smiled slightly. "You have heard of a different man."

"Have I? Careb Jasenel, the gamer, is an associate of mine." Keresgrove shrugged. "In a manner of speaking. I tolerate him for reasons of my own, and he tolerates me for reasons of his. We travel in similar circles, and I have the unfortunate opportunity to see him on a regular basis." The eyes narrowed, the lines growing more pronounced in the weathered skin. He looked at Hileshand with dubious curiosity. "Which Hileshand does he speak of if he does not speak of you?"

"My son." Hileshand said it as he always said it, and in his peripheral vision, he saw Hana glance at him.

"So it was your son who killed the dragon with his bare hands in Edimane." Keresgrove's brows lifted. "That's impressive."

Hileshand just looked at him. The dragon in Edimane? Hana had known the story, but there had been no name attached to it. She had been shocked to realize it was Myles. "Yes," he said slowly. "It was my son who killed the dragon, but I don't understand how you came to know that."

Keresgrove laughed gruffly. "The entire country knows it. Every man knows the name of Myles Hileshand, the man who fights dragons and *atham-laine* and lives to tell about it. Careb Jasenel does not keep secrets."

Keresgrove's eyes began to take on a look Hileshand had seen before. It was a look of delight and massacre, the gaze of a man who had been to the Blood Games and had loved the experience. Lord Keresgrove might not claim Careb Jasenel as a friend, but it did seem that he respected the man's work.

"Do you not know the full story? An *Alusian* told Jasenel about Myles Hileshand. She detailed his history to him and made Jasenel promise not to lay a finger on him. Drove the fellow mad, to describe it delicately. He has been insanely interested in Myles Hileshand ever since. He has made your son famous in Paxa."

Hileshand found he had nothing to say. He didn't even know where to begin.

Keresgrove turned his attention to Amilia, who sat beside Hileshand on the couch. As his gaze lingered on her face, Hileshand wondered if the old man recognized her. Jasenel, he knew, made the journey to Bledeshure regularly. Keresgrove was about twenty years older than Hileshand—not yet old enough to be immune to youth and beauty.

But then Keresgrove looked down at his granddaughter. As he realized that the little girl had fallen asleep in his arms, everything about the man seemed to relax. He sighed deeply. He leaned forward, shoulders bowed, and cradled the girl, his arms tightening around her small form.

Stephan ran to him and dropped a swift kiss on Keresgrove's shoulder.

"Pirate!" the boy proclaimed, sword held high. The blade appeared as wood now, which was good; that was a little gentler on the table legs. "Grandfather, can we go on a ship? I want to go on a ship. And I want to ride a horse. And I want to learn how to fight evil things. And I want to walk on the ridge with you—tomorrow—and see the rest of the estate. And I want to see the niessith again. I want to touch it this time! I don't care if it's stinky and dirty. Can I have one of its bones?"

Hana had told Keresgrove about the employer, the unnamed third party who had coerced Fostaine and the other guards into their betrayal, but Keresgrove didn't ask her to elaborate. He didn't press her for more information. Perhaps he knew there was nothing else she could tell him. Or perhaps he held his tongue for an entirely different reason. The color drained from his face as he stared at his grandson. His arms tightened a little more around Ramia. He had almost lost his grandchildren.

He looked back to Hileshand. "Your other son, the one named Marcus—he has the ability to heal with his hands?"

"He's a wizard!" Stephan exclaimed.

"He's not a wizard," Hileshand corrected.

Keresgrove watched Hileshand quizzically and asked, "He has a gift?"

Hileshand would not call it a gift either. He knew what Keresgrove was asking, yet he could not bring himself to agree with the wording. Quietly, he said, "He travels with the Alusian."

"The same Alusian? The female?"

Hileshand felt the grimace slide across his face. "Yes."

Keresgrove nodded. He reached out and took Stephan's forearm, held on to the boy. "I have sent for my daughter and son-in-law." He seemed to tremble as he inhaled. "They will be here in less than two weeks. Stay with me, Hileshand—be my guest. You would honor me with your presence."

Hileshand and the rest of his party stayed with Keresgrove for ten days. The son-in-law, Trind Lawvek, proved to be a short man with a high forehead, which he rubbed constantly, as if he thought it would bring him good fortune. After seeing to his children, he quickly agreed to Hileshand's request and wrote Hana's papers of freedom. Lawvek tried to offer him a substantial reward as well, but Hileshand wouldn't accept it. He had not come for a monetary reward; all he needed was a piece of paper.

Hileshand had his family off the Keresgrove estate by dusk.

They spent that night in Yomal, in a little inn off the village green. Amilia thought it rather pretty and quaint, even though the bed sheets smelled like butter. She held them to her nose and could not fathom why they would smell that way.

Eventually, the lamp was blown out, and the only light flickered from the fireplace. Hileshand and Isule had pallets on the floor. Hana and Amilia shared the bed.

In the quiet, Amilia whispered, "What are we going to do, Hileshand?"

She had purposefully waited to ask this question until this moment, in the dark. Anything he said was going to hurt her. If they stayed in the area, near Ausham, it was because of Myles and Marcus and the possibility of their immediate return. It would mean waiting in silence—hoping, when there wasn't necessarily anything to hope for. If they left the area, they would be distancing themselves from Myles and Marcus, because there was no hope. There would be no immediate return. That thought was much worse.

For a long moment, the shadowed room was quiet.

Hileshand took a deep breath. "I want to go to Furmorea."

The answer was not unexpected. Amilia knew why he said it, yet the words still stung. She closed her eyes. "But what if they return soon? What if we are not here when they do?"

"Entan is with them. He will know where to find us."

Her eyes burned. "But, Hileshand…"

"I know, little one." He hesitated. "But we simply do not know. Who can say? I do not believe this quest of Bithania's is something that has an end in a traditional manner."

He referenced Marcus, not Myles, and Amilia was afraid to ask him why. "But Marcus is due to return to Ausham. He *has* to return eventually. Perhaps in Ausham…we should wait there." Would it be so dreadful to wait there?

When he didn't answer, she began to remember what Jonathan Manda had told her about Hileshand: *Give him work. Hileshand needs work when he is hurting.* That was why he didn't want to stay. He needed something to do. He could not wait and do nothing. He had lost both his sons. She had lost her husband.

Amilia felt the mattress move as Hana sat up.

"Hileshand," Hana said.

"Yes?"

"Why do you wish to go to Furmorea?" The mattress moved again as Hana shifted position. "It is no longer safe in Furmorea. No woman should be taken there, and it would be a difficult journey for Amilia, with the baby."

Good, Amilia thought. *She will speak sense to him.*

"Myles wished to return for his sisters," Hileshand said, "for Ara and Lenay. We will go in his stead. I will not take you or Amilia into the country itself. We will find a place that is safe for the two of you, and I will go."

He was going to do it anyway, no matter the danger in Furmorea or the risk to Amilia's heart. He truly believed Myles and Marcus were gone.

Hana did not reply. Nor did she lie down again. She sat in the bed, perfectly still.

Eventually Amilia fell asleep and dreamed it was Myles lying beside her. Even in the dream, she knew it wasn't real. So did he.

"I will come home again," he told her.

"No," she answered. "You know you're not coming back. You're never coming back. Abalel told you that, too."

"He never said I wasn't coming back."

The dream repeated itself three or four times. Finally the baby stirred Amilia awake near daylight. She slid her hand through the blankets and pressed her fingers to her stomach, opening her eyes to gray darkness. The hour was early yet, and she was alone. A new wife without a husband.

She rolled her head slowly on the pillow, wishing without hope, and looked on the other side of the bed. In the pale light, she saw no one. The bed was empty on

Hana's side. As the fog cleared from her sleep-muddled mind, Amilia realized the room was quiet—Hileshand was not snoring. That was very unlike him.

She looked and saw that he was missing, too. His pallet was empty.

What is this? she wondered.

chapter **16**

Hileshand did not sleep that night.

A few minutes after the conversation ended, he heard the bed creak and the faint sounds of steps on the wooden floor. He knew it was Hana. She had sat up to ask her question, and he had not heard her lie down again.

Her steps drew near, and she touched his shoulder in the dark. She did not say anything. She just went to the door and slipped through it, and he obediently rose and followed her.

The hallway was empty, and the muted sounds of voices drifted in from the dining room. The inn was small; there was only the one floor. As Hileshand blinked in the lamplight, Hana discovered that the door to the room next to theirs was unlocked, and before Hileshand could ask what she intended, she took his hand and pulled him inside.

The room was unlocked, yes, but not unoccupied. Two sets of snores rolled from the bed.

"What are you doing?" he whispered to her.

He felt her hands on his chest. *She will be standing on*

her tiptoes, he thought and was right, for when she spoke, her voice was close to him. The occupants of this room had not built up their fire before retiring; it was nothing more than embers now. He could not see very well in the shadows, but he could picture Hana in his mind's eye, how she leaned forward, the concern drawn between her brows.

"I'm sorry," she breathed, her voice low.

He stared at her, or where he imagined her to be in the dark. "Why are you sorry?"

The words choked in the back of her throat—the sound short and quick; then she collected herself and said, "For what I said to you in Gereskow."

He stood without moving.

He remembered that day.

Korstain Elah had lost his wife shortly after she had given birth to his twin sons. Twins were considered a sign of the gods' favor. The infants would be placed side by side, and a priest would divine the child of the gods' choosing. That child would be marked with the symbol of the current moon and offered as a sacrifice in the temple. Myles had been the chosen son, and instead of taking him to the temple to be killed, Hana had run with him. Korstain had sent a hundred men in pursuit of her, but she was quick and discreet, and no one had been able to find her.

Save one.

One of Hana's pursuers, the captain of Korstain's personal guard, had been successful, because he had known where to look. Because he knew her, and she mattered to him.

"As your friend—" Hana began now. She said it again, emphasizing that certain word: "As your *friend*, I want you to know how sorry I am for saying those things. You did not deserve them. Any of them. I did not mean them. I-I just had a good reason for speaking as I did."

The moment he had learned of Hana's disappearance with Korstain's son, Hileshand had known what he would do. There was only one road for him to take, only one he desired to take.

But to his surprise, Hana had not been willing.

I did not mean them. I had a good reason for speaking as I did.

"I know," he said quietly.

The catch in her breath happened again. "How do you know that?"

One of the sleepers snorted. For a moment, both sets of snores changed their course; someone rolled and the bed groaned. Hileshand held his breath, waiting. Then the rhythm resumed.

Hana's hands on his chest tightened into fists. She gripped his tunic.

He touched her shoulder. Surely, that was a permissible action. *A friend,* she called herself. He could touch a friend this way without running into the boundaries she had quickly set up for them both. "I have many reasons for knowing that," he said. "You were crying as you said them."

"I hurt you."

"Only for a time."

"You couldn't have come with me, Hileshand. If you came and we were caught, they would have only killed me—but Korstain's guard would have injured you severely and then turned you over to the temple. You would have been punished first and then killed. You were the captain of Korstain's guard—everyone would have considered you a traitor. You could not have come."

"I know," he said again.

He had come to understand that in a brutal, painful way, she had given him the best gift she could have given in the moment—she had loved him enough to worry. He had not realized that at the time. He had seen only her unexpected rejection. He had not believed her at first, so she had taken steps to ensure that he *would* believe her. She had told him he was too old for her. That she had never considered him the way he considered her. That the very thought repulsed her. She had said many things, and in the end, she had been quite convincing.

But slowly, the pieces had fallen into place, and he had come to understand that the tears had been real and most of the words had been untrue. Perhaps none of the words had been true.

She sniffled. "You have no idea how I despised myself for what I did to you. I mourned you for years, Hileshand. For years."

She had mourned him. Those did not seem like the words one would say about a friend.

But then she pulled in a trembling breath and went on, "I don't anymore."

In the dark, his heart winced.

"When…when the Galatian soldiers killed my husband, the way in which they killed him, with pleasure and horrific talent, I was…" She was weeping now. He could feel her shoulder shaking beneath his hand. He slid his touch from her shoulder to her lower back, joining his other hand there as well, and she accepted the silent offer and leaned against him. "All of my fears came upon me in that moment. It wasn't Korstain Elah who had found us, but the outcome was the same. The soldiers butchered him."

They stood there in the midst of the snores of strangers, his hands on her back, her hands on his chest, her warmth against him. Twice he caught himself leaning down to find her mouth in the dark. *Stop it.* He couldn't kiss her. He couldn't think that way.

"Will you forgive me?" she whispered.

He considered telling her what she had not allowed him to say the day she'd left him—that he loved her more than he loved his life. That the risk hadn't mattered to him. That she had been his entire world. But what good would it do to say these things now? He knew how she had thought of him then, as a maid in Korstain Elah's house; he remembered well the warmth in her eyes and the delight in her smile when she looked at him.

As a friend, she said tonight. Those three words churned through his mind. *Why the wall, Hana?* She erected it on purpose, and he would not push her to tear it down. Twenty years was a long time. If she wanted distance, he would not try to take it from her.

"Of course," he said. "Yes. But I already forgave you—long ago."

Hana heard those words and the calm with which he said them, and she squeezed her eyes shut, feeling tears run down her cheeks. He had forgiven her long ago? She never wanted him to feel pain because of her. *Never.* She had injured herself with the ugly words she had spoken to him that day. But now, he sounded relaxed about the situation, at complete peace, like it did not matter, and she knew he had put it behind him.

Hileshand had loved her once—but that was a long time ago. Apparently, she didn't mean to him now what she had meant to him before. Her heart ached for him. What did he think of her leaning against him like this? Did he think she was trying to seduce him? In someone else's room?

She smiled sadly. Would that be so terrible? Her entire body told her what it would be like to kiss him, and she had difficulty withdrawing from the intensity that rolled through her. She had never endured with any man what she endured with Hileshand. Everything in her, body and soul, wanted to touch him, to be his. Here, now, in the dark—and yes, in someone else's room—she was fully aware of her attraction to him. She needed to calm this storm before she made a fool of herself.

She released his tunic, tried to breathe calmly. Steady. Give nothing away. "Thank you."

He did not remove his hands, so she stayed there, leaning against him. She felt his chest expand every time he drew breath. Her right hand was over his heart, and she could feel his heartbeat against her fingertips.

"You have not told me what Ethan Strelleck said to you on the road," he murmured.

Over the last week and a half, they had not been able to spend much time together. Either she had been watching Lawvek's children, or they hadn't been alone; Amilia or Isule were usually close by. Lord Keresgrove, after recovering from the shock of that first night, had asked Hileshand all sorts of questions. He had even gone so far as to offer him employment with a handsome salary. Hana smiled as the memory returned to her. Keresgrove had wanted to keep him. Everyone who met this man wanted to keep him.

At that thought, the longing was almost more than she could bear.

She said softly, "Strelleck reminded me that Abalel is trustworthy. That is all." There was more to it than that—many more words, many more thoughts. But in the end, that had been Strelleck's point twenty years ago, and it remained his point on the Yomal Road. Strelleck was nothing if not loyal.

Hileshand's hands were warm on her back. "Entan Gallowar said you gave Strelleck a gift."

"I gave him your knife," she whispered and, before she could talk herself out of it, she reached up to put fingers to his jawline. "It was the only thing I possessed that had any value. I didn't want to give it to him. I wanted to keep it, but I also wanted to thank him for everything he had done for us."

That day was firmly carved into her memory, as if it had happened only a few hours ago. She had broken Hileshand, and he, jaw clenched, face red, had still desired to wish her well, for her to be safe. He had given her a weapon he had carried for years.

You may need this, he had said and walked away.

She had felt like she was dying.

"We took a ship from Pithsbow." It was a small, secondary port three hours from Gereskow. She had hoped it would be safer for them. "But Korstain was thorough. Even in Pithsbow, his men were questioning every family, every person, who traveled with a newborn. My friend Boralan had hired a wet nurse for Myles, and neither of us told her…" Hana wet her lips and pulled her hand from Hileshand's face. "She never knew how close she came to death."

Hileshand closed his eyes. He had thought very similar words about Hana only a few days ago. They had come so close to losing her. If not for Entan and his foresight, Hana would be dead right now, cut down by a skroel. Hearing her speak such things about someone else made his knees weak. He frowned against the concern that surged within him.

"The guards boarded our ship. Myles was crying. I couldn't get him to stop. The half-moon that the priest had carved into his little chest had become infected, and his temperature was high. He was hurting, and I couldn't get him to stop crying. The guards had us. They *knew*, Hileshand. I remember the look in their eyes. They saw my fear, and they knew they were about to return victorious.

"But then, suddenly, they stopped—all of them. Only a few paces away from us, when victory was in their grasp, they just stood there and stared at us. A hand touched my shoulder, and I turned and looked up into Strelleck's face. An Alusian on the ship."

It had been planned, hadn't it? Hileshand slowly became aware of the arrangement of events, that Strelleck had known what he was doing. He had chosen the hour of his entrance very carefully. On purpose. To keep Hana and Myles alive.

What is this? Hileshand wondered. *Why is Boerak-El so interested in my son?*

"The guards said nothing to us. They returned to the port without a word, and Strelleck stayed with us. He took care of Myles and restored him, curing him of his infection. His little chest and stomach lost all their redness. His temperature lowered. The other passengers and the crew avoided us because of Strelleck. He acted as if we were his party, under his protection. He took us all the way into Furmorea and paid for all of our expenses. I was so grateful."

She paused.

For a moment, the jarring rumbles coming from the bed were the only sounds.

Hana whispered, "While we were still on the ship, Strelleck asked me what I had named my son."

Hileshand heard the tremble in her voice.

"He called him that—he said he was *my* son, even though he knew the baby was not mine. I had not considered that question until he asked it. I had not had the peace of mind to even think like that, but the moment he asked, I knew what I would name him."

She did not speak for a time. "I knew what I wanted, what I wished for." She took a sharp little breath that sounded like a shallow sob. "What I would surely have in my life, if the world were different."

This time, there was no mistaking her meaning. She qualified nothing. Even if she had made an attempt to dissuade him, Hileshand would not have believed her now.

This.

This was his fortune. This was what he wanted, what *he* wished for. *Hana Rosure.*

Amilia had told Hileshand of the first time Myles had kissed her, and remarkably, the situation had looked very much like this one. A room in an inn, to the rough sounds of someone else's sleep. A corner of Hileshand's mouth rose. It was only fitting that the son should be like the father and the father like the son.

"Hana," he said quietly, securing her against him with both arms around her, both hands. He leaned forward and brushed his lips across her forehead. He took note that she held her breath, and he thought about how time did not matter with certain women, how second chances could be sweeter and better than first ones. "I am going to kiss you in a room full of people."

And that was what he did.

chapter 17

Jeepo was a small town set on the lower slopes of a *nauno-dah,* a mountain that was alive. Smoke drained from the mountain's peak, casting a constant, steady shadow across the streets of the town. The men of Tarek and Edimane believed such mountains to be the home of their gods. Paxa was an Abaleine nation, a country devoted to Abalel and his ways, but this close to Edimane, the country folk were superstitious. The locals told stories about those who went beyond Clesser Ridge, a bald, rocky protrusion halfway up the slope. They attracted Viceese's curse.

Ethan Strelleck had explained this to Marcus because Marcus asked. With some subjects, Strelleck was very detailed and spoke for what could be considered a long period of time. With other topics, he described the ribs of the animal and nothing more—only a sentence or two. Viceese, apparently, was not among Strelleck's interests, so Marcus did not obtain as much information as he desired.

He learned much more about the mountain when he asked a townsman. Marcus wasn't fluent in Paxan, but the man spoke Terikbah well enough that Marcus could understand him. He was a bookseller. He had small, pebble-like eyes that appeared sensitive to the light, as if he had done nothing more in his life than stay indoors and squint at the pages of a book. He was older, with pale skin and a hairline that apparently began somewhere on his back. There was not a single hair anywhere on his scalp.

"Home of the skrole," the old man said, pulling his pipe from his lips and using it to gesture toward Marcus. "You know what the skrole are, boy? The children of Viceese, goddess of pain." The pipe shook at Marcus' head. "Not the most charming among the goddesses. That much is certain."

Marcus nodded, droll. "I have heard of the skrole, yes."

"Many years ago, armies came here to avenge their fallen kings, government leaders, and the other men the skrole had killed. They nearly destroyed the mountain, but Viceese taught them not to do that again. She injured them, and they knew pain. They learned. No army has come against the mountain now in several centuries." He peered at Marcus with his small eyes. "We don't get many visitors here." After a moment, he added, "Especially not those who travel with an Alusian."

Strelleck was across the street scaring people out of the mercantile. Through the bookseller's window, Marcus watched the store empty, and he wondered what the Alusian was trying to buy. Strelleck had not shared with him his list. People shivered and hurried as they scattered down the street. Some drew invisible symbols in the air above their foreheads—old signs that were meant to bring protection from death and fear.

Turning back to the bookcase, Marcus found the volume he sought and pulled it free. He tapped the cover with one finger and showed the storeowner the title. "Poetry."

The man frowned at him, not understanding.

Marcus explained, "The Alusian are fond of poetry. It is possible to converse with them at length if the topic is capable of flowing well on a page."

"Poetry," the bookseller repeated. His forehead wrinkled. He stared at Marcus with his small eyes.

Marcus almost smiled. This was the book Bithania carried. She had it with her at all times, and whenever there came a momentary lull in the activity around her, she pulled the book from her knapsack and began to read. Her copy was older and worn, the cover bowed from its many travels. Marcus turned the volume over in his hands and looked again at the poet's name. *Adraine El-Ohah.* A Ruthanian who had been dead for nearly eight centuries. The book was a series of poems describing rivers and the ocean—bodies of water with currents.

If he read this book, perhaps it would aid him in understanding what he did not understand. He, Myles, and Antonie had been traveling with the Alusian for five weeks now, and every time he addressed Bithania, it was like addressing a stranger. Nothing about her made sense. Nothing was predictable, except that she would react in anger. This book meant something to her; clearly, it was valuable in her sight, and he wanted to know why, because then, perhaps, he would be able to *see* her—who she was, how she thought—in some small way. He wanted to feel compassion for her.

"I'll take this," Marcus said.

"There is a second," the bookseller told him.

Marcus looked at him. "A second?"

"Aye, a second volume. Adraine El-Ohah wrote two books."

The bookseller came around the counter and pulled a book from a different shelf. "He writes of nature. His first book is about water and is dedicated to Issen-El, god of the sea. The second volume is about the sun, and it is dedicated to Abalel." He made a peculiar sound of laughter in his throat. "He was a Ruthanian who understood that a god can be two ways."

"Two ways?" Marcus asked.

"Of course." The bookseller nodded. "Abalel is the father of light, the creator, and the one who causes life to bloom upon the world. Yet he is also the god of the sea—of mystery and shadow, of cold and torrent. I prefer the first volume, the one about the sea, for I have never seen it. The sea is a mystery to me in many ways. So." He shrugged. "I like the first volume more."

The old man held the book out to him.

Marcus touched it, his hand closing around the cover.

As Marcus took the book in hand, the small store dropped away around him, as if someone had blown out a lamp, and he found himself standing in sudden darkness.

The change startled him. He took a step back, looking around quickly. What was this? Ethollian magic? Then he saw what stood a short distance to his right, and he knew the answer to that question. No. Definitely not Ethollian magic.

He was looking into the white face of an Alusian. As

it was with all of these creatures, it was impossible to tell his age. He could have been twenty or a thousand. And he had human blood—his eyes were blue. Entan had explained that the blood of man always produced blue eyes in an Alusian. It did not matter the coloring of the human parent; the child's eyes would be blue.

"Hello, Marcus," the Alusian said.

Marcus knew this voice, though he had never before heard it so clearly. His stomach hit the bottom of his boots. He would always know this voice.

This was Boerak-El.

Boerak-El might be the god of the Alusian, but he was not Alusian himself. He was not a physical being, with blood and a body. What Marcus was seeing right now had to be what the Alusian called a *morden*—a symbol that revealed truths about its source. This was not Boerak-El's true form. It was a metaphor, a picture of something he wished to convey. An idea.

An Alusian mixed with the blood of man? This was how he wished to present himself?

Boerak-El reached up and drew something from around his neck, bringing the thin leather strap over his head. It was like a private messenger pouch, the kind worn under the clothes, where it could not be seen. The small bag at the end of the cord was also made of leather.

"Stop running from me, Marcus," Boerak-El said.

Marcus realized he was moving backward. He did his best to hold still, to keep his heart calm and his boots in place on the floor he could not see beneath him. The only thing he could see in this room, or in this place, or wherever he stood now, was Boerak-El. There was no floor, no walls, no roof.

"This," Boerak-El said, walking toward him, "is what you have asked me to give you."

He hung the small pouch around Marcus' neck. The leather burned where it touched his skin, but the sensation quickly passed.

When Boerak-El smiled as a man would smile, Marcus nearly fell over.

"Consider it a gift," the god said. "Wear it well."

Marcus found himself back in the bookshop. He dropped the book.

His vision cleared. He began to think properly again. What had *that* been? He caught himself with his hand half lifted, about to rub his eyes.

Wear it well.

His hand changed course and went to his throat instead, but he felt no leather strap. He rubbed his chest through his tunic—he was not wearing a pouch around his neck. Yet he knew it was there.

The bookseller stared at him, puzzled. "So…no to that book?"

Marcus heard himself say, "I'll take them both."

He bent down and, with care, put a hand to the book that had fallen, touching it experimentally with the ends of his fingers before committing to picking it up. Nothing happened. He saw no pictures. Nothing unexpected occurred.

Wear it well. The words stayed with him as he paid the bookseller and walked out onto the street, both books stowed in his bag. His heart raged within him. His hands were shaking.

He sat down on the bench outside the mercantile and

attempted to relax. He did not have to wait for Strelleck very long. The Alusian appeared almost immediately. He carried a parcel wrapped in brown cloth and tied with string. It was small enough to fit in his hand.

As Marcus stood to meet him, he felt the eyes of the town upon them. Wherever they went, it was like this. People whispered about death and avoided them.

Strelleck stared at him.

Marcus waited. "Yes?"

"I heard him speak to you. You heard his voice."

Strelleck did not need to explain himself. Clearly, he meant Boerak-El.

Marcus pulled back in surprise. Strelleck had seen what Marcus had seen? *Good,* he thought at first. *I need it explained.* But then he quickly changed his mind. *No, not good. I don't know what that was. I...I don't think I want to talk of it with Strelleck.*

The Alusian's dark eyes narrowed. As the town continued to watch them openly, Strelleck said, "I heard him speak to you, but I did not understand his words. Did you understand them?"

Marcus understood nothing. "I am still uncertain," he answered and scanned Strelleck's face for any sign that the creature knew more than he let on. The eyes did not reveal any signs of knowledge. Marcus did not find anything that seemed suspicious.

The eyes narrowed further. "It is not like him to speak and say nothing. Tell me when he gives you understanding, and then tell me your understanding."

Strelleck turned and began to walk toward the stables.

Marcus hesitated to follow him. *Tell Strelleck?* How was he supposed to explain what Boerak-El had "told" him?

This is what you have asked me to give you.

Marcus had asked many questions—to which one was Boerak-El referring? It could be anything.

Strelleck stopped on the walkway and looked back at him. The creature frowned.

Marcus jogged to catch up with him.

Over the last five weeks, they had developed something of a pattern. Marcus would go into town with Strelleck; he would travel with him for the rest of the day, and they'd rejoin the others in the evening. That night after buying the books in Teepo, Marcus expected to meet up with his brother and the others around the campfire as usual. But this time, only one individual was waiting for them. She was alone. Bithania didn't even look up at their approach. It took Marcus a few moments to realize what had happened. For a moment, he felt almost ill.

They were gone. Entan Gallowar had taken Myles and Antonie and traveled a separate route.

The Alusian, Marcus thought with a sigh. *These creatures don't say goodbye.* Over and over again, they had proven they did not need companionship the way men did. Even Entan had moments when he seemed much more Alusian than he did human. This was one of those times.

"See to your horse, Marcus," Strelleck said.

Marcus frowned, unable to adapt quickly to the sudden change in his circumstances. He looked at Bithania again. She was making supper, her head down, her pale hands busy over the halfpot. She ignored him, as usual.

He was alone with these creatures. Fully, absolutely alone. He hoped he would be able to endure this.

Quiet, he went to do as Strelleck instructed.

The Alusian was tending to his own animal, and Marcus, now that he had something to do with his hands, was able to ask his question politely: "Where are they going?"

Strelleck lifted his head and gave him the same peculiar, curious look he had given him on the walkway in Teepo. But he answered the question. "They go to Helsman. Men search for you. They are envoys from Korstain Elah, and Entan will be certain they find your brother instead."

Envoys from Korstain Elah. Looking for you. So Hileshand and Jonathan Manda had been correct in their assumptions. Now that Korstain had the throne, his plans extended even to sons he had disinherited.

"Will Korstain try to kill him?" Marcus asked abruptly.

Strelleck surprised him. Humor deepened the lines around the creature's eyes. He seemed to find the question amusing, and Marcus didn't see his reasoning. Korstain Elah *had* tried to kill Myles before. The question was legitimate.

"No," Strelleck said. "Korstain serves no god other than himself. He will not do what he did in the past. He will not try to kill his son."

The words affected Marcus like a slap on the jaw. This was the first time he had heard an Alusian call his brother the son of Korstain. Everything in him revolted at the concept. *No, he isn't Korstain's son. He is even less Korstain's son than I am.* Myles went by the name *Hileshand* just as Marcus did. They had the same father, and it was not Korstain.

What were the Alusian doing? Why the interest in Myles?

With a sick rush of heart, Marcus asked, "What happened to never meddling in the affairs of men?"

Strelleck blinked at him in surprise. "I am not meddling in the affairs of men." He shook his head once and frowned, almost as if he were offended. It seemed he didn't understand why Marcus would say that. "These affairs are not the affairs of men."

Therefore he felt he could meddle as much as he wanted? Was that it?

"You do not know where we are going," the Alusian said, adjusting the conversation. "You may ask now."

Marcus was no longer certain he desired to know where they were going.

His gaze strayed back to Bithania, sensing something was different about her, yet he couldn't quite tell what it was. She had raised her head and was staring at him over the fire, her gaze dark, her expression cloaked. The afternoon was delving into evening, the sunlight fading, and the light from the fire reflected across the lines of her face. A dark streak ran down the side of her nose, Marcus realized. She had a dirty face, as if she had been fiddling with something on the ground and sometime during the process, had reached up absently to brush her skin.

The shift within him was smooth and supple, revealing itself slowly, and it took a moment for him to realize what it was. And when he did realize what it was, what he found himself thinking, it startled him with as much violence as Boerak-El's interruption in the bookshop.

Wear it well, Boerak-El had told him.

By Abalel himself, Marcus thought, his heart jumping forward in a mad rush. *This isn't good.*

Yet he knew it was very good.

This is ridiculous, he thought next, and something within him disagreed. This was not ridiculous. This was perfect.

"Marcus," Strelleck said.

Marcus awkwardly returned to the conversation at hand. "What?" he murmured. "What was the question?"

Strelleck frowned at him, seeming mildly annoyed. "Do you wish to know where we are going?"

Tapos-Dane.

The word dropped into Marcus' mind as if Boerak-El had spoken it to him. Perhaps he had. He was the god of sorrow—the Alusian with the blood of man, who gave unexpected gifts.

That was where they were headed. Tapos-Dane.

The location was logical, for the Alusian didn't care enough about others' fears to hide themselves from people. They were too proud for that, but they would seek a level of distance, for those who feared death would require that from them. Tapos-Dane sat on the border of Edimane, not far from the particular mountain that produced blue quartz and gave the town of *Blue Mountain* its name. Marcus and Hileshand had discovered Myles in that town, tossed up on the body of the dragon he had killed with his helmet.

The people of Edimane were known for their odd beliefs and superstitions. And with the Alusian inhabiting Tapos-Dane, Marcus supposed he could understand where some of their fears had originated.

"Tapos-Dane," Marcus said. "We're going to Tapos-Dane."

Strelleck pushed around the horses, and Marcus took a step back out of reflex as the Alusian invaded the space before him.

Strelleck's gaze dug into him. "Has Boerak-El given you understanding of what he told you today?"

"Yes," Marcus said, knowing it was true.

"What understanding did he give you?"

What could Marcus possibly tell him? Boerak-El had shared something with him; he had literally taken the pouch from his own neck and put it around Marcus'. Marcus now possessed something he had not possessed before, and he had no idea what would happen if he attempted to explain any of this to Strelleck.

Strelleck waited.

Shifting uncomfortably, Marcus replied, "He spoke to me about her," and nodded toward Bithania.

Bithania leapt to her feet. She upset the halfpot, and the beginnings of supper spread through the dirt.

I am just about to die, Marcus thought.

"Surprising," she said. Her head tilted, and she demanded hotly, "In what language did he speak these things? For it would need to be in a language you understood, and it's unlikely *you* would understand any—"

"Bithania," Strelleck said. He stopped her rant with a single word.

She didn't look at him. She turned and stomped off into the gathering dark.

Marcus and Strelleck watched her go.

After a time, Strelleck looked back to Marcus, his expression unreadable in the shadows. "She acted unlawfully toward you."

Unlawfully? "How so?" Marcus asked.

"It was the purpose of another to come and find you. It was to be under certain conditions, in a certain location, and in a specific hour. Bithania did not adhere to that and responds now to the pressure of impending judgment."

He meant that she was afraid. A response to the pressure of impending judgment would be fear. Strelleck said these things in a way that seemed almost apologetic.

"What sort of judgment?"

Strelleck pulled in an Alusian breath—nostrils flaring, lungs filling. Marcus was yet uncertain about this, but he had begun to suspect that the Alusian breathed in this manner when Boerak-El spoke to them. Entan followed the same pattern. He would breathe deeply and then speak something profound.

"Our council intends to remove her place," Strelleck said.

Marcus frowned.

Strelleck continued, "It is a serious matter for one of my kind to misrepresent the words of our god. We are the image of him on the earth; we must represent him faithfully." The creature nodded. "When she put her hand to you in Ausham, she acted in a way that defamed my people. More importantly, she also defamed her purpose. She is meant to bring harmony, to reconcile divided parties, but she did not act according to that purpose when she was in Ausham. There will be consequences for her actions toward you, and she knows this. What did Boerak-El say to you about her?"

Marcus made up his mind in a moment. He wasn't going to tell Strelleck anything, especially not now. "That," he said, "is between me and Boerak-El."

Again, faint signs of amusement appeared around the creature's eyes. "You will not tell me?"

"I don't think it was knowledge meant for you."

The creature inhaled deeply, waited, and in the end, he did not press his case. "He does not speak without purpose, Marcus. There is always a purpose in everything he does. Each of my kind has a purpose, for Boerak-El created us, and each word he speaks has a purpose. You do not need to share his words with me, but you do need to know he has a purpose in what he told you. An intent."

chapter **18**

Myles and Antonie stepped onto Persus Claven's property in the middle of a frigid downpour. The sky had unlaced above them. Thunder growled. The wind spoke strongly of winter. It had snowed yesterday, but here in the valley, the thin ground cover had not survived the day. The rain would likely be ice come morning.

The servants knew Antonie's face and appeared quite excited to see him. Antonie, however, never did well when he was wet and cold. He jerked his thumb toward Myles, gave his name in a shivering mutter, and asked for tea.

At Myles' name, quiet dropped through the foyer. The servants stared at Myles as if Antonie had done much more than simply mention his name. Then all at once, their senses returned to them, and they scattered. A short time later, Claven himself met Myles and Antonie in the first hall. He grinned when he saw them.

Antonie bowed. "My lord." Water ran down his forehead and into his eyes. He had recently taken to tying his hair back with a leather cord, and the wet mass of red hung off the back of his head like a sodden squirrel tail.

No part of Myles was dry. Both he and Antonie made spreading pools on the marble floor.

"Adwin," Claven called to a servant who waited near an interior door. "Take our guests and dress them in something warm. Then bring them to the North Room for a late supper." His grin widened. "And bring my son to me. Wake him. Tell him there is someone here to see him."

Antonie, who preferred order and continuity, began his tale at *his* beginning: when he had left Claven's company and joined Myles and the others at the King's Southern Inn outside the city of Bledeshure. In great detail, he told Claven and Derek about the niessith that had destroyed Claven's ship and consumed many of the crew. The horrific creature of the deep had taken Myles and Amilia as well, but Issen-El, god of the sea, had removed them from the saltwaters and deposited them in a cave three hundred miles inland.

Claven chuckled at Antonie's descriptions of old Finlan. His brows rose when Antonie told about Abalel's School of the Prophets. Fascinated with things he didn't understand, Antonie was quite interested in that part of the story and made certain Lord Claven knew that Hileshand had training as a wizard.

"Which I found surprising," Antonie said, nodding.

"That's the wrong word," Myles interrupted. "Hileshand doesn't say *wizard*."

"What is the right word? How does he describe himself?" Claven asked.

Myles shrugged. "I don't know the word Hileshand

would use, but I am certain *a wizard* is not how he thinks of himself. He does not care for sorcery. Yes, he can do odd things that some would call magic, but he tries to hide it." Myles did not yet understand why Hileshand would do that. Why would a man wish to hide an ability to use magic, especially when that magic was helpful?

Claven responded with a slew of questions. "The meusone, the niessith—what does Hileshand call it if he does not call it sorcery? What is the correct wording? How does he explain what has happened to you, Myles?"

He implied now that *Myles* used magic, too, and the notion was almost laughable. Myles knew nothing of magic. He shrugged. "Hileshand has used the word *protection* before."

"By Boerak-El. Boerak-El protects you."

Myles and Antonie both stared at him, momentarily taken aback. Where would Claven have come up with that idea? Antonie had barely mentioned Ausham in his tale, and he had not yet said anything about Boerak-El. Bithania had yet to enter the story.

"He calls it the work of Abalel," Myles said.

But calling it Abalel was not much better than calling it magic. Myles had been forced to consider this idea at length because of others, who had wanted to discuss it in his presence. It had been poked and prodded at again and again—but it still bothered him. Abalel was far beyond the boundaries of Myles' control, and his interest in Myles was unwarranted. There was no reason for it, except for Abalel's own purposes. Every time Myles thought of how Abalel repeatedly saved him from death, he felt a heavy weight on his shoulders. The burden of debt. Who could repay a god? He *owed* Abalel now. He owed him his life, for it was his life Abalel had spared multiple times—so Myles could fulfill a prophecy that felt like it belonged to someone else. It did not fit him.

Many months ago, Ethan Strelleck had told Myles that Abalel would take his life as surely as he spared it. For a time, Myles had assumed that meant the obvious—that he was going to die, that a time would come when he faced a challenge and Abalel would *not* save him. But Myles had begun to change his mind. He had started to think that death didn't always involve the physical body. Sometimes, it meant a man's future. His hopes and dreams. He never would have chosen this road. He still wanted Furmorea, as it had been, before the war. He wanted land and a family and peace. But he wasn't going to have those things now, at least not the way he imagined having them. Abalel owned his life and could direct it in any way he chose. He could take what he had saved.

Claven observed Myles quietly for a moment. "It is a peculiar thing, to be guarded by a god."

Myles replied flatly, "Yes. It is."

An hour later, Entan Gallowar unexpectedly joined them at Claven's table. The guards let him in without question, and Claven sat up a little straighter as the Alusian tossed his wet cloak to a servant and sat down in the chair on Myles' right. He acted as if he owned the house—not in arrogance, but with the full expectation of being given exactly what he wanted, knowing no one would refuse him.

Antonie was forced to pause his narration. "This is Entan Gallowar. I am *about* to introduce him in my story." Antonie did not like being interrupted, once he was knee-deep in a tale. He gave Entan a disapproving look, which Entan ignored.

Myles tried not to smile as the servants ran forward to serve the Alusian. They fumbled all over themselves in their haste, their eyes wide, their movements stiff. Young Derek, who was sitting in the chair on Myles' left, leaned against the seatback and stared at Entan with eyes as wide as the servants'.

"You have one hour to complete said story before you will have to begin it again," Entan told Antonie. He didn't explain himself. Instead, he leaned back in the chair, just as Derek had done, and looked at the boy around Myles' back. "Hello, Derek."

The boy did not unfreeze for a time. "Hello," he whispered finally, after a quick look at his father. "How do you know my name?"

It would be no magic trick to uncover the boy's name, considering the house they were in and the history Entan knew now by heart. But the Alusian answered with his typical grace. "Myles talks about you. He is rather fond of you."

Derek lost his fears. He smiled and looked at his father proudly.

This was the first time Myles and Antonie had seen Entan in four days. On the southern side of Bledeshure, late in the day, he had announced he would meet up with them in Helsman, at Claven's house. That was all he had said, and then he had ridden off on business of his own. For whatever reason, Myles had expected the creature's unexplained business to take a few days longer. The Alusian held to their own timetables. They never allowed anyone to rush them.

Entan's blue gaze flicked to Myles, and, clearly amused, he answered Myles' thoughts: "I can be quick when I've a mind to be quick."

Myles grunted and looked away.

"Are you quite finished now, Entan?" Antonie grumbled. "I mean to complete my story."

Entan grinned. "I don't know why you'd care to. You will simply have to tell it again in an hour. Less than an hour now." He said this in jest, for he and Myles both knew Antonie's great love for storytelling. A long, detailed story told twice in the same night? That would be no hardship for this man.

Lord Claven sat in silence as Antonie told about Marcus and Bithania. Boerak-El. The god of sorrow and death laying claim to Hileshand's son. Myles had never heard this part of the story before, not in Antonie's own words. The scribe managed to capture a strong sense of Hileshand's anguish. Myles could feel it, the strains of heartache, and he frowned, his thoughts suddenly in turmoil. There were nights when he simply felt distant from those he loved and other nights when he felt actual pain, as he did now. He missed his wife. He missed Hileshand and his brother. The future seemed dark and unknown, controlled by the whims of others.

Entan did not attempt to correct the sentiment stirred up by Antonie's story. His face was blank. He no longer teased.

Slowly, the mood of the story began to step out of the shadows. Derek laughed in delight as Antonie described what it had been like for him to meet Entan the first time. Entan added a few words of his own to describe Antonie, which also made Derek laugh.

"I'm telling the story, Entan," Antonie said. "My story."

Antonie would never speak a sour word to Bithania or Strelleck, but Entan was another case. Over the last several weeks, Antonie had begun to feel comfortable around him, and he now treated Entan as he would treat Myles. Claven stared at his former scribe as if he had never seen him before. Antonie was not the bravest of men, but one would never know that based on his interactions with Entan Gallowar.

"So, then," Entan said with a nod, "tell Derek about the forpin."

That was out of Antonie's intended order. With this suggestion, Entan skipped entire portions of the story, and the scribe grew red behind his freckles. "I'm getting to that part."

Entan told Derek in a secretive tone, "Your fearless redheaded scribe killed a forpin."

"I did *not* kill a forpin. *You* killed a forpin with spears you crafted yourself, which you made *me* carry for two months. It wasn't very nice of you." Lowering his voice, he muttered, "You didn't make Myles carry anything."

"You are right, of course. How heartless of me. Next time, I will make Myles carry the spears, and *you* can wrestle the forpin."

Antonie scowled. That, apparently, was not the substitution he had hoped for. It did not seem to please him either.

Lord Claven leaned forward. He looked at Myles closely. "Forpins aren't poisonous. Their venom doesn't kill, but it can make a man's life fairly miserable for several hours. How did it affect you?"

Myles replied, "I felt fairly miserable."

"So the venom did, in fact, have an effect on you, as it would any other man."

"Yes."

Claven smiled slowly. "But the goe'lah's blood did not have any effect on you?"

Antonie had not told that part of the story yet. Before Entan's interruption, he had been speaking of Amilia and the miron. The table became quiet.

"How do you know about that?" Myles asked.

"Myles," Claven said, his eyes gleaming, "the entire city knows about that. When you frustrate a gamer, he tends to talk about the loss. He exaggerates it. He makes a legend out of fact, so his name will be spread and his profits increase, despite the loss. Is it true that you are also the man who killed the dragon in Blue Mountain?"

Myles shook his head. "No one knows that story."

"My dear man, everyone knows that story."

Derek rocked excitedly in his chair. "I know it!" he proclaimed. "My uncle *saw* you kill the dragon. He was impressed. I like dragons, and I like fighting, and I think all your stories are very interesting."

Claven smiled at his son's eagerness. Then he looked back to Myles, and his dark eyes narrowed. "You remain the same, Myles Hileshand. You challenge me to my face, and yet I find myself relieved with your words. Do you understand how different you are from every other man in your position? I have never met a man who cares so little for the force and manipulation of politics." He asked suddenly, "Do you realize all that Abalel does with you?"

Myles knew this man had no allegiance to the god of the sun; for the most part, Abalel was an unfamiliar name here within the borders of Tarek. Yet Claven seemed almost compelled to ask the question, and he asked it with fervor.

"I never gave a single thought to Abalel in my life. Then I look at you, and I see something that intrigues me, something I have never seen before." Claven's dark brows rose again. "And never did I expect *Abalel* to be the one who told this story. Who knew that he was such a talented storyteller? You give fame to your god, Myles, and it is not done quietly."

Before Myles could think of a response, a servant hurried through the door at the far end of the room. He bowed before the table and rushed to speak in his master's ear.

Claven huffed and said, "What? Now?" He glanced back at the door.

Six men entered Claven's dining room.

Myles noticed the soldiers first. They bore the Ruthanian emblem of war—a red and gold eagle—over the heart of their leather breastplates. They were large men and heavily armed, as if they suspected trouble even here, in Claven's home. The other four men did not wear armor, but Myles immediately could tell by their bearing that if a point of concern existed here, it lay with these men; the soldiers served only as their support.

One member of the group was about Hileshand's age, with the same broad-shouldered, former-soldier appearance Hileshand bore. Gray was spreading through the black hair at his temples. Beneath a heavy brow, his eyes were dark and intense, but the severity didn't last. As soon as he saw Myles sitting at the table, he grinned broadly, and Myles had the distinct impression that this man believed he knew him.

This, no doubt, was Thaxon Parez. Before they'd parted ways, Marcus and Myles had sat one night before the fire, and Marcus had gone through a list of people he knew or remembered from his childhood; Parez had been mentioned several times. Parez and Hileshand had been friends for years. They had served together in the Ruthanian military and then later for Korstain Elah. Every few years, Hileshand and Marcus would meet up with Parez in Fole-Dumas, near the Ruthanian border. Parez always came armed with gossip from the homeland, and he wanted to hear all about the adventures Hileshand had been having in Parez's absence.

Like Marcus, Entan also had an opinion of Thaxon Parez. *He is a good man,* he'd told Myles. *He gambles more than he should and owes money to several men, but other than that downfall, you will like him. He considers Hileshand a friend, and in time, he will consider you a friend as well. He will be a good support for you.*

Every article that could be wet on these men was thoroughly drenched; mud slicked their boots and had splattered a noticeable height up their trousers. They appeared to have ridden here in haste.

Introductions were made.

Thaxon Parez, an auxiliary for Korstain Elah, king of Ruthane.

At once Claven began to frown, as if he had dealt with Korstain in the past and knew what to expect from future dealings with him. "And to what do I owe this honor?" He was polite.

Parez gestured toward Myles. "My lord, forgive the inconvenience and the late night interruption, but we have spent several months in search of this man. And Hileshand, his guardian." He glanced through the room, seeking a familiar face.

"Hileshand is in Paxa," Entan said, folding his hands across his stomach and leaning back in his chair to watch the proceedings. He did not look in Myles' direction, and Myles supposed he knew why.

Calm, Claven asked, "Why would Korstain Elah be interested in Myles Hileshand?"

Parez smiled warmly. "Marcus Elah," he corrected. "He is interested in Hileshand's ward, Marcus Elah." The smile turned in Myles' direction.

"Elah," Claven repeated.

He, too, looked down at Myles, who was still seated at the table. Myles saw no reason to rise.

Parez nodded. "Yes, my lord. We were going to take a ship for Paxa in the morning, but Master Gallowar found us in Bledeshure and spared us a needless journey." He nodded his head to the Alusian, adopting that reverent, dutiful look of respect that Myles had seen on countless other men who had attempted to speak to Entan. "For which we are grateful."

So that had been Entan's solitary business, the reason for his unexplained departure four days ago. He had gone for Thaxon Parez. Myles felt the grimace slide across his face, and he looked down at the table.

There was nothing he could do.

This was out of his hands.

If Parez noticed the awkward silence, he gave no sign. "Marcus." He clapped a firm hand on Myles' shoulder, the way a friend would. "I bear good news for you. I've come to bring you home. Home to Ruthane. Your name has been restored within your father's house, and you are to come home immediately, with the welcome of the nation. They're expecting you."

"Elah," Claven said again, still locked on that one point. Notes of interest began to fill his voice. "Is this true?

Are you an Elah?" He wasn't used to waiting for information, and when Myles didn't answer, he said purposefully, "Myles. Are you?"

Entan pushed his chair back from the table and stood to his feet. Hands raised, palms up in a shrug that conveyed no genuine sorrow, he addressed Parez and his Ruthanian companions: "My lords, I fear that Marcus is engaged elsewhere."

Parez's movements slowed, as if he had waded into mud as deep as his chest. He looked at Entan the way a foreigner looks at a man who has made an effort to speak the language but isn't succeeding.

"He will not be joining us. I apologize for any confusion. I can fulfill only half of your mission." Entan was always pleasant. He always thought he was helpful. "But you will find that it is enough."

Myles rolled his eyes. *The Alusian and their riddles.*

Antonie agreed with him. "By the gods," the scribe murmured in annoyance and leaned forward to rub his face with both hands.

Parez's smile disappeared. He looked sharply at Myles. And then, as understanding came, his eyes widened and the confusion drained away.

"Allow me to offer a proper introduction. This is Myles, Marcus' brother," Entan said. "This is Korstain's firstborn. This is the son you seek, is it not? You have been seeking the heir."

Parez stared. The muscles moved in his throat, and he repeated, "*Myles.*" He frowned and said more firmly, "Myles Elah."

So it begins, Myles thought with very little pleasure.

part three

The Messurah

chapter 19

Ara saw the man the moment the door opened. Her gaze ran into his, and even before she had entered the room, she knew with whom she would be spending the evening.

The man sat at the third table along the wall. He had three companions with him, but other than being aware of their presence, she did not pay attention to them. The man who looked at her so intently had clear, clean features, dark hair, and he was rather handsome. At least there was that. She felt his gaze strongly, as if he touched her with his hands.

She let her breath out slowly. For two months, she had cried every time she had seen a man look at her like this, but she didn't cry anymore. The tears had stopped as she had grown accustomed to this place and this life. Now she never cried. She took pride in that.

She stepped into the room, and as she did, she felt the strength increase in the man's gaze. She concealed the shiver that rose up her spine. Something about this soldier was different than the others. There was aggression in his look—something like anger, but not anger. She didn't know what it was. He reminded her of the first man, the first night, and she went about her duties in silence, trying to keep her heart calm. She remembered she did not cry anymore.

The inn was louder tonight than it normally was. The city of Pon-Omen had been overrun as the Galatian army returned from conquering the southern territories of Furmorea. She had never seen so many soldiers in one place before. The Galatians were rough men who took their drinking and merriment very seriously. They did not respond well to disturbances of any sort. Ara had learned this the first time her master had assigned her to a table here—it was not good to disturb a Galatian soldier when he had been drinking. She would never forget the man's face or how he had looked at her. He had frightened her, and she had responded without thought. In the end, fighting him had not done any good, and he had been rougher than necessary, to punish her.

Afterward, her master had taken her aside and warned her severely, his hand bruising her arm. *Why do you think I purchased you, girl? The Galatians have never seen eyes like yours. You are unique. Remember that. It's why I bought you for more than you are actually worth.*

Her master's name was Borili. He was not Furmorean, but he had lived in Pon-Omen, the king's city, for nearly twenty years. He understood what Furmorea was like, and he had not appreciated Ara's initial hesitance.

Another outburst like that, and I will have you and your sister whipped. Both of you. I will send your sister *to work tables—you understand me? She would not last a week among the soldiers.*

Her sister, Lenay, was nine years old and worked in the kitchen. Ara understood Borili completely, and she had not protested again.

Until tonight, she had not seen any look that resembled the reptilian, greedy gaze she remembered from the first night, but this soldier had it, and he watched her. She felt his gaze on her back as she attended to the tables along the wall. The men seated there teased her and made ridiculous comments, but she was used to such things now and they no longer affected her. One of the men put his hand on her backside, and she acknowledged him with a faint smile and then simply moved on.

Borili told her she was the prettiest girl he owned. *Because of your eyes,* he would say. So he always put her along the wall, never at the tables at the front of the room near the door. He had lost a girl that way once. Someone had grabbed her, and the next day, they had fished her body out of the river. So Borili put Ara by the wall.

Gripping the ale bottle with both hands, her knuckles whitening, she crept to the next table.

For a brief moment, none of the four men said a word. They just looked at her. One of them smiled, and it was not a pleasant smile. The man with the frightening eyes took hold of her arm.

"Purple," he said at last.

She tried to look at him but couldn't. At his hand on her arm, everything inside her started screaming. She had worked here for six months, and every night, she thought about the first time. She watched it in her head like a scene on a stage. She was used to what was expected of her now;

she was familiar with it, so this man should not scare her—but he did. Something was wrong with him. She could see it in his look.

"Your eyes," he said, his grip tightening when she didn't respond. "Your eyes are purple. I have never seen anything like that. Are you Furmorean?" His thumb moved across her skin in a caress that sent chills through her system.

"Yes," she whispered.

His look darkened. He saw her fear. "What was that? I didn't hear you." He challenged her to speak again.

"Yes," she answered, her voice firmer.

Not this one, she thought. Panic filled her. It rushed through her before she could stop it. She had not thought of Abalel in months, but she now directed her prayers to him without hesitation. *Not this one.* She saw madness in his eyes.

He spoke in Galatian to his companions, and they laughed. He smirked at the way she trembled, and then he stood from the table. She stared at him as he told her what he was going to do to her. Here. In front of them all.

He *was* the first man. This was what the first man had done. That man had seen her fear, and because she was afraid, he had broken her in front of the entire room.

She could not go through that again. She could not. Before Ara realized what she was doing, before she could consider the consequences, she jerked her arm back. It slid in his grasp, but it was as if he had expected her to fight him, for he did not let go. A wicked sort of humor rose in his expression as she struggled to get free.

"Brace yourself, girl." He leered at her.

She dropped the bottle and tried to run. He hurt her, and the man's companions laughed at her cries. The room filled with the sounds of drunken, shifting laughter as the rest of the Galatian crowd joined in. They were all watching.

No, no. The panic took her completely, and she could not think. The room grew dark around her. She couldn't breathe. Her heart shuddered violently, as if it were about to stop beating.

The grip on her arm disappeared.

She tripped and fell to the floor, where she curled up and covered her head, squeezing her legs together as hard as she could.

She realized the laughter had stopped.

A hand touched her arm. She gasped, and the touch on her hand transferred to a warm grip on her wrist. It was firm but did not hurt.

"Ara," the man said calmly. "Ara, open your eyes."

She knew this voice and cautiously did as the man commanded.

It was Jezaren, commander of the governor's personal guard and overseer of his affairs. He was a quiet man. He rarely spoke more than a few words at a time to Ara and never about his occupation; she knew only what the others said about him—that he was an important man in the newly conquered Galatian territory of Furmorea. Borili was thrilled to have Jezaren as a regular client. It brought him additional business, and Jezaren paid very well for Ara's time. Only hers. He did not even look at Borili's other girls.

He was kneeling beside her, his hands on her arms.

She lowered her arms when she saw the bodies behind him. All four men lay sprawled in various positions on the floor. There was no blood on the floorboards, nor was there any movement. Jezaren was a *messurah*; he didn't carry weapons. His training didn't require them. Her breath caught as she realized he had killed them all—in front of everyone. He had been quick, and she had heard nothing.

Why had he done this? Another sort of fear rushed through her, and she looked up quickly into his eyes. She had never seen this expression on his face before. It was dangerous. It scared her.

He had killed these men.

"You are done here," he said and lifted her in his arms off the floor. He was much larger than she, and she felt like an infant as he held her against his chest. He could crush her as surely as he had crushed the men who lay here. She was not safe with him. Nothing was safe anymore.

He glared through the room, as if daring someone to speak to him.

Borili, the master, stood behind the bar. His eyes were wide, his mouth open in surprise.

"You've just completed a sale," Jezaren informed him.

Borili made as if to speak.

"Do you wish to argue with me?" Jezaren asked, brows lifting. With deceptive calm, he said, "Say a word. Say any word."

Borili did not wish to argue. He closed his mouth.

The Furmorean king had been executed months ago, and Jezaren's lord had been instated in his place. As the governor's second, Jezaren could do anything he wanted here. Though enamored with him and pleased at his patronage, Borili had always been a little afraid of him, and Ara now understood why.

Jezaren carried her out of the building. Three soldiers followed him—his men, Ara realized, for they walked just behind him and did not speak. Her arms around Jezaren's neck, she listened for the sounds of pursuit from the inn. But all she heard was the door as it slammed shut behind them. Borili let Jezaren take her.

chapter **20**

A carriage pulled before Jezaren at the head of the next street. He did not set Ara down. He simply passed her to the man behind him then climbed into the vehicle. One of his men entered with him, and the door was shut. She watched as they pulled away.

Ara looked at the man holding her. He ignored her. She wanted him to set her down, but he didn't.

He carried her all the way to the governor's palace. *The palace?* But of course Jezaren would bring her here. This was where he lived—he was the governor's second.

The palace, she thought again. Her heart pounded. She had no idea what this meant for her, what was going to happen to her. The inn, though unpleasant, had become familiar. She could predict what would happen to her there. She could not predict Jezaren and his behaviors. He often hid himself behind a sinister quiet that gave nothing away.

The soldiers took her to a suite of rooms deep in the

eastern wing of the governor's palace. Everything in the front room was covered with blue fabric and silver trim. Her mouth fell open, and she couldn't manage to shut it as she stared at all of the expensive things. She had spent her life on a farm, with dogs running through the house and chickens scratching up the yard. She had never seen finery like this.

The soldier set Ara down.

A woman appeared out of nowhere and curtsied before Jezaren's men. They didn't acknowledge her. Once Ara was on her feet, the men left without a word.

Ara stared at the woman before her. She gathered that she was a servant of the house. The woman wore a simple gray dress with a dark blue band of fabric fastened around her upper arm. Ara had seen this strip of fabric many times; it meant the Furmorean was loyal to the new governor, Jezaren's lord, and should not be killed.

The woman looked Ara up and down, taking her in slowly. A thick line appeared between her brows. "What is your name, girl?" she asked in Furmorean.

"Ara."

The frown line grew deeper. "And how old are you?"

"Fourteen."

The woman grimaced. "Fourteen," she repeated. Groaning loudly, she reached up and ran her hands over her head, dragging at the gray bun wrapped up at the nape of her neck. A moment later, she groaned a second time and straightened the hair she had shifted out of place. "Fourteen. Naught but a child. *Fourteen*. Very well. How did you come to be here? Where did his lordship find you?"

"At the inn on Green Street." Ara realized she didn't even know the inn's name. She had never left it, once she had entered the city.

The woman glowered at her. "*Dasoshane*," she murmured in disgust.

A prostitute.

"What did...?" the woman began. She scowled and started the sentence again. "What did his lordship *do* to you? Why did he have you brought here?"

Ara quietly related the story. The words jumbled. She had difficulty speaking. "He killed four men. One of them was going to hurt me. There wasn't any blood. They just were dead."

Ara had done the very thing Borili had told her not to do—she had refused a customer. But what had occurred after that, with the dead men and Jezaren, hadn't been her fault. Borili couldn't hurt her sister, because this had not been Ara's fault. *Please don't hurt my sister.*

Her arm ached where the Galatian soldier had grabbed her. The dress she wore had no sleeves; none of her dresses covered her well, and there was a handprint growing on her skin.

"Has he lain with you?" the maid demanded.

Ara blinked at her harsh tone.

Perhaps Furmorea only *seemed* different to her, and many things actually remained the same. Ara knew this look. Occasionally, the inn saw Furmorean travelers—always men, always older, for the younger ones had died in the war and the women had been sold, as Ara had been. All Furmorean travelers looked at her as this maid looked at her now. There was always disdain, the brazen disgust, as if Ara could have somehow prevented what the Galatian army had made her. Perhaps they were right—she could have died. That was the only salvation Ara knew of.

Unmentionable. That was what the whole of Furmorea considered her now. Prostitution was a shameful thing—so sordid, so broken, that no one desired to speak of it. It was very clear what the maid was thinking. *Dasoshane.* A prostitute. The maid knew what Ara was, so why had she asked? How else would Jezaren know Ara? Ara found herself thinking that this maid must be less intelligent than others.

"Yes," Ara answered. He had been Borili's highest-paying client.

The maid rolled her eyes and thrust her arms into the air, as if the whole situation was far beneath her desire to understand. She said briskly, "I am Muriel. I have been assigned to these quarters, as have several others. There are many servants in the palace. You, however, I think, are not here as a servant. Not in the conventional way." Her brows rose with meaning. Ara did not have to wonder about her intent. "You should know I am Furmorean, from Gaines. Most of us are Furmorean here in the palace. They kept much of the former staff, and I tell you, this won't do, girl—the painted eyes and the color on your lips. Not if you expect to be treated well while you are here."

While you are here. Did that mean this was only temporary? Ara swallowed down her frustration and attempted to speak calmly. "I…I don't have to have it. I can wash it off."

Muriel stepped closer and studied her with a narrowed gaze. "He noticed you because of your eyes, didn't he?"

"I don't know."

"Peculiar color."

Borili had always talked to her about her eyes. *The prettiest girl.*

"Thank you," Ara said.

Muriel harrumphed. "That was *not* a compliment, girl. I will see to new clothes for you, something more sedated, and I will wash that garish paint off your face. We will feed you, and I will bring you whatever you need for your...stay here." Muriel gave her a snide smile.

A few months ago, Ara would have cried at the woman's tone, at the horror of this situation, but more than once, she had found herself feeling grateful for the training she had received. She did not cry anymore. She would not wish to show tears to a woman who was mean to her, simply because Ara had chosen to live and not die. Lenay, Ara's little sister, would have started crying the moment Muriel opened her mouth. She cried all the time. The cook often said he used Lenay for his kitchen salt.

Ara said, "I don't know where I am."

"Don't you, girl? This is his lordship's private chambers."

chapter **21**

$\mathcal{T}$he hour grew late, and Lord Jezaren did not return to his chambers.

Muriel would have admired his work ethic had he not been Galatian. He possessed the fortitude and diligence of a Furmorean. He was constantly advancing toward his goals, always exerting himself. Though he was young, barely thirty, he had already won marks of honor and was well-known throughout his homeland. Nothing of worth occurred in the governor's palace without Jezaren's approval—the governor did not work nearly as hard as Jezaren did. Muriel's master often came to his bed exhausted and irritable, long after the sun had gone down.

Tonight, the palace was quiet. A slight wind blew into the sitting room, stirring the curtains above the couch, where the girl lay sound asleep. Who knew how long it had been since she'd had a decent night's rest? Muriel shuddered. Fourteen years old and empty of all virtue. It was a terrifying sign of the state of Furmorea. *We have lost our souls. Nothing of worth remains.* How many Galatian soldiers had this little girl brought to her bed? It was disgraceful to think that Jezaren was one of them. He was worth more than that. Yes, he was Galatian—but Muriel could respect him because of his dedication and commitment. She did not understand how he could foul himself with a slave girl like this.

Muriel nodded off in her chair waiting for the master to return. Eventually, she registered the sound of the door opening, and she jumped up and stood straight, clasping her hands in front of her.

A few lamps burned throughout the room—he would easily be able to see Muriel standing there, but she still said quietly, "My lord," letting him know exactly where she was. It was unwise to surprise him. None of the servants entered his presence without offering some sort of distant alert.

Jezaren ignored her.

He did not, however, ignore Ara. He stopped when he saw her lying there, her hand under her head, propped up on the armrest. Muriel could not tell what he was thinking—perhaps he had forgotten he had killed for her today. A vivid image of him in bed with the girl filled her head and sent rows of painful shivers through her back. *Disgusting. I should not have to deal with this situation. It is revolting.*

"Where do you wish me to put the girl, my lord?" she asked, hearing the disdain in her voice.

He turned on her, fury in his dark eyes. "I have seen enough of Furmorean ignorance," he hissed.

Apparently, his work today with the governor had not progressed in the way he had hoped. Muriel backed away from him. *Don't show fear*, her husband had repeated during the siege. *The Galatian military is trained to exploit those who reveal their fear. They punish the fearful.* But she could not help herself. It had been a simple question—why this response?

Jezaren glared at her. "Are you really this much of a fool?"

What had she done? She hadn't *done* anything. She hadn't said more than a few words to him. She trembled at his rage.

"She will stay where she belongs," he said, and he himself moved the girl. He lifted her off the couch and carried her into the bedchamber.

Muriel's heart raced. She didn't know what to do. Jezaren had never expressed such anger toward her before. *I do not wish to die here.* For a moment, that was all she could think. *I do not wish to die.* Then yanking in a quick breath, she tried to be logical. *He won't kill me for asking a question, for doing my job. Whatever this anger, it cannot actually be because of me. I don't think I have done anything...*

She knew she was right. She hadn't done anything. Her heart began to calm.

But then he returned.

He pointed at her across the room. "You will give Ara the same respect you give me. You will answer all of her questions. You will give her everything she asks for. Do you understand? She is *mine*. She is not some poor man's child you can refuse and ignore. She is mine, and you will treat her as such."

Muriel curtsied. "Yes, my lord."

His voice rose. "Do you understand?"

Quickly, she curtsied again. "Yes, my lord! I will do everything you ask!"

He lowered his hand. "See that you do."

He glared at her. She knew a fear that suggested death.

He strode back into the bedchamber and slammed the door behind him.

chapter **22**

Ara had shared a bed with many men, but she had never opened her eyes in the morning and discovered a man sleeping beside her. Four weeks passed before this occurred with Jezaren, and she was surprised when it did.

On most mornings, he was already gone by the time she opened her eyes. She never heard him leave. He would simply not be there, and she would have the small, simple pleasure of the entire bed to herself, the room quiet and still. It was a large room, nearly as large as the main room at Borili's inn, with dark drapes at the windows, three separate dressing rooms, and a curious painting on the ceiling. The plastered dome was covered with pictures of wood fairies and flowering trees. Ara wondered if a lady had lived in this suite of rooms before the king had been killed. The dancing fairies did not suit Jezaren.

Last night, he had not returned from his work until dawn. Pale gray light was sneaking in around the edges of the drapes when she heard the door open, then close softly. The mattress moved as he slid under the blankets beside her. She felt the warmth of his presence and fell back asleep.

The next time she opened her eyes, morning had come fully awake on the other side of the windows. The gray light had become golden, and Jezaren was asleep. He did not snore. He did not make any sounds or any movements, and he slept on his stomach, his arms above his head with the pillow on top of them. The room was as quiet as it was when she awoke alone.

Slowly, Ara curled up into a sitting position near the headboard and wrapped her arms around her knees. She watched him. He did not seem frightening when he slept. Perhaps it would be good for her to see him sleep more often. At the thought, amusement turned up the corners of her mouth. He had not mistreated her. He still spoke as little as possible. Days would go by when she wouldn't hear his voice at all. Quite often, he would sleep beside her for a few hours during the late watches of the night and be gone shortly after the sun rose, and that would be the extent of their interaction. On other days, he would return at dusk, as the moon was rising, and he would be gentle with her. She found that seeing to the needs of one man was much easier than seeing to the needs of several. She imagined that marriage would be something like this and supposed that living with Jezaren at the governor's palace was the closest to marriage she would ever come.

She looked over at the door to the short hallway that led to the sitting room and wondered if Muriel knew her master was still in here, still asleep. The maid began making noises and banging things around in the sitting room if she felt Ara had slept too late into the morning.

The hour was very late today. The lines of sunlight fell across the floor in ways Ara did not often see. Muriel did, apparently, know the master was here. She never let Ara stay in bed this long by herself.

A hand touched her foot.

She looked back to Jezaren and discovered he was watching her. She had not seen him move his arm across the bed.

"Why do you smile?" he asked, his look intense.

"I do not think you are frightening when you sleep," she replied.

He did not say anything for a moment. "You find me frightening, Ara?"

She knew what Galatian soldiers did when they saw fear in another person—they crushed any person who revealed it. But he had asked her a question, and he watched her face now; she would not lie to him. The war had stripped her of much of her Furmorean heritage, but she would not lie. That she would not do. Lying was wrong.

She had seen him angry before, and this face he showed her now was not his face of anger. "Yes," she said, answering his question, "but not when you're sleeping."

You should sleep more often, she thought again.

His grip tightened on her foot. "You do not need to be frightened of me, Ara."

She did not know about that. He had killed many people. When she had asked Murial about it, the maid had grown nervous and seemed to answer truthfully. *He has killed more than you realize, my lady—many more than the four at the inn. He is a dangerous man. The servants don't want to go near him. The governor's men give him much space. They say even the governor is afraid of him.*

"Do you believe me?" Jezaren asked her.

"No," she answered.

Releasing her foot, he pushed himself up onto his elbows and just lay there like that a moment, looking at her face with open curiosity. "You are very honest."

"My people do not lie."

His head tilted. His expression grew dark. "Have you ever lied to me?"

"No."

Immediately, the rough edges grew soft again. He allowed a faint smile to appear, and then he asked, "Are you lying now?"

She heard the mild humor in his voice. She smiled, too. "No."

Taking a deep breath, he glanced over his shoulder at the door to the hallway. Murial was still very quiet on the other side. Ara had not heard her a single time this morning. Examining Ara's reaction closely, Jezaren asked, "Do you wish you were back at Borili's inn?"

He had never spoken this much to her before. His Furmorean was perfect. He did not have an accent. She shook her head. "No, I don't want to go back."

"Good. Because I will not take you back there. You are mine now. Why are you afraid of me?"

There were too many answers to that question. She could name twenty different things without having to stop and think. It was not just Jezaren alone—he scared her only a little bit. He had not hurt her, and she was here because he had protected her from his countrymen, who had, indeed, intended to hurt her.

But Jezaren was Galatian, and she could not imagine any situation in which she would *not* be afraid of the men of that country. Galatian soldiers had killed her father and made slaves of her family. They had made Ara into something horrible—it was shameful and could not be undone. Galatia had ruined everything that was valuable in her life. And it couldn't be undone.

And Jezaren was the governor's friend, the one who made all his evil plans succeed. In a way, all of this—her family's loss, the war itself—was Jezaren's doing, though she knew she could not blame him entirely.

"Why?" Jezaren repeated.

"You are Galatian," she answered quietly. She was not smiling now, and neither was he.

He studied her face. Eventually, he flipped over onto his back and folded his hands behind his head. "War does not offer a pleasant picture of anyone," he said, looking up at the fairies on the ceiling.

She wondered why he did not paint over them. If he intended to live here long term, surely he would not always want to see the fairies.

"I do not want you to be afraid of me, Ara. You have nothing to fear from me. You are mine—I will not hurt you."

He closed his eyes and was quiet for so long that she wondered if he had fallen asleep again.

"I want to ask you a question," she said.

He was not asleep at all. His eyes opened, and he looked at her. "Yes?"

"Why did you kill those men?"

Part of her wondered if he even remembered what he had done. Perhaps Murial was right and other people's deaths meant nothing to him. *He is more Galatian than others,* Ara thought. He killed so often, and he did not consider his actions. And he did not use a sword or a bow;

he killed with his hands. Could he *feel* the man breaking beneath his blows? Didn't that bother him? He must have had a difficult, hard life to kill without emotion.

The room was quiet.

"You were afraid of him," he said. "I killed him because you were afraid of him."

She had been very afraid of that man, yes; yet Jezaren did not give her the answer she wanted. Frowning, she asked, "But why did you do it? Galatians cause pain. They injure the one who fears. They do not save him." She was the one who had been afraid.

His eyes narrowed as he looked at her, but he didn't reply.

"I don't know why you stopped him," she said.

He turned his gaze back to the silly pictures on the ceiling. With a shrug, he answered simply, "You did not belong to that man. You belong to me. I will protect what is mine."

Ara lived with Jezaren for two months in relative peace.

chapter **23**

The night the governor was assassinated, Ara could not sleep. The air felt strange to her, yet it was not the air itself; very little was different about this night. It was warm for winter. Snow melted in the courtyard outside, and the star-filled sky was streaked with clouds. Earlier in the evening, she had sat at the window for several hours and watched the activity in the court below. Muriel had fallen asleep on the couch as they waited for Jezaren to return. Many evenings had passed just like this one.

But something about it was different. Ara went to bed with an anxious stirring in her chest and spent several hours on her back, watching the ceiling and trying to sleep. Eventually, she heard the bedroom door push open quietly and knew Jezaren was home. *Finally.* She waited to feel the familiar motions of the mattress as he came to bed.

Instead, he seized her arm in the dark and yanked her out from under the blankets. She was trapped against his chest before she knew what was happening. As she felt the rapid pulse of his heart through his tunic, she understood that something was wrong. She had sensed it all evening, and now her worry was proven accurate.

He did not speak, so neither did she. She didn't ask him what he was doing. He carried her across the room to the dressing room and threw open the door, closing it again once they had entered.

His feet did not make any noise when he walked. Ara had noticed this before, and she noticed it again tonight— she could not hear his feet, and she could not hear his lungs. He breathed without sound, even now, when something clearly alarmed him.

She couldn't see a thing in the darkness of the dressing room. He adjusted her in his arms and reached upward. She felt the muscles tighten through his chest, and a moment later, she heard a sound she didn't recognize. It was similar to the squeak of an old door that has not been used very often, but it was deeper than that, as if the door was very heavy and moved with pulleys. She felt a whisper of cold air across her skin, and then Jezaren walked forward—through the dressing room wall.

She jerked her breath in and held on to him. *A passage,* she realized. *A passage hidden behind the stones.* Was that why Jezaren had chosen this room with its fairy-painted ceiling? He must have discovered the passage first and chosen the fairy room on purpose.

A few steps through the wall, Jezaren turned and took the same actions he had taken before. He reached upward; the muscles grew taut in his chest as he took hold of something and put his weight to it. She again heard the squeaking door. Then there was silence.

He held her close and did not set her down. Turning

once more, he carried her down a flight of steps without light. The cold in the air grew more intense. She could hear her every breath as she pulled it in, trembling; she heard none of his. Jezaren was not given to distress and anxiety, and the pace of his heart did not slow as they descended the black steps. He acted now in response to something that must be dreadful indeed, to cause his heart to pound like this.

When they reached the bottom of the steps, he took her forward in the dark on what seemed to be level ground. An hour after they'd entered the dressing room passage, he shifted her in his arms, reached forward, and pushed open a door.

Moonlight spilled across them. Ara winced at the sudden brightness.

The landscape before them was snow covered and shadowed. There were masses of trees, their branches heavy laden and pointing toward the ground. She did not see any buildings or lights. The tunnel had brought them all the way out of the city, beyond the wall.

Jezaren stepped back into the tunnel briefly and re-trieved two full knapsacks off the floor, slinging them over his shoulder. Then he pushed the door shut, locked it with a key, and carried her out into the silver night, walking for nearly a mile.

He did not set her down until they reached a cave. It was hidden by a detailed series of trees and shoulder-high brush. She never would have seen it, likely not even in the daylight. Her toes were numb from the cold, and she couldn't tell if he set her down on dirt or rock. She couldn't feel it. She stood there and shivered as he dug through one of the knapsacks. The moonlight gleamed distantly at the cave mouth on his other side.

"Sit down," he ordered.

He put boots on her feet and wrapped her in a heavy, fur-lined cloak. He slid gloves over her hands and made certain to pull the cloak's hood over her head. He dressed her with care, rubbing her hands briskly to warm them, and only then did he set about building a fire.

He used magic. She startled as flames appeared off the ends of his fingers. She hadn't known he could do this. With the cloak pulled tightly around her, she sat on the floor and watched him. He did not speak. He explained nothing.

"What happened?" she asked eventually.

His back was to her. He was pulling meal items out of the other knapsack—a black halfpot, strips of dried beef. His movements were agitated and created noises. "Leison was killed," he tersely answered.

The governor. Jezaren's lord.

Over his shoulder, he said, "Rest now, Ara. We cannot stay here. This is your only chance to rest for two days."

She didn't think she would be able to sleep here, in the midst of these circumstances. He had preplanned a route for his escape. He had set everything in order in advance. And he had always intended to bring her with him. The boots, the cloak, the gloves—all of these things fit her perfectly. They had been made specifically for her.

"What happened?" she repeated softly.

He rose to his feet and whirled toward her, his rage sudden. "You think I did this? *I* didn't do this!"

She had never seen him this angry with her. Fear tried to grab her. She drew away from him. But then she remembered—he wanted her with him. She knew he wanted her with him. He had prepared for her presence, so she did not think he would hurt her now. He had never hurt her before.

Releasing the edges of her cloak, she stood to her feet as well and looked at him.

He thought she accused him now, and with violence he proclaimed his innocence.

"I know you did not do this," she whispered.

His shoulders bent forward. His anger melted like snow near a fire. She went to him and touched him. He didn't pull away from her; he allowed her to comfort him and didn't move except to shiver in her arms. He needed her. He needed her to take care of him, and she knew it was important that she did. She wanted to take care of him.

A long time had passed since she had sensed even a flicker of Abalel's light. Her heart had been dark to him. For months, she had believed that he had forsaken her and her family—and she'd had much proof of his disregard. But now, here with Jezaren, she suddenly didn't think that way anymore. As she held Jezaren, she realized that in a strange way, Abalel had done for her what he had done for others, in all the stories she had heard from her parents. Abalel had put her through much pain, yes—yet he had brought her out of it again and given her a companion.

Jezaren pulled in a silent, deep breath, and she felt his fear. It trembled through him. He allowed her to see what no one else saw. He trusted her, and her heart toward him warmed a little more.

"It is all right, *aufane*," she said and ran her gloved hand down his neck, held on to him. His arms went around her, and he gripped her tightly. "You are safe now."

chapter 24

Standing before the inn on the opposite side of Green Street, Hileshand folded his arms and stared up at the fading sign. *Rose Petal Inn.* The words were difficult to read. The sign was old, as if the place had been inherited several times and passed down the family line.

He heard laughter breaking through the door.

Much of the city of Pon-Omen was very different than he remembered. The streets were dirty. The market inside Central Square had been reduced to six or seven booths, when he remembered several hundred—filled with traders, shoppers, and shouting peddlers. The square had been neatly organized and easy to navigate. Hileshand had brought Marcus here when he was a boy, no more than fourteen, and bought him a proper sword from a steel merchant.

But now the square was quiet. When Hileshand had walked through it about an hour ago, he had thought about tombs and ghosts of the past.

The Rose Petal Inn Hileshand also remembered. During that same trip seven years ago, Marcus had spilled a bottle of wine all over a Furmorean gate guard, and it had taken a fair amount of pleasant words and another three bottles before the man had forgiven Marcus enough to untie him. Hileshand smiled at the memory. Back then, the paint had not been cracked as it was now. The front porch had not been as dirty. He did not recall this sense of trauma and darkness that exuded with the laughter through the door. When Hileshand had last been here, it had been a common inn, nothing more.

He went inside.

The place was filled to capacity. Every chair. Every table. It looked like an entire city patrol had stopped in for a drink. Almost every man here was a Galatian soldier. The room smelled like body odor and ale.

Hileshand made his way to the bar. He had been noticed the moment he stepped inside; in his route through the room, he felt the silent pressure of aggressive men.

"I'm looking for Borili," he told the very young, very pretty girl who stood behind the counter. She had pale hair like Amilia's, and she'd put something on it to drain the color even more. In the lamplight, it appeared almost white.

She looked disappointed. "Are you certain you came all this way for Borili?"

"Here."

Hileshand turned.

A man approached him, weaving his way around the closest table. His hair was perfectly white and stood out in contrast to the darkness of his skin. He wasn't Furmorean. The skin was too dark. Hileshand wagered he was Galatian—southern Galatian, near the islands, where the Galatian blood had mixed with a native tribe of darker skin.

The man sighed as he stopped, looking at Hileshand with clear boredom. "I am Borili. How can I assist you?" His gaze flitted across Hileshand's clothes, the sword at his hip, and he added, "My lord?"

"I am looking for someone."

"I'm certain that's true." Borili made eye contact with a girl working on the other side of the room, and recognizing her cue, she giggled at Hileshand and waved.

Hileshand scowled. "The girl I search for is Ara Gaela."

Borili's gaze jerked back to him, and Hileshand immediately knew his information had been correct. Borili knew who Ara was. The first emotion Hileshand felt was relief—after weeks of searching, he was close now—yet in the same moment, he mourned. As much as he wanted to find Hana's daughter, he had been hoping the information wasn't correct. Borili had recently developed a reputation in Abeth, where the majority of the Furmorean slaves were bought and sold—he purchased only the pretty ones for the soldiers. He had seized an opportunity, and in the aftermath of war, he had become successful and well known. Hileshand glanced again through the crowded room and saw only two or three men who were not wearing armor.

"She was sold to you in Abeth," Hileshand said.

"I know the girl," Borili muttered. He wiped his mouth and, after a brief hesitation, nodded toward the kitchen. "Come with me."

Hileshand followed him through the door.

The kitchen was clean. Considering the state of the rest of the building, Hileshand was surprised. Then he remembered—*Rose Petal Inn* had an excellent menu. Marcus had eaten three plates of *perkus*, Furmorean noodles, and had been sick in bed for a day afterward. *Very rich food. Very ill boy.*

Hileshand saw two male cooks at the ovens and two little girls chopping things at the back counter. There was a third child sitting on the floor with a large bowl of bread dough in her lap. This one sneezed and, rubbing her nose on her sleeve, glanced shyly at Hileshand. He said hello with a faint smile, and she just stared at him, eyes wide. His chest hurt as he looked at her. She was eight years old, if that, and no doubt, it was only a matter of time before Borili sent her to work the tables with the others. Ara was barely fourteen. Just a child.

You can't save them all, he thought and had to look away from the little girl on the floor before the pain in his heart overwhelmed him.

Borili took him into his office. It was cluttered and crowded, papers and ledgers stacked in piles. He dumped several stacks of paper on the floor and then gestured for Hileshand to have a seat on the newly cleared surface.

Hileshand didn't want to sit. He wanted to kill him. Drawing a breath, he forced himself to take the chair offered. Borili walked around the desk and sat down on the opposite side, looking at Hileshand closely.

"Are you," the man said, "in any way connected with Jezaren, the messurah out of Galatia?"

The question's oddity helped Hileshand to calm. He shook his head. "I am not."

Suspicion clouded the man's eyes. "You speak the truth in this? You are not Furmorean—there is no reason for me to believe that you are telling the truth."

Hileshand had heard Jezaren's name several times since entering the city. The man had assassinated the governor and every man belonging to his guard. Without aid, he had killed forty well-trained, very experienced soldiers who were trying to save their commander's life. No one knew his reasoning or his purpose behind the deaths—as far as Pon-Omen knew, the man had simply lost his mind, and the city enjoyed talking about it. Jezaren, a powerful man, had killed his lord and then magically escaped. No one knew where the man had fled. From a certain perspective, it was somewhat impressive. Messurah training was difficult to master and much more difficult to waylay.

Hileshand repeated, "I am looking for Ara Gaela. And I speak the truth to you as faithfully as any Furmorean."

"I do not have her."

Hileshand stared at him. "I was told you purchased her in Abeth. Is this not true?"

"No, it is true." Borili lowered his head into his hands. He stayed like that for a long moment; then, with a groan, he rubbed his palms through his white hair and looked back to Hileshand. His eyes were red. He appeared weary. "Jezaren took her."

"What do you mean—he *took* her?"

Borili groaned again like a frustrated child. "He claimed her. He took her. He chose her. What do you want me to say?" He lifted both hands and made a growling noise in the back of his throat. "I could do nothing. My best girl. He took my best girl. My profits dropped fifty percent and have not recovered. Purple eyes—who has ever seen purple eyes? The girl was pure gold for me, and he took her."

A severe chill ran up Hileshand's spine and skittered

across his scalp. The words repulsed him. He saw himself spreading the tavern owner across his desk and cutting him open, beginning at his mouth and tracking the blade down the length of his pudgy body. "What happened?"

Borili told him. Jezaren had stopped the girl from being raped in the main room. "Rather tasteless," Borili said, revulsion flaring his nostrils. "But it sometimes happens. The soldiers do not follow any guidelines of principle. They think they can do whatever they want, as long as someone eventually pays their bill." Jezaren had killed four men for what the one man had intended and taken the girl away with him. "I had to pay the undertaker. *Me.* When I did nothing." Borili waved his hands around and groaned, "If only I had known!"

He seemed oblivious to how much Hileshand loathed him.

"What did you fail to know?" Hileshand asked, the words barely audible.

"That Jezaren wanted her so badly! I knew he was partial to her, but I could have *sold* her to him for a profit. Instead, he just takes her, and there's nothing I can do because he's the governor's second. He paid extravagantly for her time, and he would have given me a fortune in a sale—"

Enough. Hileshand had him against the wall before the man could finish speaking. His feet dangled off the floor. His eyes were huge.

"What do you want?" Borili shouted. "Just tell me what you want! Don't hurt me!"

"That little girl," Hileshand hissed and then could not finish. The anger choked out the words. "That little girl is dear to me. If you speak of her in any way I find less than honoring, I will cut out your tongue. I will remove pieces of your body that you would rather keep. Do you understand me?"

"Yes! Yes, I understand—"

Hileshand dropped him in disgust.

The man clutched his hands to his chest and trembled. Hileshand glared at him, and Borili became desperate. He sought to appease him, gasping, "I don't have the second either!"

"What?"

The tavern master looked at him in breathy confusion. "I bought the sister in Abeth as well. The little one—Lenay. Are you not also seeking her?"

Borili had had both of them. That Hileshand had not known. He and Isule had not been able to learn anything about Lenay in Abeth, while Ara was memorable because of her eyes. Every man in Abeth had remembered Ara.

Hileshand squeezed his eyes shut, thinking of how Hana had reacted when he had gently told her that Ara had been sold to a brothel owner. Hana's mourning had broken his heart, and there was not anything he could do to heal her wound. It was not a wound he could reach. The best Hileshand could do was come to Pon-Omen as quickly as he could and buy Ara from Borili, before she was injured more than she already was.

Borili had bought Lenay, too.

"What are you saying?" Hileshand asked, each word pronounced with care.

"I'm saying I had them both, and Jezaren took them both. He took the younger one, too."

For a moment, the small, dirty office was quiet. Lenay

was nine years old. Hileshand shook his head and whispered, "You are truly odious."

The man's eyes grew with fear. "*Nothing* happened to her while she was with me! I swear it! The girl worked in the kitchen with the other little ones. She was never around the soldiers. Jezaren never even saw her before he came for her. He asked for her by name. Someone must have told him of her. Perhaps it was the sister!"

"Tell me what happened."

Borili shuddered. "The day after he took the first one, he returned for the second. That one he paid for. I will—I will give you the money, if that is what you seek."

That was not what Hileshand sought.

For a moment, he stood there in silence, considering his options.

Jezaren had taken Hana's daughters—both of them. The muscles tightened through Hileshand's jaw as he remembered previous interactions with the men of Galatia. The man who had killed Hana's husband had also strapped Marcus to a beam and tried to draw a half-moon into his chest. That event did, in essence, sum up everything Hileshand knew to be true of Galatia and the offspring it produced. He had never had a positive interaction with a Galatian. They did not think like normal men.

Jezaren had killed forty-one men in a single night. Hileshand had heard various descriptions of the state of the bodies. Some declared there had been no blood. Others said there had been blood everywhere, because Jezaren had lost his mind and no longer followed messurah principles. But all of the storytellers did agree on one point—it was Jezaren who had killed them.

A messurah like Jezaren was dangerous for several

reasons. The training was intensive and, when completed, did not always allow the man to live as a normal man would—the trauma he had endured in the training process sometimes left the mind with "gaps." Hileshand had heard stories of messurah who had slipped in their sanity and committed murder on a broad scale—never drawing blood, never making a sound.

To keep such things from occurring, certain messurah were assigned Ethollian handlers, who observed their activities and stepped in if the messurah began to show signs of disorder. As much as Hileshand despised sorcery, there were few things capable of stopping a messurah who desired to kill.

Both of Hana's daughters.

"Where did Jezaren take them?" Hileshand asked.

chapter 25

According to his word, Jezaren pushed them for two days. Ara was exhausted by the time he stopped to make their first camp since the cave. Her entire body hurt. Her feet had blisters. She sagged to the ground and just wanted to sleep.

He had chosen an area that was sheltered by a tight cluster of tall pines. Snow covered the interwoven branches overhead, and very little of the white powder had been able to filter through to the soil, which was deeply lined with old pine needles. The trees formed walls on all sides. As it had been with the cave, Ara doubted that she would have found this place on her own, but Jezaren knew where everything was and exactly where to take her. She assumed he had been here before.

He cleared away a small section of the pine needles and built a fire in the same way he had in the cave—the flames appearing off the ends of his fingers. Light flickered on the frozen bodies of the pines, standing guard around them.

As he went about making supper, Ara sat bundled in her cloak, the hood pulled over her head, her arms around her knees. She watched him work. She had not asked him where they were going. In fact, over the last two days, they had barely said more than five words to one another. The destination was not important to her right now. It would be important eventually—she knew that, but for now, all she truly desired was to be with him. To do that, she did not need to know where they were going. He would tell her when he was ready.

Jezaren filled the halfpot with snow, and as the white melted and the water began to boil over the fire, he pulled the last of the dried beef from his knapsack and stirred it into the pot. His food was rather bland, but she doubted it had anything to do with his cooking ability. He was a man of talent. If he desired to be a good cook, he would be a good cook. More likely, he simply cooked like a Galatian. Borili, her former master, liked to say that Galatians knew cooking the way virgins knew intercourse.

Jezaren took a knife out of his knapsack. He did not carry the blade directly on his person, in order to use it as a weapon; he carried it in his bag as a tool, like the halfpot. Stepping around the fire, Jezaren walked to Ara and knelt down before her.

"Give me your right hand," he said.

Cautiously, she brought her hand out from beneath the cloak. He pulled off her glove and took her hand firmly. She did not fight him as he drew two deep lines on her palm with the knife's edge. The first was long—a semi-circle that cut into the heel of her hand. The second was blessedly shorter, crossing through the center of the semi-circle and aligning with her middle finger. It hurt badly. Tears ran down her cheeks, but she squeezed her lips together and tried not to cry out.

He did not speak to her until he had finished. His voice was quiet. "This is a sign of your commitment to me. It is a sign you are mine. Every man of my country who sees this will know you belong to a man. You belong to me."

The knife had her blood on it. He transferred the blade to his left hand and drew the same mark into the palm of his right. He did not make a sound, though his hand bled much more than hers. He had cut himself more deeply.

"This is the sign of my commitment to you," he said as he pulled the knife away.

She looked at him.

He continued, "Every man of my country who sees this mark will know that I am not a man alone. I have committed to sharing my strength with a woman." He lifted his head and met her gaze. "With you."

Her palm pulsed with fantastic pain. Blood dripped off her skin and wet the layer of pine needles near her legs. She pushed up onto her knees and reached for him, putting her hands around the back of his head, drawing him close. Blood spilt on his cloak. She accidently left a red smear across his cheek.

"Yes," she said. "Yes."

That night, Ara slept on Jezaren's chest, her cloak open to him and covering them both. He did not move her during the night. She awoke several hours after dawn and discovered him still asleep beneath her, his arms locked tightly around her shoulders. He had not left her to stand watch. She wondered where they were that would allow him to sleep without concern. He had been greatly concerned for two days, and now he wasn't. She had never seen him off guard like this, for such an extended period of time.

The fire still burned brightly. The original pieces of wood had not dissolved into ash, nor had Jezaren replenished it during the night. He had powerful magic.

She could feel the rise and fall in his chest as he breathed; she could feel the air move across her face as he exhaled. Yet even this close to him, she could not hear it. He produced no sound, even in his sleep.

His eyes opened and focused on her.

She smiled at him slowly. Could he feel her gaze as he slept? Was he that aware of his surroundings, even when unconscious? This was not the first time he had awakened at her stare.

Drawing up his arm, he traced her cheekbone with the fingers of his bandaged right hand.

"Mine," he said quietly, with contentment.

"Yours," she agreed.

She felt the muscles grow taut beneath her, and he sat up, pulling her up with him. He adjusted her on his lap until she was sitting on him sideways, her legs beneath his arm.

"This is Paxa," he said.

Ara had not been in the country of Paxa before. The border was several weeks' journey from the small town of Nan in southern Furmorea, where she had been born and raised. "Is it always this cold?" she asked, hoping for a smile from him.

Lines appeared beneath his eyes. That was how he smiled the most—with his eyes. The laughter was often harder to see with him than with others, but she slowly had come to understand that it existed with him, as surely as it existed with anyone. He had a different way of displaying it.

"No," he answered, "not always. You have not asked me where I take you. Are you not interested?"

"I am interested," she hurried to tell him.

"Then why have you not asked?"

She considered her words a moment and then answered, "I knew you were taking me to a good place."

He looked at her in silence, and what she read in his gaze made her few remaining doubts vanish like smoke in a strong wind. In this moment, she did not think she would ever need to ask him anything again, for he took care of everything and looked after her, and she was safe with him.

His look of love transitioned into a more serious study. He watched her for a long time, and finally, he said, "I am going to kill someone."

She grew still.

"It will be dangerous," he added. His gaze made a slow loop through their little house of trees. "But here in Paxa, the danger is less. The country's border is protected by Abaleine magic, which will slow him down. It will take him time to enter, but enter he will. He will try to kill you, for you belong to me and he wants to kill me."

He reached for the fingers of her right hand and touched them with his own, his bandaged hand to hers. "Mine," he repeated, looking at her. He waited for her to respond in kind.

Ara's heart ran. She thought of how he had saved her from the soldier at the inn. Then she thought of how he

LAUREN STINTON

had revealed his fear to her and trembled in her arms. He trusted her.

Leison is dead, he had told her then.

I am going to kill someone, he said now.

She put the words out of her head. She did not have anyone other than Jezaren. Everyone else had been stripped away from her, by death or by slavery—but Jezaren had fought for her. So she chose to believe his worth and that he was as good a man as she desired him to be. She needed to take care of him. She knew that, so she would not believe what his unexpected words suggested.

She put her fingers to his mouth. "Yours," she said and leaned forward to kiss what her fingers touched.

chapter **26**

Jezaren took much time with her that morning. He made her breakfast and changed the bandage on her hand and was so tender toward her that she almost forgot what he had said about killing someone. The hour was approaching noon when he finally announced it was time for them to leave.

The route Jezaren chose for them was meandering and slow, avoiding settlements and cities. He kept them in the mountains. They left tracks in the snow. Every night, he cast his magical fire that did not go out until he put it out; he would make supper and want her near him, and she was happy to oblige. They traveled unhurriedly like this for six days.

The morning of the seventh day began like the others. They did not break camp until midday, and then for four hours, he led her over white terrain. It had snowed again last night, and the drifts were deep and tried to capture their boots. The going was even slower than usual, but the day was clear, without a single cloud to mar the blue expanse above them, and the snow glittered.

Ara had always enjoyed the snow. When she was little, she had pretended it was full of diamonds and she was the only person who could find them. She found she was not very good at pretending now. Instead, the snow made her think of her parents and what she had lost, and she fought against the sorrow that rolled up her throat. It was not tears, yet it captured her breath just as severely.

The sun was setting when they came upon the cave.

The flickering light of a campfire drifted out of the opening in the rocks. The snow reflected orange, and Ara could see several sets of footprints leading up to the cave mouth. She hadn't seen anyone but Jezaren for days, and their departure from Pon-Omen had been an escape. Why did he bring her to people now?

She looked at him.

Pulling the glove off his left hand, he drew his fingers down his face in a gesture that was more nervous than anything she had ever seen from him. He was nervous? Why was he nervous? It made her heart jump. She began to feel nervous, too.

He glanced at her. "Wait," he commanded. "I will call you."

She nodded.

He held her gaze. The smile lines appeared beneath his eyes again. She could see them, despite the gathering shadows.

He stepped into the cave.

Ella was eight years old. Audra and Crisi were both ten. All three had lost their parents in the war, and all three required stories. All the time. Crisi was particularly fond of perusan, for some reason—the glowing, yellow-skinned creatures of the woods that killed people with their icy hands—and Audra wanted to hear about Hana over and over again.

"Is she pretty? Does she have long hair? Does she have an accent?" Hileshand had yet to ascertain why having an accent was important.

Every time Audra asked a new question, Ella's eyes would brighten, and she would lean forward, as if she had asked the question herself. She liked to know about Hana, too. She carried a mangled doll in her arms; the little thing's head was falling off and cock-eyed, the dress torn in several places. It was missing both feet.

He was a bad dog, Ella had explained to Hileshand two days before, shaking her head solemnly. *He tried to eat her.*

All three girls were precious. He hadn't been able to leave them. He was not returning to Hana with Ara or Lenay—but he had not been able to leave these little children behind in Borili's keeping.

Crisi wanted to be a boy. Hileshand told her about Marcus and how he had fought the perusan, and she stared in wonderment.

Audra wanted to be older. She hated her hair. She hated her fingernails. She wanted a bath with rose soap. "It has to be roses," she insisted.

Ella just wanted her doll to have feet again. Hileshand told her he would do his best.

After leaving Borili's tavern, Hileshand had exhausted every lead he could find and had uncovered a story that made him ill. Jezaren, as the governor's second and chief of his guard, had resided at the palace. When he murdered his lord and the man's entire bodyguard, the Galatians responded according to common Galatian law and killed everything belonging to him. Jezaren was a traitor, and they had left no one in his household alive. Hileshand could discover nothing definite about Lenay, but Ara, the girl with the purple eyes, would sit for long hours at the window. She had been seen several times. There was no doubt that she had been killed, along with the rest. The bodies had been burned the day before Hileshand had stepped foot through the city gate. He had been so close to finding her, and he had failed.

He mourned the loss of Hana's daughters. Crisi, Audra, and Ella helped numb the pain. Hileshand closed his eyes, considering the horrific news he would be forced to deliver. He would hold Hana and comfort her. He would do everything he could, but he knew he would not be able to spare her the pain of this blow. She, Amilia, and Isule waited for him in a little town called Bisbay, near Brassen Lake. Hana expected him to bring her happiness, and he had no happiness to give her.

"Hileshand!" Ella exclaimed loudly.

He looked at her across the fire. "Yes, little one?"

She pointed at the spoon in his hand. "I need to stir the stew. I am very good at stirring. Cook always said so."

Hiding a smile, he passed her the spoon.

"Hileshand!" Crisi cried next.

"Yes, my dear?"

The girl pointed toward the cave entrance. "There is a man!"

The words didn't register at first. *A man?* Hileshand sat facing the opening of the cave. If anyone entered here, he would be able to see that man.

But somehow, Crisi was right. Hileshand focused on the presence in the cave mouth and came to his feet, reaching for the hilt of his sword. How had the man entered unnoticed, right in front of his face?

The intruder pulled back the hood of his cloak, and the firelight washed across his skin. He was somewhat young, his features dark. "I want to travel with you," he said, the words simple and very odd.

He spoke Ruthanian perfectly, yet Hileshand doubted Ruthane was his homeland. His features were heavier, earthier, than those commonly found in that country. Hileshand would guess the man to be Galatian, which raised a series of questions.

They were three days' journey into Paxa. The nearest town was four hours east. What was a Galatian doing here, appearing out of the dusk like this? It was uncommon for a Galatian to request companionship. They were not amiable people.

"Where are you going?" Hileshand asked politely.

"The destination is not important," the man replied. "I will go where you go."

Hileshand began to feel like he was having a conversation with an Alusian. He studied the features a second time, half wondering, but knew it was not a possibility. Even Entan Gallowar, whose Alusian blood was thin, had skin as white as the snow bordering the cave mouth. This man was not Alusian, but, as it was with Entan and the others of his kind, something about this man was strange.

It was not merely the sudden, awkward request he presented; something unnatural lurked in his gaze. Hileshand did not wish for trouble, not when he was by himself looking after three little girls.

"What is your name?" Hileshand asked.

"I am Jezaren."

Silence thudded across the cave.

Every muscle in Hileshand's body stiffened. He asked slowly, "The messurah from Pon-Omen?"

The man nodded.

He had already given a demonstration of who he was. Hileshand did not need to ask for further proof of his words—the man had *appeared*. He had stepped up to the fire like a ghoul, offering no sight or sound beforehand. A warning tolled in the back of Hileshand's mind. *Careful.* What was he doing here?

"I want to travel with you," Jezaren repeated. "You cannot refuse me."

Unfortunately, there was truth in those words as well. This man possessed skills that were far beyond Hileshand's. Any altercation between them likely would not end well. Hileshand would never willingly stand against a man trained in the messurah arts. Not without a bow. He would also require a substantial distance between himself and his target.

Yet because of Ara and Lenay, he quietly challenged the man. "And why is that?"

Jezaren had anticipated the question. He stated calmly, "I am married to your daughter."

Hileshand knew Hana's story, what had happened to her family. She had told him of the brutal death of her husband, the horror she had felt leaving Myles behind in the slavers market, her sale in Tarek and her life in the home of Lord and Lady Lawvek. Hileshand had heard the entirety of her story. Alone in Paxa, she had mourned until the pain had become too much for her, and she had finally closed down her hope, so she could live.

Hileshand knew what it felt like to lose one's hope. Bithania had taken both his sons. Both of them. He could not predict the future. He did not know what was going to happen with anyone he wanted safe and protected. The world seemed in turmoil.

And yet on one issue he felt no concern whatsoever. There had been no hesitation, no confusion. Hileshand had taken the only step he considered logical, considering the circumstances—he had married Myles' mother.

They hadn't given anyone time to get used to the idea or wonder about it; they had married in the little town of Yomal, the morning after he had kissed her in someone else's room. There had not been a single question in his heart. It did not seem quick to Hileshand. Indeed, it seemed like he had endured a twenty-year engagement and only now could be with his bride.

Hileshand had not seen Hana, his wife, in four weeks. She had not entered Furmorea with him; she had remained behind in Paxa with Amilia, who was about to give birth. Wizened trappers and local hunters knew the cave Hileshand used tonight; it was three miles off the road and difficult to find. No one in Pon-Omen had known Hileshand's destination, and he was certain his small party had not been followed. He had taken precautions, just in case.

Perhaps Jezaren and his network of sources could uncover one or two facts about Hileshand and his family, but Hileshand did not see how the man could have arranged this meeting tonight. How did Jezaren know where to find him? Nothing should have been able to lead him here, yet here he was.

"You would not refuse the daughter," Jezaren told him, "and she goes where I go."

Hileshand stared at him as faint hope lifted its head in his heart. The man meant Ara. He had to mean Ara. He had *married* her. "She lives?" Hileshand asked softly.

"Both of them live. I will take you to the second. She is not far from here. Permit me to travel with you, and I will give you what you want."

The man was so convinced of the power of his argument that he did nothing to conceal his attempt at manipulation. And for the moment, Hileshand didn't care. "May I see her?"

Jezaren turned and called Ara's name. The girl cautiously entered the cave and approached the light of the fire. She looked like her mother. The resemblance was undeniable, and as little Ella shouted, "Ara!" and seemed happy to see her, Hileshand's heart twisted within him.

"Ara Gaela?" he whispered.

Her brows came together in concern. She looked quickly at Jezaren, then back to Hileshand, nodding slowly.

Hileshand forced himself to remain where he was. He did not wish to alarm her further. He had to keep his peace and his head. He let go of his sword hilt and put his hand on his chest. "My name is Hileshand. I am your brother's father. Myles' father."

A moment passed without any change in her expression. Then her eyes widened, and she understood.

"I came to find you. Your mother waits for you in Bisbay. Are you all right?" He glanced at Jezaren, who had killed forty-one men in a night.

"Yes," the girl replied. Her mouth opened, closed. The words did not easily come. "My mother...?"

There were no tears with Ara, but he watched the surprise, the intensity, go through her face, and it moved him. He answered when he could. "Yes. She is fine. Healthy and whole. Your brother also. There is much I have to tell you."

He wanted to tell her she was safe now. He wanted to put his arms around her and tell her that after months of war and pain, everything was all right. But he couldn't bring himself to say those things because of the man who stood at her side. *Her husband.* Hileshand fought off a wave of disgust as he remembered the messurah's words: *You cannot refuse me.* What sort of man manipulated a defenseless child in this way? He had chosen his steps with a keen sense of intelligence. He was right—Hileshand was not in a position to refuse him anything.

Why did Jezaren wish to travel with him? Why the effort, just to travel with him? The man made no sense. He was unstable—a broken man, who knew how to kill.

Ara turned to her husband. "You did this for me?" she whispered as she looked up at him.

He did not answer her, but his silence didn't matter; apparently, she had grown used to him and his ways. She reached for him, slid her arms around his chest, and held on to him. Her trust in him was evident; he had come to possess great power over her.

Jezaren met Hileshand's gaze over her head. His

eyes were blank and empty, like stones that bore no life. Something was wrong with him. The look in his eyes gave him away.

A chill raced across Hileshand's arms. *No,* he answered in silence. *You have won nothing. This little girl you will not keep.*

chapter 27

Ara had rarely seen Jezaren in the company of anyone other than his servants, and it was interesting to observe him with Hileshand. Neither man relaxed. Jezaren didn't look at him, for the most part, and Hileshand frowned a lot. They were like two bulls in a small pen. She could feel the tension exuding from both of them and found she could barely eat the meal Hileshand had prepared.

My mother. Several times that evening she looked at Hileshand just to look at him, just to be certain he was real. How had Jezaren found him? She had never told him her last name, nor had she told him of her brother, Myles; yet in the midst of his own peril, he had somehow managed to find Hileshand on a mountain in a different country.

Immediately after supper was completed, Hileshand leaned back against the wall and said to Jezaren, "You should take the first watch."

Jezaren walked out into the night without a word, and

for a time, his absence was almost a relief. The cave seemed to sigh as the tension lowered. Hileshand took out his pipe and lit it with a glowing scrap of wood from the fire. Pipe in hand, he put the little girls to bed. He bundled each of them up in their blankets and bedrolls, taking time with them and making them giggle. They eventually did what he asked and lay still, their eyes squeezed shut. Ara noticed that Ella, the littlest one, kept one eye open whenever Hileshand wasn't looking. Ara's sister, Lenay, had talked about Ella. She liked her. They were friends.

Her gaze strayed back to Hileshand. Hana had spoken of him many times, but her mother had never given certain details, certain stories—Ara had assumed he was dead, and Hana simply did not want to talk about it. Death clearly was not what had happened to him, and she wondered what *had* happened. He was gentle with the girls. There was nothing harsh or unkind in his interactions with them.

Hileshand returned to his place along the wall and settled down, his boots near the fire. His gaze met hers. "You are certain you are all right?" he asked.

"Yes."

"Does Jezaren tell me the truth? Are you married to him?"

"Yes." She had spoken no vows, but that didn't concern her. If Jezaren said he was her husband, then she was his wife.

His wife. As she thought about what those words actually meant, a deep sense of relief rolled through her. It no longer mattered what Furmorean women like Muriel thought of her, because Ara was not one of Borili's girls any longer. She had a husband. He had accepted her, giving her value.

Hileshand hesitated as he watched her. For a moment, the frown was heavy and noticeable. Then the line between his brows shallowed, and he said, "You look so much like your mother. I can see her in your eyes and in your chin. A good resemblance."

There was warmth in his voice, a queer sort of melodic tone that set needles of apprehension to Ara's spine. Hileshand was not like Jezaren. Jezaren knew how the world was and interacted with it carefully. He was wise and cautious. Hileshand was not cautious at all, and she found herself wondering what his secret was. Every man had one—something he concealed. The cave began to feel small and stifling. She could not sit in here, alone, with him. This was not safe.

She tried to remember how she had felt about strangers, about men she did not know, before the war, but the answer simply was not there anymore. She couldn't remember. Why was Jezaren outside? She would feel safer if he were here, for Hileshand was looking at her and speaking his soothing, untrustworthy tones, and she wondered what he intended.

Her palm ached. She cradled her right hand with her left and saw Hileshand's gaze drop down to the bandage wrapped around her skin. Her fingers were cold without the gloves, even here beside the fire, but she did not like the way the gloves kept her from feeling the things she touched. She felt separated from what was real when she was wearing gloves.

Hileshand had mentioned her brother, but he hadn't given details about him, as he had with Hana. Her mother waited in Bisbay—Hileshand had not said that Myles waited, too.

"Where is Myles?" Ara asked.

Hileshand pulled the pipe from his lips and sighed, glancing at the cave entrance and the dark of night beyond it. "He travels with friends," he said at last. The frown returned in full strength. "I haven't seen him in several months." He paused and amended, "I suppose it has been about three months. Feels longer. His wife is with me; she waits in Bisbay with your mother."

Ara straightened. "He has a wife?"

Hileshand smiled at her reaction. "Aye, that he does. She is now well into her ninth month, and it is possible I will find myself a grandfather when we return. I haven't seen them in four weeks." He nodded to himself. "In fact, it is likely that you are an aunt now."

In his incautious way, he told her about her mother and brother, what had happened after the soldiers had taken them. He was a good storyteller, even when the topic was dark and scary. He said many interesting things, yet a few minutes into the narrative, Ara realized the story felt hopeful because he was telling only the hopeful parts. He did not describe anything that was painful. He had located her brother in Edimane. Her mother had been sold to a wealthy family in Paxa that needed a nursemaid.

At one point, Ara noticed that Ella watched with both eyes. The other two girls appeared to have gone to sleep, as they had been instructed, but Ella gripped her ugly little doll in her arms and watched Hileshand as he spoke.

Eventually, Hileshand said, "You should get some sleep, Ara." He sighed heavily. "I do not know what tomorrow holds."

Hileshand continued to prove himself different than

Jezaren. He slept like a dragon, roaring in his sleep. Ara was unused to snores like this and found she could not sleep to them. Gathering her cloak around her, she crept to the entrance of the cave.

The night was silver and moonlit on the other side. The land looked like something from a painting. Everything was quiet.

She took three steps out into the snow and waited.

Jezaren appeared without sound. He anticipated her desire and opened his cloak to her, and she leaned into the warmth of his embrace.

"I can't sleep," she said. He didn't answer her, and she looked up into the darkness beneath his hood. The moonlight did not touch any part of his face. "Why didn't you tell me what you did for my sister?"

He had removed Lenay from Borili's tavern and sent her into Paxa with one of his men. *There is a farm near here.* Those few words were his only description. He would not tell Hileshand where the farm was. *They know I am coming for her.*

"Why would I tell you what I did for you?" Jezaren asked.

"Because it's important. Because it means something to me."

The hood bent as he looked toward the cave and the sound of Hileshand's ferocious snores. He turned back to her. "You belong to me. This means I will take care of you and do what needs to be done for you. There was no reason for me to tell you what I was doing."

She removed the glove from her bandaged right hand and reached up with two fingers into the dark expanse beneath his hood. She found his cheek and felt the whiskers that, in Furmorea, he had been faithful to remove. "Mine," she said quietly.

The hood came toward her and blocked her face from the moon. He kissed her in the dark, warming his lips against hers. He touched her slowly and firmly, and she wished they were alone, as they had been the last several nights. He had moved her heart.

"Yours," he agreed.

"The next time you do something for me, I want you to tell me."

"Why?"

She put her fingers on his face again, to his jawline. She would have to go back into the cave eventually, and he would have to remain out here. Hileshand kept watch, she realized suddenly, when Jezaren had not stood watch in days. *Why does Hileshand keep watch and Jezaren does not?* "Because you are important to me. And what you do is important to me. I want to know."

He lifted his head and scanned the slope once behind her. Nothing seemed to hold his interest. Her eyes adjusted, and she was beginning to see his features hidden beneath the hood.

"I don't understand why you want me to tell you," he said. "I will not boast of my actions to you, nor do I do them to compel you toward making an action in return. I do them because they need to be done. Why would you want…?"

She tugged on his hood, and he moved according to her request, bending toward her. But she did not kiss him again, not right then. She pushed her face into his hood, her cheek to his, her lips to his ear. "Jezaren," she whispered.

His arms went around her back, and he pressed her against him.

He hadn't told her he loved her, but she knew he did. It was possible that such words were never spoken by his people. She had rarely heard them said by her parents—once, possibly, after her mother had miscarried and her father was distressed at her tears. Ara didn't know how many children had been carried briefly and lost, but her mother had been sick often, much sicker than other women; her body had not responded well to pregnancy in any way. Ara remembered several different times of tears and much heartache. This particular time, Hana had miscarried in the eighth month. The baby was a boy, and Hana's pain at his loss had been severe. Rand, Ara's father, had told her he loved her then—in that moment, when she was hurting. He had been trying to comfort her.

Those three words were special. They meant something deep and full and important, and Ara chose not to say them, simply because they were true. Because one did not need to say what was already known. Jezaren knew her thoughts toward him, and she knew his thoughts toward her.

She returned to the cave and didn't fall asleep until the watch changed. Finally, Hileshand's snoring stopped, and a short time later, Jezaren lay down behind her, wrapping her in his cloak, his arms around her. He knew she was awake. His hand came up, and he traced her nose in the firelight.

Once again, she thought, *It doesn't matter where we're going.*

Hileshand hesitated at the cave entrance. He did not want to leave Ara alone with the messurah—he did not want any of the girls left alone with him, particularly Ara. But she had been alone with him for two months. The man had carved the *charsahn,* the Galatian symbol of marriage, into her palm. She still treated that hand with care, so he had marked her recently. In Galatian weddings, there were no vows or witnesses, no presiding priest. In most cases, the mark was brutally carved into the woman's hand, but sometimes there was not even that; sometimes, the man would simply claim the woman. He would take her as his own, and she would be his. When did Jezaren believe he had married Ara—when he had marked her or when he had taken her from Borili? Either was possible.

Grimacing, Hileshand stepped out into the moonlight. Away from the fire, the night was frigid. He rubbed his gloved hands together and hunched his shoulders against the cold. If something were to happen, he could do very little against a messurah at close range. *No blood. Without sound.* He realized he was grimacing again and tried to reduce his expression to a mere frown.

He squatted down and studied the footprints in the snow. He had heard that the most advanced among the messurah did not leave any signs of their presence. It was said that the earth itself sheltered them and hid them from man. Hileshand didn't know the accuracy of that idea, but still, he wondered—how much training had Jezaren received?

He backtracked the steps in the snow until the trails parted a stone's throw from the cave. He knew which tracks were his and the girls'. Two other sets came up from the south. *Two sets.* One larger than the other. Jezaren and Ara.

It would seem Jezaren was capable of leaving a footprint. This was good. At least there was that.

Hileshand sighed and started back toward the cave.

chapter **28**

The next morning shortly after dawn, Jezaren took them northeast at a pace that was manageable for Crisi and Audra. They kept up without trouble, but Ella stumbled every few steps. She slowed them down, and eventually, she gave way to uncontrollable crying.

She kept repeating, "I don't want to die. I don't want to die!"

Hileshand squatted down in the snow before her, his hands on her small shoulders. "You're not going to die, Ella."

She sobbed.

"What is it, little one? Why are you so scared?"

"I can't do it. I can't make it. The wolves will eat me."

"We aren't going to leave you behind."

She didn't seem to hear him. Her voice rose. "I can't do it! I can't make it through the snow. I'm too little!"

With a frown, Hileshand turned on his haunches and looked at the other two girls. Standing behind Ara near the front of the line, Audra was fixing the hood of her cloak. Crisi was making a snowball and eyeing the hood that Audra so carefully arranged. Neither of them appeared concerned—they knew they were going to make it just fine. Apparently, they had witnessed Ella's outbursts before.

Ella stood beneath Hileshand's hands and wept without restraint.

"Ella. Ella, look at me." Hileshand ran his hand over her hair and wiped away snow that clung to the strands after her last fall.

She tried to quiet herself. As she met his gaze, he was stunned by the emptiness in her eyes. There was fear, but more than that, he did not see any life. She sincerely believed that they were going to leave her behind if she failed. He touched her hair again, his heart bending inside of him. What had Borili done to this one? What horrible things had he told her, playing on her Furmorean upbringing that exulted strength and self-sufficiency?

"Well, my dear," he whispered. "I suppose there is only one thing to be done."

Her eyes welled. She didn't fall to pieces again, but it was close. "I don't like dogs—I don't want to be eaten! I can't do it."

"Then I will carry you." He slung his pack around his left shoulder, put his hands under her arms, and lifted her out of the snow. She clung to him, her arms around his neck. He would not have needed to support her; her arms were like small bars of iron. She was terrified.

"Shhh, Ella. You're all right now. It is going to be all right." He tried to move her onto his back so they could continue a little more easily, but she wouldn't lessen her hold. He smiled at her strength, the backs of his eyes beginning to sting at her desperation. "Don't be afraid, little one. I will carry you."

It was not an easy road. There was a reason they travelled on foot and not on horseback. The terrain was rocky, and the snow hid their options for secure footing. Eventually, Ella allowed him to transfer her to his back. She gripped his neck and shoulders.

Hileshand was aware of the way Jezaren watched him stagger through the snow. The messurah waited at the front of the line. He was barely sweating. He did not seem winded. Ara reached him and stood there next to him, breathing hard. Jezaren did not acknowledge her. He was watching Hileshand.

Hileshand looked away and shook his head. Jezaren could think whatever he desired. It would not affect Hileshand's decisions to act.

They traveled for another two hours before the snow-covered stones seemed to part like drapes before them, and they began their descent into a valley. Another two hours, and they came upon a wide patch of snow that had been trampled flat by booted feet. Hileshand counted six or seven different sets of boot prints mixed through the flattened area, and there appeared to be many others as well, the tracks unclear.

Shouts rang out across the snow.

Three girls ran toward them out of the woods. They were around Audra and Crisi's age, and Audra and Crisi were their targets. In a very brief period of time, all five began to jabber excitedly in Furmorean, and Audra and Crisi started grinning. Hileshand heard something about kittens with blue eyes—did they want to see them?

They did. Audra and Crisi ran off with the other three.

"Jezaren," Hileshand began.

"This is Gresten Farm," the messurah answered. "They take children who have been orphaned in the war. He is Furmorean. His wife is Paxan."

The ample farmhouse appeared below them as the well-packed trail circled Hileshand and the others out of the pines. Situated at the bottom of the slope, the old stone building was the size of a barn, with many windows and red chimneys that puffed gray smoke into the cloudless sky. Even from a distance, Hileshand began to smell baking bread and roasted chicken. Several large barns and storage sheds sat behind the house.

Tracks marred the snow every direction he looked. There were no signs of Audra, Crisi, or the other girls.

Hileshand was about to slide Ella off his back when a dog barked, and the little girl stiffened up like water in winter. A longhaired black sheepdog bounded out of the closest barn and came toward them.

"It's all right, Ella," Hileshand told her.

"No dogs."

"It is for the animals. It helps the farmer—it's a good dog."

"No dogs," she repeated.

He pried her grip off his neck and pulled her around him, holding her on his hip. "It will not bite you if you are friendly toward it. This is a nice dog, *goshane*."

She looked at him quickly. The dog barked once, and she didn't even jolt. He wondered at her sudden stillness, the surprise in her little face. Was it because he had called her *goshane*? It was a Furmorean endearment, a word parents used with their young children. He smiled at her and kissed her cheek. *Fine.* They could work on her fears slowly.

The dog raced toward them, bounding across the packed snow. Ella came alert and stopped breathing. Hileshand patted her back, repeating, "It's all right..."

In between the dog's energetic barking, he heard Galatian words and a voice he did not recognize. He looked over and saw that a man had joined them, speaking with Jezaren. Hileshand had not seen or heard his arrival—he appeared to have stepped out of the woods after them. He wore a long gray cloak that swung just above the heels of his boots. He was young, perhaps twenty, and he looked like a Ruthanian. The features were cleanly cut and somewhat reserved; he was dark, his eyes brooding but alert.

Ara stood a few paces from Jezaren, her gloved hands bunched into fists at her sides. Hileshand knew this look of concern she displayed; he had seen it often enough with Hana, when she was this age. It meant Ara didn't know what to do. Her husband was in deep discussion, and he ignored her. Hileshand did not speak Galatian very well. He thought they said something about guards, or standing guard; there had been no signs of activity. As far as Hileshand could tell, Jezaren didn't say anything about Ara, though the newcomer studied her with curiosity. It wasn't interest, the way a man would tend to study a beautiful woman, but curiosity. No obvious introduction was made until Jezaren unexpectedly turned to Hileshand.

"This is Sevoin," he said in Ruthanian. "He is from Gereskow."

The man shifted position. He took a single step so he could focus his attention directly on Hileshand. Something seemed peculiar about the movement, and Hileshand eventually realized what it was—the step made no sound. It should have made sound; the man moved on snow.

He was messurah, the same as Jezaren.

Sevoin studied Hileshand with the same sort of curiosity he had used with Ara. "I have heard of you," he said.

Hileshand had been listening to their conversation, and he hadn't heard his name. He might do poorly with the language, but a man could understand his name, even when it was spoken by a foreign tongue. He had not been mentioned, yet this second messurah somehow knew him as well, just as Jezaren had known him last night in the cave.

"Myles Hileshand," Sevoin said, apparently attempting to be helpful.

"You've heard of my son," Hileshand answered.

Ara seemed to rise off the ground a bit. "Myles?" she asked.

Hileshand nodded. "Yes. Myles."

With a brief glance at Sevoin, she asked Hileshand, "Why would he have heard of my brother?"

"You know the story about the man in Edimane who killed the dragon with his helmet?"

"Everyone knows that story."

Hileshand nodded again. "Yes. Everyone does."

A faint smile went across Sevoin's mouth. With the slight movement, he showed more positive emotion than Jezaren had ever displayed. He was messurah like Jezaren, yet he was not like Jezaren. Hileshand looked into his eyes and did not feel that same sense of loss, of brokenness.

"Myles," Sevoin said, "your son, did not serve Korstain Elah twenty years ago in Gereskow. I have heard of your son, yes—the man who killed a dragon and chopped the head off the *atham-laine*. But I have also heard of you. From my father."

Hileshand could not think of a single man he knew in Gereskow whose son was a messurah. Sevoin had been trained in Galatia, for he spoke that tongue proficiently.

"My father has spent time with a man you consider a friend," Sevoin offered. "Thaxon Parez."

The name jarred Hileshand. He hadn't heard it uttered by a stranger in years.

Thaxon Parez was the head of Korstain's auxiliary. A good man. A loyal man—too loyal, perhaps. For years, Hileshand and Marcus had made weeklong stops in Fole-Dumas, on the Paxan side of the Ruthanian border, where Parez would join them. He wanted to know everything that had happened to them and what their plans were. Hileshand knew what Parez did with this information, because he knew Parez. Parez was loyal. Everything they told him would eventually make its way back to Korstain.

Was it possible that the events of today and last night were actually much simpler than they first appeared? Jezaren worked for Korstain Elah. Immediately, Hileshand thought, *No*. The idea was ludicrous; it gave Korstain a level of power and control he couldn't possibly have. But for a moment, Hileshand still considered it. He weighed the probability and examined it from different angles. He knew what Korstain was. He knew what the man was capable of. Now that he was king, Korstain could not afford to have a disinherited son. It gave his enemies too many options, too much power.

No, Hileshand thought again. This couldn't have anything to do with Korstain. If Korstain wanted Marcus, all he had to do was send Thaxon Parez. He didn't need the service of a messurah. He didn't need to kill the new governor of Furmorea and his entire bodyguard.

As Hileshand thought of Marcus and Myles, the situation suddenly began to overwhelm him. He lost his strength and had to set Ella down. She protested initially, but the dog had run back to the barn, so she eventually allowed Hileshand to set her feet in the snow.

He gripped her small hand and turned his glare to Jezaren. "Where is Lenay?" he demanded.

Sevoin nodded toward the barn. "There, with the others. I will fetch her."

Jezaren acknowledged Ara's presence. The moment his head began to turn her direction, she looked up at him, waiting. Eager for his interaction. The fear left her as she looked at him with hope, and with a sinking heart, Hileshand realized she was in love with him.

"Go with Sevoin," Jezaren directed.

The happy look disappeared. Her eyes narrowed. She seemed to suspect him of something, yet she obeyed without protest. Sevoin walked down the hill toward the barn, his boots silent in the snow, like the steps of a spirit. Ara followed more carefully. Every move she made produced sound. The snow crunched under her heels.

Jezaren studied Hileshand for a long time after Ara and Sevoin had gone.

Hileshand wanted to hit him.

"No," the messurah said in Ruthanian, which Ella did not understand.

"No?"

"You are angry."

"Yes," Hileshand said. "I am very angry. What are you doing?"

"Sevoin trained as a messurah in Galatia, which is where I met him and offered him rights of travel. His primeran-level training completed last year, and he has been in my service since that time. He has not spoken with his father, or Thaxon Parez, in ten years. He travels with me, and I travel with you."

Rights of travel. Hileshand realized he was running into a Galatian paradigm he did not understand. His knowledge of Galatian ways was incomplete. "Why do you wish to travel with me? What do you want?"

The study continued. The dark eyes blank and eerie. Hileshand waited for his answer.

Jezaren finally told him, "I desire to kill someone, and you will teach me how."

Needless to say, that was not the answer Hileshand anticipated. "What?"

Jezaren took a step toward him. His voice lowered and grew intense. "In the last eight years, you have defeated two Ethollian sorcerers who stood against you, and in Tarek, you killed one who had as much training as any handler. I intend to kill my handler, and I will learn from you how to do this. I cannot kill an Ethollian. My training forbids it. His magic protects him from me. I cannot put a hand to him, but you know something I do not know, and you will teach me how this killing is done."

"Why...do you wish to kill your handler?"

The intensity eased slightly. Jezaren glanced down the slope, in the direction of the barn. "He condemns me for his actions. If he kills me, he will also kill Ara, for she is mine."

"Actions? What actions?"

"He killed Leison, the governor. I do not know why, but I intend to discover that as well."

Hileshand could guess how Jezaren "intended to discover that as well," yet his methods of torture would fall short if his training kept him from touching his handler. Was it some sort of spell that made killing his handler impossible for him? "All of Pon-Omen believes *you* killed the governor."

"Yes." Jezaren nodded. "The Ethollian is talented in magic—yet he is no more skilled than the Ethollian you killed in Tarek. I will learn how to kill him from you, and then I will kill him. I will not let him harm your daughter. I would accept a great loss myself before I let him harm Ara."

Ella rocked in her boots and pulled on Hileshand's hand, seemingly for no greater purpose than to remind him she was there. He gave her bright eyes a distant smile and squeezed her hand.

Jezaren didn't know what he was asking. The Ethollian in Tarek—yes, the man had died, but it had not been Hileshand's decision to kill him. That life had not been his to take, and he had not taken it. "Why would your *handler* kill the governor and his bodyguard? Do you have any idea what he was after?"

This didn't make sense. The messurah was the point of weakness, the table leg that wobbled when pressure was applied. The Ethollian handler was entrusted with keeping the man under control, should control become necessary; the *handler* was not to be the source of concern.

"I killed the bodyguard."

Hileshand looked at him.

Jezaren said, "They believed the Ethollian's words. They were my men, under my authority, and I killed them when it became clear they intended to arrest me. But I could not kill the Ethollian."

Forty men. Jezaren freely admitted to these deaths. Hileshand was overwhelmed by the lack of concern in his eyes, the inhuman void he saw there.

The messurah looked down at the farmhouse. "We are five hours from Bisbay. The farmer's wife will want to feed us, which is unfortunate, but if we leave within the hour, we can reach Brassen Lake shortly after dark."

chapter 29

Lenay was just as pretty as her sister. Her eyes were light brown and, after nearly two months on the farm, did not bear the shadows that were visible in Ara's gaze. Her curly hair had been tied up with red ribbons that Carlane, the farmer's smiling wife, told her she could keep.

Lenay was given one of the blue-eyed kittens as a goodbye gift, and she promptly named it Green Marble King, which Hileshand thought creative. She put the little mewling animal in her bag and tied the top flap down carefully.

Audra and Crisi hugged Hileshand goodbye.

"Thank you," Audra whispered in his ear as he knelt before her. "Thank you. Thank you—Carlane is so pretty, and she says she has roses in the summer time."

Carlane heard Audra's loud whispers and smiled. There were five girls and seven boys on the farm. Audra, Crisi, and Ella brought the number to fifteen. When she realized there were boys here, Crisi had shouted like a warrior and thrust her fists into the air. Both she and Audra seemed very pleased with these arrangements. They wanted to stay and did not seem to have any question about the future. Clearly, this had been the plan all along—for Hileshand to bring them here.

To Hileshand's disappointment, Ella did not join them on the front steps to say goodbye. After the meal, she disappeared somewhere into the house and did not return when he called for her.

"It is time," Jezaren told him. The messurah pressed them to leave.

Hileshand took one more moment to watch the back hallway, hoping to see Ella run around the corner.

"We will tell her you said goodbye," Carlane said.

They were entering the pinewoods at the top of the hill when a small voice shouted behind them. Hileshand turned around to see Ella chasing after them, her cloak in one hand and her broken little doll in the other.

Carlane stood on the front porch, watching her in her mad run.

"Hileshand!" Ella screamed. "Hileshand, don't leave me! I want to go with you! I'll be good! I won't make any mistakes—I want to go with you!"

Hileshand dropped his pack and started running down the hill.

Hearing the commotion, the sheepdog raced from the barn. Carlane put her fingers to her lips and with a short whistle, redirected the dog's sprint toward the house, but Ella didn't see the dog veer away. Her face filled with terror.

Running with all her might, she held out her arms as Hileshand approached, and he grabbed her, skidding to a stop on the slippery snow. He held her against his chest, and she began sobbing.

"I will be good. I will be very, very good. I will always stir things and I won't spill anything and I will be happy and smiling all the time. I won't make you sad—"

"Ella." He put his hand on the back of her head. "Ella, *goshane*, you can be naughty. You can spill everything and cry as often as you want. Yes, come with me. I want you to come with me, Ella."

"You won't leave me here?"

"Not if you don't want to stay."

"I don't want to stay! I want to be with you. Please—"

"Yes, Ella. Yes."

She wiggled in his arms, and he relaxed his grip so she could twist around and look at him. "Truly?" She sniffled loudly, her face covered with tears.

"Truly. I want you with me. I will take care of you."

She rubbed her eyes with one hand. "I couldn't find my cloak. Then I couldn't find my doll. I didn't know where they put them, and I was afraid you would leave me." She shuddered as she thought about it. Her chest heaved with emotion.

Then she looked at him more closely. Her little brows came together, and she asked him, "Why are your eyes wet?"

He drew her head close and kissed her wet cheek. "You have made me very happy."

Mistaking the reason for his emotion, she said again, "I will be good."

"You don't have to be good, Ella. I would love you even if you were bad." He checked on the whereabouts of the dog and then began to set her down. She stiffened, and he said, "Just for a moment, little one. Trust me. You can trust me." He took care of her, sliding her cloak over her arms, pulling up her hood, searching for her mittens in her pockets, and covering her hands. "You don't have to be good. You are mine now. You will be mine whether you are good or not."

He swung her up into his arms. "My girl," he whispered into her ear.

She squeezed him until he couldn't breathe, her tiny arm against his throat.

Turning toward the house, Hileshand gave Carlane a broad wave. She grinned and waved back.

Ara had never seen any man do what Hileshand had just done. As he walked up the hill, little Ella in his arms, Ara stared at him. She saw his expression and did not understand why he would act this way toward a girl who was not of his blood.

This was not his child. He had no obligation to her, yet he *allowed* her to obligate him. Ella was not someone who would ever be able to boast accurately about her quick wit or intelligence. She interacted with the world as if she were younger than eight. Borili had complained about her and how she had been a poor purchase. The cooks would set her in a corner with a bowl of flour and a wooden spoon and not let her anywhere close to the ovens or the sharp knives. Ella was a sweet child, but she was not going to be a woman of significant worth. She wasn't even pretty, and no one had understood Borili's reasoning when he had brought the child home from the market.

Surely, Hileshand could see these things about her as well. Unlike Ella, he had expressed a strong intellect. Ara had been able to hear it in his choice of words and in the way he told stories. He was wise, cunning—so why would he want Ella with him, as he had put it? All of them had heard his words. His voice had carried up the hill.

Reaching the top of the slope, Hileshand lifted his pack off the ground where he had dropped it and tossed it around his right shoulder, his left arm supporting Ella firmly.

His steps paused in front of Jezaren. "All right," he said, holding the man's gaze. "I will give you what you want." He adjusted Ella in his arms in a movement clearly meant to draw attention to her. "*This* is lesson one."

Ella giggled, as if she knew exactly what he meant, and buried her face in his neck.

Hileshand walked away.

chapter **30**

They entered Bisbay after dark. It was a town, not a city; the walls were made of oak beams. The pungent odors of old fish, manure, and wood smoke roiled through the air as the guards opened the gate.

Ella had slept on Hileshand's back for the last hour of their journey. Once the gate was shut behind them, he slid her to the ground and had her walk on her own, clutching his hand. She stumbled on her first step, not yet alert, and Jezaren was the one who reached out to catch her before she put her knees in the mud.

Ara could see very little in the torchlight. She was not aware that her husband had moved at all until Hileshand quietly thanked him for his effort. Lenay, who loved Ella, seemed to believe that whatever Ella liked was good for her, too, so when Hileshand held out his other hand to her, she went forward and took it right away. Ara watched this and wondered at her sister's simple trust. Didn't the girl realize what had happened to them? Did she not understand that their father was dead, and they would never be able to go back? They had no home. Lenay should not trust men so easily.

Hileshand had a little child on each hand.

He took them to an inn on Main Street. On the second floor, he opened the fourth door on the right, and Hana was waiting for them.

Ara saw the ring on her mother's hand the moment they walked into the room. Hana had not worn a ring during her marriage to Rand, Ara's father. Ara had thought rings to be a romantic gesture, but Rand had disagreed. *I am married to your mother—she doesn't need a ring to prove it to somebody else.*

Hileshand had married her.

The initial greetings were loud and wild. Then Hana kissed all the girls a second time, exclaimed over Lenay's new height and hugged little Ella, welcoming her as warmly as she had welcomed Ara and Lenay. Ara was watching, and she noticed when Hileshand put his hand to the side of Hana's head and leaned close to kiss her temple. In response, her mother looked up and smiled at him, and Ara saw the unfamiliar warmth in her eyes. She had not looked at Rand this way. Hana adored this man.

Why? Ara wondered. She did not understand this sudden turn of events. What had happened to keep them apart, when this situation obviously made her mother happy? Why had she married Rand if Hileshand was the one who made her smile?

Ara's thoughts grew dark. *Perhaps it is the war.* Perhaps the glow would not be so great if the loss had not been so painful.

She looked up at Jezaren. His face was like a wall of plaster—there was no expression, nothing that gave away his thoughts. He stood near her yet did not touch her. He didn't seem to mind what his friend Sevoin or the little girls observed, but when Hileshand was present, Jezaren became as affectionate as a stone. The warmth sucked out of him.

Ara expected Hileshand to put words to the frowns he had given Jezaren all day, but he didn't. For the time, he said only the good things, leaving her to wonder, again, what his plan was, the secret he was hiding. Briefly, he mentioned the marriage and how Jezaren and Ara had met up with him in the mountains.

After a moment's hesitation, he added, "Jezaren saved the girls' lives—both of them."

Ara had never seen her mother cry except in times of death and mourning, when she buried children. Hana was fearless, and she was strong. Even if she had known that Jezaren was a messurah running from a crime he had not committed, it wouldn't have changed her actions. She still would have treated him the way she treated all men.

Hana went to Jezaren and put her hand on his arm. It was just a touch, and Ara realized this was the first time she had seen any person touch Jezaren other than herself. He did not react negatively, or positively, to the weight of Hana's hand.

"Thank you," Hana whispered. "*Thank you.*"

He nodded stiffly.

Ella stepped forward with a shy smile and embraced Hana again. She seemed quite pleased with the decision she had made today. Her face was flushed. Crisscrossed marks ran across her cheek from the way her head had lain against Hileshand's cloak.

"I have a doll," she said, one arm around Hana's waist. With the other hand, she held up the ugly, miserable creature she had mentioned. Its eyes were mismatched buttons. One red, one blue. "A dog ate her feet. She needs feet again. Do you think you know how to make a doll have feet? It will take a needle and some thread. Maybe some buttons."

Hana leaned down. She squeezed the girl tightly and said, "Yes. I think I could manage that for you."

Lenay pressed in from the other side, and Hana put an arm around her as well. Hana's eyes grew glassy and full, and she met Ara's gaze and smiled. It was a smile that mocked the war. It mocked pain and sorrow and all the things her family had experienced. Ara just looked at her, not knowing how to respond.

There was a door set in the room's back wall. When Hileshand looked at it, Hana informed him, "I think Amilia fell asleep."

"And Isule?"

"He's in the room next door. He has winter lung and did not want to give it to the baby."

At those words, Hileshand froze, just for a moment. Then he laughed once—a short burst of sound—and smiled the same sort of smile Ara had just seen from her mother. A smile that despised all of the things Ara knew were true. Hileshand was happy. Extremely happy.

He told Hana, "I will be back," and slipped inside the adjoining room, closing the door softly behind him.

A lamp burned on the side table. In its warm glow, Hileshand could see Amilia lying on her side, the blankets pulled up around her, one arm stretched out in front of her in a sheltering gesture. He approached with quiet steps.

Amilia slept, but the baby did not. His eyes were open—blue eyes, like his mama's. Hileshand smiled and leaned down for a closer look. He was a beautiful baby. Hileshand had never thought that about another child, not even Marcus, whom he had watched grow up.

"Hello, Westland," he whispered. "I am your grandfather."

Only the baby's small face was visible. His mama had him wrapped securely in his blankets.

It was not right that Myles could not be here for this. He needed to be here. This was his son.

All at once, Hileshand realized something. Surprise roared through him like a strong wind, and he looked at the baby more closely.

"By Abalel himself," he muttered.

Little Westland looked like his father. He had Myles' nose—he looked like Myles. *How is that possible?*

Keeping an eye on Amilia's sleeping form should she stir, Hileshand eased the wrapped bundle from the blankets and held him. He was so small. Hileshand had not held a baby in years, and he always forgot how small they were.

The baby watched him. The little lips parted, and Hileshand nearly groaned.

"Hello, Westland," he said again. His face began to hurt from his smiles.

Ara and Lenay would surely like to see their nephew, but for a time, he could not bring himself to move. *Myles and Amilia's son.* The baby was so beautiful.

"Westland," he said quietly, "you have come into a good family. Your *dabi* is the best of men. Your mother will love you and care for you better than any woman, save your grandmother. Your grandmother will always win that war, in my opinion."

Crossing the room, he opened the door with one hand, eased through into the first room, and shut the wooden panel after him.

Conversations stopped. He looked up to multiple sets of eyes. "This is Westland," he announced and held the baby so Myles' sisters could see him. They immediately came close and made noises, as girls would, in admiration.

Lenay declared him lovely and perfect.

Ella touched his cheek and told him they were going to be friends. "I will be friendly with you," she said.

"He looks just like Myles," Ara whispered, putting fingers to the little chin. Hileshand offered the baby to her, and she took him from Hileshand's arms almost reverently. He watched the weight of the war, of death and pain, momentarily leave her.

Just like Myles. Hileshand lifted his head and met Hana's gaze. She gave him a soft smile across the room, each of them knowing the other's thoughts.

"Yes," Hileshand said, "he looks like his father. As is fitting."

"Amilia."

Hileshand woke her, putting his hand on her shoulder as he sat beside her on the bed. She released her breath in a sigh and opened her eyes. The first place she looked was the empty space before her on the mattress. The baby wasn't there; he was being delighted by his aunts.

Hileshand, with a smile, gathered that this was not the first time little Westland had disappeared while Amilia had slept—she did not seem alarmed at his absence.

She rolled over and looked at him. For a brief moment, the sleep did not part from her eyes.

"Hello, *goshane*," he said quietly.

"Hileshand!" Her arms went around his neck, and he held her.

She began asking questions—quickly, the sentences flowing one after the other. "When did you arrive? How long have I been sleeping?"

"An hour ago, and I don't know."

"And the girls? Did you bring the girls?"

"Yes, both of them. Plus one more."

"There will always be one more with you," she said with affection. She let him go and moved backward on the bed so she could see his face. Her blonde hair was tousled. Her cheeks were marked from the pillow. She looked lovely.

"Well done," he said. "He is truly beautiful."

Amilia grinned. "Did you see his nose?"

He nodded. "I saw his nose." Young Westland took after all the males in his bloodline—the bloodline that, in truth, was not his bloodline. When Hileshand looked at Westland, he saw Myles. He saw Korstain Elah. He saw Korstain's father, Ullan, and the generations before him. Korstain's estate was filled with portraits of his ancestors, and among them Westland would look at home. Hileshand wondered again, *How is it that he looks so much like his father?*

The pleasure in Amilia's eyes grew morose. She looked at the door as quiet voices drifted into the room beneath it.

He said, "You know that Myles will not be able to stay away for long." He hoped that was true.

She glanced at him.

"You know that he will not let any of those near him have peace until you are with him." That was certainly true, but it likely would not do any good in Korstain Elah's company.

Perhaps she heard it in his voice. The doubt. She did not appear convinced. Lines ran between her brows, and she turned her face away.

He put his hand on her shoulder. They had received no word concerning his sons, even though Marcus and Myles traveled with Alusian who would be able to find Hileshand, Hana, and the others—they would be *able* to send word, if the Alusian were concerned enough to send it. Every day, Hileshand had to tell himself not to dwell on that. The Alusian did not think like men. They did not desire what men desired; they felt no need for companionship.

"Westland. A good name," he said.

He saw her face again. The concern eased slowly, and she returned his smile. "It is the name Myles wanted him to have. Westland Hileshand."

The words moved him. Westland might look like an Elah, but he had Hileshand's name. He was a Hileshand.

Hileshand squeezed his daughter's shoulder and said gruffly, "Come meet your sisters."

part four

The Ruthanian King

eseraut Nelsan killed the skroel himself as the king watched. The creature was strangled, the skin left uncut, because Nelsan felt no need for fanfare. In some ways, the blood of this spindly, disgusting creature was even more dangerous than that of a goe'lah. He did not care if the king was watching—Nelsan would do it his way, without theatrics. He would not risk his life or those of his men for the drama that others so often wished to employ in the king's presence. Since Korstain had become king of Ruthane, Nelsan had seen more wide-eyed praise and drooling adulation than he'd beheld in his life.

Nelsan shook his head, disgusted. Today's attack had been predicted. The Nauget were the king's seers—ten men who, through training and natural talent, had learned to see into the hidden realms of the gods. They had sent word of the skroel two hours ago. Immediately, Korstain's son Athland had been taken into the North Tower and sealed within an upper room guarded by thirty men, twelve of the king's best hunting dogs, and a number of falcons trained to hunt snakes. The skroel did not require doors. They could come from anywhere.

The skroel had been sent by the Temple of Mal-len, located in Gereskow on the coast. During Habeine's rule, the Temple of Mal-len had been the chosen place of worship, and therefore, the Mal-len priests were the ones who felt Korstain's newly established rule the most severely. Korstain had no intention of allowing the temple to retain the power it had wielded during Habeine's reign. In retaliation, the Mal-len priests had declared him a traitor to the gods and had sent the skroel to slay a member of the king's family—it would be the king's life or that of his son Athland.

The skroel always came in pairs. One skroel was dead. Its partner was yet unaccounted for.

Fools, Nelsan thought, unwinding the metal cable from his gloved hands. He knew what Korstain could do when he was angry. His vengeance would be brutal. Why had the Mal-len acted so stupidly? Didn't they have fortune readers and seers of their own? The attack today had not been a worthy risk. This would destroy them.

Korstain Elah employed an impenetrable wall of protection. Nothing could pass through this force. Nelsan had never seen anything like it. Korstain slept well at night, and he could afford to do so, without fear. No other king had ever been as defended as this man.

"Bury the body," Nelsan ordered. "Outside the city." He tossed the cable to one of his men, who caught it and looped it around the creature's neck.

They carried the body out of the courtyard.

Ensign Brate, Nelsan's second, lowered his voice and said, "No sign of the second, my lord."

Nelsan motioned for the skroel's weapon, and the mole blade was delivered to him. It was a knife of unique design, instilled with a unique magic. The handle was made of black ore. Symbols were etched into it and painted white. He ran the thumb of his glove over the markings and then shifted his grip to examine the three-headed blade more closely.

He had only heard of these. They were called *mole blades* because the metal pieces moved. The blades twisted and wound through the victim's system. Apparently, the weapon's magic was strong enough to pierce bone, driving through muscle and sinew. Not a pleasant weapon, yet it was rather remarkable—all the more so because of the blood, still wet, that glistened on the blades. Skroel blood. Very dangerous. If the weapon itself didn't kill the man, the blood would. The smallest scratch, and the target would be dead within a few hours.

Without lifting his head, Nelsan glanced sideways at the king, who stood a few paces away with his steward and finance manager, flanked by two of his personal guard. The king and his immediate staff had been in the middle of a panel when the Nauget had interrupted them. Lord Sten, the finance manager, appeared ill. Mason, the steward, spoke with the king quietly and nodded toward the gate through which the soldiers had just dragged out the skroel's body.

The king ignored Mason and watched Nelsan. Korstain missed nothing. He was not like his predecessor, who had embraced fanaticism and fear; Korstain had strength in his blood. He had been born for this position of king and had taken what rightfully should have been his. Nelsan smiled slightly. Sensing Korstain's curiosity, he left Brate standing there and took the weapon to the king.

"Your majesty," he said and offered the expected bow. He held out the mole blade to the king. It was an awkward pass, for Nelsan kept his grip on the handle, having no intention of touching any of the blades.

The king wrapped his hand around the black haft and twisted his wrist. The sunlight reflected off the metal. Nelsan had never seen Korstain touch a weapon he did not carry well. Another mark of a true leader. The man's presence could be felt on every occasion. He controlled a room just by entering it.

Lord Sten cleared his throat and twittered. Weapons made him nervous. A small man, he carried a knife, not a sword; a sword would have overwhelmed him.

Sten jerked and cried out, hands lifting, as a wild commotion sounded on the street near the gate. Shouts of alarm.

"There would be the second," Brate said dryly.

Nelsan jogged toward the gate. The guardsmen cluttered the opening and didn't step aside until he shoved them.

The street was crowded. Most of the men Nelsan saw were soldiers. The third division had returned yesterday from running drills at the garrison in Tarek, and many of them had yet to receive their orders; so they congregated here, outside the walls of the palace courtyard, waiting for the general's aide to direct them.

Much of the crowd was making for a point about fifty yards away. The sound of their shouts had altered. They were goading now, cheering; they no longer seemed alarmed. Nelsan pushed his way through the bystanders. As the men recognized him, they made way, and when he came to the edge of the inner circle, he saw the reason for their entertainment.

It was, indeed, the second skroel. A man in traveling

clothes had captured the creature by the ankle. Both of them, man and monster, were on the ground, one behind the other. The skroel had dug gray fingers into the stones of the street and now resisted valiantly as the man tried to loosen its hold by force.

The men laughed and placed bets on whether or not the fighter would succeed in killing this creature.

In appearance, the man on the ground seemed well built and strong, yet he wasn't quickly overpowering the creature locked in his grip. He wasn't using a blade to kill it—that was good. Nelsan would have his head if he endangered any of the king's soldiers by spilling the skroel's blood unnecessarily.

No one moved to assist the man who was brave enough to wrestle a skroel barehanded. He did not appear to need assistance—he was just having trouble getting the skroel where he wanted him.

Nelsan lifted his hand to send men into the crowd to break it up. But then he paused. For the first time, he saw Thaxon Parez standing nearby. What was Parez doing back in Oarsman? He had been commissioned to locate Marcus Elah, the king's son. Had he been successful? Nelsan scanned the immediate crowd. No one stood out to him. He did not see any man who fit the description he had been given of the king's son, whom Nelsan had never met.

With a strong heave, the fighter on the ground ripped the skroel free of the street. The creature squirmed in his grasp, fought him, resisted death, tried to sink its snake-like fangs into the man's throat, but the fighter pinned the creature down. He maneuvered his hands around its head, one on the jaw, one on the back of the skull, and broke the skroel's scrawny neck. The body went limp in his arms, and he shoved it away.

The men congratulated the fighter, but their praise was somewhat half-hearted. These men were stationed in Oarsman nine months out of the year. They were used to the Ruthanian Blood Games and had witnessed much more entertaining excitement than this.

Ensign Brate stepped around Nelsan and extended a hand to the man on the ground. "Not bad," Brate said with a wicked grin. "Seen better, but not bad. Who are you?"

The fighter did not take the proffered hand.

He rocked onto his hands and knees, head down. A groan lurched out of him, and he spat blood onto the stones.

The cheering hesitated. Surprise rolled through the soldiers.

The man had been injured. Nelsan did not see any wound upon him, but a long cloak concealed much of the body.

Brate withdrew his hand.

The fighter arched his back as two metal blades punctured the fabric of his cloak and grew out of him like weeds. The skroel had stabbed him—the man was dead where he knelt. The multi-headed blade roiled inside his torso, the individual blades twisting as they rotated upward. He grunted. Deep in his throat. Intense.

Nelsan released his breath and regretted his earlier thoughts. This fighter was not weak; he was valiant. For his act of bravery, this man had paid a very high price. Korstain would want to compensate the family, for their loss had helped ensure the life of the prince.

Even now, with the third blade still hidden and moving within his body, the fighter did not die easily. He did not go down. He wheezed as he tried to fill his lungs. His body jerked.

Thaxon Parez stood there in shock. Then he dragged in breath and dropped to both knees, grabbing the man's shoulder as if he could keep him conscious. "Myles!"

The man called Myles pulled away from him. "Care... careful," he mumbled.

Parez moved his hand, and a moment later, the third head of the mole blade twisted out of the man's skin, right where Parez had been touching him.

The crowd responded with whispered groans. It was truly grotesque. A horrific way to die. How was the man still alert and upright?

"Hold this."

Nelsan heard the words, but with his eyes fixed on the gruesome sight before him, they did not make sense until the man beside him repeated himself.

"Hold this, commander."

Nelsan turned and looked into the white face of an Alusian. The creature appeared young, hardly more than a boy. The sight of blue eyes was startling.

Not only did this fighter kill a skroel, but an Alusian came to attend his death.

Wordlessly, Nelsan did as instructed. He held out his hands, and the creature tossed his cloak upon them, handing him his pack as well. The Alusian now held only a large set of smithy's forking shears, used for cutting metal.

Parez looked up. "Entan—"

"Hello, Myles," the creature said and stepped closer to the man on the ground. "Sorry about the delay." His brows rose, and he said with mirth, "Took me a moment to locate the smithy."

From the crowd, a man said, "You aren't amusing, Entan." He was standing a few paces away, his arms folded, his shoulders bent, as if he were cold. Nelsan was familiar with war and battle and the emotions inspired by both; he knew what discomfort and trepidation looked like. This man, with his freckled pale skin and brilliant red hair, spoke to cover his fear. "You still aren't amusing. You are never amusing."

"I am about to be amusing," the Alusian answered.

Entan used the shears on the blade that protruded from Myles' shoulder. The metal bent first and finally snapped. The shaft dropped to the ground and spiraled about on the stones like the body of a snake that had lost its head.

Parez jumped to his feet and stepped back.

Myles grunted again as the decapitated blade jerked down into his body. Nelsan was not a weak man, without experience—he was not this redheaded fellow who was familiar with concern and trepidation. Yet even he grimaced as the man's body flexed with the moving blades.

Entan cut the remaining two blades and laid the shears on the ground. Retrieving a pair of thick gloves from his pack in Nelsan's hands, he looked at Myles and said easily, "On your feet."

A second time, surprise washed through the crowd. Nelsan stared. This white creature could not be serious.

But he was. "You have to get on your feet. It will stop, if you get on your feet."

Entan extended a gloved hand to Myles, but he did not bend down to help him off the ground—he made Myles reach for him.

Once on his feet, Myles staggered. Entan supported him. Keeping one hand on Myles' arm, the Alusian untied the man's cloak and let it fall to the street, revealing the inscribed haft of the mole blade protruding from Myles' side. The weapon was buried between his ribs all the way up to the hilt. A solid hit. This strike had been on purpose.

Why had the skroel attacked him? This man had not been the target. The skroel never attacked anyone but the target.

Nelsan drew his gaze from the blade to Myles' face. It was red and tight, the jaw clamped shut in pain. Brows lowered. Blood covered his lips, across his chin.

Nelsan halted. He knew this face. He had seen this man somewhere before. *Where?*

A man in the crowd swore, and that single syllable of awe worked like a sudden break in a dam. A wild, crazed flood of cheering swept across the street. Nelsan could not tell how far down the street it continued. This was Oarsman, home of the Ruthanian Blood Games. The soldiers were intrigued when their entertainment came in unexpected ways.

Myles frowned at the crowd. Entan leaned forward and said something to him quietly, and a grimace went through Myles' expression. He snapped a response back to him, and the Alusian nodded, insistent, but Myles shook his head—he disagreed with an Alusian. Nelsan released his breath slowly. *Daring.* The man was very daring. The fascination built tenfold in Nelsan's chest.

Eventually—after several minutes—the soldiers began to quiet, and Entan put a firm hand on Myles' chest, as if to reassure himself that the man's heart was still beating.

"Are you all right?" Entan asked. His voice could be heard now that the screaming had stopped.

Myles rubbed the shoulder where the third blade had exited his skin. "Uncomfortable," he replied.

He was *uncomfortable*? Three broken blades inside

him, moving with a bitter sort of magic, and he was simply uncomfortable? A flurry of questions dropped through Nelsan's mind. How was the man standing? How was he "all right"? What was this—more magic? What was his training? What was his background? Nelsan was going to give this man a commission and a significant salary.

The handle of the mole blade suddenly sagged in Myles' ribs and dropped, clattering across the stones. Nothing remained of the three-pronged blade but a silver stump, jutting from the handle. The metal did not move. It lay twisted and dead, as if it had been heated and then ripped to pieces. Myles closed his eyes, opened them. The tension eased from his face.

Entan gripped him. "Better now?"

Myles nodded slowly. "Better." His breathing grew steady and even.

What is this? Nelsan shook his head, trying to shake away the pulsing confusion.

"Shall we make the introduction?" Entan asked.

At once, the grimace reappeared. Myles ran his hand over his mouth and looked down at the ground. "Now?" The word was quiet. Nelsan could barely hear it.

"It will need to be now," the Alusian returned. "He's here. He saw."

Myles scowled. For a delayed moment, he did not answer.

Entan waited patiently.

"As you wish, " Myles said stiffly.

Entan nodded to Parez, who turned to Nelsan.

"Where is the king?" Parez asked.

The realization struck Nelsan like a sword blade. *That* was why the man looked familiar. Parez had returned to Ruthane because his task was finished. He had found Elah's son. Nelsan had difficulty dragging his gaze from the man with blood all over him. The king's son.

It can't be.

"Here."

Korstain's voice behind him. Nelsan turned. When had the king and his bodyguards joined them? Nelsan's attention had been violently preoccupied.

The jubilant men saw their king, and silence dropped across the street.

Myles leaned over and spat a mouthful of blood on the stones, wiped his lips with the back of his hand. He had not looked at the king. It appeared that he hadn't heard the king's voice.

Entan tapped him on the shoulder. Pointed. Myles looked up and met the king's gaze.

He looked like the king. The same nose. The same hard refusal in his expression. Nelsan immediately knew many things about this man, simply from this look he gave now. *Myles,* they had called him. This was not Marcus, now grown. Marcus was the son Nelsan had expected, but all at once, he understood what this was, what Parez had done. He had gone and located the chosen son, the son who had been stolen by a nursemaid as an infant. He would have a half-moon scar on his chest, from where the priest had marked him for death.

Where had Parez managed to find him?

And why was he not dead? He recovered—he grew *better,* not worse, despite the blades that had twisted through him, despite the skroel's poison in his blood stream.

"You were correct," Entan said.

Nelsan discovered that he himself was the focus of the creature's odd blue gaze.

"The priests of the Mal-len Temple, with their fortune tellers and prophets, saw that they would fail in their attempts to kill the king. They knew. And the Nauget, your king's seers, were not mistaken in their predictions either." Entan nodded toward Myles. "They simply made an assumption about which son was the temple's target."

Entan took a step away from Myles and pointed at the man with the red hair. "Now, Antonie," he called. "Now is the time when I'm amusing." Lifting his voice, he swung his hand toward Myles and shouted to the crowd, "This is Myles Hileshand!"

The street exploded with sound. Nelsan had to fight to keep his footing as men rushed forward—sane men, men who didn't act like this. Trained men.

Myles Hileshand.

All of them knew this name. Myles Hileshand was the man who had fought the dragon in Blue Mountain and killed it with his bare hands. He had killed the goe'lah with only a stick of wood. He had cut the head off the *athamlaine* and sold it to Careb Jasenel. He had battled a meusone and somehow survived. If one were to believe the rumors, he had scars on his neck in the shape of the meusone's fingers. The beast had punctured him and tried to destroy him, yet he had lived. There were numerous other stories about this man, other things that could not possibly be true, yet they were repeated as truth. Every man in Oarsman who was interested in war knew the name of Myles Hileshand.

None of them had expected him to be the son of the king.

chapter **32**

Careb Jasenel became aware of the silence suddenly.

The papers quieted in his hand, and his form grew still as he realized he could no longer hear the thick, heavy breaths of the guard at the door. The man's peculiar breathing was the main reason for his assignment here, at the door of Jasenel's study. There was no need to watch him—his nose was like a flaming torch in the middle of a dark room. Jasenel always knew exactly where he was.

But now he didn't.

Reaching to his thigh, he jerked the knife free and stood to his feet in the same motion. He whirled to face the door.

And stopped, knife raised.

The guard lay facedown on the marble floor. There was no blood visible, and there had been no sound, even as he had fallen and his armor had connected with the stone. Soundless killings. Works of art. Jasenel stared at the body.

Then he recovered. Took a deep breath. Came to his

senses and lowered the knife. He sheathed it and returned to his chair, gathering the pages of his list. A sigh escaped his lungs. *Not again.*

"Have you reconsidered my offer?" he asked eventually. He waited, shuffling the papers, pretending disinterest.

The quiet broke with a deep, accented voice. "The king desires an audience."

Jasenel could feel the messurah's eyes. Other than the voice floating through the room, the weight of his gaze was the only sign of the man's presence. Jasenel couldn't even tell from which direction the voice came. The messurah had chosen a location in the room that caused his voice to echo off the walls.

Scowling, Jasenel goaded, "So you've become the king's messenger boy now? Do you find the occupation agreeable?"

A presence filled the space to his left. He felt it before he saw it, and his body stiffened. When he turned his head, the messurah was smirking at him.

The man's name was Quillan. He was Galatian; every word he spoke was difficult to understand, but his ability to speak Ruthanian had no bearing on his talents. He had been in Korstain's service for seven years. A story circulated that in Gereskow, while Korstain was still governor, a nobleman named Karn hadn't appreciated one of Korstain's rulings. He had sent a team of fifteen men to teach Korstain to make different rulings in the future. Quillan had stopped them, and, as the story went, no one ever found the bodies. Korstain then sent Quillan to Karn's house, and at this point, the story left the land of rumors and what-if's and entered the arena of fact. Everyone knew how Karn had died. The story had been repeated over and over. Quillan had taken his time, completed his task well, and Korstain's rulings were never treated lightly again.

"I would make you a god among mortals," Jasenel said wistfully, trying one more time. He did not expect to win Quillan's interest. The messurah were a determined group of individuals. They never did anything they did not want to do; they were very difficult to manipulate and very easy to offend. They did not enter the arena for sport. *Too bad.* For if they ever did, they would be remarkable.

"You are very talented at that, are you not?" Quillan responded. "Making gods of men."

Jasenel frowned at him, not understanding.

Jasenel was escorted to Red Haven, the king's palace on River Street, and left for two hours in a sitting room attached to the king's study on the third floor. The guards at the door would not let him leave. Jasenel sat in the chair and sulked, feeling miserable—he was under arrest, for some reason he could not even begin to guess.

What have I done? The king liked him, at least a bit. In the past, Korstain had attended the games every time he was in Oarsman, and he made regular appearances now that he lived in the city. Jasenel had once even had an invitation to his table. Korstain approved of Jasenel and his work, so what was the protest now? Why had he been arrested?

When the door opened and Korstain Elah finally appeared, he had a man with him whom Jasenel did not recognize. He was somewhere near his fiftieth year and wore his clothing as if it were armor; Jasenel knew immediately that this was a man of some authority, used to being obeyed.

No one introduced him.

Korstain did not sit down. Instead, he leaned his weight against the table in the center of the room and folded his arms.

"Your majesty." Jasenel offered him a low bow.

The king looked at him hard. "Tell me about your interactions with Myles Hileshand."

The guard closed the door to the hall, and the king's nameless companion reached over and locked it. Jasenel was quite aware of the sound of the bolt clicking into place. This meeting could go very poorly for him, and he wasn't even certain why he was here.

Myles Hileshand? Why was the king asking about Myles Hileshand, the man who had evaded Jasenel's arena solely because he had an Alusian friend? The king already knew this story. Jasenel had repeated it two dozen times at a party on the North Row last month, and Korstain had been in attendance; he had even asked Jasenel questions about the dead goe'lah's size and what had happened when the diluted blood had been poured across a man's face. Jasenel remembered these questions well, for he had been pleased with the king's interest. *The man melted, your majesty. That is the only word for it. His face ran like water. If you would like, I could arrange a demonstration.* Jasenel had bottled the water from the spring and had brought several bottles with him for exactly that purpose.

"What do you wish to know, your majesty?" Jasenel asked slowly. He needed to be cautious. Careful. There was nothing polite or civil in the king's gaze right now.

Korstain shifted position against the table. The line grew between his brows. "The Alusian female told you that the man was preserved by Boerak-El?"

An interesting first question. Korstain cared nothing for religion. He had proven that quickly enough. After the military had secured the throne for him, he had executed King Habeine's counselors—priests who had, at one time, counseled Korstain in his service to the gods. He had killed them the same day he'd beheaded the king. Korstain had not hesitated, nor had he feared to touch a priest, as many others would.

"Yes, your majesty," Jasenel said.

"She specifically said that the Alusian god of sorrow preserved him? Those were her exact words?"

And so, Jasenel began the story again, starting with the Alusian and her reference to Boerak-El. There was no reason for him to hide any details from the king, for the details made the story that much more remarkable. Myles Hileshand had killed a goe'lah with a splintered piece of wood, and the creature's searing blood hadn't killed him. He had fought *atham-laine* and survived, his body and soul somehow still intact. For three months, Jasenel had repeated no story other than that of Myles Hileshand. *A man preserved by a god of death.* He shivered. Simply thinking about it was too much for his heart. He had to calm himself.

An hour later, Jasenel drew the story to a close. He could have continued; he could have said many more things, but he attempted to control his tongue. This was the king before him now, not a lord of the court. Not a soldier, who would remain fascinated no matter the length of the tale.

Korstain looked at his companion, the nameless fellow who had followed him into the room. As the man nodded once, apparently agreeing with Jasenel's story, Jasenel frowned, intrigued. What did this man know? He clearly knew something—and *why* was the king asking about Myles Hileshand? The familiar shaking began within

Jasenel. The excitement, the fervor, struck the chains of his soul, and the tremors made it difficult for him to remain still. He had to ask questions. He had to know what had happened to bring this meeting about. He drew breath to speak again.

The king's gaze swung back to Jasenel. "And," he said coolly, "do you intend to keep your vow to this Alusian? That you will not attempt to touch or manipulate Myles Hileshand, who is protected by this god of death?"

Jasenel stared at him. *Why the questions?* "She would know if I failed in this, your majesty."

The king offered an obscure smile. "A safe answer."

"Yes, I will keep my vow—I would not dare touch what Boerak-El preserves. Not now, when I have seen the god in the very act of preserving him." Jasenel could hear the elevated tones of his voice, but he could not help himself. This story loosened the strings of his resolve and calm. "Myles Hileshand should have died. Multiple times, the man should have died. He was a slave, completely vulnerable to the power of other men—he was incapable of success. He should have been dead right in front of me, yet he *wasn't.* I have never seen anything like that before. I have never heard of anything like that. I have spent every waking moment for three months asking myself why Boerak-El would stand in a man's stead, and I am confounded with the answer—indeed, I have no answer. A man preserved by a god of death. Who could predict that?"

These words seemed to mean something to the king, something Jasenel could not read. Korstain shifted against the table again, turned his frown toward the carpet as he thought.

Then he straightened and abruptly left the room.

The king's man without a name remained behind. As the sound of the king's steps faded down the hall, the man reached over and closed the door.

"I am Thaxon Parez," he said. "My errand was to find the king's son. We discovered him in Tarek—with an Alusian." Parez's brows rose. "It would seem that Boerak-El has had a vested interest in this situation long before anyone supposed."

What did that mean? Again, Parez implied he had hidden knowledge. Secret understanding. Jasenel asked eagerly, "What are you saying?" He had to know all this man knew. Had Parez met Myles Hileshand? Was that the source of his information?

Parez was not impressed with Jasenel's enthusiasm. He looked at him blandly. "Did you not see the scar on his chest?" He crooked his forefinger and made a flipping motion near his sternum. "The half-moon. Myles Hileshand is Myles Elah. The king's firstborn."

Jasenel had difficulty breathing.

He remembered the scar. Myles Hileshand had been standing in the pool, his chest bare, the half-moon carved into his skin. Such a mark was the death sentence of Temple Law. Twins were considered a sign of the gods' favor. One child would be marked with the sign of the current moon and sacrificed in the temple. The other would live. Myles Hileshand had such a mark. And his brother had been with him. *Ruthanian twins.* They had looked exactly alike, save for the scars on Myles' body.

Myles Hileshand was Myles Elah? It could not be. Jasenel's heart raced. *Boerak-El has had a vested interest in this situation.* The words tore through his system.

Parez watched him. "A good thing, your resolve not to touch him. The Alusian saved your life with that command. The king would have had your head several times over."

Jasenel was shaking in earnest now. He had to calm himself, just so he could breathe. "Myles Hileshand is Korstain Elah's son?" The thought was awesome. It was beyond his comprehension or his—

Stop. He needed to breathe.

Parez's watchful gaze became a frown. He glanced at the door. "You may go, Jasenel. Return to your house and try to function as a man who retains his sanity."

Jasenel bristled at that word. Sanity had nothing to do with this. This was passion. "I'm not under arrest?"

Smoothly Parez returned, "Why would you be under arrest? Did you, in fact, lay a hand to the king's son? Did you buy him from your slaver? Did you injure him?"

The king's son. Chill bumps raced across Jasenel's arms. Down his spine. "No. No, I did not." The story he'd told today was the truth.

Why would Boerak-El protect a man? Why would the gods of Ruthane—Etnyse and Oelemah—do nothing as Korstain executed their priests, while *Boerak-El,* a god of death in his own right, would choose the king's son and repeatedly saved his life? *Why?*

Etnyse and Oelemah did not intimidate Korstain. He knew they were not strong enough to retaliate for the public abuse and offense that Korstain heaped upon them. But Boerak-El was an entirely different matter. The god of the Alusian would not be weak. He had already proven himself more than capable. And he had done so with the king's son.

Myles Hileshand was the king's son. *Incredible.*

chapter 33

Prasilla had been with the House of Elah for two generations. She had nurtured young Korstain when he was a child; she had comforted him when his little heart was broken after his mother's death. She knew all his faces, and even now, as a man of fifty-five, his thoughts were not hidden from her. She knew all the expressions of his children as well, for they took after him.

She might be old now, her back slightly bent, her movements growing slow with all the wrinkles, but she had her secrets. She knew things that no one else knew, things about Korstain, that would cause the entire nation to reel in shock.

Yet Prasilla would never reveal those things. No matter his faults, in her mind, Korstain Elah was still just a child. Every time she heard a new story about him, every time he did something surprising or horrifying, she would remember holding him night after night when he missed his mother—that was what she thought of. Prasilla would never betray him, and she often reminded him of that. He would smile and tell her he knew.

His only daughter, Gracile, was four years old and liked building cities. She did not care for dolls or lacey things—she wanted blocks and rods and glue and pieces of fabric that she could lay down as roads. She used books for bridges and had once stripped a plant out in the hallway and used the individual leaves for trees and bushes. Every city was detailed and, in its own way, quite magnificent.

Four years old and more intelligent than the lot of us, Prasilla often thought with pride. Korstain had two other children with his second wife, and they were intelligent as well—all of them took after their father—but none of them responded to life the way this little one did, her brow creased with concentration as she built her towers and laid her bridges.

Right now, Korstain was sitting on the floor with his daughter. He did not touch her, nor did he help her as she carefully set up her structures. He simply watched. The child knew he was there and had greeted him upon his entrance half an hour ago, but beyond that, she ignored him, intent on her task. Today the city was very large. Gracile had curled a long piece of blue fabric through the center of it, which Prasilla supposed was a river.

Prasilla remembered how the king of Ruthane had played and dreamed when he was this age. He had built cities, too.

"I heard the news, my lord," Prasilla said at last. *My lord,* she called him, not *your majesty.* That was what she had always called him, long before he was king, and she saw no reason to change her ways.

What sort of man would this *Myles* be? Marcus had been a happy child. He had been able to communicate well from a very young age, and his favorite pastime was conversation. His second favorite was reading. When his father had pressured him, he had eventually come to enjoy fencing as well, but it had never been a true desire of his heart. Nor did it always come easily to him. On one occasion, he had accidentally stabbed the hunting dog, and afterward, he had cried all over Prasilla's shoulder, utterly distraught that he had injured the creature. The dog had limped for a week.

Young Marcus had not been the clear leader his father had hoped for. *What will you be, Myles?* The chosen son.

She remembered well the day Korstain's twins were born. The entire house had wept for Lady Elah and her unexpected passing. Korstain could be vicious, and Tamra Elah had calmed him; she had been the balm of peace in his house. Not all the tears shed at her death had been in mourning. A few had been shed in fear, and rightly so.

When Korstain had married again, he had chosen a woman from a prestigious family. She was quite beautiful, but he had certainly not married her for the brilliance of her mind. She was too simple to be helpful in politics, and she was too selfish to care. Now that she had been elevated to queen of Ruthane, most people never saw her. Korstain encouraged her to be out among them, for the people praised her and he knew it softened his appearance in their eyes, but she frequently complained of headaches and sorrow. She hadn't wanted to come to Oarsman. She preferred the wind-swept coastland of Gereskow. Most of her friends were there, along with her mother. She had been tiresome before the journey across country, and she was positively dismal now that Korstain had decided to stay in Oarsman.

Korstain's head lifted. He looked at Prasilla, his gaze unexpectedly intense. "You should speak with him."

"My lord?"

"I want you to meet Myles. Tell me your thoughts about him."

For a moment, it seemed he was seeking her approval. *No*, she thought, *not my approval. He seeks reassurance.* Her brows came together as she studied him. Gently, she asked, "My lord, why are you alarmed?"

He scowled at her. The others in this house would have trembled in fear at such a look, but she knew she had no reason to be afraid. He would never put a hand to her, just as surely as she would never betray him.

"You seem to be alarmed by something," Prasilla said.

The scowl retreated into something that resembled a grimace, and he glanced away. "I did not expect this," he said after a moment had passed in silence. "I expected Marcus. I know Marcus. I know how he thinks, and I know how to direct his hand, but this one..." The words faded.

He did not have to say it. This one was supposed to be dead.

Korstain took a deep breath. His gaze on his daughter, he said, "What am I to say to him? How could this man give me what I want?"

So that is your fear, Prasilla thought. She heard the self-centeredness, but more than that, she heard the depth, the display of heart that she did not see very often with him. *Ah-ha, my lord. You give yourself away.* "You are afraid he will not agree with your worth."

The royal head rose again. "That isn't it at all."

"Yes, it is."

"No, Prasilla—it is not."

She nodded, undeterred. "You tried to kill him."

He glared at her.

"And now you are *concerned* that he will not receive you."

"I am concerned that he will not give me what I want."

She smiled. "Exactly."

He put a hand to the floor and pushed himself to his feet. Coming toward her, he said again, "No, Prasilla. In all your avenues of gossip this day, did you hear of how the soldiers shouted and cried his name? He comes to Ruthane as some sort of hero—Jasenel has turned him into legend, and legends are much more than men. The men want legends. They want strength and cunning. Jasenel made certain this man had all of that. A few well-placed steps, and *Myles Hileshand*—" Korstain sneered at the name. "—could secure the military's support and then the throne. I can see those steps. I can predict them; I know what I would do in his place, what I *have* done. It would not be difficult."

"What would a Furmorean do with a throne?"

Korstain scowled. "He is not Furmorean."

"He was raised in Furmorea. Looks like a Furmorean. Speaks Furmorean. Kills dragons like a Furmorean."

The scowl increased. "He isn't Furmorean."

"Think this through, my lord. You overreact, surely. The men of Furmorea hold strongly to their morality. They will not lie or cheat you. They will not kill, and they will certainly not steal your throne." Prasilla's gaze softened. "Be calm about this. Even if he did intend to take what you have taken…"

Her choice of words brought his head around. She

looked at him purposefully, and he hissed something un-intelligible beneath his breath.

"Even if he did intend such a thing, what would he do with it? He knows about plowing fields and farming—what would he do with a throne and a nation?"

Korstain looked away, and Prasilla reached out and put her hand on his shoulder.

"My lord," she said, gripping him. "You worry where no worry is due. Give it time. I know you will walk with care and make your final determinations when the time is right."

And you are afraid he will not receive you, she silently added, because she knew his look now as much as she knew all the others. She knew what he was thinking.

"I want you to meet him," Korstain ordered. "And then tell me your thoughts about him. You are the wisest among my counsel."

She smiled and patted his arm, teasing, "I *am* your counsel, my lord. I always give great wisdom."

The tension on his mouth began to ebb. He looked down at his daughter. "We will see if that remains true in this case," he said quietly.

He remained unconvinced.

chapter 34

Three hours later, Prasilla took a tea tray to Korstain's son. A servant named Roce opened the anterior door for her, and he gave her a look that was both hopeful and concerned. Prasilla knew Roce fairly well. He was a good man who had experienced much heartache through the actions of his son—he embodied what Korstain feared. A son's betrayal. Bitter blood. Prasilla smiled at Roce reassuringly, and he closed the door behind her.

The front room was empty, save for the object of Prasilla's mission. Myles Hileshand, firstborn of Korstain Elah, was sitting at the table with a large book spread out before him—a map, she realized eventually—until he saw her and came to his feet.

"Would my lord care for some tea?" she asked and then gave the man a thorough study.

Immediately, she was amazed at how much he looked like his brother. It was an older version of little Marcus standing before her now. *Identical twins?* she wondered. That phrase turned over a few times in her head. Many of her "avenues of gossip," as the king put it, included multiple versions of Careb Jasenel's story. It had been twisted and retold countless times by hundreds of people. She had heard of the brother, a man who had been with Myles that day at the hot springs, when the goe'lah's blood had washed off of him and filled the pool. No one had used the term *identical* to describe the brother. Her heart began to hurt. She looked at Myles and missed his brother, who had never been shy in expressing his affection for her.

There would be twenty-two summers to Myles' name now. He did not look younger or older than that. He carried a Furmorean build that clearly had seen many hours of labor, and a network of interesting scars spread across his forehead and jawline. They were noticeable but not disturbing; he was handsome in spite of them. The sleeves of his tunic covered his arms, but she caught sight of additional scar lines on his wrists. This was a man used to battle, to ruckus. Prasilla had been told that Myles Hileshand had dispatched the skroel today all by himself even after he had been stabbed. The mole blade had dug through his body, but he bore no sign of it now. It was as if the attack had never happened.

This is a curious thing. Marcus might not be the warrior his father desired, but perhaps Korstain had been given a second chance.

"Yes," Myles said momentarily. "Thank you."

Prasilla did not hear an accent. *Good.* He sounded as if he had grown up here, within Ruthanian borders.

Moving across the room, she set the tray on the table beside the book of maps and went about preparing him a cup. She would make it the way she made it for his father and then see what he said about it.

She was glad his friend the Alusian was not with him.

She had seen an Alusian once before—a male—and the next day, Lady Elah had died. The Alusian brought death everywhere they went. It was said they could see the future more accurately than any seer among men, and Prasilla began to wonder if that was why Entan Gallowar favored Myles' company. Because he knew Myles wouldn't die the way other men would die.

Myles watched her as she watched him. She smiled warmly and hoped to set him at ease. "Welcome to the palace, your highness."

His grimace was unmistakable. She knew at once that he did not like being called that, and she paused, the teapot suspended in her hand. He had the same look of displeasure as his father. Korstain worried that Myles would make an attempt for the throne—but this man had no such intention, not if he couldn't even bring himself to accept his rightful title. *Furmorean dragon-slayer. Fighter of meusone and naught more than a farm boy.* She laughed aloud and set the teapot aside.

She met his gaze with a large smile. "I will call you *my lord* instead. Would that do? That is what I call your father. He will never be anything more than six years old to me. A little boy I love very dearly." She looked Myles up and down and said, "So you are Marcus' brother—I am glad to meet you. I have missed Marcus dreadfully. He was always happy, always full of pleasant words. I was Marcus' nurse, as well as your father's. My name is Prasilla."

She could see the tension in his form, so she worked him the way she would work Korstain. She teased him. With a purposeful smirk, she said, "Relax, my lord. This, clearly, is not your day to die, and I, clearly, am not here to kill you."

That, finally, produced a small response. First, he

looked at her with surprise. Then his shoulders lowered slightly, and a faint light of humor trickled in along the corners of his eyes. He nodded. "Marcus told me about you."

"Where did you meet my dear Marcus?"

"In Edimane."

Her interest rose even more. "When you killed the dragon?"

"Yes."

"At the same time or...?"

"He and Hileshand were watching from the stands."

Marcus and Hileshand were in the stands. What a surprise that must have been! "Is it true you had no weapons with you? That you killed the dragon with your hands?" She had traveled back and forth between Oarsman and Gereskow for years with Korstain's family. She had never been to the Blood Games and never would, but perhaps their proximity was beginning to influence her.

The signs of humor faded from his face. "I had a helmet," he replied.

He shrugged, as if such a feat meant nothing, and she shook her head. *Farm boy.* This was truly amusing. The sniveling gossips of the court would try to pull him to pieces, yet he wouldn't run from them. He fought dragons—he could certainly handle a court filled with insane noblemen and senseless women. She looked at him and marveled, once again seeing his father in him.

"Why do the Alusian call you *Hileshand*?" she asked. Korstain would want to know the answer to that question, and Prasilla wished to be prepared. Not only that, but she was insanely curious. Careb Jasenel the gamer had been clear in all his stories: the very beautiful Alusian female had called Myles by the surname *Hileshand*. She had not called him Myles Elah. Why was that?

A moment passed, and then Myles said, "I call myself Hileshand because Hileshand is the only man who has fathered me."

She frowned at him. "But he is not your father."

Calmly Myles replied, "He is my father. I don't carry any other name."

He looked down at the tea tray, and she wordlessly handed him the cup and matching saucer. They looked awkward and tiny in his hands. Was Marcus as large a man as this?

Myles continued quietly, "If I do anything of worth in my life, it will be because of Hileshand. I am aware that saying such words in Korstain Elah's house could cause stress. I mean no disrespect. However..." A faint smile crept across his mouth, and Prasilla knew his thoughts. He wouldn't care if he offended the entire nation. He said, "My mind cannot be changed on the matter. Hileshand is my father, and my son is of his blood."

"Your son?" she repeated. In every version she'd heard of Jasenel's story, the woman had died—creatures in the Paxan woods had killed her and her child. Was she still alive, or was it just the child who lived? "You have a son?"

"I do."

"And his mother?"

Myles frowned, and sadness turned over in Prasilla's chest. The woman he loved was dead, wasn't she?

"She remains behind in Paxa," Myles replied. "With Hileshand."

Prasilla's "avenues of gossip" had failed her. Did Korstain know about the son of his son? Did he know he had a grandson? *Three generations,* Prasilla thought. *That is a number far more powerful than two.* This was important. A legacy stretched before her.

"You have many questions," Myles said.

She laughed. How many times she had heard that same statement from Korstain! Of course, Korstain usually said it when he was upset and disgruntled. Myles was still being polite with her. "I will always have questions for you, my lord. That is my nature—my calling, if you will. But there is one answer I must know straightaway."

He waited.

"How did you amuse yourself as a child?"

"Excuse me?"

"I know what Marcus did when he was a boy. Tell me of yourself."

Myles shrugged. "There is not much to tell."

Prasilla could only imagine how a boy in Furmorea spent his time. Was he herding cattle by the time he was five? Could he harvest a crop at seven? "But you were *very* young at one point, my lord. What did you do before you were sent out to the fields?"

He reached up and rubbed the back of his neck, and it was a motion she could read. He felt awkward. "It's difficult to say," he offered after a moment. "I was told I built things."

He built things. *Of course you did.* Never mind this nonsense about Hileshand—Myles was an Elah as much as any other man in his bloodline. He built things.

"What sort of things?" Prasilla studied him carefully. "Cities and bridges?"

He shook his head and smiled ruefully. "No, I had far greater plans. I would build kingdoms with stacks of wood. They'd go to war against one another. I had no patience for things as small as cities and bridges."

chapter 35

Entan did not want his own rooms down the hall. He wanted Myles' rooms. He directed the servants, and they, of course, were willing to give him anything he asked for. The blue eyes didn't make him appear more like a man; people feared Entan Gallowar.

Myles didn't know if it was common for one man to request to stay with another in circumstances such as these, but he didn't care. Nothing about this situation felt comfortable to him. He wouldn't have requested Entan's presence—but he was glad Entan had requested his. They had discussed their plans several times during the journey here, and Entan apparently had no inclination of leaving.

Do you know what my purpose is, Myles? he had asked. *An Alusian's purpose is his lifeblood and his reason for walking the earth. Do you know what my purpose is?*

The first time Entan had asked that question, Myles had been expecting something grand and unique—something worthy of the mystery of the Alusian race. But Entan had surprised him.

My purpose is to be your companion as your prophecy comes to pass. I make a good friend, Myles.

The words had seemed somewhat childish and simple the first time Myles heard them, but they did not seem that way to him now. He didn't like this situation. Nothing about it appealed to him. He could use a friend, especially one who could look into the future and scare people.

The palace was massive. Two kings ago, it had been renamed Red Haven, and apparently, it was the smallest of the king's homes. Myles did not have the ability to comprehend that statement, now that he had seen the building. Ruthane, the land of his birth, was completely foreign to him in many ways.

Shortly after Prasilla departed, taking the tea tray with her, Entan emerged from the left bedroom, blinking his eyes and rubbing his face. He had collapsed on the bed shortly after they arrived. There were days when he slept very little and other days when he slept like a sluggard who saw no reason to hold a decent occupation. His sleeping patterns were difficult to predict.

Entan paused in the doorway and looked around. "Was someone here?" he asked.

Strelleck had called it vision of the past. Its proper name was *eshtareth*, and it was the opposite of prophecy. Entan could see what *had* happened as easily as he could see what was about to happen.

"You know that someone was here, but you don't know who it was?" Myles asked.

Entan must have heard the goading, for he frowned at Myles. "I was asleep."

"That has never hindered you before."

The Alusian inhaled deeply. A single, full-lunged breath. "As always, I choose to ignore your blatant disrespect. I shall think of you as vastly overwhelmed by your new circumstances and feel pity for you instead of annoyance. You had tea. But I do not know with whom."

"Marcus' nurse." Myles expected those two words to be enough, but at Entan's blank stare, he added, "Prasilla. The nurse named Prasilla."

Entan blinked. "Oh, yes. And what did you tell her?"

"Why do you want to know?"

Entan returned, "Why are you being difficult?"

Hiding a smile, Myles dropped his gaze back to the book on the table. He had been carrying this book of maps for weeks. It calmed him to know his position in a country, his exact location. Even if nothing else could be known or predicted, at least he knew where he was. "I'm not being difficult."

The receiving room was quiet as Entan again drew long breaths. "He tells me nothing," he stated at last. "He gives me no details."

Myles looked up. He and Entan had discussed how the god of sorrow spoke to his people. Boerak-El was the source of their revelation; he showed them the future and the past.

Curious, Myles asked, "Why would he keep his silence?"

"For the same reason he would speak," Entan answered. "There is always a purpose. He is always moving. He is always acting. There is always a purpose in everything he does."

After her short visit with Myles, Prasilla returned to Gracile's rooms and waited for the king to come to her. She did not have to send for him. He knew the placement and movements of every person in his palace. He would know she had been to see his son.

Korstain entered the nursery, and Prasilla rose from the rocking chair and went to meet him, folding her hands before her.

He looked at her expectantly. "Well?"

"Congratulations, my lord," she said.

A frown appeared between his brows. The king folded his arms. "Explain."

She could see the apprehension crawling through Korstain's form. "He is your son." She would say that first, because it was the most true. Everything about Myles spoke of his bloodline. "Myles is everything you wished Marcus to be. He is just like you but easier than you and…" She paused. "And trustworthy in ways you are not."

The frown increased.

"You do not need to be concerned about any attempt from him to take your throne. He doesn't want to be here. Indeed, I believe that one day, your main concern will be whether or not you are successful in forcing the throne upon him. You will want him to have it, and he will try to convince you otherwise."

Surprise flickered through his gaze. "That is your prediction?"

"Yes. He is just like you, my lord, just like you—but his goals are different than yours."

He looked away as his thoughts adjusted and shifted within him. He considered her words with a familiar frown. "You are certain of your counsel in this?"

She reached up and put her hand on his cheek. "Spend time with your son, my lord." She smiled coyly. "He is different than the others. You will see that I am as wise as I ever was."

chapter **36**

"**I** have a brother."

Prasilla heard the announcement yet again and added another notation to her mental list. She was at eleven so far—eleven times she had heard little Gracile say those words in the last hour.

Sara was finishing up the child's hair. The maid glanced at Prasilla with a small smile and told Gracile, "You have four brothers, my lady. You have Athland and Baenan, who live here with you, and *then* you have Myles and Marcus. They are your oldest brothers."

"New brother," Gracile said.

"Well…yes. I suppose you could call him that."

The girl's long dark hair had been braided and wrapped into a pretty bun at the nape of her neck. She had asked for blue flowers, and Sara had picked them from the water-way garden herself, returning only a few minutes ago. The little girl looked like a dancer for the King's Parade, with dozens of tiny flowers mixed in through the braids. Later, she would pull the flowers out and use them as people in one of her handcrafted cities.

Gracile pushed up onto her tiptoes. "He is a soldier. Dabi says so."

Sara glanced at Prasilla again. "Yes, miss."

"He kills monsters. I don't like monsters."

"Yes, miss."

The girl lifted her voice. "Prasilla!"

"What is it, dear?"

"He will like me."

It was not asked as a question, but it was a question. This was how little Gracile often communicated things she was uncertain about—she made declarations. She was much like her father in that way, too.

Prasilla leaned forward, setting her hands to her knees, and said, "I know a secret, my dear."

The girl waited with wide, excited eyes.

"Your brother Myles has a son. He has his own baby; his name is Westland. Do you know what this little baby means?"

Gracile shook her head.

"You are an aunt. Little baby Westland will grow up and call you Aunt Gracile. Does this make you happy?"

Gracile nodded. "I have a brother now."

Sara sighed, a worry line appearing between her brows. "You have *four* brothers, my lady. Four of them. You have always had them. Your father has told you all about Marcus. You've even seen pictures of him. Remember the painting in your father's study? And you see Athland and Baenan almost every day."

But Gracile was not listening to Sara. She never listened to Sara. "New brother."

"Come along, dear." Prasilla held out her hand, and the child reached up to grip three of her fingers. "Your brother Athland and your brother Baenan wait for you in the North Gallery. You are going to meet your brother Myles now."

"He likes me," Gracile announced.

"Yes." Prasilla squeezed her hand. "Yes, he likes you."

Leaving the nursery, they walked through the Hall of the South Winds, then through the Gated Hall, and eventually arrived at the tall red doors of the North Gallery. The guards opened the doors for them, and Prasilla had to enter the large room slowly because Gracile had decided to tiptoe. She crept into the room with her back bent, her shoulders lifted with tension. Her steps made small *tap, tap* sounds on the marble floor.

Athland, Baenan, and their personal guards waited in the center of the long, rectangular room. Prasilla scanned the group and saw that the queen was not among them. She breathed a relieved sigh. *Good.* The queen's presence would only cause additional distress. She would not see this meeting as something of value. She didn't spend much time with the children, and Marcus especially had not been able to win her compassion. For the few years he had lived with her as Korstain's prized son and heir, Lady Namalinia had proven to be as excessive and self-righteous as her name. She had never let Marcus forget that he was not *her* child.

Athland frowned as Prasilla approached with his sister.

"Korstain is coming," he said sourly. His displeasure was a common occurrence. Athland brooded. The day could be bright and full of sun, his needs fulfilled, his expectations met, and still he brooded.

"I know, my lord," Prasilla said.

She looked at his brother Baenan and watched as the boy carefully matched Athland's expression. That was typical behavior for him as well—whatever Athland did, Baenan made certain Baenan did. He was sixteen and possessed a noticeably happier disposition than that of his elder brother, but this was true only when he was away from him. Neither boy cared much for their father, so not all of Baenan's dark sentiment now was due to Athland.

Baenan pouted. "I don't know why this is necessary," he said.

"My lords," Prasilla chided.

Gracile did not let go of Prasilla's hand. She might not fully understand the situation, but still, the child was nervous. She bounced up and down on her tiptoes, unable to stand still for long.

"He is your brother," Prasilla said.

"Just one of several we haven't met, I'm sure," Athland whined.

Even as a young man with nothing but the hopes of eventual power and fame, Korstain Elah had not been familiar with the concept of faithfulness to his wife. He had loved Tamra Elah, the twins' mother, but his interest had been taken by several others as well. No doubt Athland's statement was true, but there was no helpful reason for him to point it out now.

"My lord, calm yourself." Prasilla frowned at him.

"If he is capable of killing a dragon, he will likely be a soldier," Baenan said.

"Is it true," Athland demanded, "this story that Careb Jasenel repeats about Myles Hileshand?"

She began to answer, but he interrupted.

"Is Myles Hileshand Korstain's son?"

"Killed a dragon," Baenan muttered.

Prasilla smiled slightly, well aware of Baenan's interest, which he was trying to cloak with annoyance. "Yes, it is the same man. And yes, the story is true."

Athland's frown began to ease. "Good. Perhaps, then, he will distract Korstain."

"He is bound to do so," she answered. *In one way or another.*

Athland sighed, the tension in his shoulders sliding away as he repeated, "Good. Then let Korstain have him."

"Yes," Baenan agreed. "Let Korstain have him."

Gracile announced loudly, "My brother will like me."

Her brothers scowled at her, and Athland snipped, "What are you worried about?"

"Now, my lord..." Prasilla began, as she always did when the boys said things like this, but today, she couldn't remember what she normally told them. Athland wasn't mistaken in his response to his sister. Korstain had a favorite and did nothing to mask his affections for her.

"He will like me," Gracile stated again.

"Yes," Prasilla told her. "Yes, he will."

Myles Hileshand.

The guard at the end of the hall signaled to Prasilla, and she squeezed Gracile's fingers. "Here he comes," she said.

The little girl began to bounce with gusto.

Her brothers turned.

Myles Hileshand stepped into the room, followed by the Alusian with the blue eyes and Antonie Brunner, the redheaded scribe out of Tarek. The servants had seen to Myles' clothes, but it would seem he had been opinionated about their choices. Based on his garments alone, Prasilla would think him a landowner and nothing more. Strong but relaxed, wealthy but without arrogance; his clothes were not presumptuous. They were not the clothes of a prince.

Thaxon Parez had assigned Myles a brace of guards, and Myles did a fine job pretending he didn't see them behind him.

He stopped a few paces from his brothers and sister and folded his arms. For a time, no one spoke.

Myles pointed at Athland. "You must be Athland."

Athland nodded mutely.

Myles held his hand out to Entan, and the white creature reached into his bag and brought out a small stick.

A stick? What sort of thing is this?

A small smile turned the corners of Myles' mouth. His expression softened. "I have gifts from Marcus."

The words were like a knife on the tension, cutting it in half. Prasilla felt the entire room take a breath. Even the guards seemed to relax.

"You've seen Marcus?" Athland asked. Athland had been seven years old when his beloved elder brother was turned out of the house—old enough to remember him. Athland had often spoken of Marcus, especially as a boy. Through the years, Marcus' memory had become idealized and perfect, without blemish.

"Yes. I have seen him." Myles nodded. "He speaks highly of you. Told me about the time you threw flour all over the cook and then accidentally locked yourself in the beef cellar when you were trying to get away from him. Marcus laughed very hard as he was telling me that story."

Prasilla saw Athland's smile for the first time in months.

"Do you know what this is?" Myles held up the stick.

All of Korstain's children possessed good minds. Athland readily asked, "Is it something more than it appears?"

Myles showed him. He twisted the tip, and as they all watched, the stick became a sword. Baenan cursed in surprise, and Athland grinned.

"From Marcus?" Athland asked as Myles passed the weapon to him hilt first.

"Aye. From an Alusian armory. You will find this blade to be a ready companion in battle, more so than a sword made by the hands of man. Alusian weapons can be trusted."

Athland looked very pleased. He spent as little time with the fencing masters as possible, but that didn't matter in this moment, when Marcus had given him a gift.

Myles turned his attention to the next son. "You must be Baenan."

"I am, sir."

The Alusian produced a second stick, and in Myles' hand, this one lengthened into a horseman's ax, with a single, engraved blade and a pointed shaft jutting from the head. There was a small hole in the haft so the weapon could be fastened to the wrist. Baenan, when he was not pretending to be his brother's shadow, was often found in the stables. His horse, a stallion named *Atham-laine*, descended from famous warhorses and served as a difficult but sometimes loyal companion for Baenan.

Baenan could not have been more pleased. He felt the weapon, running his hands along the haft, and pricked his finger on the point. He did not express any signs of pain as blood trickled down his thumb. If anything, his smile widened.

Prasilla smiled. Marcus remembered his brothers well.

Gracile released Prasilla's fingers. The nurse looked down as the child stepped closer to Myles and waited expectantly, holding up her hand, palm exposed. She wanted a gift, too. She responded very well to gifts but already possessed far more toys and little pretty things than any sane child should have. Her father saw to that. When he was pleased with someone, he gave a gift. That was his way, and he was very pleased with Gracile.

Gracile had been born seven years after Marcus' departure. It was possible Marcus knew of her existence, but for a moment, Prasilla was concerned that there would be no gift, that the girl would leave empty-handed and Korstain would be upset.

Myles, without hesitation, looked over at the Alusian, who produced a long, rectangular book out of his bag.

Myles knelt to one knee and placed the heavy book in Gracile's hands. She had to adjust her weight to hold it; it was a very large book. "*The King's History of Paxan Architecture*," Myles read, adding, "With pictures."

Gracile looked at him as if he had fulfilled all her dreams in a single moment. "You *do* like me," she said.

Prasilla almost missed the guard's hurried signal. The king approached. She opened her mouth to issue a quiet warning to the children, as she always did when the king was coming. Athland had asked her to do so. But this time, she held her tongue, and Korstain stepped into the room and saw the delight on his children's faces—things he did not often see with them, with the exception of little Gracile, who had not yet learned to be afraid of him.

As the children saw their father, a heavy blanket of silence dropped across their excitement. Again with the exception of the youngest, all of Korstain's offspring lost their smiles. Myles rose to his feet as his father approached.

Gripping the book against her chest with both arms, Gracile staggered forward. Her father caught her just as she lost balance. "Look, Dabi! Look—Myles gave me a book! He likes me!"

"Of course he likes you," Korstain answered, not perceiving the reason she would say such a thing. He swung her up into his arms, book and all.

Athland and Baenan bowed before him. They had started doing so a few years ago, long before he made himself king, and he had not corrected them. Myles did not do as his brothers did. He noticed they did it, and it seemed he purposefully chose not to follow their example.

Well done, Prasilla thought.

Myles held out his hand to the Alusian again.

A moment passed before Prasilla noticed her mouth was open. She tried to close it. *Truly?* There was a gift for Korstain as well? She had not expected that. She had imagined bitterness in Marcus. Marcus had been a sensitive child, with the heart and thoughts of a poet. He had loved his father and, to a certain degree, had perceived that he was not what his father wanted. A man could not experience that level of rejection as a child and suddenly be able to forgive and offer peace later. *What is this, Marcus?*

Myles twisted the end of the small stick, and the wood transformed into a double-headed ax. The blade, like that belonging to Baenan, was etched with flowing designs that looked almost like words, but if they were words, they were not in any language or script Prasilla recognized.

The double blade gleamed in the lamplight.

"From Marcus," Myles said and held out the hilt to his father.

Korstain studied him briefly before setting Gracile on

the floor. He took the haft of the weapon and drew the head close to study it. Though heavily masked, there was uncertainty in his look. Prasilla knew the man was still deciding what to think about the situation.

Prasilla was unfamiliar with weapons, but she had no doubt that each of these gifts from Marcus was worthy of his father's house. *The magic of the Alusian.* Powerful weapons. When had Korstain's twins crossed roads with Entan Gallowar, as well as the ill-tempered female Jasenel spoke of so often? Such a relationship had to be highly uncommon. Prasilla had never heard of this before.

Korstain Elah stood there and contemplated the immediate future. He stared at his firstborn, and Prasilla could see the decision as he made it. In a single moment, he elevated Myles above the others and did as Prasilla had counseled him.

"How does this work?" he asked, turning the weapon in his hand.

Myles stepped closer to explain the weapon to him, and Prasilla breathed a sigh. It was done. He had found favor with his father, as Prasilla had known he would. Korstain's face lost that familiar look of tension. He seemed almost eager as he asked questions and pointed at the flowing script on the blade.

Athland began to look relieved. Myles' favor with the king meant Athland would no longer be Korstain's focus.

Baenan, meanwhile, remained quite taken with the horseman's ax. His thumb was still bleeding. He left red fingerprints on the blade.

Gracile sat on the floor with the book of Paxan architecture spread open on her lap. It did have pictures, as Myles had said; his sister made quiet exclamations as she ran her little fingertips over the ornate spikes on the bridges and touched the windows of the sketched buildings. It was a perfect gift for her, and her pleasure automatically meant Korstain's pleasure.

"I understand you have a wife and son," Korstain casually stated several minutes into their conversation about Alusian weaponry.

Prasilla glanced at him in surprise and then realized that Thaxon Parez must have told him.

At the king's words, suspicion dropped through Myles' gaze. It was so strong that Prasilla felt it, even several steps away.

"Yes," Myles replied.

"Send for her," Korstain said. "Send for your son."

He gives you a gift, Prasilla silently told Myles. She knew how Korstain often communicated his acceptance or gratitude. If he was pleased with a man, he gave him a reward. *He gives you honor, Myles.*

Myles looked at the king hard. "No," he answered.

At that single word, all other sounds disappeared from the room. The children stared at their brother. Prasilla tried not to react.

Korstain's expression darkened. "No?" he repeated. He did not do well when he was surprised, and no one ever refused him anything.

Myles said firmly, "My wife and my son mean more to me than my life. I will not entrust them to your keeping."

Tense moments passed before Prasilla's heart calmed enough for her to realize what Myles was thinking. Of course he would assume the worst of his father. Of course the worst would be his opinion. In Myles' mind, Korstain had attempted to destroy both of his sons from his first marriage. Who knew what Marcus and Myles had discussed about their father? Myles, being like Korstain, would not willingly do anything that jeopardized what he wanted, and what he wanted was to protect his wife and son.

Korstain's glare reduced itself into a look that remained serious and inflexible, but the anger slowly dissipated. He seemed to be considering Myles' words. He turned back to the Alusian ax. "I will change your mind," he said, his tone calm.

Myles looked at him a moment longer, and then he also shifted his gaze to the ax. There was a definite challenge in his words as he quietly stated, "You can try."

chapter 37

Marcus Hileshand stood on the bluff overlooking the valley of Sporans Brook. The mountain called Tapos-Dane formed a barrier on the distant side, jutting up into the sky with a snowy cloak spread heavily upon its bony shoulders. Snow did not cover the circular rim of the mountain; the uppermost peak was completely clear, and a faint line of smoke drifted from its mouth to mix with the clouds. Tapos-Dane was a *nauno-dah*, a living mountain, full of fire and molten rock.

Marcus could smell wood smoke wafting up from the town. Sporans Brook filled the valley's base. He wagered he could see about fifty houses from his current location on the bluff, plus several additional buildings that lined the main street. Snow-laden farmland and enclosed pastures ran along the hills. It was a town of men.

Bithania came up behind him, her steps muffled in the undergrowth, and he sensed her presence before he saw her.

For a few moments, they stood together in silence.

"An ugly place," she said, watching the town below.

He was surprised to hear her speak. Over the last three weeks, she had said as little as possible to him. This was, he thought, the first time she had initiated a conversation with him in that same length of time.

She lifted her hand and made a loose gesture toward the north. "We will be going around the town," she said. "Avoiding the valley."

He looked in the direction she indicated but couldn't identify the road through the trees. Paxa had trees enough to rival the grains of sand on its beaches. He hadn't seen a clear, unhindered sky in months. It was consistently filled with the dark veins of tree branches.

Bithania's right hand returned to her side, and he noticed that in her left hand, she gripped her book of poetry, the one she always carried with her. Marcus had read both volumes by Adraine El-Ohah and had found that the second, the book dedicated to the sun god, intrigued him more. His studies with Hileshand had been in that arena: *Abalel is the father of life. He causes growth and warmth in a world given to cold and fear. He is both teacher and plumb line. The sun is a symbol of who he is. Without him, there would be no life on earth.*

Bithania carried the first volume, the one dedicated to Issen-El. It spoke of rivers. Oceans. Water with currents. Cold elements. Darkness—yet there was life concealed in its depths.

Bithania looked up into his gaze. Just briefly. Turning back toward the valley, she said, "I know Boerak-El has given you words for his council."

"Bithania," he said with care.

She didn't look at him. She frowned at the town. "And

I know the words he has given you pertain to me."

An owl hooted across the ridge.

"Tell them what you will, Marcus. It doesn't matter."

"It does matter," he said softly.

"No." She shook her head. Her eyes narrowed. "I know how you are. I know how you think. I don't need you to save me."

He just looked at her.

She turned and walked back into the woods, in the direction of their camp. Strelleck was making supper about half a mile behind them. Bithania was a miserable cook; the meal was a much more enjoyable experience when Strelleck was the one who had prepared it.

Marcus watched her go.

The late afternoon light was fading. Tapos-Dane blocked the sunset; the mountain was ringed in a cold orange haze. They had perhaps half an hour of daylight left.

Breathing a sigh, Marcus looked down at the town. *Sporans Brook.* Nearly five hundred people—men who had dwelt in the shadow of the Alusian mountain for generations. *Hard men,* Strelleck had told him. *Men familiar with fear.*

Marcus was beginning to hate fear. He had looked down upon it because Hileshand had taught him that it was unnecessary, but Marcus had never despised it as he did now. Why did the men of Sporans Brook live in fear of the Alusian? There was no reason for the effort; the Alusian intended them no harm, nor did the Alusian god intend them harm. Their proximity to the Alusian should actually be considered a promise of safety, not a threat. But still they lived in fear.

He felt a sudden breeze flow across him. It was as if he no longer wore his cloak—the draft cooled his arms, his shoulders, ran down his spine.

The trees around him were quiet, nearly silent. They felt no wind.

His heart jumped. He knew what this was.

"Marcus." His name spoken into the evening.

Boerak-El had joined him.

Two hours later, Marcus walked down Cartographer Street and knocked on the front door of the second house on the left.

A woman answered. In the lantern light, it was difficult to tell her age for she bore that haggard look of a person who has lost her will, having discovered her efforts are not enough. A child gripped her legs, and the little girl's brow was furrowed with a look that matched her mother's.

"Yes?" the woman asked, her tone dark.

"I am here for your ax," he told her.

Her eyes narrowed. "That is all? You want only the ax?"

"Yes."

"Fine."

She shut the door in his face. He waited. It was colder in the valley than it had been on the bluff. The wind found a way through the slopes and raked the valley floor like the currents of a river. He folded his arms and hunched his shoulders. The street was dark. He held one of the only lanterns visible for about a hundred paces.

The door opened again.

"Here."

The ax was thrust into Marcus' hands, and the door slammed.

The woman's name was Larsa. Her husband had died in the beginning winter months and left her with substantial debts and three small children. Collectors had been coming for four weeks now and slowly stripping her house of her belongings. She had no means and no family. No one to take care of her in her despair.

Marcus shouldered the ax and walked behind the house.

Soon after he started, Larsa heard the sounds of the ax head on the logs and came outside. She was wrapped in a large worn cloak that had clearly belonged to her husband.

"What are you doing?"

"Filling the rack." He paused in his work and nodded toward the empty metal brace by the back door. "It is empty, so I am in the process of filling it."

She stared at him. "I do not want you to do this."

"Why?"

She frowned. "I cannot pay you."

"I do not wish payment."

She tried again. "I don't know you."

He nodded. "Marcus Hileshand. That is my name. Now you know me, so you can lay your fears aside."

In anticipation of sweat and solid, honest work, he slid off his cloak and draped it over the fence rail. Lifting the ax again, he said, "I will be finished in one hour. You may tell me to leave then."

Eventually, she went back into the house, and he finished the woodpile. He loaded the wood rack by the back door and piled the pieces that did not fit in the rack in thick rows along the back of the house. When he knocked on the door with his boot, Larsa opened it, and he came inside to fill the rack by the fireplace.

The fire was close to dying out. With the exception of the wind's fierce bite, the air inside the house felt no different than the air outside. Three little children looked at him from the bed in the corner. They had covered themselves with blankets. Their faces were dirty.

The entire house sat in disarray. There was a table, but all the chairs had been taken. Cabinets had been removed from the walls, leaving behind large squares empty of paint. The countertops were bare. Dirty laundry lay scattered across the floor. He saw a large rat scurry across a ceiling beam. This was more than lack and the debilitating chains of poverty—Larsa had given up hope.

It took him three trips to fill the indoor rack.

"Leave," Larsa told him.

He nodded. "I will build up the fire, and then I will leave."

When the fire was singing cheerfully in the hearth, he tipped his head to Larsa and left through the back door, retrieving his cloak and his lantern.

Marcus returned to Larsa's house two hours later. The night was deep and silent by this time, the sky full of ice and stars. Most streets in the town stood as dark as Larsa's, with no lanterns, all the windows heavily shuttered, as if the townsfolk wanted to conceal themselves from what lurked in the shadows. He imagined that Bithania's comment on the bluff was correct: *An ugly place.* Eerie during the day, and the night only increased the sense of crawling fear.

Larsa scowled at him.

"What do you want now?" she asked.

He turned and motioned to his companions—three men who had "volunteered" to assist him outside the butcher's house. Having been diverted from their original plan to rob him, they now obeyed quietly, eyes small and darting, mouths tightly shut. They followed Marcus into the house and began to empty their bags, depositing their packages on the counters. He had needed all three men—there were many packages.

No one in the house was sleeping. The children had moved from the bed to a warm spot before the fireplace. They stared as the counters began to disappear beneath all the bundles piled on top of them.

Larsa stood there, her face blank, as Marcus set the receipts in her hands. "Your account has been settled with the mercantile and the butcher. Here are the final papers closing your accounts with the creditor on Second Street and the creditor on West Street. The landowner has been paid in full—here is the receipt for that. This means the house is yours. No one is going to take it from you. Keep these papers in a safe place, Larsa, but don't be afraid anymore. You no longer need to worry about collectors."

She slowly lifted her gaze off her paper-filled hands and looked at him.

"Do you understand?" he asked, but the expression did not change.

So he turned to the children. "Betsy," he called.

The older girl didn't even pause to throw off the blanket. She jumped to her feet and caused her younger siblings to rock over onto their sides, grasping at the fabric and pulling it back in place around them.

She smiled shyly. "It is my birthday this week," she said.

He smiled back. "I know. And I have a gift for you." He reached into his bag and pulled out a doll made of porcelain. It had blue eyes and hair that was almost pale enough to be called white. He looked at it and thought of his sister.

Betsy's eyes filled with a hunger that wasn't childlike. He held the doll out to her, and she grabbed it with both hands, as if she feared he would change his mind.

"That is yours," he told her. "You don't have to fear that someone will take it from you. No one will."

She gripped it tightly, holding it against her chest. "Thank you! Thank you. This is the most beautiful doll I have ever seen."

"Hovelant," he called next.

The middle child rose before the fire slowly. He looked at Marcus with suspicion.

Marcus put fingers to his lips and whistled, and Sam, the butcher's ten-year-old son, pushed open the front door and stepped into the lamplight, a puppy in his arms. The creature was half wolf and half some sort of sheepdog, and Hovelant was going to name it Kiley.

The puppy was transferred from one child to the other. Hovelant was six. He held little Kiley and trembled, and when the puppy reached up to lick his chin, the boy's eyes filled and he started sniffling.

"Anna," Marcus said, looking at the third and lastborn of Larsa's children.

This one was three, and she had a fever. Her eyes were unfocused and shiny, like glass. Marcus did not require this child to move. He went to her instead, sitting down beside her and pulling her into his lap. He was becoming able to recognize the subtle thrum of Boerak-El's power. He felt it in his hands—a faint tingling, as if his hands were numb. The child blinked at him several times and sighed. He put a hand to her forehead and felt her temperature lower beneath his touch.

"Do you know what I have for you, little one?" he

asked quietly. He reached into the interior pocket of his cloak and pulled out a small silver locket on a thin chain.

Anna squirmed in his arms until she was able to touch the glittering object with two fingers.

"Someday," he whispered, "this will keep you safe from evil men. Wear it always."

He fastened it around her neck, and she smiled up at him.

Leaning back, he braced himself with a hand on the floor and climbed to his feet, holding Anna in his arms.

The three men and Sam the butcher's son waited at the door. He paid them for their time, and with the exception of one, all of them scattered out into the night. The one who remained had been the instigator outside the butcher's house. He was almost forty years old, his face lined with hardship, his features thick and heavy.

He rubbed his hands together nervously and bowed and said, "Anything else, my lord? Anything…at all?"

Marcus knew this man had four children of his own. Despite the desperation that had driven him to attempt to rob Marcus tonight, the man understood about gifts and family. He, like Larsa, had bills and accounts with creditors. Also like Larsa, he knew the sting of hopelessness; Marcus could see it in him.

"Yes," Marcus answered. "There is something more." He dropped ten additional gold pieces into the man's hand. "Now you may go."

The man left quickly.

"What are you doing?" Larsa whispered, finding her voice at last.

He passed Anna to her, and she clutched the child to her chest.

"Fulfilling my purpose," he told her gently.

She looked at Betsy, who was braiding ropes of blonde hair before the fire. Then she turned her head toward Hovelant, who sat in the corner of the room and cuddled his wolf puppy.

"I don't understand," she said.

He pulled his purse off his belt and dropped it on the table. The coins clinked together, and he frowned at the shallow sound. That wouldn't be enough. He looked at the bag, and it began to spread out, growing fat, pushing at the seams, until the ties unraveled, and a handful of gold pieces escaped and rolled across the table.

Better, he thought.

Marcus looked back to Larsa. Choosing his words carefully, he said, "The night your husband died, he told you not to fear, that Abalel was going to take care of you."

Her face paled at first; then it turned as brilliant red as a spring flower. "How do you know that?"

"Abalel has not forgotten that promise." Marcus leaned close and kissed her forehead and said, "Don't give up hope, Larsa. There is always hope with Abalel. He is the god of the sunrise—of new times and new days."

He motioned toward the packages on the counters. "You now have everything you need. You are going to be all right. Your children will be all right. Abalel will continue to take care of you, and you can *expect* him to do so. Let go of your fears. There is no reason for you to fear."

Marcus left the town of Sporans Brook and started back to camp. Halfway up the hill, yellow light fell across his path.

He looked up to see five perusan staring at him from behind the trees. The creatures appeared as men. They had different shapes and sizes, as men would—tall, short, thin, long hair, short hair. Two of them even wore the uniforms of the Paxan royal guard. The other three were dressed as peasants. The bodies glowed as if with lamplight.

He sighed. *Not again.*

The perusan had a touch like ice. They killed men with their hands and immediately recovered when injured; to kill the perusan, the neck had to be severed. Marcus and his father had been fighting perusan for years. The creatures seemed to follow them from city to city, appearing as they did tonight—suddenly, in the dark, out of the trees, shedding cold yellow light. Marcus used to be thrilled to see them. They always meant a fight. Excitement. Action. He and Hileshand had so many stories…

But all of that was over now. The perusan no longer came near Marcus. They watched from behind trees and did not allow him to get close enough to use his sword. They used to be adventures; now they were lamps that walked around.

It was rather disappointing.

As he neared, they backed away, pulling deeper into the woods.

The hour was long after midnight when he walked into camp. The area Strelleck had chosen was sheltered by a series of leaning boulders and bent trees; the cold ground was snow-less here and shielded from the north wind.

Bithania was asleep, her arm crooked beneath her head. It was a cold night, even close to the fire. The blankets were pulled up tightly under her chin, her cloak hood low across her face.

Strelleck was waiting for him. He used the trunk of a fallen tree as a chair, his legs stretched out before him, his boots crossed near the fire. "Where were you?" he asked.

Marcus heard an unfamiliar tension in Strelleck's

voice, and it slowed his steps. *Strelleck concerned?* It was quite uncommon for Marcus to catch any signs of worry with this creature. At times, Strelleck showed surprise; it seemed all of the Alusian could be caught off guard. But Strelleck—and Entan as well—appeared earth-like in their emotions: quiet, calm, sensible, not given to outburst or concern. What room would they have for fear? They could see the future.

Bithania, however, was different. Distress, concern, anxiety, anger—Marcus had seen all of these reactions from her in the last few weeks, and he didn't understand why. She could see the future, too, but she didn't seem to accept it calmly, as her male counterparts did.

He watched Strelleck a moment, considering, and then sat down on the opposite side of the fire. The warmth reached him slowly. Yanking off his gloves, he rubbed his hands together and held them toward the flames.

Stars peered through the tree branches overhead. His breath left him in clouds.

"I was in town," he answered finally.

Strelleck frowned at him. "You should not go into Sporans Brook. Sporans Brook is dangerous."

Yes, thank you. Marcus had discovered that. "Do the Alusian ever come down the mountain and into the town?"

"No." The creature took a full-lunged breath and amended his statement: "Not anymore. The people do not wish to see us. They do not venture far up the mountain, and those who do report the presence of *atham-laine* and great evil. Our community has become naught more than a legend among them. A rumor without substance. Why did you go into Sporans Brook?"

Strelleck could be persistent. Marcus eventually replied, "Boerak-El wished to keep a promise to someone in the town."

Marcus waited for another question about Sporans Brook, but Strelleck said nothing. He stared at Marcus for a long time, and Marcus returned his gaze, still waiting for the response, for additional questions.

Boerak-El wished to keep a promise.

Yellow light drifted through the trees. Marcus leaned away from the fire and shielded his eyes. The perusan came within twenty paces and stopped, watching silently from around the tree trunks.

"Tell me about the perusan, Strelleck."

Strelleck followed his gaze. "What do you wish to know?"

"Why do they not attack?"

"They are guardians."

Guardians? The description made little sense. The perusan killed men; they did not guard them. What, then, did they guard if their interest was not in men? "Guardians of what?" Marcus asked.

Strelleck didn't seem to understand the question. "Guardians," he repeated.

"Were they men?" Marcus asked next. Some believed the perusan were ghosts of the dead because they resembled men so closely.

"No," Strelleck replied. "They were never men."

Marcus considered that a moment and then asked the question in a different way: "Why do they not attack us?"

Strelleck stood up and added wood to the fire. Sparks rose into the night. A gust of wind grabbed them with invisible hands and carried them off to die in the tree branches.

"They are guardians."

Marcus groaned. "You know," he said, hoisting himself to his feet, "sometimes, talking to you is as helpful as
talking to a tree."

Curiosity flared in Strelleck's eyes. Marcus sensed the
question that was coming and groaned again.

"You speak to trees, Marcus? I did not know this."

arcus awoke at first light, consciousness seizing him with violence. His heart raced, and he didn't know why. He couldn't remember his dreams, and the morning was quiet. He heard a dog barking at a great distance. That was the only sound—what had awakened him?

In the early morning shadows, he saw Strelleck sitting on the fallen tree. It was the same position he'd held last night as Marcus had fallen asleep. Marcus couldn't tell if the creature had slept at all. His bedroll appeared untouched next to his bags.

Marcus sat up and looked on the other side of the fire, where Bithania had been lying, but the area was empty. Her bedroll was missing, as well as her bags. The horses occupied the eastern end of their shelter, and when he looked, he saw only two.

"You are awake," Strelleck needlessly announced.

Marcus rubbed his eyes and willed his heart to calm. Why did he feel so anxious? "Where is Bithania?"

Strelleck stood up and came to the fire. Opening his bag, he removed the halfpot and other items and began making breakfast. "She has gone to appeal to her father. He is a member of the *Aroyaphel* and has the authority to speak on her behalf."

Her father was a member of the Alusian council? Marcus hadn't known this. He had trouble judging Strelleck's tone and couldn't tell what the Alusian intended with that statement. "*Will* her father speak on her behalf?"

"No. Going to her father is merely protocol. He will not speak for her. She will surely lose her place."

Strelleck had mentioned this before. *Our council intends to remove her place.* Marcus wasn't sure what that meant.

"Several of us have seen it," Strelleck said after a moment's quiet.

"What, exactly, have you seen?"

"We have seen that she does not remain on the mountain. In a short time, there is a loss in her father's house." The creature nodded. "Bithania's place among our people will be removed."

Strelleck spoke calmly, as if the words carried no weight, the topic unimportant.

Heat spiraled through Marcus. Bithania wasn't like Entan Gallowar, who could make a home for himself in two different worlds. If the Alusian did not claim her, where would she go? Who would protect her? Marcus had seen the way men looked at her. There was fear, yes— fear of death. Fear of the Alusian god. But none of these men had looked away from her with fear in their minds. Bithania was beautiful, and that fact was not lost on any man who saw her. It would not be good for her to be alone.

Words came to Marcus, angry words, but he tried to hold his tongue. What was wrong with the Alusian that they acted this way? It was as if they had no concept of life and family. There was no concern for others. Was it selfishness? Was it ignorance?

Frustrated, he finally said, "Do you not see any good in her future at all? What about fulfilling her purpose? You said Boerak-El has given her a purpose of reconciling divided parties, of bringing unity. Harmony."

"I see nothing in her future," Strelleck replied. "Her future is dark to all who have looked, which is another reason we know her place is removed—Boerak-El no longer speaks of her after today."

The Alusian town of Tapos-Dane shared many similarities with Sporans Brook, the town of men in the valley below them. Much of the town was old, the buildings made of wood and stone, the streets clogged with hard-packed, muddy snow. There were pastures and barns, undecorated storefronts and warehouses. He heard dogs barking.

But there the similarities ended. Tapos-Dane was consumed by stillness. As Marcus and Strelleck rode down the main street, he didn't hear any voices. He saw no colors other than gray and brown; he saw no signs of the presence of children. The Alusian they passed stopped and stared at them. They did not appear pleased, nor did they appear upset. No one greeted Strelleck, whose face was well known here. It was as if the town were filled with ghosts that had nothing to do with real life.

Marcus had been to nearly every country north of the desert with Hileshand; he hadn't been able to speak every language they encountered, and some of the cultures had been harsh and difficult to understand, but nothing had felt as foreign to him as this town on the mountain. Nearly two hundred Alusian lived here; most of the creatures did not prefer town living. Most were like Strelleck, who sought solitude, the woods, and open air.

Strelleck turned down a side street and stopped in front of a stone house. "You will stay here. Your needs have been anticipated; however, if there is anything you need and it has not been provided, it will be provided shortly." Strelleck opened the front door for him. "Refresh yourself. I will come for you in three hours. The council will see you this afternoon."

Strelleck took the horses and left.

Marcus couldn't imagine the Alusian having a "guest-house" and supposed this was actually someone's home. The interior of the house looked exactly like the exterior. There was no color or warmth, no signs of expression. The floor was made of the same stone as the walls, and everything blended into similar shades of gray.

What was their interest in poetry, if they could not translate that interest into normal life? The house resembled the entire town—there was nothing of life here.

He dropped his bag on the table and heard a loud popping sound on the other side of the room. He looked over in time to see a fire crackle to life in the hearth, all on its own.

Very well, he thought and went about doing as Strelleck had directed. He tossed his cloak across a chair and pillaged the cabinets for meal supplies.

The *Aroyaphel,* the Alusian council, met in a building outside the Alusian town, high up on the mountain.

Just a few paces beyond the doorway, the trees faded into snow-covered boulders, and the mountain stretched upward at an impossible angle, ending at the rocky circular mouth with its constant line of smoke rising into the sky.

Marcus paused at the front door and looked over his shoulder. Miles and miles of snow and stone and trees sprawled behind him. A magnificent view.

"They're waiting," Strelleck said when Marcus stopped for too long.

"You read poetry, don't you?" Marcus asked, knowing the answer.

Strelleck frowned at him.

Marcus nodded toward the horizon. "I think much could be written about beauty such as this. Do you ever take notice of the view?"

"I read poetry," Strelleck replied. "I do not write it. You can't stay here, Marcus. The council waits for you."

He held open the door, and Marcus stepped inside as the sky began to drop snow.

For some reason, in his head, he had been expecting the Alusian council to have a similar feel as the council in Ausham. Everything Ausham did was large and well lit. The council met in the midst of extravagance and vastness, surrounded by lamps, open windows, and mirrors that reflected the light and drove away the shadows.

Conversely, the Alusian council met in a short stone building that had only one room. A single window had been cut into the eastern wall. Tall staff lamps stood in the corners; the glass panels in each of the lamps were stained and dingy, as if no one had touched them with a washrag in years. It took a moment for Marcus' eyes to adjust to the sudden shadows. No, this was not like Ausham at all.

But then, all at once, that began to change.

He felt a cool breeze whisper across his skin. Wind that was not wind. With it, his confidence came to life. Every time he rode through the gate at Ausham, he felt the same thing. Every time, he lost all his doubts. His questions and his worries became like unimportant whispers, childish arguments. He began to think clearly. At the gate of Ausham, he realized, again, that everything Hileshand had taught him about Abalel was true.

Marcus almost sighed with relief. *All right,* he thought. *Good. Perhaps this isn't such a foreign land after all.* The cold, dark room around him began to feel warm and familiar. He knew the one who lived here, the god who bore his sorrow for him.

Ten Alusian males sat at the table in the center of the room. Marcus looked through their faces and then scanned the room a second time. He had assumed Bithania would be here. This was, after all, her quest.

Strelleck inhaled deeply, held it, then leaned close to Marcus and said, "They wait for you to speak. They know Boerak-El has given you words. His words are more important than their own, so they will not speak to you until you have completed your quest by speaking his words."

"Where's Bithania?" Marcus asked quietly.

The creature's frown returned. "It does not matter," Strelleck replied.

Strelleck was mistaken. It did matter.

The purpose of Bithania's quest was to remind the *Aroyaphel* of something they had forgotten. Marcus knew what Boerak-El had given him to say, and he wanted to say it so badly that he wondered if he would be able to say it at all.

"Eserak Amary," Marcus said.

Bithania's father. He sat at the end of the table. He appeared young, somewhere near twenty-five, when he actually approached his two hundredth year. His purpose was not yet completed. Marcus could see the resemblance between father and daughter. Even here among the council, Amary bore a mildly haughty expression that Marcus had seen before.

"Yes?" Amary replied with obvious caution.

"I have a gift. For your daughter." Marcus reached into his bag and pulled out the second book by Adraine El-Ohah. The book about the light. About Abalel. The volume Bithania had not read.

The entire room stared at him.

After an extended period of silence, Bithania's father asked, "Why?"

He sounded as if he sincerely did not know why Marcus would want to give her a gift, when Marcus had a list. A list of reasons he did this. It was a list too long for a single sitting.

"Your daughter," he said finally, when he could, "is beautiful in her thoughts and in her actions. There is not a single quill stroke out of order with her. Every word is true. Every description is perfect. She is not a matchstick. She is not *like* fire—she is fire. Nothing about her is passive. Nothing about her retreats from the task she has been assigned. She hears Boerak-El's voice and follows it, unmindful of the cost and the weight of his words. There is nothing missing in her person, nothing flawed."

No one said a word.

"I don't know if she acted correctly in Ausham," Marcus said. "I don't know if she did what Boerak-El intended her to do, and with no intention of disrespect, simply to be honest with you—I don't care. It doesn't matter to me, because either way, I want her with me."

Marcus walked across the room and held the book out to Bithania's father.

Amary took a deep breath once, then again, and listened to the voice of his god. A long moment passed before he lifted his hand to take the book. "I will accept this gift for her," he said, his voice quiet. "You are..." He stopped and looked around the table at his companions. "You are giving her a way to complete her purpose. You do not know the value of such a gift. It is without price."

"Yes," Marcus said.

Amary stood to his feet. He gripped the book in his hand and drew it near his chest. "Do you understand what you do here?"

He was no longer speaking of his daughter.

Marcus nodded. "Yes, this is *morden*—a symbol of something else. Truth presented in picture and story. I show you something that cannot be expressed with words. And..." He smiled. "By doing so, I win a prize that is far beyond all my efforts."

chapter **39**

$\mathcal{T}$he night before the Feast of the Full Moon, Jonathan Manda, abbot of the School of the Prophets, waited by his fire for a guest.

He knew someone was coming to see him. He knew the man would come late in the evening, long past Jonathan's normal hour of retirement. He also knew the man would surprise him, but Abalel hadn't told him how or why. Jonathan didn't know who the man would be.

So he made himself a pot of tea, built up the fire, and read a book as he waited. The night was cold for early spring. He hoped that whoever this guest was, he was prepared for travel in harsh conditions. They would likely have additional snow come morning.

Jonathan fell asleep before midnight. Two hours later, the book slipped from his hands and banged against the floor, and he awoke with a start, his heart running.

"What? What is it?" He slowly realized he addressed an empty sitting room. "Oh. Dear me." He ran his hand down his beard. *What time is it?* Had he missed his visitor's call?

A few minutes later, his question was answered when someone knocked on the door. Pulling his house robe about him, Jonathan climbed out of his chair and went to answer the summons.

Abalel was correct—the man was certainly a surprise.

"Marcus Hileshand," Jonathan exclaimed. After several moments of open-mouthed study, he remembered to step aside so the man could enter the warmth of the house.

A cold draft of wind gusted in behind Marcus. "How are you?" the young man grinned, stomping snow off his boots. A thin layer of it covered the shoulders of his cloak as well.

When had it started snowing again? "I'm…I am doing well. Surprised to see you. Come in and sit. I will make a fresh pot of tea."

"That would be excellent."

Jonathan made them both tea, and they sat down across from each other at the table by the kitchen door. Marcus answered every question Jonathan asked—what he had been doing over the past months, the last time he had seen Myles, what Entan was doing and how long the boy would be away from Ausham.

Jonathan did not ask about Boerak-El and the Alusian's quest. Not yet. He didn't know how to word the question—and he was hoping his worries were hollow. Looking at Marcus tonight, there didn't seem to be any cause for concern. Marcus smiled without pause. He was happy. He seemed himself, even though Boerak-El had laid claim to him for a period of time longer than five months.

About an hour into their conversation, Marcus stood

up and disappeared into the kitchen. He returned with two additional cups.

"What is this?" Jonathan asked.

Marcus replied, "They wanted to stop at Bryce Gallowar's house first. Entan made a request of them. They will be here shortly."

Marcus traveled with someone?

At Jonathan's curious look, Marcus said, "You remember Bithania, don't you?"

All of Jonathan's feelings of peace and hope were suddenly gutted. He had been imagining Hileshand's joy at the safe return of his son, but with the young man's words, Jonathan didn't know what to think. "You mean the quest is yet unfinished?" How had Marcus been able to return if the quest was unfinished?

"Oh, the quest is finished," Marcus assured him. He picked up the teapot and set it on the nearby stove to reheat. "They travel with me because they desire to do so. It has nothing to do with the quest." He paused, smiled, and said, "Well, not in the way you are thinking."

"My boy, you don't make any sense. Why do they remain with you if the quest is finished?"

Marcus folded his hands behind his head and watched Jonathan across the table. He smiled. There was cause for alarm in his words, but there was nothing alarming in his look. His posture was relaxed, almost teasing. This was the Marcus Jonathan remembered, the man as he had been, before he had heard Boerak-El's voice.

Marcus seemed quite pleased with something. A rich sort of pleasure filled his gaze. "I like their company. Do you know what I have learned on this venture, Jonathan?"

"What have you learned?" Jonathan asked.

"I have learned that Abalel is perfect."

The sincerity behind the words took Jonathan by surprise. He looked at Marcus for a moment, hoping the young man would say more, but all Marcus did was stand up a second time and walk to the front door.

No one had knocked, but Marcus apparently no longer required such conveniences. He opened the door and welcomed into the house the Alusian that traveled with him. Jonathan recognized Bithania's features immediately, even as they were half-hidden beneath the fur-lined hood of her cloak. He had not seen the male before. Marcus introduced him.

"This is Eserak Amary, Bithania's father."

Her father? Marcus had brought her father?

Jonathan had trouble forming words. "Welcome to my home."

Bithania tossed back her hood, flinging snow against the door. Her white face lit with a smile, and Jonathan nearly toppled backward into his chair.

Her voice light, she said, "Entan sends his greetings. He anticipates seeing you again in the next several months. He wanted you to know that it will be months, not years, when he sees you again."

Jonathan's brows rose, and beyond his nephew's name, he didn't retain a word she said. She was smiling. Why was she smiling? "When...when did you see Entan?"

Amary leaned forward. "She hasn't seen Entan. No one has seen Entan. He's in Oarsman with Korstain's son. One does not need to see a man to hear his words. You know this, Jonathan. Entan sent his greetings and she heard them, just as she said. I say, Marcus—is the tea ready yet?"

"Give it a moment more."

"May I sit?"

Marcus nodded, trying not to smile. "You may sit."

Amary tossed his cloak on the hook by the door and sat down at the table. He folded his hands in front of him and looked around the room with curiosity while Jonathan gaped at him. Amary was nothing like Entan. He tied his hair back like a soldier from Tarek, and he carried a sword. His folded hands were riddled with pale lines and puckered indentations, as if he'd lost a fight with a very angry, very determined blackberry vine.

Not a blackberry vine, Jonathan immediately knew. It likely had been something with an intent much fouler than a blackberry vine.

Jonathan felt like a foreigner in his own home. What was this?

Bithania sat next to Marcus, and Jonathan tried not to stare at her. She was beautiful when she scowled; she was devastating when she showed pleasure. Jonathan was certain that in his many years, he had never seen anyone or anything as beautiful as this creature.

Jonathan sat next to Amary because that was the only seat available, and some time passed before he rediscovered the use of his voice.

"Are you here to stay?" he asked Marcus. He didn't know what to expect, as he stared at two full-blooded Alusian sitting at his table.

The young man shook his head. "No, but soon. We actually need to leave tomorrow evening. We have an appointment."

With another quick glance at the Alusian, Jonathan asked, "All of you?"

"Yes."

"And where are all of you going?"

Bithania grinned. It was not a smile but an actual grin—something larger and more delighted than a smile. A noise slid up the back of her throat, and it sounded much like a single roll of laughter.

Marcus leaned back in his chair. Humor gleamed in his eyes. "My brother requires our assistance."

Jonathan examined the young man's face, unable to tell if he was being serious or if he was making sport. The spark in Marcus' eyes made reading him difficult. Warily, Jonathan said, "Your brother is in Oarsman—in Ruthane, heavily surrounded by Korstain's guard. What situation is so dire that he would need your assistance?"

Marcus shook his head. "I am not speaking of Myles."

Now Jonathan was truly confused. Korstain Elah had four sons. The younger two were called Athland and Baenan. Athland was studious and enjoyed learning. If permitted, he would lock himself away in a school somewhere and never leave the grounds. Baenan, on the other hand, enjoyed battle and horses, and Jonathan had always been curious about the boy's name. Korstain had chosen a Paxan name for this son. *Baenan* meant *bringer of light*. It was a name typically ascribed to Abalel.

Athland and Baenan were both in Oarsman as well, and what was true for Myles was true for them; surrounded by Korstain's guard, what harm could reach them? Korstain employed the most experienced, most talented guard of any country. He had seized Ruthane by force and cunning—and had taken steps to ensure that the same thing would not happen to him.

Marcus turned to Bithania. "If Myles is my brother…"

She nodded. "Yes."

"And he has a sister…"

"Yes."

"Then his sister would be my sister, because Myles is my brother."

The smile twitched across her lips again. "Very good, Marcus."

"Which would also make her husband my brother. In a manner of speaking."

"Indeed, your wisdom gleams like the sun."

She teased him. Jonathan felt his mouth drop open. His last interactions with this female had greatly disturbed him, and he had no way of understanding the smile currently on her lips or the light smirking in her eyes. If not for the milky whiteness of her skin, Jonathan could almost imagine her a woman, born of human parents, and he didn't want to think of her that way. It seemed unnatural.

What had happened during her quest?

Marcus looked back to Jonathan. "What has Abalel told you about a man named Jezaren?"

The name hit Jonathan like the butt of a spear.

"He is a messurah out of Galatia, who has—"

"I know who he is," Jonathan said.

chapter 40

Amilia awoke to the weight of Hileshand's hand on her arm. He leaned forward and deposited Westland beside her on the bed, and she realized that the baby was crying. Westland's face was red. Tears ran down his temples as he lay on his back and shook his fists in the air.

She pushed herself up, blinking to clear her vision. "I didn't even hear him."

"He kept you awake last night. You're tired."

He had kept all of them awake last night. They had set up camp some distance off the road to Narsal Bay, and no doubt, everyone within two miles had heard Westland's screams and assumed he was being tortured. Westland usually didn't fuss, but last night, he had raged until first light. Amilia frowned as she lifted the baby off the blankets. *Surely he will not do the same tonight, too.* At least tonight, he would have a bed. He seemed to sleep longer, and cry less, in a bed. Or perhaps she simply heard him less, because she was in a bed.

"Any word from Myles?" She asked the question without looking at Hileshand, for she knew what his answer would be; he would have told her straight away if there were news. But still she asked. She asked every time he awakened her like this. Myles' absence became harder with time, not easier. Myles had told her it would be easier, and he had been mistaken.

I'm tired, she thought, leaning down to kiss the baby's forehead. *I'm only tired.*

Hileshand put his hand on her shoulder. "He will send word."

Send word of what? Hileshand didn't know what Amilia knew. He didn't know that Jonathan Manda had put his hand on Myles' chest and looked through his future. Myles didn't have a future in Paxa, in Tarek, or in any other land. He was to be in Ruthane for a long time—and he didn't want her with him, because of the king. *Send word of what?* she thought again. *Myles is stubborn, and he doesn't want me with him.*

Amilia had been considering a certain outcome for months, and she put words to it without thinking. "The king will not want me," she whispered.

Hileshand didn't say anything. She sensed she had surprised him, but the words were true. Indeed, it was possible he had been thinking about this already and simply hadn't told her. There was only one way Amilia would ever be accepted in a palace. She had been in palaces before.

"And he will not want Westland either." She grabbed the little hand as the baby flailed in her arms. He looked like Myles, but he was not *of* Myles. The moment the king discovered that, he would make arrangements to have Myles' small family stripped from him. This was going to be her life—this emptiness in her chest, this distance from her husband. She felt like her soul was bleeding. Everything was awful without Myles here.

"Amilia, *goshane*," Hileshand said softly, "what is the matter? This sadness is not like you."

"I'm just tired." She glanced at him. "You were right before. I'm tired."

Hileshand headed for the door. Westland cried for a few short moments and fell silent as Amilia began to nurse him.

Hileshand closed the door softly behind him.

Hana, Lenay, and Ella were curled up in one of the beds against the wall, the blankets wrapped around them, cups of tea in their hands. Hana had been telling the girls stories about Myles when he was a baby, and the girls were very pleased to hear them.

Lenay's kitten, Green Marble King, played on the bed. He pounced on a string coming off the corner of the blanket, and Ella giggled, sloshing tea on the sheets. *Green Marble King* was the name of Myles' first dog. *Myles* had come up with that name, not Lenay. That story had been of particular amusement to Hileshand.

Why Green Marble King? he had asked Hana.

He liked your story of the thieves in Ruthane—the time when you and Thaxon Parez uncovered the thieves in the quarry and chased them all the way to the coast. He wanted to hear it every night for three months, so he named the puppy after the story and, of course, made him a king.

But, Hana, Hileshand replied, *it wasn't a quarry. It was a wheat field. There was no green marble involved. Or any marble, of any color.*

Hileshand, you told me it was a quarry!

I said it was a field near a quarry. You were not listening.

He walked to the edge of the bed, and Hana reached a hand out to him.

"Is Amilia all right?" she asked.

Hileshand didn't know the words to describe Amilia's current mood. He frowned and tapped Hana's fingers with his own. "She is not herself."

"It happens sometimes, after a woman has given birth. It will pass on its own."

Hana smiled at him, and he didn't know what he had done to make her happy in this moment, when he was being serious. He scowled at her good humor. "I'm concerned for her. Why are you happy?"

She laughed quietly. "Put away your discontent, my lord. I simply admire the way you adore her. The melancholy will leave. Consider her circumstances—the very small amount of time she has had with you, with Myles, and with good support. Much was handed to her in a short period and then much was removed. She needs compassion, which you are giving her in full."

"And me!" Ella shouted, sloshing her tea again. "I am compassion!"

"Yes, *goshane*. You are compassion, too." Hana ruffled the child's hair.

Lenay peered at Hileshand over the rim of her teacup. "Father," she said somewhat woefully, "I like her, too, you know. I have compassion as well."

Lenay had never hesitated. When she had learned that her mother had married him, from that point forward, he had been called *Father*. She spoke like an adult, and her choice of words made his "discontent," as Hana put it, quite slippery to hold. Hileshand felt his frown soften. "I know, little one. I know you like her, too."

"You like everyone," Ella told her sister, repeating something she'd heard from Hana.

Lenay's eyes darkened with a deep frown. Drawing her teacup close to her chest, she whispered, "Not everyone. I don't like *everyone*."

She had one exception. Whenever Jezaren entered the room, Lenay quieted, and her smile disappeared. She would retreat as far from him as possible and watch him in silence. Ara had spoken to Lenay about her behavior toward Jezaren, but nothing had changed. When Jezaren was nearby, Lenay wasn't comfortable.

Lenay was similar to Marcus—she enjoyed spending time with other people, so her dislike of Jezaren was all the more peculiar. It left Hileshand wondering what had happened during that brief period of time when Jezaren had taken Lenay from Borili's tavern and sent her with Sevoin into Paxa. Something must have happened to injure Lenay's opinion of him. What had he done?

Hileshand sighed, unable to fault the child for her dislike. He was steeped in his own opinion of Jezaren, the messurah who claimed innocence in his lord's assassination. The man was difficult and unsociable. Even after weeks in their company, he acted like a stranger who had never seen any of them before. With Hileshand and Hana, he didn't speak unless addressed. He treated Ara coldly, as if he didn't want her, which made Hana glare and mutter things her younger children shouldn't overhear. It was more than just the discomfort of dealing with multiple cultures and languages—Jezaren did not respond to life as a normal man would respond. This awkwardness went beyond Galatian social customs.

And yet...

Every time Ara looked at her husband, Hileshand could see the adoration. Jezaren could ignore her. He could speak to her tonelessly, as if she were a servant girl and he didn't even remember her name—and nothing changed. The glow in her eyes remained the same. *Why?* What did that little girl see in this man? The more Hileshand observed her interactions with Jezaren, the more he felt he was missing something—that she knew something he did not. So he attempted to keep an open mind, if for no other reason than to satiate his curiosity.

Hileshand looked out the window nearest him. The sky was beginning to darken with the evening. He hadn't seen Ara and Jezaren return from the shop across the street, and he wondered where they had halted on the short journey back. Knowing an Ethollian tracked him, Jezaren never ventured far. It was not like him to be gone for more than a few minutes at a time.

Releasing Hana's hand, Hileshand walked to the bed on the opposite side of the room and retrieved his pipe from his bag. "I will be on the porch," he said.

Hana smiled as she watched him pull on his cloak.

chapter **41**

Hileshand was sitting on the front porch, his boots elevated on the rail, when Jezaren and Ara walked up the street.

Jezaren was holding Ara's hand, and she was supplying him with a steady stream of words that did not pause or have any apparent stopping point. She did not speak like this when she was with the rest of them. Indeed, Hileshand had never heard her say more than one or two sentences together. The change baffled him.

She appeared relaxed, comfortable. He hadn't seen this expression she bore now, and it made her look like the child she was. There was excitement. Delight, even. He could see her as she had been, before the war.

Hileshand turned his attention to the husband. A real smile passed across the messurah's mouth as he listened to her, and Hileshand nearly dropped his pipe. What was this? *What has caused this change?* The answer came to him—the reason Ara's eyes never lost their love, no matter the way Jezaren treated her. It wasn't a change at all, was it? What Jezaren presented to her in private was very different than what he presented in the presence of her family.

Hileshand waited, and sure enough, all signs of pleasure disappeared the instant Jezaren's sharp gaze landed upon him sitting there. The messurah dropped Ara's hand and actually took a step away from her.

I know what you're doing, Hileshand thought. *This is Galatian behavior I recognize.*

The world suddenly seemed like a much simpler place.

"Ara," he called as she and her husband came up the stairs.

The girl startled. She hadn't seen him until now.

"I require your husband for a moment."

She looked at Jezaren quickly. He nodded to her, and with caution, she walked inside the inn, closing the front door behind her.

Narsal Bay was a small town along the southern loops of the Redaman River. The people were fishermen, for the most part, and had been much more friendly toward travelers than the men of several other towns they had encountered. They were five weeks beyond the Paxan border now, and the sentiments and hardships of the Galatian war with Furmorea had not touched this small gathering on the river.

Hileshand motioned with his pipe toward the chair next to him, and Jezaren warily sat down.

For several minutes, they sat in silence. Through the rails of the porch railing, Hileshand watched the people passing by on the street. Jezaren watched Hileshand.

"Did you understand your first lesson?" Hileshand asked finally, keeping his gaze forward.

Jezaren didn't hesitate in his response. It seemed he had given this considerable thought. "You care more for others than you do for yourself."

"Close," Hileshand said agreeably, "but there is more to it, something I do not think you are able to understand right now."

Jezaren's stare didn't falter. The words didn't seem to offend him.

Hileshand could imagine it unwise to offend a messurah. "That is why I am going to let you put it together for yourself. Some things in life you cannot be told by others—you have to learn them on your own. You have to experience them. This is one of those things." He gestured with his pipe. "I am certain of your intelligence and your ability to see truth, even when that truth has not been explained to you." Jezaren had, after all, been able to find the cave at the Furmorean border. He had known Hileshand's name and history. Hileshand still couldn't explain how the messurah had come to know these things. "I suppose you already know that my son Myles is not of my blood anymore than Ella is. Or Ara."

The man didn't say anything, so Hileshand added, "Or you."

That produced a response. Jezaren frowned in the gathering dark, unable to process the reason Hileshand would group him with the others. Hileshand turned away and smiled to himself, greatly amused at this man who did not comprehend the worth Hileshand was ascribing to him.

Hileshand continued, "But that doesn't mean these children aren't mine. If you want to stop an Ethollian, or any other strain of dark magic—*that* is something you have to understand right away. And it also introduces your second lesson."

The porch was quiet.

Jezaren looked out through the porch rails at the street. "You give me a second lesson before I understand the first. Your methods are different than those of Galatian trainers."

"Of course they are." Hileshand nodded.

"Why give a second lesson so quickly?"

It had not been quick. Ella had been calling herself *Lady Hileshand* for weeks. "The innkeeper told me that *atham-laine* have been seen in the hills a few miles from here. I suspect your handler has finally made it through the border. He may be closer than you think."

Ethollian sorcerers could summon creatures called *atham-laine*, the children of the gods of death. Many Ethollians preferred to fight their battles that way, instead of with magic or sword. They would stand back and observe as their enemies were mangled and destroyed by creatures found in myth and legend. Facing an *atham-laine* in some ways was much more alarming than facing a man with magical talent. Creatures of the spirit world were not subject to the rules and laws of the natural world; therefore, the weapons of man could not kill them.

"I do not wish to endanger your wife and children," Jezaren said at last.

The typical Galatian would see no reason to make such a statement. Most men from that land would consider it unbecoming. Something about this Galatian was different. *Courage or great arrogance?* Hileshand shook his head. *Who can say?*

Hileshand pulled the pipe from his lips and looked at the man fully. "Jezaren, I do not fear your handler. I do not fear his finding us. I do not fear his *atham-laine*, or his dark magic, or his association with the gods of death. Do you understand why?"

"I want to understand," Jezaren replied. "That is why I have come to you—to be taught."

Hileshand nodded. "Then accept my words. All of this belongs to me—it is my family. *My* wife. *My* children. They are all mine, because I desire them to be mine. Do you understand? Do you yet have questions for me?"

"How will this teach me how to kill my handler?"

"It will teach you what is most important in killing your handler."

Jezaren scowled.

Hiding a smile, Hileshand said, "Speak your thoughts, Jezaren."

"You are mistaken," the messurah answered.

He was *mistaken*? Hileshand's brows rose. He highly doubted that was the word Jezaren was actually thinking. "Still polite, I see."

"This is not warfare. This is not how you killed the Ethollian. You waylay me. You do not teach me."

"Jezaren, consider your words right now. How will training you in warfare give you what you want? You have been trained in warfare, and clearly, it has not answered your questions."

Jezaren didn't reply, but his expression revealed his thoughts.

"Look." Hileshand set his weight against the arm of the chair and leaned toward the man, lowering his voice.

"Everything I say here is a picture of something else. I speak of things you do not see. When you understand what I am talking about, you will have a much better understanding of how to defeat your handler."

chapter **42**

They left Narsal Bay the next day in the late morning. The sun had cleared the eastern foothills and was casting long shadows across the town.

The journey between Pon-Omen in Furmorea and Port Soren in northern Paxa could be made in six weeks, but Hileshand set a slow pace for his party and, as much as he could, avoided major waterways. After the niessith's attack, and then the river pirates who had sold her to the miron, Amilia did not travel by boat. She simply didn't. Perhaps Myles or Entan Gallowar could have encouraged her, but in their absence, she had difficulty even crossing bridges. She paled in the presence of bodies of water. The pattern of her breathing altered. She would hold on to the sides of the wagon until her hands appeared frozen in place. Watching her, Hileshand felt helpless. He couldn't remove his little girl's fear.

Their final destination was yet undetermined. The city of intent was Port Soren, but Hileshand held to that plan loosely. He didn't care where they were going; he just wanted his sons to be returned to him, healthy and whole.

Marcus he would see again. It could be a year, five years—he had no idea when, but Ausham wanted Marcus, so Marcus would eventually return to the frozen, tree-covered regions of northern Paxa. *But Myles…*Hileshand had prepared himself for the possibility that Myles would never come home. Korstain Elah wasn't blind. He would see the worth in Myles, just as Hileshand had, and then he would make his plans and position Myles according to his own will and purpose. It wouldn't matter what Myles did or did not want. It wouldn't matter what anyone wanted, other than Korstain.

No, with Myles, Hileshand knew better than to plan for a return. He would *hope* for a return, but he would not expect one.

Six miles out of Narsal Bay, they unexpectedly came upon Jezaren's companion, Sevoin. Hileshand hadn't seen him in nearly a week. Until this moment, he had no idea what Jezaren did with him—if the Ruthanian traveled ahead of them or if he lagged behind as a rear guard. Apparently, he scouted the way.

The man was leaning against a heresen tree and watching the Redaman River that flowed about a hundred paces beyond him.

Jezaren spoke with him privately and then motioned for Hileshand to join them.

"Something you need to see, my lord," Sevoin told Hileshand.

The three of them walked down the slope toward the water, leaving the others in the wagon. The road led to the Seddington Bridge, one of the oldest wooden bridges in northern Paxa. King Stellwark had built it nearly two hundred years ago. The piles were covered with various species of moss and red snails. The bridge was tall, set very high above the water, allowing boats to pass beneath it. Hileshand suspected this would be a particularly difficult bridge for Amilia to cross due to its age and appearance.

Sevoin took them within twenty paces of the river and stopped.

"Something is in the water," he said, nodding toward the surface of the Redaman. "It has a noticeable stench and swims backward."

"Backward?" Hileshand repeated.

"I have not seen it clearly, but the bulk of the body seems to move backward, not forward—away from the head."

The three men stood there and waited for the creature to show signs of its presence. Several minutes passed, and the water remained undisturbed. Eventually, a ten-port fishing vessel meandered by, and no one aboard seemed alarmed or cautious. It appeared that they hadn't seen what Sevoin reported.

"We do not have to cross here," Jezaren said to Hileshand. "The next bridge is in Kings Port."

Kings Port was more than twenty miles away. If they crossed here at the Seddington, they could spend the night within the walls of Cendarin, a small town known for its wood carving; otherwise, it would be another night on the ground, and they wouldn't reach Kings Port until tomorrow.

Hileshand looked behind him up the hill. Hana had climbed out of the wagon and was standing now beside the horses, her arms folded against the morning chill. Springtime in Paxa was exceedingly different than springtime in Ruthane, near the southern sea. It hadn't snowed in nearly two weeks, but on days like today, the air still felt like winter.

Hileshand met Hana's gaze, and she smiled.

Jezaren watched him. "We will go to Kings Port."

The river's surface broke into an incalculable number of water shards as a gray mass rose into the late morning light. It was covered with scales like a fish but was shaped more like a niessen-nal—a giant squid. The stench Sevoin had mentioned hit Hileshand hard. His eyes watered. His throat tried to close. *What is that?*

The head looked like that of a beak-nosed lizard, the jaws long and narrow. The creature held in its teeth a large fish that fought violently and started hissing like a cat when it did not find its freedom. Hileshand had never heard such a sound from a fish before. The squid-like creature leaned backward and sank into the water, the fish's screams sucking beneath the surface.

The three men stood on the bank for a period of silence.

"A good decision," Sevoin said, "that of waiting until Kings Port."

When they reached Kings Port the following afternoon, Hileshand made inquiries about the creature in the river.

The bridge keeper was a short, gray-bearded man with only one eye. As he gestured, Hileshand noticed he was missing some fingers as well. They had been chopped off just below the first knuckles.

The man immediately knew what Hileshand described. "Folks call him the balkinmoore. Don't know his rightful name, if he has one. He's *atham-laine*."

The offspring of one of the gods of death. Hileshand looked at the bridge keeper in surprise. "How do you know?"

After an *atham-laine* had been summoned into the natural world by a sorcerer, it commonly sought higher ground. The Redaman River was one of the longest rivers in Paxa, yet the balkinmoore had chosen to stay here, near the coast, instead of heading higher. That was irregular behavior for an *atham-laine*.

The old man shrugged as if the answer to Hileshand's question was common knowledge. "Can't kill him. Those who want to kill him can't find him, and those who don't want to kill him can't kill him when they need to. Don't be concerned, though, boy—you've seen him now. That means he doesn't want to kill you. It's the *not seeing* that can be scary."

Hileshand hadn't been called *boy* in many years, and it amused him. "How long has he been running the river?"

The old man scratched his head. "Don't rightly know. Long time. Folks have been talking about him for generations. He scouts around between Gar'rodd in the south and Dorsare in the north. Some folks post signs along the water—no swimming. No one touches the river here without using a spell or two first. There's stories." He laughed. "Lots of stories of swimmers in the old days. Nobody swims now."

Hileshand remembered something Myles had said about the Redaman River, a warning Bithania once had given him: *Do not enter the water. Do not touch it at all.* She must have been speaking of the balkinmoore.

"I appreciate the warning," Hileshand said, distracted.

Could an Ethollian sorcerer command a creature he had not summoned—something that had been summoned by another sorcerer several years before? Hileshand folded his arms and studied the dark water rushing under the bridge. He did not like the possibility. It was far too open, left too many options.

The bridge keeper nodded. "Heard a story once about a man who lost his leg to the balkinmoore. He was sitting on this very bridge, fishing with a pole, and ol' Balkinmoore rose up and took off his leg without even upsetting his seat. Didn't lose the pole. He just didn't have a leg no more. Some of the men of Edimane come up here and throw dead things into the river—say they're an offering to Etnyse." He snorted. "They should stay in their own lands and worship their own gods of death."

chapter 43

They spent the night in Kings Port.

Just before they left town the next morning, Hileshand stepped into the cobbler's shop on Norsen Street to buy a pair of sturdier boots for Hana. Hers were growing holes in the heels. A few days ago, he had teasingly accused her of ruining her boots with fire walking, trying to ward off evil spirits. Jezaren, overhearing this remark, had seemed to think him serious, for he had turned and given Hana an odd look. His response had been much more amusing than the remark itself.

When Hileshand came out of the cobbler's shop, boots in hand, the bridge was gone.

Only the piles remained, sticking up like jagged teeth in the water. Shards of wood floated downstream and slammed into boats docked nearby. Townsfolk had gathered on both sides of the river. Hileshand heard exclamations and whispered curses. People pointed at the water.

The bridge was gone.

Less than a quarter hour ago, Hileshand had walked Amilia across the bridge himself, her arm in his, and then he had doubled back to make what he had expected to be a quick purchase. He'd almost sent Isule to the cobbler instead, but the sea captain had not fully recovered from his bout of winter lung. He needed to be locked away in a bed in a warm room; when he coughed, his lungs sounded as if they were made of mud.

So Hileshand had come. Only two streets away from the Redaman River, he had heard nothing as the bridge had been torn apart. He stood there on the corner, his arms folded, his jaw tight, and stared at the river.

He grabbed a little boy as the child ran past him. "What happened?"

Breathless and red-faced, the boy sputtered, "The balkinmoore ate the bridge! It ate the bridge—came out of the water and swallowed it whole!"

Hileshand had seen the creature's jaws; the boy's narrative couldn't be completely accurate. The balkinmoore had not *eaten* the bridge.

The boy struggled in Hileshand's grip. "Let me go! I have to tell my father!"

Hileshand released his tunic, and the boy ran off.

Hileshand watched the water and the crowd gathered a safe distance from it. The Seddington Bridge, twenty miles from Kings Port, had stood untouched for hundreds of years. This bridge in Kings Port hadn't been nearly as old as the Seddington, yet it, too, had been in place for years—the balkinmoore did not attack bridges. It left ships intact.

What was responsible for the creature's sudden change of heart?

Hileshand could think of only one possibility.

He had instructed Jezaren and the others to wait for him at the west gate. They were still in town but on the other side of the river—far from the water. The balkinmoore was restricted to the river; it was a useless weapon, unless Jezaren was standing somewhere near the bank. So what was the Ethollian doing? The man had a poor sense of timing. He had missed his target. He hadn't even been close.

Unless—

Hileshand paused. Unless Jezaren was not the target.

He scanned the crowd on the distant bank. Immediately, his gaze collided with a man who stood apart from the rest. His hands were folded loosely in front of him; it was not a position of fear or concern. He did not worry or tremble, as did every other person near him. He paid no attention to the river and the damage the balkinmoore had caused.

When he was certain of Hileshand's study, the man smiled slightly and tilted his head back to look at the sun. The sky responded to his movements, and the air filled with sounds of thunder, though there were no clouds. The day seemed to darken. The temperature lowered as if the wind came off the mountains.

Cries of fear grew among the crowd. Several female voices began to shout incantations and prayers of protection.

The Ethollian was not old; he appeared to be no more than forty. A young man, to be so advanced in his dark arts. Hileshand couldn't tell the man's nationality. He had smooth, dark features that could have been from a handful of countries. When he turned and began to walk away, he displayed a severe limp. His entire torso rotated when he moved his right leg.

He walked west. Toward the gate. Toward Hana and the girls, Jezaren and Captain Isule.

Hileshand almost laughed. *Oh, you'll have to walk faster than that.*

He strode across the street and entered the crowd. The people pressed against him. Thunder rolled overhead, and screams began erupting along both banks. The Ethollian had ignited the beginnings of pandemonium. And then he had just walked away.

Someone nearby muttered about dark magic. Someone else made vows to Abalel in return for protection.

Careful.

Hileshand heard the warning twice before it registered enough to slow his steps. He paused, looking around him with an impatient scowl.

Careful? he repeated hotly. The warning did not fit his intentions. He saw the Ethollian step onto Baker Street and disappear behind a stone archway. The man was not walking quickly. The limp slowed him.

Abalel, why do you tell me to be careful? Be careful of what? He moves like an old man.

Hileshand stepped off the street onto the rocky soil of the riverbank and saw familiar movements out the corner of his eye. He recognized the stance, the swing of the arm, and he pivoted on instinct. The knife bounced along his ribs.

He lunged sideways and caught the attacker by the hair. The man was young, hardly beyond boyhood. The beard growth was still patchy, and the eyes were set too close together, full of surprise. This child had not expected to miss, and he certainly had not expected to be caught. He dropped the knife, lifting both hands in fear.

Heat spread down Hileshand's side.

The warning came again: *Careful.*

Keeping a firm grip on the man's hair, Hileshand twisted around and nearly ran into his second attacker. The man's knife missed his intended target and instead cut through Hileshand's side, just below his ribs.

For a moment, Hileshand stood face to face with the man. This one was young, too. He had freckles like Antonie. *What is this?* Nearly fifty people stood on this side of the river. Fifty immediate witnesses.

Hileshand planted his left fist in the man's chin. The blow knocked his assailant off his feet and into the men behind him. People shouted, the threat of the balkin-moore momentarily relieved.

This had to be one of the worst plans Hileshand had ever encountered. Two inexperienced men attack him in the middle of a crowd?

Hileshand never saw the third man. Something clubbed him from behind. Light and dark flashed before his eyes. He staggered to keep his balance on the loose soil, lost his grip on the first man. He reached for his sword, but rough hands grabbed him and shoved him head first down the embankment, toward the water.

As he fell, Hileshand suffered a quick change of mind. This wasn't a stupid plan at all, was it? The Ethollian didn't need to attack Hileshand with magic—it was far simpler to hire men to do his fighting for him. He then could watch from a distance. Hileshand hadn't anticipated this. He hadn't expected cunning.

He put his hands out and struck the earth hard, breaking skin. He nearly collapsed. The slope was steep; his feet were elevated above his head. The pain rolled through him in a sudden rush, and he couldn't breathe without agony flaring through opposite sides of his body.

Abalel.

He shifted his weight, pulling back on his knees, the heels of his hands in the dirt. The world darkened around him, but he didn't know if it was the results of his wounds or whatever spell the Ethollian had cast on the sky. He could still hear rumbles of thunder. The air still felt piercingly cold.

Abalel, do not let that man hurt my family.

He slid his sword from its scabbard, but the weapon was heavy in his hand. Too heavy for him. The weight felt foreign. The blade tumbled out of his grip and clattered down the short distance into the water. He stared at it, tried to breathe.

A loud shriek filled the air. It drove spikes of color through Hileshand's vision, and he looked left to see the balkinmoore rising out of the river about a hundred paces away, beyond the bones of the bridge that jutted up from the currents. The creature threw itself backward and swam for him, the water breaking across its scales.

Just once, Abalel, Hileshand thought. *Just once, I would like something to be easy.*

He had to get on his feet, get his sword back. He tried to rise, and his boots slipped. His arms trembled. The river seemed to overlap and twist around on itself right in front of him, and he had difficulty remembering which way he needed to go for his sword—was it up? Or was it down, in the water? Where was his sword? *Abalel...* He had been wounded before. He had experienced much worse than this, though in this moment, he couldn't seem to recall any of the details. He had to get on his feet.

Hands grabbed his arm.

"Hurry, hurry!" the man said.

Hileshand recognized the old bridge keeper—the man with only one eye and several missing fingers. The man shouted to someone on the street, and a second man scrambled down to help him. Taking Hileshand's other arm, they dragged him away from the river.

At the top of the bank, Hileshand fought to find his footing. He stood there, bent over, breathing hard, gripping the bridge keeper's shoulder. He was aware of people screaming and running. He had trouble thinking around the pain in his body.

The balkinmoore was almost to the destroyed bridge.

The bridge keeper's companion let go of Hileshand's arm and fled with the crowd. The keeper remained behind, his fingers digging into Hileshand's shoulder.

Hileshand put a hand to his side and felt the blood on his tunic. Nausea rushed through him. His vision moved of its own accord. He needed a plan. He needed to clear his head. *Deep breaths.* The balkinmoore was coming.

A plan. Abalel.

He said it aloud. "Abalel." So much rested on that one word.

The ground itself seemed to be pulling Hileshand down to meet it. He couldn't go down. He had to get to his family. "Abalel, I need you." Powerful words. Words of magic and salvation and the defeat of his enemies.

Sit down, Hileshand.

What? That couldn't be right.

The words came to him again. *Sit down.*

He knew this voice—he just didn't know these words. He was to give up? Now? He had never walked away from a fight in his life. This did not seem like Abalel.

Sit down.

He hesitated. He was having trouble keeping his eyes open.

His hands lowered. *Fine.*

The balkinmoore rose out of the water. The head was grotesque. Almost as ugly as the niessith. It screamed, jaws wide, tentacles flailing across the river. At the force of the creature's roar, Hileshand lost his footing, and he and the bridge keeper hit the ground both together. A horrific stench filled the air.

The street had cleared. Other than the old man crouched and moaning beside him, Hileshand did not see a single other person.

The balkinmoore slapped the water with its tentacles and bellowed displeasure. Pain slid through Hileshand's head like the motions of a knife. The beast was larger than he had realized; when they had seen it swallow the fish at the Seddington Bridge, apparently it had not been fully erect. This creature could have sunk a barge with its weight alone.

This could be a short fight, Hileshand thought. But the balkinmoore didn't attack. It did not approach Hileshand's sword, lying half-exposed in the current. Faint light glowed along the metal.

Fine, Hileshand thought again and did as Abalel instructed. He adjusted his position and sat there on the embankment, groaning for breath. It used to take much more than this to bring him down. Used to be more of a fight.

When the bridge keeper realized they were going to live after all, he leaned close to Hileshand and said, "Your sword has magic. Is that why you threw it—because you knew it would stop him?"

Hileshand had trouble focusing on the man's face. The bridge keeper was an unkempt man who had seen many hardships. His hand with the missing fingers still clutched Hileshand's arm.

"Dropped the sword," Hileshand said.

The creature screamed in frustration, and something within Hileshand's skull came dangerously close to exploding.

"You *did* throw it. I saw you."

Hileshand didn't have the strength to argue. "I need to… to…" His mind refused him. The remaining light of day continued its trickle into darkness.

He couldn't stay sitting here, not when Hana and the children waited at the gate. The Ethollian. He couldn't sit here.

"Easy, my lord." The old man turned, putting his shoulder against Hileshand's to steady him. He wrapped an arm around Hileshand's waist.

Hileshand groaned and leaned forward. *Abalel, this is not what I want.*

The light disappeared.

chapter 44

Delain Speck no longer had a bridge to keep, and he enjoyed a good smoke as much as anyone, so he hoped the wealthy Ruthanian traveler wouldn't mind if he borrowed his pipe.

It was a very good pipe. The maker had carved his initials on the bottom of the bowl. The injured man had good tobacco, too. And thirty gold pieces in his purse. Delain left *most* of them, which he didn't normally do, but the Ruthanian had earned it. Stabbed twice and clobbered across the head, and still he managed to best ol' Balkinmoore. It made for an interesting story.

Delain had one other reason for leaving the man's purse intact—he admired the man's scars. Not only had this traveler survived being knifed yesterday, but he had, apparently, survived many other attempts on his life as well. Sitting beside the bed, pipe in hand, Delain leaned forward and examined the Ruthanian's chest. This fellow must have been a soldier. This particular scar on his ribs had been made with a Galatian ax, a weapon that always left a recognizable scar because the blade was curved. The scar looked like a snake sliding along the ribs.

Another interesting scar had left deep pockmarks in the man's shoulder. This scar had been made with a tri-headed arrow, also a Galatian weapon—one usually carried by pirates and highwaymen. Delain grinned. All night long as he sat here waiting for the Ruthanian to wake, he had been wondering if he himself had shot this man, many years ago. Some of Delain's greater adventures had happened with military patrols along the coast of Ruthane. For a year or two, he had used tri-headed arrows exclusively.

He couldn't tell if the man looked familiar to him or not. With a sigh of gray smoke, he decided it was impossible to know for certain. A retired Ruthanian soldier, who had fought pirates. Delain grinned. *This is very interesting.*

Delain had left the sea behind many years ago. He had lost his eye, lost his fingers, had drunk himself into stomach trouble, and had eventually returned to his homeland of Paxa to be a bridge keeper. No one thought to look for an old pirate on a bridge. On a boat, yes. But on a bridge? No one cared about the man who tended a bridge, as long as he did his job without complaint.

The unconscious Ruthanian wouldn't think Delain a pirate. He would think him brave. Delain grinned. *Well, it's true, isn't it? Just look at me. I went down the hill, and I saved him.* That would be worth the weight of this man's purse—all of it. Delain deserved every coin.

But no. He wouldn't do that. Delain could respect a good scar when he saw it.

Warsen the physician had come and sewn the

Ruthanian back together last night. The cut in his ribs was a deep scrape. The cut in his side was a shallow puncture. Warsen had said some sort of drivel about keeping the Ruthanian clean and in bed. Delain rolled his eyes. What did physicians know? They were handy with needle and thread, and that was all. Delain had survived many knife wounds. He had lost his fingers to a knife—and not once had he appeared weeping before a physician. They pretended to know things, but the steady hand and pretty stitchery were really all they were good for.

It was morning now, but the Ruthanian hadn't stirred. He snored with violence, which made Delain enjoy his company even more, for men who snored could be trusted. Every pirate, former or otherwise, knew this for a fact.

The man did not wear any jewelry. He'd had a knife in his boot and another in his cloak. Delain let him keep both of those, too. What would he do with another knife? He had more knives than the king of Paxa—than *all* the kings of Paxa there had ever been. Someday when he died and this house passed to someone else, they would go through Delain's things and discover he was a much more interesting person than any of them had thought.

The traveler's sword, the one fashioned with magic, Delain had left in the river. He had never heard of a weapon that could keep the *atham-laine* at a distance. He would have returned for the sword—he would have—if he'd been a man of a little more courage. He could pull a man away from danger, when he could see the danger clearly and could judge the distance, but returning for the man's sword? The very sword that kept the balkinmoore in the water? *Well.* Delain did not run from anything, but neither did he forget his age.

He and his pirate-fighting unconscious friend shared one another's company for two more hours before the injured man began to groan. He opened his eyes and blinked in the daylight that swam in through the windows.

"Hello again," Delain greeted him. "You have decided to live after all. This is good news."

The Ruthanian stared at him for a moment and then looked through the small room. "Where am I?" His voice was rough with sleep and the remains of a difficult night.

"This is my house." Delain waved the pipe. "This is the front room. Redaman Street is right through those windows there. You have not come far."

Concern tugged the man's brows together. "How long have I been here?"

"Several hours. A day. Overnight." Delain pointed at the man's ribs. "You have some fine stitch work there. Took the physician a long time. He was expensive, too. I paid him from your purse. Hope you don't mind. Remember—he was expensive."

The man tried to sit up, wincing, and Delain stood from the chair and helped him reposition himself on the bed, his legs over the side.

"I was traveling with others," the Ruthanian rasped. "Do you know what happened to them? Did something happen?" Making a face, he put his hand against the bandage on his side. Grimaced.

Delain drew on the pipe and shrugged. "Don't know anything, now that there's no bridge. I have lost my source of news. Used to be that I knew everything that happened in this town." He scoffed. "Now I don't know what will happen. I suppose they'll rebuild—very carefully. And probably hire a magician or two to stand guard. Are you a magician? I saw your sword."

"Was there any...?" The Ruthanian hesitated and re-phrased the question. "Is the town intact? Were there disturbances of any sort?"

Delain chuckled. "You mean, other than *you* and ol' Balkinmoore? No. Kings Port hasn't had this much excitement in years. Where did you come by a magic sword, boy? I have never seen anything like that." And Delain Speck, retired pirate, had seen many, many things of interest.

"Nothing happened last night?" The man was repeating himself now.

Delain looked at him pointedly. "I'm answering your question. You can believe me. Nothing happened. No one died. You were the highest point of excitement, and you didn't even die."

The man blinked at him a few times and finally appeared to relax. "Good."

"What are you all worried about, anyway?" Then Delain remembered something. "I don't know your name. I'm called Delain Speck." He was just *called* that. It was not the name his father had given him. He had left that name, the first name, behind in Ruthane. He smiled as he thought about it. In his youth, he had been rather famous.

"I'm Hileshand." The Ruthanian looked through the room again. "I need my clothes. Where are they?"

"Hileshand," Delain repeated in surprise. He *did* know this man.

Hileshand looked at him abruptly, and Delain shrugged, pretending disinterest. "I have heard that name before. I think. You...are from Ruthane?"

The man spoke Paxan with a Ruthanian accent—

Delain knew exactly where he was from. The age, the build, the number of interesting scars—it could be the Hileshand he remembered. Delain had never met him in person—not to his knowledge, but among Delain's company, there had been many stories about this man. After yesterday, Delain no longer wondered if all of them were true.

Where had Hileshand obtained a sword that possessed magic? No wonder he had been such an admirable foe on the coast—he had magic. Magic was not commonly found among Ruthanian soldiers. Men of magic worked in the temples; they typically did not fight pirates.

"Clothes," Hileshand repeated.

"I will get them for you." Delain stuck the pipe back in his mouth. "But I will need to rewrap your wounds before you dress. The expensive physician left salve that is sure to sting. He left rhusa bark, too. You should use it. Help your wounds heal faster."

"I know what rhusa bark is," Hileshand answered. "And absolutely not."

Delain snickered with delight. Rhusa bark *did* help a wound heal. It also made certain men sicker than a first timer on a ship, and Delain felt a severe sort of pleasure knowing Hileshand was one of them.

Pushing up out of his chair, Delain went to retrieve the man's clothes.

chapter 45

Hileshand felt the weight of his purse and glanced at the old man across the room. Delain had not taken all of it, or even most of it. Peculiar for a thief. He had, however, helped himself to Hileshand's pipe, and remembering the state of the old man's teeth, Hileshand was content to let him keep it.

Hileshand needed to leave. There was no extra time, yet at the door, he turned back. "Thank you. I am in your debt." He thought of his purse and smiled a bit. *But not very much debt.*

The old man grinned, clearly pleased. "Imagine that," he said. Then he reined back his odd excitement and said politely, "Thank you for gettin' yourself injured on my doorstep."

Hileshand moved across the street like a grandfather, one of those old men who reach for grandchildren and great-grandchildren instead of a sword. As long as the motions were slow, he could walk. As long as he took shallow breaths, the wounds in his torso didn't scream at him. They protested every movement, slow or not, but he could ignore their voice.

He stopped at the top of the riverbank, looking out across the river that now ran peacefully. There were no signs of the balkinmoore. With the exception of the destroyed bridge, the area appeared undisturbed. The boats had been removed from the nearby dock and taken to another dock farther down river. He could see them through the trees.

He did not see his sword.

He *did* see an Alusian.

Bithania Elemara Amary sat on the soil halfway down the bank. She was wrapped in her traveling cloak, the hood hanging down her back, and she was leisurely smoking a pipe.

After staring at her profile a moment, Hileshand looked in the direction of the west gate. If Bithania was here, surely that meant Marcus' presence as well. *Surely.* He stood there, hesitating. Then he grimaced and made his way carefully down the slope.

She didn't look at him, nor did she greet him. "Why do you like this?" she asked, holding the pipe away from her. "This does not amuse me, and the smoke is disturbing. This cannot be healthy for the lungs. It could, in fact, be the reason you snore so incessantly."

"Where is my son?" Hileshand asked.

She lifted her head and looked at him, shading her eyes in the late morning light. "Which son?"

Something about her was different, and he wasn't certain it was a positive change.

She smiled at him beneath the shadow of her hand and greeted him properly. "Hello, Hileshand. You're looking remarkably well. Remarkably. And in all likelihood, the greatness you display this morning is because you did not smoke this horrible thing last night." She scowled at the pipe and shook it a few times.

By Abalel himself, what was this?

Standing to her feet, she swished the grains of dirt off the back of her cloak and held the pipe out to him. "Here you are. To replace the one you just gave away. I trust you will find nothing amiss with *my* smile."

She gave him the unfamiliar turn of her lips again, smiling in a mocking, pretty sort of way, blinking her eyes several times, and he didn't realize he was staring like an imbecile until she shook the pipe in his face. "Take it! Quickly! Before I decide to curse it."

He didn't move. "What are you doing?" he managed. The question had to be asked. This boggled him.

"I am *attempting* to give you a gift. Though I do not know why you would want this. It is foul and revolting."

A gift. "Oh." A gift meant something to an Alusian. It was important. He watched her and eventually reached out to take the pipe from her hand. "Thank you."

Bithania smiled at him slyly. "I forgive you for your previous ignorance."

This new Bithania was just as disturbing as the old one.

She squatted down on the slope and slapped the earth with her open hand. His sword jumped out of the ground like a surprised cat. She caught the blade and turned it, offering Hileshand the weapon's hilt. He accepted it without words. She slapped the earth again, and the boots he had purchased for his wife responded in the same manner as the sword. One shot up on her immediate left; the other shot up a short distance to the right, and she had to reach out and grab it.

Straightening, she tied the boot laces together and said, "I will carry these. You have been injured."

"You..." Hileshand cleared his throat. "Where is Marcus?"

"Marcus and the others wait for you at an inn on the other side of town."

She didn't seem concerned as she answered his questions. She didn't tell him to hurry. She wasn't alarmed. Hileshand let his breath out slowly, trying to dispel his expectations of evil and harm. *What happened?*

"What of Jezaren?"

"What of him?"

Frowning, he asked, "Is he all right?"

"Why do you ask about him?" She wasn't smiling now. "What is your interest in Jezaren?"

"Why will you not answer my question?"

She waited.

"He asked to travel with me, which I'm certain you know."

Bithania shook her head, frustration building in her gaze. "Do you know what it means when a Galatian asks for rights of travel?"

"He wants to learn from me."

She muttered something he didn't understand and said, "Fine then. And have you been teaching him?"

"Yes." At least Hileshand knew the correct answer to that question.

"Do you know how many men he has killed, Hileshand? He is not friendly toward you. He does not compel a sense of safety and trust within you, or within those who know you. *Why* do you ask about him, Hileshand? Answer the question. Why do you include him in the group traveling with you?

Yes. That was her true question. He could see the fire in her eyes. "What happened, Bithania? Is he all right?"

"The Ethollian was successful in his quest."

Hileshand stared at her. "What?"

Bithania turned and glanced across the water to the opposite embankment. It was as if she could see where the Ethollian had stood yesterday. "This Ethollian is different than the others, Hileshand. He has wisdom and skill in strategy, as you briefly experienced. His level of skill is equal to Jezaren's level of skill. That is how it is done—the handler must be an able match. He knows that you are capable of besting him, and so he took measures to remove the possibility. He will not fight you himself. A different strategy is required."

"Tell me what happened. What does this mean—the Ethollian was successful?"

A moment passed in quiet.

Bithania studied him as he studied her. Then she stated, "Ara has lost her husband."

The words physically hurt him.

"His handler will take him into Ruthane—"

His heart staggered a second time. "He's alive?"

"Yes. Jezaren is alive."

If he was alive, there was still hope. Hileshand's thoughts jumbled, and he tried to sort them. "How is he still alive? His handler intended to kill him."

"His handler did not intend to kill him," she answered.

She was being most unhelpful. For the first time, he noticed that passersby had stalled on the streets on either side of the river. People stared at them. He heard whispered voices. The presence of an Alusian always drew attention, but *Bithania's* presence drew it the way dry brush drew fire. At the sight of her face, men forgot their names.

Bithania ignored the townspeople. "Do you believe Jezaren killed the governor?" she asked suddenly.

Hileshand's brows lifted. "Why would you ask me that? Do you not know the answer?"

It took a moment for his thoughts to obey him and allow him to consider the question. The topic felt distant, like something that no longer mattered. Hileshand rubbed his face with one hand and knew there had to be a reason Bithania would ask such a thing. She had a purpose.

Did he believe Jezaren was innocent?

"I don't know," he replied. "He speaks of his innocence."

"You don't believe he speaks the truth?"

Hileshand scowled at her. "I don't know," he repeated.

The knife wounds complained against him. He needed to sit down, but even when he was off his feet, his needs met, what then? He wouldn't have full relief. *Abalel, I don't understand.* His heart broke for Ara.

"What happened?" he asked.

This time, in typical Alusian fashion, Bithania answered in scattered detail. "No one was injured. Many of those nearby on the street did not even know what occurred right beside them. The Ethollian knew how to manipulate him, for Jezaren wished to spare Ara's life."

And the Ethollian had kept his part of the bargain? He had let Ara live? That did not adhere to Hileshand's understanding of Ethollian thinking. *I should have been there. I should have suspected.* He had been separate from them for only a few minutes. "The Ethollian didn't hurt Ara?" He had to be certain.

"Yes, he did hurt her. She knows she is the reason for Jezaren's loss."

That shy, wounded heart didn't need any more pain. It was not her fault.

Bithania stepped close to him. "Hileshand," she said with urgency. "Do you understand what the Ethollian has done? The spell he used is a difficult spell to break, for it is an accepted spell—the one to be spelled must agree to receive the spell, which Jezaren did. Understand that he made a significant sacrifice for his wife. Perhaps that knowledge will improve your opinion of him."

"Do you know what the Ethollian will do to him?" He didn't appreciate her reluctance, and he urged, *"Bithania."*

She pulled in a full-lunged breath and stood there quietly, looking at him. She inhaled a second time and said, "It doesn't matter what happens to him."

"Why? Why is that?"

"Because you are not his father."

Heat spread through him. "He is married to my daughter."

"That does not make him yours."

"Bithania..." Why was she being so very difficult? His head was pounding. Her image seemed to be shifting and shimmering in front of him. One way or another, this conversation was about to end. "What do you want me to say? I don't know with certainty whether or not he killed the governor—I simply don't know. And if that isn't a satisfactory answer, then I will tell you no, I don't think he did. If he had killed the governor, why would he search me out and ask to travel with me? Why would he have fled his handler? He is capable and intelligent—if he killed his lord, the assassination would have been perfect, and no one would ever have known his hand was in it. That is my answer—he didn't do it. Is that enough for you?"

He thought of Ara and her delight in her husband. He remembered the tender way Jezaren had held her hand.

Bithania inhaled. Deep. Full. An Alusian breath. "I am to ask you if you will consider him yours."

He looked at her.

She hesitated. "Abalel," she said and then repeated the name, as if it were a foreign word and she wasn't certain of the pronunciation: "Abalel desires to know if you consider Jezaren your son, if you think of him as you think of Marcus and Myles. You have the opportunity to see him become more than he is, but *you* have to make the decision. Do you claim him? Or will you allow him to be claimed by another?"

Her eyes narrowed. "Abalel will abide by your decision. It is in your hands."

She spoke of Abalel as she would speak of Boerak-El, as if she had heard his voice. Hileshand considered that, but the thought couldn't stay with him long.

Marcus and Myles were his sons; they carried his blood. Nothing could break that commitment within him. Nothing could stall it or injure it or cause it to fail. They were his sons—his boys. How could he make the same decision about another man, especially when that man was Jezaren? It was not a commitment that could be randomly assigned. Every day, he felt the distance between himself and his sons the way he felt a break in his skin—the knife wounds in his torso. Their absence was a constant ache within him. The commitment he made to his children was a bond of joy and of sorrow. How could he commit his heart and his strength to a man like Jezaren?

Yet how could he *not* make such a commitment? There was only one answer he could give Bithania—only one, if what he had been trying to teach Jezaren was true and real, something to be trusted. The foundation of every truth Hileshand possessed was the commitment Abalel sought from him now.

Hileshand reached up and put fingers to the bridge of his nose, closed his eyes. The swimming sensation in his head grew worse, so he opened them again and tried to breathe. He grimaced at the trembling in his legs. "Yes," he said simply. "I will consider Jezaren as I consider Marcus and Myles—so he will know that what I am teaching him is trustworthy."

Apparently satisfied, Bithania turned and walked up the slope. The crowd gathered on the street scattered at her approach.

"You need to lie down," she said over her shoulder, Hana's boots dangling from her hand.

chapter 46

Hileshand made it halfway down the street before Bithania turned back to take his arm. He flinched as she touched him, remembering what her touch had done to Marcus in Ausham. She had dropped his son to the ground with nothing more than the weight of her hand.

Yet at her touch now, nothing horrific occurred. Hileshand remained on his feet. He did not sense anything amiss or beyond the ordinary within him.

As if she had been doing such things for years, Bithania entwined her arm through his and told him to lean on her. He realized she was trying to help him.

"Thank you," he said, embarrassed.

Every person who saw them stopped and stared. Whispers flowed like mountain streams down both sides of the street. Hileshand wondered how Marcus had managed to endure six months of this—the gaping mouths, the startled expressions, the fear of death in every person's face. He glanced at Bithania beside him and found himself thinking a little more softly toward her. Perhaps not all of her temperament came from her Alusian blood. Perhaps some of it had been learned on streets such as this one.

He decided to be gracious. "How is Marcus?" he asked, wondering if she'd answer.

"You are often in his thoughts," she replied.

She had arranged for a private ferry to take them across the river. The small, flat-bottomed boat was manned by a tense, scrawny individual who kept his eyes on the water. Bithania sat beside Hileshand on the boat seat, her hand on his arm, and talked about the spring rains.

He studied the side of her face. He hadn't expected to see her again. What was she doing here? And how long did she believe she was staying? She seemed calm, and it did not make sense to him. In all of his dealings with her, he had never seen her so relaxed.

On the other side of the river, she took him to an old moss-covered inn that sat near the western wall of Kings Port, not far from the gate. The side street was quiet, and every building for the length of the street was surrounded with ornate trees and small pieces of garden. Available spaces between walkways had been filled with flowers.

The inn itself had not seen as much care and concern as the grounds surrounding it. The paint was peeling off the front porch. Several of the windows on the first floor had lost their shutters, but the nails were still there, poking crookedly out of the walls. The entire building had a *tousled* look, as if it had never quite recovered from some drunken stupor several years ago.

He looked at Bithania, and she shrugged. "They serve very good ale here."

"Who chose this place?"

"Marcus did—because of the ale."

The front room was empty, save for two middle-aged servants who became like statues when they saw Bithania. It was enough of a reaction that Hileshand frowned at them, but Bithania didn't seem to notice that anyone else was in the room. She took Hileshand around the tables and down a back hallway. Doors lined the left wall, windows the right; the last door was situated some distance from the others, and this was the door Bithania opened.

Hana met him first. She was there as the door opened, as if she had been reaching for the handle. She was kissing Hileshand before he could complete his step, and he sucked in breath as the wound pulled in his ribs.

She instantly reduced her displays of affection. "Are you all right? Hileshand…" Her hands on his shoulder. She took hold of him and brought him in, away from the door. "Come in and lie down."

He had not been mothered in a long time. There was sweet concern in her eyes, worry running across her brow. He wished for privacy, so he could remove the signs of her fear. He hurt, but he wasn't dying—and he could prove it to her, as a new husband should.

Ella slid off the bed against the far wall and ran to him. Hana told her to be gentle. Amilia had the baby in her arms. Hileshand kissed her forehead and touched Westland's cheek. The baby stared up at him with clear blue eyes.

"Westland thinks you shouldn't ever do anything like that again," Amilia whispered. "Westland requires you to come home every night. You are to stay away from sharp objects and evil men. Westland feels quite strongly about these things, and he intends to write a contract, which you will be forced to sign."

"The baby is very wise," Hileshand answered, his hand on her shoulder.

When he looked through the room, there were three faces he did not see. Marcus, Ara, and Lenay were not present.

Hana told him, "Ara thought he was Myles when she first saw him."

"Me, too!" shouted Ella, who had never seen either twin before yesterday. "He looks just like Myles!"

Hana glanced down at Ella with a faint look of humor and then returned her attention to Hileshand. Warmly, she said, "Myles has always been very good with his sisters. Marcus appears to be the same."

His sisters, she said. Hileshand saw the look in her eyes. Hana did this to him on purpose. She knew how he thought, what moved his heart, and she said these things now with intent—to remind him of her love. And for her effort, he was going to remove all her worry. He hadn't been injured *that* severely.

He remembered to speak. "Where are they?"

"The back porch," Hana replied. "He took them away just a few minutes ago."

Ella grinned and wrapped her hand around Hileshand's thumb. "I was asleep. I like to sleep. I didn't hear him wake her up."

As she stared up at him, her grin faded into a trembling line. He watched as her eyes welled.

Her voice softened. "Are you going to die?" The question was heartrending in its concern.

"I'm not going to die, *goshane*." He rushed the words. He had to tell her that right away, before the sound of her voice and the sight of her eyes impeded his ability to speak. He forced a shrug through his shoulders, tried not to wince at the movement. "This? A scratch. Naught more than a bruise—like stubbing your toe. No one dies from stubbing his toe."

Her grip tightened around his thumb. She didn't say anything more, and he wished she would speak, just to relieve the pressure he could see building in her face.

"Ella." He shook her hand, squeezed her fingers, saying calmly, "Ella Hileshand."

She stilled.

He didn't know how long those two words would work their magic and affect her with such strength, but he would use them every day. And he would continue to use them, even long after the magic had become commonplace. The distress bled from her eyes. The smile returned. *Little Ella Hileshand.* It didn't matter what her fear was. It didn't matter the worry—all he had to do was remind her of her name, and everything else was immediately forgotten.

"Don't worry, little one," he said.

Hileshand looked at Bithania next, and the Alusian shook her head. "They're at the end of the hall." She pointed. "Right through that wall. He would not take them far."

The inn had two sitting areas. The main dining room overlooked the front street. There were curtains on the windows, and the air smelled like fresh bread and winter ale. The secondary sitting room was a glass-enclosed porch that overlooked one of the inn's many flower gardens. A wooden walkway stretched through the greenery and bright colors, running the length of the wall from one backyard to the next.

The enclosed porch was six steps away from the suite of rooms Marcus had reserved for his ever-expanding family. From the porch, Ara could sit at the table and see her mother's door. It could not be safer for her. Six steps—that was all. In his quest to put her at ease, Marcus had brought Lenay along as well, and he wasn't certain the girl truly understood what a *twin* was. Sitting on the floor, she looked at him and smiled, went back to playing with her kitten, looked at him again, smiled happily. Did she realize he wasn't Myles? He couldn't tell.

In certain ways, Lenay seemed almost untouched by the Furmorean war. She was still a child who acted like a child. The same could not be said for her sister Ara. Ara's husband had been taken from her yesterday. Marcus and Bithania had come upon them at the west gate shortly afterward, and Ara had been still and silent. Those were the only signs of grief she displayed. She hadn't cried. She hadn't mourned. There had been only the stillness and the absence of her voice.

Marcus brought the girls cinnamon bread and tea from the kitchen, and then he settled in at the table with Ara. They sat for a long time in silence. As he watched her from across the table, Marcus wondered if Ara was capable of showing emotion. She had a look he had seen before—there was death in her eyes, and it was not new death. This was something that had existed long before yesterday.

Boerak-El was the god of sorrow. Marcus couldn't seem to get away from that. The longer he was with the Alusian, the more adept he became at seeing the sorrow in others and feeling compassion. He could see the sorrow in Ara so strongly that he could actually feel it himself, to a small degree.

Myles had told him that Ara was frank. When something needed to be said, she said it. So Marcus would do the same and see how she responded.

As Lenay tried to feed cinnamon bread to her kitten, Marcus asked Ara, "What do you think of Amilia?"

Ara didn't look at him. Her gaze remained on the porcelain cup that was cooling in her hands. "She doesn't say very much to me." The words were quiet.

Amilia was in mourning. Ara was not observing her at her best. In truth, Marcus had never seen Amilia around other women—considering the life she had known, it was possible she didn't see a reason to be friendly.

"Do you know where Myles met her?"

"In Tarek," Ara said.

"Yes, in Bledeshure." Marcus nodded. "Amilia was a prostitute. She was owned by a businessman named Olah."

Ara did look at him then, and he gathered that this story she had yet to hear. Why hadn't it been explained to her? Hileshand would not have been blind to her need to hear it.

"They called her the Jewel of Bledeshure," Marcus continued. "Every man in Tarek knew her name and told stories of her. She was taken as a slave at a much younger age than you and lived that life for a much longer time. The men of your country avoided her and ridiculed her, while Tarek promoted her. She was at home in palaces and the private chambers of important men."

He paused. He glanced at Lenay, and for propriety's sake, he lowered his voice. "Westland is not of Myles' blood. The blood he carries is that of a client, who will never know his moment of passion produced something that will endure." Indeed, that nameless man had a purpose in life that was far beyond anything he had ever dreamed of. His offspring was suddenly in line for the Ruthanian throne.

Marcus set his hands on the table, lacing his fingers together. "Do you know why I say these things to you?"

She didn't avert her gaze. "No."

He smiled. Myles had been accurate in his description of her. She was very frank. "The first time Amilia saw Myles, it was in the North Square, where the slaves are sold. Amilia saw him that one time and fell in love with him because of how he treated your mother, even in a time of hardship and pain. My father spent a good deal of time and effort trying to find your mother, and he bought Amilia from her owner when he discovered she knew of Hana's sale. That is how she came to be with us." He smirked at various memories of that time and said, "She was terrified. Do you know why?"

Ara shook her head. She was listening.

"She thought Myles would reject her. He is Furmorean—raised in that land, and she had become something no Furmorean would love." Marcus watched Ara's face as he said these things. "She was pregnant with another man's child. She thought she had nothing of worth to give him."

Marcus saw Ara's sudden frown.

"But Myles loves no one more than he loves Amilia. He loves his son. It does not matter to him that Westland was fathered by another. It will not affect his heart or their future together. He knows what he wants, and he wants her."

"Why does he love her?"

The transparency of the question caught him by surprise. Marcus chose to be as frank with her as she was with him. "Why does Jezaren love you?"

The girl became like a fence post. Stiff. Quiet. She swallowed. "I belong to him."

Marcus could only imagine how his father had reacted when he'd heard that statement the first time. He nodded. "Amilia belongs to Myles. He chose her. She is his. And he is proud of her. You should hear the way he talks about her. You should see the way he looks at her. You would think him a poet." Marcus laughed quietly. "The last time I saw him, he was *ridiculous*. You think *she* mourns for *him*? You should see him. You would think him a different man."

The corner of Ara's mouth rose. The darkness in her eyes momentarily lightened.

"Jezaren knows about you what my brother knows about Amilia—that there is *great* worth here, that you are deserving. You should believe him, for he wouldn't lie to you." Marcus didn't need to know the man to understand the truth of that statement; all his information concerning Jezaren came from another source.

Jezaren the messurah. Jonathan Manda had almost slid out of his chair when Marcus had told him that Jezaren was Hileshand's son-in-law.

You can't be serious. Do you know who Jezaren is?

Yes, Marcus did.

He saw movement out the corner of his eye and turned to look through the window. A man was coming up the walkway, approaching the inn's garden. He was middle-aged and fair, tall and sinewy. There was no beard or other physical markings, no visible weapons. His cloak was dark brown, like tree bark. *Of course,* Marcus thought.

Marcus looked back to Ara. "You are worth saving. I will help Jezaren prove this to you. Starting now."

He stood up. She looked at him, immediately apprehensive.

"Stay," he told her, gesturing toward the table. "Drink your tea. I will be back."

She blinked at him. "I don't understand."

"Do you remember when the Ethollian promised your husband he would not hurt you?"

"You weren't there. You…couldn't have heard him."

Marcus shrugged like it didn't matter, because it didn't. "The Ethollian did not speak the truth. He has sent you a little gift."

He started walking backward toward the door to the garden. He smiled at Ara. "But you do not have to worry about it. You can just sit there and observe the steps Abalel has taken to provide for your safety."

chapter 47

Marcus hadn't had a good fight in months, and he was looking forward to this one. He needed a distraction, something capable of securing a good amount of his energy and attention.

Folding his arms, he leaned up against the porch window and waited for the tree sucker to reach him.

Watch the head, Bithania had told him. *They like the eyes the best.*

Marcus would try to remember that.

"Ho there, friend," he said as the creature made to pass by him.

The boots froze on the walkway. The agile body stopped its forward motion, and the pale head swung around toward him. Green eyes.

Makes sense, Marcus thought.

"Juniper," he said. Then he snapped his fingers and held up his hand. "Wait, wait—an orange tree. I haven't seen an orange tree since...How old was I? Sixteen? Seventeen? I can't remember. I was on the Passaline Islands with my father, and there was an orange grove. They had lemons, too, and a fountain of green marble. You should have seen it. Very beautiful."

It truly was remarkable how much this thing looked like a man. Marcus would not have been able to tell it was anything else, but Bithania had given the information to him as a peace offering of sorts, and he had accepted. She had described the face and the cloak, had detailed its appearing and how the Ethollian had sent it. No one would be able to tell these creatures in a crowd, which made them deadly. They weren't necessarily skilled fighters, but they didn't need to be.

The green eyes narrowed, and a deep-throated gurgle rose in the creature's throat. Marcus imagined it to be a noise of offense, and he nodded.

"I know, I know. I have no respect." He shoved the creature's shoulders. Both hands. Both shoulders. The thing stumbled back a step and snarled at him. "What are you going to do about it?"

Watch the head, Bithania had said.

The tree sucker pushed off the walkway and flung itself at his throat. Marcus ducked and caught a boot in the face. He didn't see it coming until it was upon him, and the force of the blow propelled him backward into the window. The pane rattled in its frame.

When his vision had cleared, two tree suckers stood in front of him. There would be three. Bithania had told him that, too. But she hadn't mentioned they traveled *together*, as one person, before they began fighting in sets. They had magic that enabled their traveling abilities; the appearance of a man, obviously, did make things simpler. Three as one. *That would have been helpful to know, girl,* he thought, taking a moment to put his fingers to his cheek and nose. The skin was broken. He was bleeding at a steady pace. He could feel warmth dripping off his jaw.

"Already bleeding. First blow, and already bleeding." He looked at the two creatures in front of him and grinned. This was what he had needed. He'd been needing this for weeks. "Well done, boys. Let's have it again." He pulled the knife from the sheath on his belt.

He clipped the first one across the hand as it lunged at him. The second died as it ran for the porch door and caught Marcus' knife in the side of the head. The blade made a peculiar sound as it penetrated the skull, like an ax against wood. The creature crumpled to the walkway. Once they were dead, their power dissipated. This one would have to be buried in its current form—as a man.

Marcus pulled his sword.

He felt a cool, earthy presence behind him and spun around in time to block a sharp metal rod that came at his face. The third tree sucker had overextended its swing, and as it stumbled, Marcus grabbed it by the throat. He dragged it around and flung it into the one with the injured hand. They went down in a heap of boots and brown cloaks and flailing arms. They looked exactly alike and wore the same clothing.

Standing near the porch door, he leaned up against the window, putting a shoulder to it, and watched as the tree suckers tried to untangle themselves. There was no reason for him to rush this. He was going to enjoy it while it lasted.

The one with the poker managed to free itself first and jumped to its feet. Its ear was mysteriously bleeding, as if it had cut itself in the fall. The sucker squealed at a pitch that hurt Marcus' ears and rushed him with the poker. For a few moments, something resembling a first-year fencing lesson took place. The sucker handled the poker the way an angry eight-year-old would.

"Lower your elbow," Marcus instructed. "Rotate your arm down. You'll have much better luck if you don't hold your arm out like it's a goose wing."

The creature hissed and whined, clearly displeased.

The second tree sucker, the one with the bleeding hand, slid along the wooden slabs of the walkway toward the porch door. Marcus blocked another awkward poker swing, then bent down and jerked a knife from his boot. He flung it at the creature's injured hand and pinned it to the boards. The sucker started hissing.

But not for long.

"There you go," Marcus said. "Be brave now."

The sucker began to melt back into its original form. It did not like it, and it squawked loudly, struggling to free its hand. It wasn't quick enough.

A tree suddenly sprang up in the middle of the walkway, its roots breaking the boards and penetrating down into the soil. It cast a thick shadow across the porch. The upper branches stood beyond the second floor of the inn—a tall tree, advanced in years.

Marcus scowled. "An oak tree. I didn't guess oak."

The remaining tree sucker waved the poker wildly. Marcus sighed. This was not turning into the fight he wanted.

Throwing the poker at Marcus' head, the tree sucker turned and ran. Marcus couldn't allow it to leave. Once summoned by a sorcerer, tree suckers would continuously seek out the one they had been summoned for. The creature would return for Ara eventually.

Marcus gave chase.

The sucker fled down Vale Street, turned right on Norsen, and headed straight for the river. It jumped the edge of Redaman Street and disappeared down the riverbank.

Marcus put one boot over the edge, took his first step down the embankment, and the balkinmoore broke the water's surface. The oily gray mass reared into the early morning air, mouth gaping, its screams shattering the town's sense of calm and quiet.

The tree sucker adjusted direction and ran right, along the length of the river. Away from the *atham-laine*.

Marcus skidded on the rocky soil as he tried to double back on his steps.

Scaled tentacles lashed out of the water and slammed into him. He was jerked off the ground, elevated high enough to see the town's wall behind the inn. He could hear people shouting in alarm. He saw the tree sucker running as fast as it could to get out of town. It looked like a man—the guards at the town gate would not suspect anything else and would surely let it out into the woods.

I spoke too soon, he thought.

This could turn out to be interesting after all.

chapter 48

*T*he balkinmoore intended to drown him. Cold arms as thick as tree branches strapped Marcus to the bottom of the river and dragged him. He couldn't push himself out of the muddy silt rubbing his back raw. The currents tangled his cloak around his sword arm.

Finally, he thought. A challenge. Excepting today, Bithania hadn't allowed him to pull his sword in weeks. If he even thought about it—literally, if he had a single thought of doing so—she stepped forward and took care of the problem herself. The thief outside Harenstown probably wouldn't be able to sleep in a dark room for months. The mountain lion in Oak Dale had taken one look at her and, no doubt, was still running. Marcus didn't understand Bithania's sudden urge to be in complete control in every skirmish, minor or otherwise. It was annoying.

Marcus unclasped the cloak and let it flood away from him. The water was dark this deep in the river. He could see the surface shimmering far above his head and very little else. The balkinmoore's tentacles were the same color as the shadows. His sword arm now unencumbered, he felt for the reptilian muscles extending from his body and thrust the sword through the darkness. He felt resistance then freedom as the blade punctured flesh. A muffled cry shredded the water. He tasted the *atham-laine*'s blood on his lips.

He brought his feet underneath him and pushed upward toward the bobbing surface. He'd take a breath, submerge again, and rid the river of the creature that roiled beside him. He could feel heat building in his right hand, spreading through the hilt of his sword. He felt the presence of magic and knew the balkinmoore would not survive the next encounter with his sword.

The balkinmoore crashed into his skull and chest, wrapping around him with vengeance. He couldn't see. His sword arm pinned against his ribs. As he wrestled to free himself, he slowly became aware of burning in his lungs. A growing need to get to the surface.

He almost lost his remaining breath in laughter. *Finally. This is what I wanted!*

Arching his back, he twisted sideways and found enough room beneath the mass that held him to carefully transfer the sword to his left hand. His right was still caught beneath moving, slithering layers of cold that were growing tighter.

Pulling his arm back, he slashed the sword through the water and hit nothing.

The weight dissolved from his chest. The tension around his skull faded. Pressure disappeared, and he nearly took a breath of frigid river water in surprise. *What?* He hadn't been released—the creature was simply no longer present.

The water cleared. The ugly taste of the creature's blood weakened in his mouth.

As he realized what had happened, a storm of curses thundered through his head. He kicked toward the surface, broke into the air, and threw his head back. Hauled in breath.

Surprisingly, he was not where he expected to be. Trees stood on both sides of the river—there were no signs of the town of Kings Port. Apparently, he had been carried a fair distance. The balkinmoore had moved quickly and smoothly.

"Bithania!" he shouted when he saw her. He wiped water out of his eyes and fought the river to stay above the surface. "How many times are you going to do this to me? Stop it! I had everything under control."

The morning light trickled through the trees and gave her face the quality of a painting. Brush strokes. Every one of them in perfect order. He wanted to be upset. He *was* upset. Upon occasion, he shouted just so he could start to think again, an activity that was *incredibly* hard to do when he was looking at her.

She held a bow in her hands. The magic of Alusian weaponry had a powerful effect on various children of the gods of death. She had probably used no more than a single shaft. One puncture. The balkinmoore had died quickly. As Marcus glared at her, she put fingers to the bow's tip and gently twisted, and the weapon shrank down into its original form—a short stick that fit easily against her palm. She slid it into her cloak and calmly walked downstream, following the current as it carried him.

Swimming toward shore, he caught hold of a broken tree and pulled himself onto dry land.

He *was* winded. He could give her that, he supposed,

but there were certain times when a man just needed a fight. She didn't understand.

"Yes," she said smoothly. Her eyes narrowed, and she stepped closer to examine his face. "I can see you had everything under control."

Warmth rolled down his face. He realized his cheek was still bleeding. He snorted as he shakily stood to his feet. "A small bump."

"I told you to watch your head."

He heard the accusation in her voice and growled back, "I *did* watch my head." He jerked his hand up and pointed at his cheek. "This was his boot! You failed to mention certain aspects of their magic."

She nodded, as if he should have expected that. "You said you were interested in a challenge."

"*That* was not a challenge! In its most exciting moment, it was not a challenge. That was…was a group of children knocking wooden swords together. It wasn't a fight. And this—" He gestured toward the river. "—was not a victory. I appreciate the concern, but I am most certain your purpose in life is not to be my watchdog, stripping me of danger."

Her eyes narrowed further. For a time, her stare was purposeful and somewhat frightening. She said quietly, "I have seen your death."

That drew him up. He frowned at her.

In the same patronizing, aloof tone, she stated, "You do not die by drowning."

"That is exactly my point. I knew what I was doing. I had my next move."

"Next time, perhaps, I will let you take it."

Amazing how a few simple words could sound so much like a threat.

She turned around and stomped back toward Kings Port. He watched her go and then groaned and followed her. If her behavior over the last several weeks was any indication of the future, he soon would not even be allowed to *carry* a sword.

He had given her a gift. That was all. He hadn't intended it to be a request to save him from mice, and falling leaves, and other creatures of evil intent. He didn't know what she was thinking in all of this, and he truly wished she would begin to think something else.

He lost sight of her in the woods on the way back.

"Ow."

"Sit still, Marcus."

"Whatever you're doing, it hurts."

Coolly, Bithania replied, "I am stitching together the outcome of your diversion. I will do a very good job and leave a minimal scar—if you can manage to hold back your sobs and sit still."

Hana had been observing this conversation for the better part of an hour now, and she wasn't sure which individual amused her more. Marcus followed Bithania's movements with his eyes. The small things. The way she breathed. How she moved her hands. The tilt of her head. Despite his words, he seemed quite content to sit beneath her ministrations. And Bithania, meanwhile, spoke poetry with her fingertips. Her every touch was a caress. The Alusian communicated violence with her words and romance with her hands. When had this happened?

Did Hileshand know about this? Somehow, Hana doubted it.

Her husband was asleep in the adjoining room. If she listened carefully, she could hear his snores coming through the door. Rhusa bark made him violently ill, so she had filled him instead with crimseur, a medicinal wine. It wasn't as potent as rhusa bark, but it had a similar effect and would help him heal more quickly. She had then allowed him to abate her concerns—*remove the worry,* as he had put it—and had slipped out from under the blankets as the wine put him to sleep. She was a very good nurse, very skilled. He had told her so with his last bit of consciousness. Alcohol of any sort made Hileshand prolific with his compliments.

His wounds did not appear serious. The attending physician had left discrete stitches. She had touched the fresh lines in Hileshand's skin and spoken an old Paxan blessing over him as he slept:

Precious light,
Father of life,
Keep this one safe
From pain and strife…

Every moment with this man was precious to her—more so now, she thought, in these circumstances, than it would have been if they had spent the last twenty years together. The wait had made it all the sweeter, and she found she did not feel robbed by life.

Lenay was worried about him. She didn't understand sickness and wounds and how some brought death while others didn't. The little girl saw Hana looking longingly at the bedroom door, and she stood up off the floor and came to her, touching Hana's arm.

"Will he be all right, Mama?" Lenay whispered. Hileshand had been kind to her.

"Yes, love," Hana said.

"Will he get sick from the knives?"

"No, love. He will be fine. You don't need to worry."

She kissed Lenay on the cheek, and the girl eventually returned to playing in the corner with Ella and her kitten.

Marcus sat on the bench with his head back, his body immobile beneath Bithania's care. She finished her stitch work and smeared some secret ointment across the wound.

"Ow," Marcus said again.

The Alusian rolled her eyes.

He saw her do it—of course he saw her do it, for she was like magic to him—and he insisted, "It stings. It feels like needles."

Bithania made a comment beneath her breath, muttering words Hana couldn't make out, and put away her materials. Marcus watched her several moments longer, until Hana wondered whether or not he remembered other people were present, and then he turned his gaze to the door.

It opened, as if Marcus had answered an inaudible knock.

The first thing Hana saw was a white hand on the door handle. It became an Alusian male, one she had never seen before. Her heart jerked once, as it always did around these creatures, and then it grew calm again. She had nothing to fear. Ethan Strelleck had taught her this.

The creature stepped inside, closed the door behind him.

Hana realized he was handsome. She had never thought that about Strelleck, not a single time, but there was something about this male that was different than Strelleck—very different than Strelleck. He made her think of Hileshand, who had been her set standard of attraction and masculinity for decades. Unlike others of his race, this Alusian didn't look like a silent specter whose presence meant someone's death; he looked like a soldier. He carried a sword, and something about him suggested that he was quite comfortable in its use.

"Hana," Marcus said, standing from the bench. "Allow me to introduce Eserak Amary."

Amary. The name stood out to her, but she couldn't place it.

Marcus explained, "This is Bithania's father."

The pale face and dark eyes turned toward her. Amary smiled warmly, as a man would smile at an old friend, and the movement somehow made him seem more intimating, not less. Again, she thought of Hileshand, this time for a different reason. Hileshand could do anything he wanted. If there was no way to accomplish his plans, he simply made one. He did not listen to others' opinions of what he could or couldn't do. He was the strongest man she knew, and never in her life had she met anyone who carried that same innate sense of strength, until this moment.

"Hana," Amary said, as if he had known her name for years. Perhaps he had. "A pleasure. Your husband has raised a fine son. That is the highest compliment I could pay either of you."

As Hana tried to interpret those words, Amary turned back to Marcus. "Well? What have you decided?"

Marcus hesitated. A slight wince passed through his features. Then he said, "I want you to come with us."

Come with us. Hileshand had muttered something about Jezaren before he had fallen asleep. Something about an Ethollian and a promise and a difficult journey into a difficult land. Hana had not yet allowed herself to consider what these things likely meant. She didn't want to think about what Hileshand had promised in her absence.

Amary nodded. "Very well. I will see to the supplies and return in a week."

Marcus cocked his head. "Is a week enough time?"

Amary's smile drew close to a smirk, but he didn't put words to it. At least not out loud. Something silent was exchanged between them, and Marcus nodded. "A week it is."

Nodding at Hana, Amary went out the door. Hana heard his steps on the wooden floorboards as he walked away, and the sound had a peculiar effect on her. *Wait,* she wanted to call to him, though she didn't know why. Why should he wait? What did she possibly have to tell him? There wasn't anything. It took a moment for her to piece together a reason she reacted this way. He felt like Hileshand, and Hileshand was something she always wanted to hold on to.

Marcus turned and looked at Bithania. Her movements became more and more violent. She finally threw the bag to the floor and spun around.

"Amary?" she demanded. "You're taking *Amary*?"

Marcus was calm. "Yes, I am."

"I am not going to Ausham," Bithania declared.

Her words dragged a heavy frown across his face. Marcus replied, "I would like you to accompany Hana and the others to a safe haven, but we do not have to discuss this now. We can do so at a later time. In private."

Bithania didn't seem to care about privacy. "Amary can go with Hana and the others."

Westland lay in the bassinet beneath the window. He awoke to the sound of Bithania's voice and started to cry.

"You're angry with me," Marcus said.

"You are making a mistake," Bithania answered tersely. The tenderness had seeped from her eyes. Her glare possessed claws.

"Bithania," Marcus said quietly, "I want you to go with them."

Bithania's white face was, in this moment, a fearsome thing to behold. She expressed her displeasure with force as she stomped out the door into the hall. Hana waited, and sure enough, the inn's back door slammed shut a few moments later.

Marcus' frown deepened into a scowl.

Hana went over to the bassinet and lifted the baby from the blankets, cradling him against her chest. Westland quieted as she rocked him. *Oh, how you look like my son,* she thought as she studied Marcus' profile. She missed Myles dreadfully, but Marcus made the burden more manageable. He had no idea the good he did his father by being here.

It was a good thing, to have one's burdens made more manageable. Hana wished to return the favor.

"Marcus," she said and gave him a sly look across the room.

The signs of frustration eased from his face. His brows rose as he waited for her to speak.

"Come sit with me on the porch."

She couldn't keep the amusement out of her eyes, and he saw it and studied her with suspicion.

chapter 49

Hana nodded toward the chair she wished him to take, and he obediently sat down across from her.

The porch was empty, the chairs neatly arranged around the table. The fire had wilted into faintly glowing embers on the hearth in the far wall. Hana smelled the scents of fresh bread and spiced venison wafting in from the kitchen.

"Marcus," she said and transferred Westland up to her shoulder, setting him in such a way that he had a clear view of the garden. He was sucking his thumb. She could hear the soft sounds he was making, now that he was close to her ear.

"Yes, Hana?"

"I am married to your father. Do you know what this makes me?"

He hesitated.

She didn't. "Queen. I am queen of everything you hold to be dear and true."

The suspicion relaxed. He grinned, laughing quietly.

She watched him, watched the smile she knew so well, and asked, "Has it been difficult?"

"Travelling with the Alusian?" he said.

No. That was not what she meant, but she would accept it as a beginning. "Yes."

His normal study was deeper and more intense than what she was used to with his brother. He was different than Myles. Several weeks ago, Hileshand had told her about Marcus in depth—his likes and dislikes, his fascination with books and his sword. He liked music, particularly the mandolin. He enjoyed conversation and sometimes debate, but the purpose always was to spend time with the other person, even when it was in argument. Companionship was important to him.

She could tell that Marcus wanted to say something, but he seemed cautious, as if he could not fully decide whether or not she would appreciate his words.

I will appreciate them, she silently promised. *You can tell me anything you desire.*

He leaned back in his chair. "This is what I have learned," he said at last. "*Boerak-El* is the Alusian's name for Abalel. There is no difference between them. It is the same god."

That was a curious statement. She tried to keep her face still and not reveal how much it startled her.

When she didn't respond in violence, Marcus' concern seemed to loosen. His shoulders lowered. He relaxed. "I know this because they have the same voice. I don't know how it comes together. I can't explain it, yet I know it's true, because I know his voice."

They sat in silence.

Hana didn't know how to process his words to her. Boerak-El? Had Marcus spoken of this with Hileshand? Her heart jumped, but she took slow breaths and tried to keep her sudden tension to herself. The Alusian were beyond her understanding. She thought of Ethan Strelleck and how he had taken care of her and her son, when they had been helpless. Considering it now, she realized all at once that in their conversations, he had *implied* his meanings; he had never mentioned Abalel by name. She frowned briefly, wondering if she had missed something, doubting she had. It was just that the Alusian were decidedly difficult to fathom.

Then she thought of the reason she had brought Marcus out here, to speak with him in private.

Westland pulled his thumb from his mouth and grunted at her, and she rubbed his back.

"I have a question," she said slowly.

Marcus looked at her, waiting.

"I have heard many stories of Bithania. I know how she behaved in Ausham, and Hileshand has told me many other things as well. He would see her at the bottom of the river, I believe, because he worries far more than he should. He thinks she hurt you and that she continues to hurt you."

Marcus nodded. "He dislikes her. I am aware of this." A moment passed, and he added, "So is she."

"And his concerns are not necessarily ill-founded. She does not understand anything of propriety." Hana chuckled, thinking about it.

He nodded again. This was true.

She stirred the words in her head a few times before deciding on the route she would take. Her eyes on his face, she asked, "What happened, then, to cause you to form a very different conclusion than that of your father?"

He did not react. "What do you mean?"

"You do not dislike her."

He looked away.

For years, Hana had imagined what it would be like to watch Myles fall in love with the woman who would be his wife. On most days, she had looked forward to the prospect; on other days, it had alarmed her, and she had started to miss him, even when he was near her. She hadn't been able to see him fall in love. He had married Amilia weeks before Hana's path had crossed with his.

She smiled as she studied the side of Marcus' face. This was to her liking. Perhaps she had not been present to watch Myles fall in love, but she could be present for this one. However, based on what she had observed in their room just now, she suspected she had missed much of the process already.

"Have the two of you spoken of this? Are you open with her?"

"Hana…"

"Yes, Marcus?"

He met her gaze. Indecision swirled through his eyes, and he said, "I think I told her."

"You *think* you told her? What did you say?"

He brought his hands up and rubbed his face. Around his palms, he said, "I gave her a gift. I think that means I told her." His hands lowered. His face was flushed. "Do you think I should speak to her?"

She knew he didn't ask that question because he hadn't thought about it. Not Marcus, the thinker of deep thoughts. He asked because he was concerned.

What Marcus dealt with now—Hana didn't think this was common. It was in none of the stories Hileshand had told her of Alusian quests in the past. The chosen man would accompany the female on her quest and then return to his home. As far as Hana knew, no companion had ever suffered what Marcus now suffered.

This was not how it was done.

She smiled. "It is a unique situation, is it not?"

"Uniquely difficult," he answered.

"Returning to my earlier query, what happened that began to make you think this way?" She wanted the story. She wanted the details.

For a moment, she felt Hileshand's concerns. Was this shift in Marcus' heart the result of foreign magic? Was Marcus wrong in his conclusions of Boerak-El, and this was some sort of manipulation—a spell he could not fathom?

Marcus adjusted his position in the chair, the awkward movement revealing his discomfort. It would seem he did not wish to answer the question. She wouldn't force him. She was opening her mouth to tell him so when he sighed.

"I saw her heart." He sighed again and added, "It is very difficult to see someone's heart, who she truly is, and remain unaffected by the sight. Everything she does is lovely. I have never met anyone who is so...so captivating."

Hana put all of her husband's worries aside. This was what she had missed with Myles. She was happy not to have missed it with Marcus.

Bithania did not return until dawn the next morning. Marcus had been awake for an hour, and from the corner table in the dining room, he watched her walk up the street. She came from the north, which allowed him to see her from a distance. He could hear the servants banging pots and pans in the kitchen, preparing for breakfast.

Bithania was carrying a branch. It was about the size of a shepherd's staff, and one end was covered with leaves—a fresh branch. Off an oak tree.

She set it on the table in front of him. She didn't set it down roughly; her movements were gentle. She was no longer angry with him.

"Where did you find him?" he asked, leaning forward to examine the wood.

"Eight miles west."

He gave her a scrutinizing look. "Did he give you trouble?" She appeared to be fully intact. There were no scratches, no obvious signs of trauma.

Her brows rose in dry humor. "No."

They watched each other. Every time he looked at her, he remembered how he had never seen anything like her. It was distracting. The heat in her eyes, the smirking turn of her mouth—he would not be able to dream of anything better. He'd had trouble sleeping last night, knowing she was gone.

He stood from the table slowly. "You don't have to go to Ausham."

She stared at him. "I know."

"We will be giving pursuit to an Ethollian sorcerer, who has a plan in all of this—something he wants and will kill to possess."

She nodded and said again, "I know."

"I *prefer* you to go to Ausham."

A moment passed in quiet. Even the kitchen sounds had fallen silent, and he wondered if he and Bithania were being watched through the keyhole.

There were moments when she pretended she did not understand what he was talking about. This would be one of those times. "I will go with you to Oarsman," she said.

He looked at her steadily.

She returned the look. A smile pulled at her lips. Stubborn, she was. So very stubborn, but she was not mad at him. "You gave me a gift."

He nodded, his gaze moving across her face. Could she hear his thoughts? Is that why she said those words now?

"It is a very good gift," she said.

"Have you read it?"

"Several times now."

He looked at her for a long time, because he had difficulty remembering his last question, the reason they stood here like this. Hadn't there been a reason?

"I will go with you to Oarsman," she said.

He groaned. "Why? Why are you so determined in this?"

Her eyes flashed. "Why are *you* determined in this? I will go with you."

"I do not want you to go with me."

Her mouth dropped open in shock. She bunched her hands into fists and drew them to her temples. "No," she said, shaking her head. "No, you do not speak truth to me. Why do you lie to me? That is not truth, Marcus. I will not listen to your lies. I know you want me with you. You gave me a gift."

The choice appeared before him—push on or retreat? He could not do the latter; his reason for the former was too strong. He reached out and touched her shoulder, two fingers to her cloak. She stilled.

"I do not lie to you," he said quietly, moving his hand away. "I wish you to be out of harm's way. I do not say this because I doubt the strength of your arm or your abilities. I simply wish you to be out of harm's way. Do you understand me? Can't you…Can you not hear my thoughts toward you?"

Her hands lowered from the sides of her head. She looked at him and inhaled, filled her lungs; she was listening to Boerak-El's voice. The god spoke to her.

Marcus watched her.

Gradually, Bithania's shoulders lowered. She relaxed. "I will go to Ausham," she said.

Boerak-El had told her to go to Ausham? *Good.* Surprise moved through him, quickly followed by relief.

"I will go with your sisters and your mother. I will show them the road."

Your mother. He had not heard those words in years, and never had they been spoken in reference to someone who yet lived.

Bithania reached forward, the movement slow, and put her hand on his chest. It was the first time she had touched him since that day in Ausham, when she had claimed him for Boerak-El before the men of the school. He felt a brief flare of heat flood his entire body, and he took a breath. Then the sensation passed.

She was beautiful beyond his ability to describe. She looked at him, a question in her eyes, and he wanted to answer. With everything in him, he wanted to answer, though he had no idea what she was asking. *Yes.* Whatever it was. *Yes.*

Gradually, he became aware of the familiar feel of Boerak-El's power tingling through his hands. He had learned what this meant. He had felt it the night little Stephan was healed. He had felt it when he had gone into the valley of Sporans Brook and chopped wood for Larsa. There was something for him to do, someone to touch.

Lifting his hand, he touched Bithania's shoulder. He felt the magic move through him, flooding without weight or sound through his hand, but he didn't know the reason or purpose for it.

She had to go to Ausham. She had to be kept safe.

She smiled at him, and he considered the outcome of obeying a strong inner urge and bending forward to kiss her. He wondered what her response would be. Then, for the hundredth time, he wondered if an Alusian female would respond to a kiss the same way a woman would. He wondered many things.

With a sigh, she pulled her hand away from his chest,

and immediately, he ached. The absence of her touch felt cold and empty. In his head, he saw himself taking her hand and returning it to him, but he held his breath and refrained.

For a moment, neither of them moved. He needed to release her shoulder, but the thought of doing so hindered the action.

"Thank you for going to Ausham," he said softly. He adjusted his grip and, finally, had the presence of mind to pull away. "I know you do not wish it. I know it is a…a sacrifice on your part."

The look in her eyes grew intense. "Yes, it is. If, in my absence, you choose to do something stupid or foolish, I shall surely know of it, and you shall not enjoy my knowing."

No doubt, this look had made other men tremble to the very core of their being, but Marcus could not have the same response. Unable to help himself, he laughed at her seriousness, and she scowled at him.

He tapped her lightly on the chin. Something sparked in her eyes, and he wondered if he had, with his touch, crossed yet another invisible Alusian line of propriety. "Be at peace, woman. I daresay we shall—"

She wrapped both hands around the back of his head and drew him forward. The kiss was brief, far too brief. Startling. A single touch of her lips. Then she jerked back, and the warm strength of her hands on his head disappeared.

He gaped at her.

She glared. She appeared furious. "You," she whispered, "are not allowed to touch me in jest."

In jest? He was not allowed to touch her *in jest*?

It did not have to be in jest.

He returned his finger to her chin. The same movement as before, but this time, he left it there and felt again the warmth flood his body—the peculiar sensation of Alusian magic. One finger became three, slowly tracing the line of her jaw. She had kissed him. She wanted to kiss him. What other assurance did he need?

In jest, he thought again. She was ridiculous.

He bent down and kissed the end of her nose. That was all he kissed. He met her gaze and smiled, toying with her, and the glare blazed bright in her eyes.

"Marcus, if you even *think*—"

He was done with thinking. He had made his decision about Bithania Elemara Amary months ago. This land was unknown to him, vastly unknown, but that suddenly seemed like a small concern. He lowered his head and met her lips.

She was fierce, and she was wild. True to form, she held nothing back, and everything in him came alive in response to her passion. He bumped into the chair behind him, lost his footing, landed heavily in the seat, and pulled her down with him, barely breaking stride. He was able to use words only at certain points. "You know I love you—"

"Yes."

Her hands on his neck, on his jaw, on his chest along his ribs. Her mouth was beautiful in a compelling, consuming way that had little to do with sight.

Talking had never been such a hardship.

"But I have to go back to Ausham, and I don't know how this is—"

"Stop talking, Marcus."

Had she worried about this? Was she worried now? Marcus wanted to know everything. All of her thoughts.

All of her concerns. All of her hopes. Did she have any idea what they were doing or how this would affect the future? Did she know what Marcus wanted? He wanted the cliff and the final step that would take him over the edge. He wanted the danger. He wanted all of it, here, in his arms, just like this.

He felt the chair suddenly shift beneath him. *That's not good.* He tried to pull away, to gain the distance necessary for speech. It was difficult. "Wait, wait, love. We broke the—"

One of the back legs snapped. Marcus and Bithania toppled backward onto the floor. She made no move to let him up. Instead, she curled there in his arms and laughed.

All of his concerns about the future disappeared like morning mist.

chapter 51

Hileshand did not recover from the crimseur wine until the following morning. Hana was in the chair when he opened his eyes, and she moved onto the side of the bed, running her hand across his forehead.

"How are you feeling?" she asked quietly.

He took hold of her, his hand on her forearm. "I do not wish to leave you," he said.

That was how he was feeling. Her heart hurt, and she hesitated.

For a moment, the only sounds were the voices drifting in from the other room. Marcus was entertaining the baby. Lenay and Ella were laughing at his antics. Hana could hear Bithania's voice as well. The Alusian had returned early this morning, and she seemed to have forgiven Marcus for his apparent indiscretions. Hana didn't know what had happened between them, but whatever it was, Bithania smiled about it in a sweet little way, and the kitchen staff all appeared confused.

"Are you certain of this road?" Hana asked her husband.

His hand tightened on her arm.

"I do not wish you to leave me either," she whispered.

He sat up slowly, wincing. She moved back a little and gave him room, and when he was situated, she climbed up on the bed and sat facing him. He held her hands in his lap.

"Yes," he said. "I am certain of the road."

The shortness of the reply was terrible. She wanted many words. She wanted a good reason he was leaving her and the girls. Jezaren, by himself, wasn't a good reason.

Hana turned her hands over and took his thumbs, enclosing them in her fists. "My daughter is fourteen years old. Jezaren sought her out in a brothel, and it was not to save her. Not in the beginning." She looked at Hileshand, knowing he would understand the subtle challenge in her words. "I care for him as much as I can care for him."

Hileshand shook his head. "He doesn't make caring for him an easy task. This is true."

"No, he doesn't." Hana listened to the voices of her children in the other room and asked, "Do you believe you will be successful? Will you be able to recover him?"

A slow smile moved across his lips. "Entan once told me that Myles learned from me to heed Abalel's voice." He brushed his fingers across the backs of her hands. "Myles is willing to go where he does not wish to go, because of that. I will do what I know I am being asked to do. Myles respects me—it was hard-earned on my part, and I would like to keep that respect intact."

He smiled. She made an attempt to do the same, for he had made his decision. She could see it in his eyes. Once he knew his next step, there was nothing anyone could do to change his mind. She loved that detail of his character. *In most situations.*

Wetting her lips, she asked again, "But do you think you will be successful in recovering Jezaren from the Ethollian?"

For a moment, Hileshand simply looked at her, considering her question with seriousness. His sudden sobriety did nothing to alleviate her concerns.

Then mischief slid through his eyes. He leaned close to her, lowered his voice, lacing it with mystery. "I happen to know a secret about Ethollian spells."

"And what is that?"

He squeezed her hands. "Ethollian spells are much like those who cast them. They are never quite as permanent as they would lead you to believe."

The sun was high, the early afternoon warm. Myles was unfamiliar with spring in the south. This felt more like a Furmorean summer. He half expected to hear the lowing of cattle, and sometimes when the clean breeze rushed across him, it took him by surprise. He had grown up with smells of the earth—of cattle, of barns, of damp hay in the fields. He was not used to winds that smelled of flowers and spices. Oarsman was nothing like the hill country of Furmorea.

He and his brother Baenan stood in the eastern practice field. A single archery target faced them at thirty yards' distance.

"Something I want to tell you," Baenan said.

Myles removed a small stick of ash wood from a pouch at his belt and gently twisted the top. "And what is that?" he asked as the ustrian bow grew to life in his hand. He ran his fingers lightly across the four words inscribed beneath the grip: *Myles Elah Rosure Hileshand*. Four names.

This was the bow Issen-El had given him in a cave three hundred miles from the Paxan coast. It had a few unexpected, interesting properties.

"The king does as he sees fit," Baenan said. "He does whatever he wants to do, and he doesn't care whether or not you want it, too—he's going to do what he wants."

Myles knew this. He had been in Oarsman for several weeks, and every day during that time, Korstain had proven his character. The king was everything Baenan said he was.

"I suppose there is a specific reason you're telling me this," Myles replied.

Baenan nodded. "Korstain sent thirty men north into Paxa. They left four days after you arrived."

Baenan was surprisingly intelligent, and he went to great lengths to hide it from his father. He directed his attention to horses, and when that didn't work, he looked to Athland, who was also intelligent but in a different way. Athland liked books. He was Antonie Brunner, but with enough melancholy to satisfy a hundred poets. Baenan, on the other hand, could look at the elements of the story and see what had already happened and what was about to happen. He thought like a general. Given time and experience, he would be everything Korstain wanted him to be. The boy just hid it well. He didn't want his father's attention, because Korstain's gaze was not an easy thing to endure.

Myles had learned that if he wanted to converse with Baenan at any length, he had to draw him out by asking questions. "What do you know?"

"Julmas Triven went with them."

"I don't know who that is."

"He's Paxan. From Port Soren." When Myles just

looked at him, waiting for more information, Baenan sighed and said, "Julmas Triven used to run stock and deliveries to Ausham. He knows the road. He's been there countless times."

Myles squeezed the bow's grip between his fingers and palm, realized what he was doing, tried to soften his hold. "And?"

Baenan grunted in the back of his throat. "I think it's fairly obvious."

Yes, but Myles still said, "You'd best tell me."

"Korstain has sent for your wife, even though you told him otherwise. He doesn't care about anything that is important to others. He does only what he wants, Myles. You'll come to understand this."

Myles already understood it. Korstain was not a difficult man to read.

The king, Thaxon Parez, Commander Nelsan, and several others had come to the practice fields this afternoon. This was the training ground for Korstain's private guard. Baenan was at home in these fields. General Claninger, who had beheaded the last king and brought Korstain into power, was quite proud of Baenan and his accomplishments. At sixteen, the boy was a better soldier and horseman than several of the ranked officials of the king's guard. When the king allowed it, Myles was out here with Baenan almost every afternoon.

This was the first time in four weeks that Korstain had accompanied them. He and his men sat in raised seats at the edge of the field. The distance was great enough that Myles and Baenan could speak with one another in normal tones, and their words would not carry. When he thought about it, Myles could feel Korstain's gaze pushing against his back. Even from a distance, the man was aggressive. So Myles chose not to think about it. He brought his focus to Baenan alone and ignored the seats behind him, as well as those sitting there.

"Why do you think he sent for her?" Myles asked. It was good for Baenan to voice his thoughts and know they had value. And the boy was wise. Myles would believe anything Baenan told him.

"Well, if you won't bring your wife here, it looks like you don't trust him, doesn't it? He wants to give the appearance that all is well. The entire city reveres you. If you don't trust Korstain, that will not help him reach his goals."

Myles was strangling the bow again. He relaxed his grip and tested the weight of the string. "And?"

Baenan leaned forward eagerly. "And I think he wants to manipulate you."

There it is. "How so?"

Baenan shrugged. "Korstain doesn't have anything you want, and he knows this. But that would change if Amilia were here."

Many things would change if Amilia were here. With a sigh, Myles lifted the bow and directed his attention to the target.

"You don't have any arrows," Baenan reminded him.

"Arrows are for children," Myles replied.

He took a step forward and turned, arm straight, drew back on the string, pulling it across his chest. The bolt appeared as he released. It was not an arrow. There was no head, no fletching. It shimmered with faint light, as if someone had managed to capture a single blue flame from a wizard's fire and bottle it. Myles never missed with this weapon. He didn't even have to aim. During the journey to Oarsman, he had tested the bow's magic and discovered he could shoot in a westerly direction and hit a northern target. It was a rather remarkable gift from the sea. Issen-El was unique and clever, in all his ways. Myles smiled.

The glowing bolt hit the center of the target without effort. Myles heard exclamations in the crowd sitting across the field, where the king was.

Baenan swore in pleasure and disbelief. "Can you do it again?"

Myles did it again.

A short time later, Myles felt a presence behind him and turned.

The king had joined them.

Baenan's eyes instantly lost their shine. He stepped back, fumbled, recovered, and attempted a bow. "Your majesty."

The king didn't even look at him. "May I?" Korstain asked Myles.

"Of course." Myles passed him the bow.

The king had a ready stance and a practiced grip. It was immediately apparent to Myles that Korstain was an experienced archer.

But experience can be fickle. The string snagged on the king's sleeve and snapped down his forearm before the bolt formed. He swore and dropped the bow. Surprise flooded his face.

It was so unexpected that Myles laughed before he realized what he was doing. He tried to swallow it down, his mouth closed, his face stiff, but failed. He could not imagine that Korstain Elah had been many times in this predicament.

The king glared as he lifted his arm and pulled back his sleeve to inspect the damage. An angry red mark ran down his skin. Myles had injured himself like this before; give it a few hours, and the king was going to have an impressive bruise.

Myles bent down, picked up the bow where it had fallen. He knew he was smirking. He could feel it in his eyes and on his mouth, but there was nothing he could do. The sight of the king cradling his arm was the most entertaining thing he had seen in weeks.

"Second try?" He held the bow out to the king.

The king met his gaze and didn't look away.

Myles saw them as they occurred—the first faint signs of amusement. The corners of the king's mouth pulled down. His eyes began to gleam. He grabbed the bow out of Myles' hand and forced a scowl through his features, as if good humor went against his principles.

This was the first time Myles had seen the king anywhere close to a genuine smile. He suddenly knew what he was going to do. It was as if the path appeared beneath his feet, and he took it with confidence.

"If you desire, your majesty," Myles said, "I can have the target moved closer for you."

Baenan stared at one man then the other, his mouth open in horrified surprise.

Myles saw the glint in Korstain's eyes.

"That won't be necessary," the king replied. He lifted the bow.

THE ALUSIAN'S QUEST

end of book 2

Made in United States
North Haven, CT
06 June 2022

19920006R00264